REALM

ALEXANDREA WEIS

Realm

ISBN: 978-1-944109-48-6

VESUVIAN BOOKS

Published by Vesuvian Books
www.vesuvianbooks.com

Printed in the United States of America

10 9 8 7 6 5 4 3 2 1

To the woman who taught me to love history and always fight to be heard, no matter what. This is for you, Mom. I miss you.

IN THE FOO

ROX

BLACK SEA

GREECE

PELLA
AMPHIPOLIS

ISAURIA/
LARANDIA

EUIA
SARDIS
CAPPADOCIA

PHOCIS

MEDITERRANEAN SEA

HELIOPOLIS

PELUSIUM
BABYLON

EGYPT

ARABIA

RED SEA

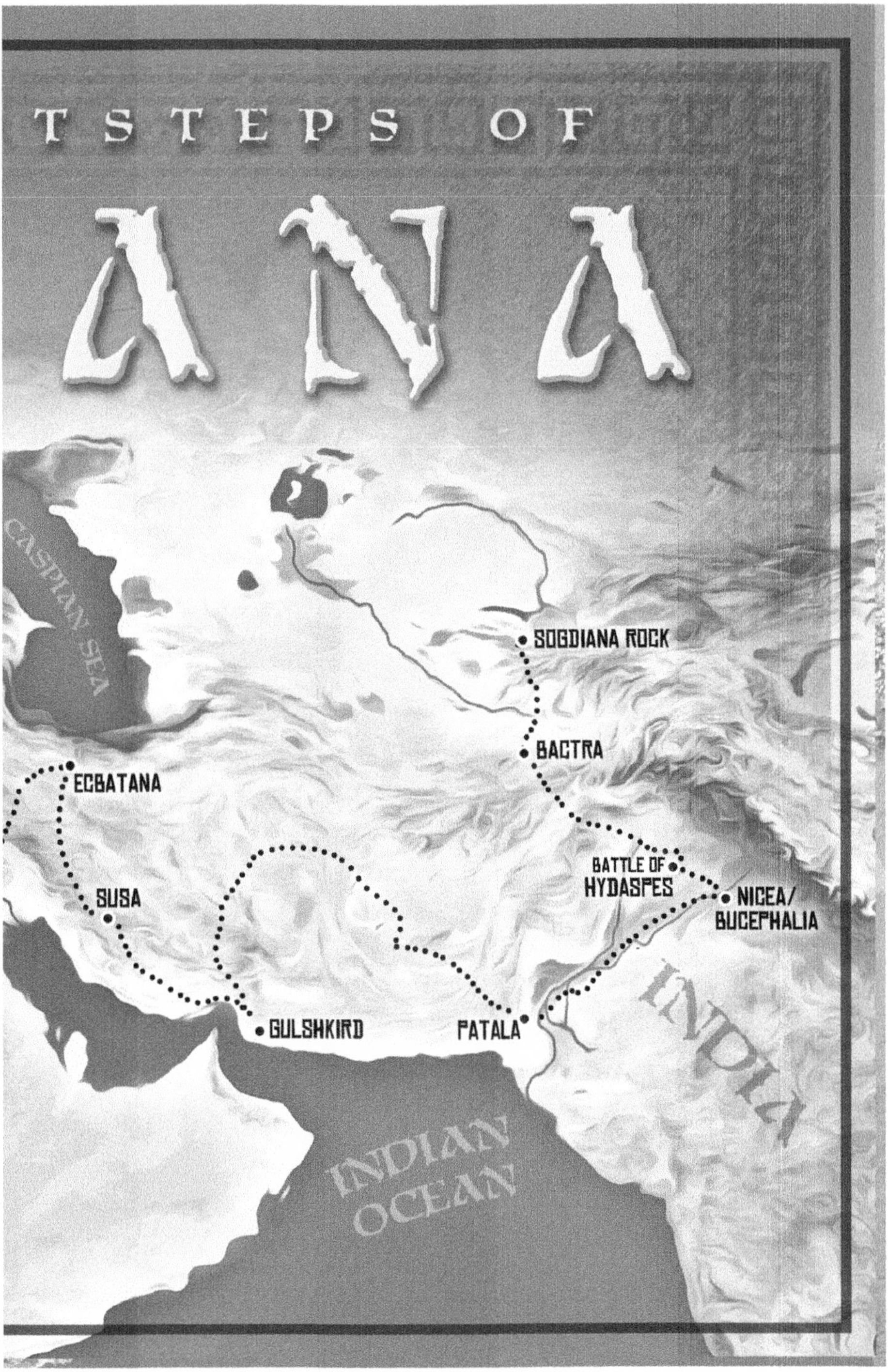

TSTEPS OF
ANA
CASPIAN SEA
SOGDIANA ROCK
BACTRA
ECBATANA
BATTLE OF HYDASPES
NICEA/ BUCEPHALIA
SUSA
GULSHKIRD
PATALA
INDIA
INDIAN OCEAN

CHAPTER ONE

My sweet Persia. What will become of you?"

Baron Oxyartes peered out the entrance to his family's tent observing the winds blowing in from the arid plains. The brisk breeze pestered his soldiers as they stockpiled spears, swords, and quivers loaded with arrows. In the distance, the rhythmic *ping, ping, ping* of a blacksmith's hammer ignited a fearful churn in his belly. Women hurriedly packed food and belongings into woven baskets while children herded groups of sheep, geese, and goats toward the winding path that led to the top of the great Sogdiana Rock. Anticipation saturated the camp as preparations occupied the minds of his people. With the war already lost, Oxyartes felt certain the battle to come would be his last.

"Who are you talking to, Father?" a soft, feminine voice asked behind him.

When he turned, a young woman stood at the back of the tent. Dressed in a man's baggy pants and dirty top, she could have passed for a common stablehand, but her stunning smile took his breath away.

"Roxana."

She glided forward, and her movements reminded him of the lightest linen caught up in a breath of wind. The hint of round curves beneath her loose-fitting clothes made him mourn the loss of his little girl. Where had the time gone?

He admired her long brown hair shimmering in the afternoon light, and how her skin resembled the purest goat's milk—creamy and without blemish. Then he noticed the flush of exercise on her sculpted cheeks, and the light film of sweat covering her high, regal brow.

"What have you been doing, child?"

"Exercising your horse." She wiped the dust from the front of his red robes. "You told me I could this morning."

"Ah, yes, I did say that, didn't I?" Oxyartes debated how to share his concerns with his daughter. "You should be packing to go to the great rock with the other women in the camp."

She planted her feet. "I want to stay with you."

He chuckled at her resolve. "Your grandmother would never allow it."

"Atimexis wouldn't care what I do. She hates me."

Oxyartes sighed as he inspected the young woman. "Atimexis cares for you like a daughter, so try and get along with her. Can you do that for me?"

Roxana's shoulders slumped. "Then why is she always angry with me?"

His heart broke for the poor girl. A half-bred, part Persian and part barbarian from the north, she never truly fit into his world.

"Mother is angry with me, not you. She's never forgiven me for marrying your mother, so you must work especially hard to show her the respect she deserves."

Roxana smiled, instantly dispelling his doubts about her future in his tribe.

"You will break hearts with that smile." He frowned at her filthy outfit. "If you ever hope to catch a suitable husband, you'll have to dress like a woman. I should have insisted you start behaving like a young lady years ago. I was wrong to let you scamper about with your brothers."

Roxana's lively green eyes flickered. "I don't want a husband. Why would I want a man to tell me what to do and take me from the people I love? And what's wrong with learning the things a man learns? I can ride, hunt, administer to the sick, and even fight—"

"Who have you been fighting?" Oxyartes demanded, crossing his arms. "I told your brother to watch out for you. Histanes should not let you get into any more skirmishes."

Her skin paled, and she lowered her head. She reminded him of her mother in that instant. She had Tasia's fair beauty, her seductive mannerisms, and her notorious temper.

"You must learn to control your anger." He raised her chin. "You must think before you attack. Use your head to solve arguments, not your fists. I need you to be very careful and remember all the things I've taught you."

"You're worried about the Greek who is coming for us. He's the reason we left Bactria, isn't he?"

He let her go, nodding. "Ever since Gaugamela, I've refused to accept this man as our Great King. That has made me his enemy, and why we had to flee our home. There's no way to predict what he will do when he arrives in Sogdiana. If we're lucky, and our supplies hold out, perhaps we can survive for eight months … maybe even a year in the fortresses atop the great rocks. I wonder if Alexander will be able to last that long in this valley with a large army to feed."

"Do you fear this Greek?"

"I'm not afraid of this Greek or any other Greek, my love." His arm went around her, and he detected the fragrance of spring in her hair. "He's just another general; another invader who will, in time, leave us as he found us."

He wished he could tell her they would weather the storm, but he feared what would happen if Alexander got hold of her; or worse, if his men took her for themselves.

Oxyartes stroked her cheek, amazed by the contrast of his dark hand against her pale skin. "I survived for years in the courts of King Darius, I can do the same with this Greek. After all, he will need Persians who know the Persian way of things and the Persian people." He pulled his hand away and touched his oiled black beard, debating his plans. "It will not be the first time I've had to bend with the winds."

She stepped closer, coming right up to him, distracting him from his thoughts of war.

"Let me fight alongside you."

Oxyartes bristled at the notion and clasped his hands behind his back. "You're a woman, and a woman's place is with other women. You must help Atimexis and your stepsisters to the top of the great rock." Oxyartes stooped down to one knee. "I would feel much better knowing you are with them." He paused and switched from Persian to Greek. "Please, little star."

Whenever he spoke her name in Greek, Oxyartes knew his daughter could not resist the request. The language of the barbarians he'd learned from her mother. He used it to calm her and chase away her unhappiness.

She tilted closer, a wrinkle marring her smooth brow. "You're not going to be with us on the great rock, are you?"

Oxyartes ushered her to the tent doorway and pushed back the large flap. Pointing across the valley to the steep mountains, he said, "I will be there. On top of the small rock, I will wait for Alexander while you, your mother, and stepsisters remain safe on the big mountain."

Roxana darted her eyes back and forth between the two craggy peaks. "And where will the army and soldiers be?"

"With me, on the smaller rock. A few men will be garrisoned with you."

"What if Alexander comes for us?"

He kept up his stoic demeanor, not wanting to frighten her. "Alexander is known for his kindness to women. If he makes it to the top of the great rock, he will not harm you."

"Will the Greek fall for your deception? Making him chase women on the big mountain while you hide on a smaller one with your army could be dangerous for all of us. Look what happened to Troy when the Greeks deceived them."

Oxyartes tapped the tip of her nose, impressed. "You're truly a wonder. You're smarter than any man I know."

"Even smarter than this Alexander?"

"Yes, perhaps, even smarter than Alexander." He nodded to the tent flap. "Go and help your sisters. We must have you settled on the great rock by nightfall."

She stepped outside and turned to him.

"Will I see you again before we leave?"

He offered her a fleeting smile. "I will come and say my goodbyes."

She made her way across the camp, dodging goats, children, and soldiers. Then he lost her behind several tents.

Oxyartes wanted to rush after her and hold her once more, but such affection would be frowned on by his people. She was a woman and not worthy of his devotion, but he'd never embraced such prejudice. Roxana had been his one true treasure in life, and now he feared he would lose her.

He glimpsed the shadow of the large rock stretching across the ground. Daylight was slipping away, and there was so much still to do before the mighty army of Alexander arrived.

CHAPTER TWO

Roxana peered over the edge of the cliff next to her new home atop the great rock. Dust clouds swirled along the valley floor—clouds that came from the hooves of horses running over the barren ground. She hugged herself as the bitter wind smacked against her face. The Greeks had arrived.

Despite what her father had professed, he feared the Greeks, and suddenly, so did she.

"What are you looking at?"

In her blue coat with a matching long dress, her stepsister, Yasmin, came alongside her. She was a tall, brown-eyed beauty, who shared Roxana's slender build.

"The Greek army is in the valley." Roxana stepped back from the edge of the cliff. "I heard the soldiers stationed with us talking about it. They think they will attempt to climb the rock."

Yasmin pulled her coat closer, fighting against the stiff wind. "I thought no one could climb this rock."

Roxana gazed into the afternoon sky, not liking the change in the air. "Perhaps these Greeks can."

"Do they have wings?" Yasmin snickered. "Because I don't see how else they can get up here."

She wished she had her confidence, but her father's uncertainty had become her own.

"Father said this Greek general, Alexander, is very clever, and very determined. He will try to find a way."

Yasmin twisted her lips—something she always did when thinking. "You know what's going to happen to us, don't you?"

Roxana turned away, wanting to hide her fear. "Men in time of war can be unpredictable. You've heard the stories in the camp."

"Yeah, I've heard. But father won't let that happen to us." Yasmin peeked over the edge of the cliff, taking in the swirling dust below. "Perhaps we should tell grandmother of the Greeks."

Roxana chafed at the mention of the woman. "Let the captain of the guards tell Atimexis. She wouldn't believe it coming from you or me."

"You could try and be nicer to her. She does have our best interest at heart. She means to make you, me, and Irania wives to noblemen, and perhaps mothers of great men one day."

The idea of marriage to a nobleman tied Roxana's stomach into knots. "I'll never marry. I know it's what they expect for us, but I would rather die than give up my freedom to a man. Why can't we hope for more?"

"Like what? Women were made to marry. You need to get your head out of the clouds." Yasmin stepped back from the cliff's edge. "Do you think it's true what they say of the Greeks? That they hate all Persians?"

Roxana remembered something her father had once said. "Doesn't the conqueror always hate the conquered."

Yasmin frowned at her. "Are we the conquered?"

Roxana gave her an encouraging smile. "Not yet."

Roxana awoke with a start from a fitful dream about Greek soldiers caught up in the brutality of war. The blackness around her was occasionally interrupted by streams of light from the torches burning in their camp. An uneasiness settled over her. She was not alone.

Then something nudged her arm.

Yasmin stepped into the light next to her cot.

Roxana let out a relieved breath and tossed her blanket aside. "Again?"

"You're lucky grandmother doesn't make you share a cot with our little sister." Yasmin settled in, tugging on the blanket. "Irania's snoring is driving me mad."

Roxana punched her pillow. "Could be worse. Could be your husband's snoring keeping you awake and then where would you sleep?"

"Let's hope when the time comes, Father marries us off to wealthy Persian noblemen who have many bedrooms in their homes and don't beat us when we leave their beds in the middle of the night." Yasmin yawned then stretched out her arms. "That would be a happy marriage for me."

"Do you think Father would force us into marriage? Maybe he will let us live out our lives with him."

"You need to accept the fact you will have to marry, Roxana. From what I hear around the tents, marriage is a strange business. The women talk about how they cater to their men. Then they get pregnant, bear the children, cook, clean, and must continue to let the man have his way, whenever he pleases."

"'Have his way'?" she asked, drawing her knees to her chest.

"You know … sex." Yasmin sat up. "The older women always talk about sex and—"

"Oh, by the gods, enough!" She waved her sister's thoughts away. "I swear all you talk about is sex."

"Aren't you interested in sex?" Yasmin poked her shoulder. "Or do you plan on spending all your time with horses instead of men?"

"I prefer horses to men. On a horse I'm free. With a man, I would be—"

A faint cry came from outside their tent.

Yasmin tipped her head. "Did you hear that?"

A shrill scream pierced the air.

The two girls scrambled from the cot. They were about to run to the front of their family's tent when Yasmin halted.

Roxana turned to her. "What is it?"

"What if it's the Greeks?" Yasmin's hand went to her throat. "What if they have climbed the rock like you said they would?"

Another scream cut through the night.

Heinous visions of Greeks swinging blood-covered swords terrified Roxana.

Then, the curtains dividing their sleeping quarters parted.

Her youngest sister, Irania, stepped inside, rubbing her sleepy brown eyes.

"I heard someone shouting." She clutched a doll made of rags and horse hair. "What's going on?"

Roxana straightened out the nightgown clinging to Irania's short, chubby figure.

"We're not sure, but—"

"I have an idea," Yasmin called out.

She went to some trunks set up at the edge of the room and flung open the lids. Yasmin rummaged through Roxana's colorful coats and long pleated dresses.

Roxana gaped at her as if she'd lost her mind. "What are you doing?"

Yasmin picked up two thick red coats and tossed them to her sisters. "Put these on over your nightgowns and cover your heads with shawls. Place all the bracelets and necklaces you can fit under your clothes. If we have to escape, we might need them to barter for food later on."

Roxana hugged her coat. "Don't you think you're getting carried away."

Yasmin took a long pearl necklace from one of the trunks and wrapped it around her neck. "No, we must plan ahead. Grandmother always speaks about the wars she's witnessed and how …" She went quiet, a glimmer of fear rose in her eyes. "Roxana, no matter what happens to us, I want you to promise me you will save yourself. Use your Greek. Speak to them in their language. Stand up to them."

The images of bloodshed and death from Roxana's dreams still haunted her. "But what if …?"

"Oh, Roxana." Yasmin cupped her face. "For years, I've envied how men have looked at you. Now you can use what you have to save our lives. Use what Tasia has given you."

When the three young women arrived in the reception area, the oil lamps flickered. Their grandmother, the gray-haired, steely-eyed Atimexis, stood in the center of the room.

She raised the oil lamp in her hand, the lines in her brow cutting deeper into her skin. "What is this? I didn't tell you to dress."

"The Greeks have come to kill us all!" a woman shrieked outside their tent.

Roxana's heart sped up as frantic footfalls echoed around her. "Is it the Greeks?"

"I don't know." Atimexis searched the tent behind them. "Where is your sister? Where is Irania?"

Irania came out from behind Yasmin, covered from head to toe, allowing only her eyes and the bridge of her nose to peek out from beneath her clothes. "I'm here."

Roxana rushed toward the tent flap. "We need to find out what's going on?"

Atimexis put an arm in front of her, stopping her from leaving. "Don't go out there."

The fright in her grandmother's quavering voice made Roxana want to flee. But where would she go? Trapped on the high mountain rock, with only one steep road out that could never be negotiated in the darkness, she could not escape if she tried.

Irania clutched her doll, tears welling in her eyes. "The Greeks!"

"Hush up!" Atimexis pointed at the girls with her bony finger. "We must stay here and wait—"

The tent flaps billowed as if unseen hands pushed them aside.

Roxana grabbed for Yasmin, noting the iciness of her skin.

A handful of muscular men, wearing white chitons and cuirasses made of layers of thick linen, entered the tent. The coldhearted stare of the Greek soldiers sent a shudder through Roxana, knocking her knees together. The men formed a line at the entrance; their long spears gripped tightly in their hands. They stood at attention, and when the last soldier held open the tent flap, Roxana's heart stuck in her throat.

Atimexis fell to the ground, kneeling before the soldiers. Yasmin gave a quick, pleading glance at Roxana to do the same, before grabbing Irania's hand and pulling her down with her. Roxana swore she would be sick, but she didn't move.

She remained standing, and held her head up, determined to meet her enemy on her terms.

I will not grovel before a Greek.

Roxana held her breath as two men in bronze cuirasses, short tunics, and purple woolen cloaks strolled into the tent.

The first was older, with reddish hair and large brown eyes set into his leathery skin. He had a very prominent chin and an even larger hooked-nose. The second man to enter was taller, with brown curly hair, soft brown eyes, and a handsome, clean-shaven face. He scanned the furnishings in the room, then discovered her stepsisters and Atimexis cowering on the floor.

When his gaze landed on her, he asked in Greek, "Who is that?"

"Must be a daughter of Oxyartes," the hooked-nose man said. "This is his family tent, or so the interpreter says." His eyes lingered longingly on Roxana. "Quite a beauty."

Her cheeks burned, but she did not lower her head. She had to appear strong, resilient, and unafraid, just like her father had taught her.

"Yes, Ptolemy," the tall one agreed in a deep melodic voice. "Indeed, she is. If she's a daughter, then who are the rest of these people on the ground?"

"What are you thinking, girl?" Atimexis barked at her in Persian. "Get on the ground, or they will cut you down."

"What did the old one say?" The taller man snapped his fingers at a one of the guards. "Go find out where that damned interpreter is?"

Roxana summoned her courage and said in perfect Greek, "She's scolding me for not bowing before you, Great King."

The men's shocked faces almost made her giggle. Initially, she thought speaking up the smart thing to do, but as time passed and the men did not respond, anxiety gripped her.

Ptolemy stepped closer. "You speak Greek?"

The sword attached to his belt glistened in the lamplight and she swallowed hard. "Yes."

The taller man folded his arms, glaring at her. "Who are you?"

She fought to control the trembling overtaking her limbs. "I am Roxana, daughter of the Baron Oxyartes. This is his family, my king."

The general's brow creased. "Why do you call me *king*?"

Roxana clutched her coat, her confidence waning. "You are the king. Are you not Alexander?"

A few soldiers standing behind the tall Greek snickered.

Ptolemy loudly cleared his throat and cast a wary eye at the men. "This is Hephaestion Amynatos. Not Alexander, my lady." Ptolemy smiled reassuringly. "Not to worry, for in many ways he, too, is Alexander."

Roxana searched one Greek face and then another, mortified by her error. She felt sure she would be sliced in two by their swords.

Hephaestion stood before her. "I am a general under Alexander's command. You have nothing to fear from me, my lady."

"Where did you learn Greek?" Ptolemy's gruff voice carried through the tent. "You speak it very well."

Roxana wrung her hands. "My father, the baron, always said it was wise to learn the ways of one's enemies."

The two men chuckled.

She hoped it was a good sign, or at least a reprieve from the certain death she'd imagined for herself.

Hephaestion nodded to her sisters. "How is it you're not on the floor like the others?"

Roxana kept her eyes on the brilliant star on the breastplate of his cuirass. "Because I'm not afraid."

Hephaestion lifted her chin, taking a closer look at her. "How old are you?"

She did not like his touch. She would never have let a man other than her father touch her in such an intimate way. Was this how men treated women in Greece?

"I have seen sixteen summers, General." Her voice came out shaky, but she was proud of her bravery in spite of the man's rude behavior.

"You're not dark like the rest of your people. Why is that?"

For the first time, Roxana dropped her gaze to the ground. She had endured thousands of jokes and many days of teasing from the other children in the tribe. Because she was lighter than the rest of her family, she'd been an outcast of sorts. For her, being different was a curse, not a source of comfort.

"My mother was from the northern lands around the Aral Sea."

Hephaestion turned her head, inspecting her face. "Beautiful, quite exquisite." His hand fell to his side. "You and your family are now under the protection of Alexander of Macedon. Do you understand?"

She slowly nodded.

"No harm will come to you. You have the king's word." With that, he marched out of the tent, followed quickly by Ptolemy and the guards.

Yasmin, Irania, and Atimexis rose from the floor and came up to her.

Atimexis clasped her hand, yanking Roxana to her side. "Well, what did he say?"

"He promised no harm would come to us." She let out a long, ragged breath as the ordeal finally sank into her bones. "We have the king's word."

Hephaestion strolled across the army camp that was set up in the shadow of the great rock. Smoke hung heavy in the morning air, and the aroma of roasting meat tempted his empty belly. Men sat around fires or camped outside of small tents appearing to enjoy the respite from the days of marching they'd endured to get to Sogdiana. He wished he could join them in some wine, taste the goat on their spits, and listen to their stories of the long campaign, but he had more pressing matters—an audience with his king.

He made his way to the tallest tent in the camp—the one with the gold pike at the very top. A surge of energy hit him when he noted the way the pike glistened in the sun. He had good news for his king, something to appease the foul temper he had suffered for days.

He approached two members of the king's guard stationed at the entrance. Each soldier held a spear and wore a bronze cuirass with the sixteen-pointed star, the symbol of the king's Argead dynasty, emblazoned on the breastplate.

"Where is he?"

One of the young men opened the tent flap. "He's inside, General, at his desk."

Hephaestion brushed past the guard and followed the familiar route to the back of the spacious tent.

He arrived at an area decorated only with a small wooden desk and some stools. Hunched over and furiously pounding a stylus into a wax tablet was Alexander of Macedon.

"You must be here to report about the goings on atop the rock."

Alexander looked up, and the intensity of his deep-set gray eyes struck him. Perhaps his square jaw and bulging forehead added to their piercing quality; Hephaestion wasn't sure, but he'd seen Alexander use his gaze to intimidate many in the past. He wasn't very tall and had a stocky build with broad shoulders and a thick chest. His ruddy skin, prone to burning in the sun, flushed whenever he was angry, a warning to those who knew him well to stay away. His disheveled, reddish-brown, wavy mane seemed perpetually in need of a good brushing, and his tunics never stayed clean for long. But it was his scars which intrigued the general most. He had one along his left cheek, another on the right side of his forehead, and another across his lower neck. Hephaestion couldn't remember Alexander without scars. It was as if he had been born that way, a gift from the gods.

"How did it go?"

Hephaestion walked around the desk to Alexander's side. "You're chipper, considering you've been up for almost two days."

"You know I hate to sleep. There's always too much work to do." Alexander returned his attention to one of the numerous scrolls scattered about his desk. "What news have you brought me?"

Hephaestion read one of the scrolls over Alexander's shoulder. "Scouts are already on the second rock. Now that we know how to climb the damned things, we should have them under control by nightfall."

Alexander dropped the stylus to the desk. "And what did you discover on top of the first rock?"

"The family of Baron Oxyartes. They're now in your custody—his mother and three daughters." Hephaestion raised his hand, anticipating Alexander's next question. "Orders have been given that none of the women atop the rock are to be touched on pain of death. The men are well aware of your feelings about rape. At least now you'll have something to bargain with to get Oxyartes to surrender. Holding the women hostage should speed things along."

Alexander closed the wax tablet. "Any problems?"

Hephaestion shook his head. "No. They were too afraid to organize an attack. The men and women went screaming when they saw the soldiers arrive at the top. After that, it was pretty much routine."

"The family of Oxyartes? You saw to their comfort?"

"Of course." Hephaestion folded his long arms, itching to tell him about the girl. "You won't believe this, but one of his daughters speaks Greek."

Alexander's eyes danced with interest. "Did this daughter, who speaks Greek, say anything to you?"

"It's not so much what she said but how she said it. Not like a barbarian at all. She had a kind of bearing, a certain dignity I've not seen before in these people. She was very …" He hesitated, knowing it would spur his friend's curiosity.

"What?" Alexander insisted.

Hephaestion grinned. "Spirited."

He could almost see the wheels turning in Alexander's mind. He never stopped thinking or planning. Alexander was always one step ahead of everyone else. He had to be. It was the only way to remain king and stay alive.

"Was she pretty or did she have the face of a pig?"

"The girl?" Hephaestion smiled, knowing his answer would please his king. "She was the most beautiful woman I've ever seen."

Alexander raised his eyebrows. "What was the name of this beautiful girl who spoke Greek?"

Feeling that nudge of satisfaction at seeing Alexander beguiled, Hephaestion angled closer and whispered, "Roxana."

CHAPTER THREE

Atimexis paced the reception area of their tent, waiting for word on the fate of Oxyartes. The old woman's hands twisted as she remembered how the Greek generals had interacted with Roxana—lust on the faces of conquering men was dangerous.

"Why are you worried, Grandmother?"

Yasmin's beauty stirred visions of her fate at the hands of soldiers. She quickly wiped the pesky teardrop from her cheek.

"Your father's surrender to the Greeks will bring shame to our family. How can we go back to Bactria now?"

Roxana sauntered out from a corner of the tent. "You would have preferred Father's death to the shame of surrender, is that it?"

"You don't understand." Fear squeezed Atimexis' throat. "With your father a captive, there is no telling what they will do ... with you or your sisters." Her strength leaving her, Atimexis took a seat on a stool.

Yasmin stood and came to her side. "The general told Roxana we would not be harmed."

She scowled at her granddaughter. "Barbarians are never to be trusted. Conquerors have no word, and the conquered have no hope."

The tent's flap flew open, letting in the chill of the early spring afternoon. Suddenly, the robust figure of Oxyartes strutted inside.

Roxana ran to her father's open arms, quickly followed by her sisters.

Oxyartes held and kissed each of his daughters while Atimexis stayed back, keeping an eye on her only son. She ached to feel the reassurance of his arms, but that was not her place anymore.

"And your sons? Where are Histanes and Estander?"

Oxyartes lovingly touched each girl's cheek. "The boys are coming. They stopped along the way to examine a Greek soldier's sword. They're fascinated by everything Greek."

Atimexis could not help but notice how he lavished his affection on Roxana. A sharp slice of dread passed through her.

"What are the terms of your surrender?"

Oxyartes moved closer, his dark eyes staying locked on hers. The girls didn't seem to notice the tension emanating from her son, but she felt it. Something had happened with the Greek king.

"Alexander and I have made a great pact for the future." He stood before her, his mouth a rigid line of warning. "We are to be honored members of his kingdom."

The furrows in his brow told Atimexis there was more to this pact than he wanted his children to know.

Yasmin tugged on his sleeve. "Father, what will happen now?"

Oxyartes faced his eldest daughter, masking his misgivings. "We will have a banquet in the Greek tradition to honor our guests and celebrate our peace. You all must help me plan it."

Irania jumped up and down like an excited puppy. "Me too?"

"Yes, my little one." He tweaked the end of her nose. "You will have the great privilege of being the only maidens dancing at this banquet. I told Alexander what beautiful daughters I have, and he insisted on meeting each one of you." Oxyartes placed a hand on Roxana's shoulder. "Now let me have a word with my daughter."

The old woman's heart sank. She wanted to question him more about his pact with the Greek, but it would have to wait. Uneasy about their fate, she ushered Yasmin and Irania quickly toward the back of the tent.

"We can pick out your costumes and plan a dance. By the gods, Irania, you must try not to burp in public. Come, come."

Before she reached the curtain hiding their sleeping quarters, Atimexis glanced back at her son and granddaughter. She envied the young woman's place of reverence in her son's heart but had a feeling their bond would disintegrate when Oxyartes married her off to a man of wealth or influence. Atimexis had adored her father, too, and had believed him when he'd promised her a happy marriage. She feared Roxana's fate would soon mirror her own, and she pitied the beauty.

With a last sad smile, she escorted Irania and Yasmin out of earshot. In a few short days, their once peaceful life had been turned upside down, and Atimexis knew nothing would ever be the same.

Roxana stood patiently, waiting for the others to leave. She felt her father's eyes on her. Her muscles twitched with anticipation.

"What are you not telling them?"

He came around in front of her. "You always could read my thoughts, little star," he said in Greek.

Why had he switched from Persian to their secret language—the one her mother had taught them?

"What really happened with the king?"

He hesitated, stroking his thick black beard. "Histanes is to join Alexander on his campaigns. He will leave with the army when they go."

"You gave them your son as a token of your surrender." She rubbed her forehead, repulsed by the idea.

Oxyartes tilted closer, dropping his voice. "I had no choice. It was the only way to guarantee the rest of the family would be safe."

"What if they kill him?" She kept her voice steady, hiding her anger. "You know the Greeks hate us. You have told me about our history with them. The wars in Greece, the battles this Alexander has waged against our dead king, and now they're here. Do you think they want peace with you, or is this a ruse for some greater treasure?"

At the word *treasure*, a strange gleam sparked in her father's eyes. He folded his hands, something she'd seen him do whenever he searched for the right words.

"I've heard it said Alexander likes—no, that's not right—he admires beautiful things. He's a barbarian, this is true, but such taste denotes a softer side not usually seen in a general or a king. I think you have the ability to bring that side out in him. I've seen you do it before in others—me, for instance."

A tickle awakened in her belly. She didn't know why, but she sensed her life was about to change.

"What are you asking?"

He rested his hands on her shoulders. "Alexander mentioned you spoke to his generals in Greek. He's intrigued by you, I can tell. When you meet him at the banquet, I wish for him to be impressed with you. If he is impressed with you, then he's impressed with me. It makes my position with him stronger. Do you understand?"

The icy fingers of dismay squeezed her heart. "Are you planning on marrying me off to this barbarian? Offering me as a term of surrender, like you did Histanes?"

"No, nothing like that. Alexander has never married. He's even refused Darius's daughter. From all accounts, he has no desire for a wife, and I have no wish to see you married to a Greek." His face became grave, and his dark eyes burned into her. "I want you to be on your best behavior when you're around the king. Listen to him, talk to him if he wishes it, and when you dance at the banquet, I want you to do your very best. Everything you do must please him."

Her shoulders heaved forward as she sighed, feeling both relieved and troubled. "How am I to please anyone with my dancing? I move like a goat on the rocks. I have none of Yasmin's grace, and Atimexis says I can't keep time with the music. I'm sure I will embarrass you, and then you will be ashamed of me."

"No, my little one." He gathered her in his arms. "You forget how graceful goats can be when dancing on the high cliffs. You will be just as graceful. I know everything you do will mesmerize these Greeks and please Alexander."

The weight of her responsibilities pressed against her chest. She pushed away from her father.

"And if I don't please Alexander, what will happen to us then?"

He tapped her nose. "I have a feeling you will please the king very much, my love. Possibly more than you will ever know."

CHAPTER FOUR

Hundreds of burning torches guided their way to the feasting tent set up in the shadow of the great rock. All around her, Roxana could hear the laughter of men, the echoes of music, and smell the meat cooking throughout their camp.

The cold air against her skin only made her shiver harder. She walked along, the giant tent looming ahead, adding to her nervousness.

"Yasmin, do you think these Greeks will like our dancing tonight?" Irania tugged at the snug blue belt around her waist.

Yasmin took Irania's arm, urging her to keep up with her. "That's why we have been practicing all week, little sister. So we can be perfect before the Greek king at the banquet."

Roxana attempted to shove her braided hair under her gold shawl. "I'm not sure I can do this."

Yasmin clucked with disapproval and stayed her hand.

"No, the Greeks must see your beautiful hair." She smoothed the thick plait over her right shoulder.

"Atimexis will think I'm immodest." Roxana bit her lower lip.

"Our father wasn't concerned about modesty when he gave you this expensive cloth to wear." Yasmin touched the sleeve of Roxana's golden pleated dress. "You belong in the heavens."

Roxana held her shaking hand against her stomach. "I feel like I'm going to throw up."

Yasmin patted her shoulder. "You always say that when you're nervous."

At the entrance, Atimexis turned to the fidgeting girls, hissing last minute instructions.

"I must go in and take my place with your brothers. When you hear the music, then walk into the center of the tent, as I showed you. The musicians will change their tune once you are in position. Don't look at the Greeks while dancing. You're the daughters of a Persian governor now. Mind your manners." She released a heavy sigh. "When you have finished, go to the king's table, and your father will introduce you. And for heaven's sake, keep your eyes on the floor. You must bow to the king as I taught you. Can you remember all of that?"

Roxana nodded along with her sisters.

"If the king invites you to dine, you must sit next to your brothers. Eat quietly and eat only small amounts. Please, no fighting with Histanes, Roxana. No burping, Irania. And none of you are to touch a drop of wine. You hear me?" Atimexis rolled her eyes. "The last thing I need is for you children to get—"

"It will be fine, Grandmother," Yasmin interrupted. "Go on. Father and the boys are waiting."

Atimexis checked the girls over one last time, and then fixed her attention firmly on Roxana. "Your father will be so proud." She ducked into the tent.

Roxana almost stumbled forward. She'd never heard her grandmother give any hint of kindness or encouragement, but tonight when she had least expected it, the words had helped.

Yasmin blew out a loud breath. "Let's get this over with."

"Yeah," Irania added, tugging at her blue costume. "I'm hungry."

"What else is new?" Yasmin laughed and then turned to Roxana. "Are you ready?"

Roxana wanted to scream she wasn't ready, but instead, nervously bobbed her head, unable to speak. She prayed to the gods for strength to keep from being sick all over the king.

Lutes, harps, and flutes came to life inside the tent.

Irania walked into the open tent flap first, her head held high, followed by Yasmin. Roxana brought up the rear.

Spiced meats and sweet smoke filtered through the air. Low dining tables circled the room with pillows as chairs. The girls rushed to their spot in the center of the open floor. The crowd grew quiet. The music's tempo changed, and Roxana took her position, her gaze lowered to the mats covering the ground.

In time with the music, she twisted and twirled, concentrating on every movement, mindful of her duty to please the king. She arched her hands and arms gracefully, attempting to imitate the blowing of the breeze.

Her nerves settled as she lost herself in the strains of the pleasing tune. But then she became curious about the men in the room. Her grandmother's warning repeating in her head, she peeked up until she saw the golden table reserved for their honored guest. She reached out to do a tricky bend, lifting her head ever so slightly, and a pair of intense gray eyes almost took her breath away.

She gasped and quickly dropped her head, never losing her place in the dance. Her fingers and toes tingled as if struck by lightning.

Who is that?

At the head table, seated next to Oxyartes, Alexander became mesmerized as the beautiful girl in gold moved across the floor. She resembled a cloud floating in the sky—delicate, graceful, and like no woman he had ever seen. He found himself unable to look away, and when he finally did, he discovered the rest of the rowdy

Greek men had gone silent as their greedy gazes devoured her.

"Is this the girl you told me about?" he questioned through the side of his mouth, so others could not hear.

Hephaestion leaned in closer. "That's her."

The music stopped. Alexander tore himself away from the girl and remembered his duty. He stood from his place behind his table while the three young women approached.

When they bowed before him, Oxyartes came to his side, beaming from ear to ear.

"Great King, I would like to introduce my daughters." He gestured to the first child standing in front of the table. "My youngest, Irania."

Irania bowed obediently, and then stepped to the side.

"My oldest daughter, Yasmin."

Alexander politely dipped his head, and then she quickly moved out of the way.

His heart thudded as the daughter in gold walked right up to him. The scent of jasmine drifted off her skin, and her hair shimmered in the torchlight.

"And finally …" Oxyartes motioned to his last daughter. "Roxana."

At first, she kept her head lowered, hiding her face from him. But then her chin tilted upward, raising her gaze higher to his knees, and higher still to the hem of his tunic. When she reached his ceremonial bronze cuirass, decorated with the sixteen-pointed Argead star, Alexander held his breath. Without a word or even a smile, she'd captivated him completely. How could he, the king, be so bewitched?

Then without warning, Roxana raised her head all the way, looking directly at him.

A collective gasp ran through the tent. Tension filled the air.

Fire. Her green eyes radiated an innate spirit, the kind he'd admired all his life. To find it in a woman from such a backward land could mean only one thing—the gods had sent her to him.

"Roxana," Alexander whispered.

She dutifully bowed.

He noted the flush of color in her cheeks and the way her hands trembled. He feared what others had told her of him. The Greeks and Persians had a long history of hate. Had she taken such animosity to heart?

Alexander sighed, wishing he could talk to the young woman more, but it was time to get back to formality.

"Would you ladies care to join us for the feast?"

Oxyartes directed his daughters to a smaller table behind him where Histanes and his youngest son, Estander, sat next to Atimexis.

Irania and Yasmin took their seats while Roxana remained standing in front of the king.

"If you will excuse me, my king," she said in Greek. "I'm unable to dine with you this evening. Forgive me." She turned around, showing her back to him, and walked directly out of the tent, leaving Alexander dumbfounded.

Her father's mouth fell open. "I don't know what to say. Great King, I apologize for her behavior."

Alexander gave a dismissive wave as the young woman strolled away. "Think nothing of it, my friend." He tipped his head slightly to the left, as he often did when thinking. "Perhaps I've offended your daughter." He smiled at his host. "I will go and make amends for my bad manners. If you will excuse me."

The entire tent was silent as Alexander hurried to the entrance and dashed into the night.

CHAPTER FIVE

Roxana gulped in the cool air, fighting the thunderous explosions resonating in her being. The eyes of the man she had seen, the one who had set off a firestorm in her, had belonged to the king. She'd never experienced such intensity from anyone before.

And what had she done after meeting the man? She'd left the tent, terrified by the encounter.

Roxana wanted to sink into a hole and never come out. She grabbed the roughhewed pole holding a torch next to her, convinced her legs would give way.

I am cursed.

What to do? Did she go back in the tent and apologize? No, she couldn't go back in there. She would face the wrath of her father and Atimexis a thousand times over before having to endure the king's presence again. Her fate was probably already sealed. The best she could hope for now was marriage to a lowly goatherder or banishment from her home.

She bent over, the bitter burn of regret rising in the back of her throat.

"I must apologize, dear lady."

Roxana spun around. At first, she noticed the king, but then she became distracted by the two soldiers standing next to him, clutching long spears.

"Am I under arrest?" She clenched her fists, ignoring her father's warning to please the man standing before her. "For leaving a banquet?"

"These are my bodyguards." He coyly grinned. "One can never be too careful when one is king." He gestured for his escort to fall back.

Roxana relaxed when the soldiers moved away. Her focus shifted to Alexander. The all-consuming way he studied her made her believe he could see through to her very soul.

"I wanted to apologize if I offended you. I thought perhaps you were angry and that's why you didn't stay for the feast."

She dropped her head. How could she tell the king that if she had not left, she would have been sick in front of him?

"I still would like you to join me at the banquet." Alexander inched toward her, waiting for a reply. "Roxana?"

When he said her name, she snapped her head up. Confronted by those eyes, a flutter of tingles overtook her.

"I cannot ... I had to ..." She fretfully searched the campsite. "I had to leave. I couldn't ..."

"You're shaking." He lowered his voice into a soothing whisper. "I don't bite.

I just wanted to make sure you're not angry with me."

Like a skittish horse calmed by her master's voice, Roxana settled down. She took in the lines around his eyes, the scar on his cheek, the way his thick, wavy hair fell across his forehead. Then his gold diadem—the crown worn by Macedonian kings—sparkled in the torchlight.

"I'm sorry I ran out on you." She let out a breath, her shaking easing. "You're the king and my father's guest. I have insulted you."

He lifted the corners of his mouth into a dazzling smile. "If I were insulted, would I be standing out here, abandoning a sumptuous feast and begging your forgiveness?"

She put her hands to her flushed cheeks. "I guess not."

"Well, I'm glad we've established that." He took another step closer, and this time, she wasn't afraid but intrigued. "So, will you come back to the dinner?"

She pictured the crowded tent, the curious stares, the odor of meat and wine mixed with the sweat of men, and the tightness in her chest intensified.

"I can't go back in there. I feel unwell when I think of the noise, the crowd, and …" Her voice died away.

He raised his hand to a path leading from the banquet tent to the Greek camp. "Perhaps we could take a stroll in the night air, to help you feel better."

Roxana was thankful for the suggestion. For the first time that evening, her worries left her, and she smiled.

"You're captivating when you smile, Roxana. Hera herself would kill for your smile."

Roxana knitted her brow. "Who?"

"Hera is the queen of the gods, to us Greeks anyway."

She was astounded by how easy he was to talk to. Definitely not what she'd expected from the Great King.

"I remember my father mentioning your curious gods to me. How they fight with each other and have contests to see who's the strongest."

"Yes, they can be a bit dramatic." Alexander came alongside her, a gentle breeze tossing his hair. "But they are the judges of our souls. We must do their bidding."

"My father doesn't think much of the gods, mine or yours, so I've never wasted my time with them." Realizing what she'd said, she hurriedly added, "I meant to say, I'm so busy with my studies, my womanly work, and the—"

Alexander chuckled, cutting her off. "I seem to remember your father mentioned something about you spending most of your time at the stables. He said your love of horses got in the way of your womanly work."

Roxana found herself strangely drawn to his broad chest and muscular arms. She liked that he wasn't tall like his other generals. His stocky, powerful physique appealed to her. The uneasy feeling in her stomach abated, only to be replaced by a new and very different sensation.

"My father spoke of me?"

"Yes. I inquired about you after you made such an impression on my generals. I wanted to know more about you." Alexander cleared his throat, sounding nervous. "How long have you been riding?"

"Ever since I can remember. I love horses."

"Then there's someone I think you should meet." He moved swiftly past her and started quickly down the path.

Roxana struggled to keep up in her tight dress. Not far behind, the heavy footfalls of the soldiers followed. Their constant presence bothered her. Did the poor man ever have time alone?

She arrived at a makeshift stable made of timber and rope. Below a tented roof, horses, secured in narrow stalls, pawed the ground.

Alexander waited for her at the front of the stable, his hair shimmering in the light from nearby torches.

"This is for my horses and those of my Companions."

Roxana breathed in the essence of the animals and then wrinkled her nose.

"Companions?" She slowly approached him. "I don't know this word. What does it mean?"

"Companions are the men who have earned my trust and friendship. They are the generals who fight alongside me, and the members of my court who advise me. You can't miss them around the camp. They wear purple cloaks and receive the best of everything."

She motioned to his outfit. "But you wear a purple cloak as well. How will anyone know if you're the king?"

"A king must set himself apart from others by his deeds, not his dress." He took a step toward a row of stalls.

Her father had warned her about the peculiar customs of the Greeks, but she had not expected to share such an intimate exchange with the Great King. Why was this mighty conqueror spending time with her?

Alexander petted and greeted each of the horses with soft murmurings. He seemed so relaxed with the creatures. Nothing like the formidable king she'd met at her father's side.

"This is my general Ptolemy's horse. Ambrosia. A fine mare." Alexander patted the horse's head lovingly.

Roxana moved in step behind him as he rubbed the white blaze on the chestnut's forehead. He then walked down a few stalls to an impressive red roan.

"This is Thunder, Hephaestion's horse."

"I met this man." Roxana gently stroked the horse's soft nose. "He came to our tent that first day on the great rock."

"Yes. Hephaestion is a good general, and also one of my closest friends. He was the one who first told me about you. He called you spirited, I believe." Alexander moved back to observe her.

Roxana continued petting the horse, hiding her face to avoid blushing again. "I'm surprised he troubled you with such trivial matters."

He crossed his arms and rested his shoulder against a post. "Great beauty is never a trivial matter, especially to a Greek."

"Perhaps." She turned to Alexander, eager to appear confident. "My grandmother was once revered as the most beautiful woman in Persia. It's hard to believe such a thing when you look at her today. Beauty does not matter because it does not last."

Alexander clapped. "Spoken like a true philosopher. I wonder what Aristotle would make of you."

"Who is Aristotle?"

"Aristotle of Stagira. My tutor. My father sent him to me when I was thirteen. Taught me many things, the old man did. Philosophy, science, strategy, medicine. He was also a great friend and a second father to me." His cheerful grin fell. "But that was a long time ago."

A shrill whinny rose from the end of the stable. A black head jutted out of the stall entrance and bobbed excitedly.

"All right, old friend. I'm coming," Alexander called to the anxious horse. "This is who I wanted you to meet." He hurried down the aisle.

Roxana arrived in front of the last stall where Alexander cradled the head of the largest horse she'd ever seen.

An all-black beast, he had a half-moon shaped white mark on his forehead. He had gray around his mouth and ears, but the rest of his coat still shined like onyx. The stallion reminded her of a child with its mother as he rested his head against the king's chest. The horse snorted with disapproval when Roxana neared.

"This is Bucephalus." Alexander stroked the stud's head. "I've had him since I was a boy, and we've ridden in many campaigns together. We've had great adventures, haven't we?" The horse nodded as if he understood every word. "He was even captured by the Mardians and held for ransom for a time. Weren't you, old man?"

"Who would want to ransom a horse?"

His eyes filled with fire. "Someone wishing to hurt me."

She cooed gently to the steed and reached out to stroke his soft nose. The horse objected at first, but she persisted, and finally, Bucephalus gave in.

"He likes you." Alexander rubbed the animal's neck. "He's old and ornery, so he doesn't give his affections readily."

Bucephalus turned and nipped his master's arm.

"Hey, there." Alexander chuckled and pulled away. "He's showing off for you."

Their lighthearted play momentarily stilled the fluttering in her stomach.

An awkward moment of silence passed between them. Roxana felt the king's eyes on her, and her butterflies burst into flames.

"Why did your father teach you Greek?"

She stepped away from the horse, her nervous energy getting the better of her. "It was my mother who taught me. She was the daughter of a Greek merchant. She also taught me to ride, hunt, to heal the sick, and to fight."

Alexander raised his eyebrows. "Fight?"

"Yes, sir. I can hold my own, as long as my opponent isn't much bigger than me." She dropped her gaze, embarrassed at her pride in such an unwomanly skill.

"What did your mother teach you about healing?" He moved in next to her. "I've always been fascinated with local medicinal treatments. I often instruct my court physician to learn all he can from the native people. Perhaps you should speak with him."

Roxana raised her head, reassured by his interest. "My mother was the skilled healer, not me. But she did teach me about treatments for wounds, broken bones, and fevers."

"She taught you to hunt, too?"

His voice rose in the most charming way.

"Nothing big, only fox and small game. My father never allowed me to go on boar hunts."

Alexander's musical laugh surprised her. He didn't come across as menacing.

"I love to hunt. Lion is my favorite." He paused, inspecting her with a renewed interest. "Is your mother the one who taught your father Greek?"

"Yes. It's something we share, sort of like our secret language. His mother never approved, which only made me want to speak it more. She says it's not proper, but my father insisted. Father and Grandmother have had many intense discussions about my speaking Greek."

Alexander snickered. "Oh, the things my parents used to fight about when I was growing up."

Roxana frowned at him. "Did your parents also fight about your future and try to plan what they thought was best for you?"

"I think all parents do that. But mine argued about other things, too. Politics mostly. They used to go at each other like cats and dogs sometimes, but my father always got his way in the end."

He grew colder when he spoke of his parents, eliciting a twinge of concern. "Was your father also a great conqueror?"

"No, not quite, but he aspired to be one."

"Now, you are what he aspired to be." His face remained a little sad, perplexing her. "I'm sure he would be very proud."

He turned to the camp surrounding them. "I sometimes wonder what he would have made of all this."

There was something different about Alexander's eyes; something she couldn't define. Longing, restlessness, an avid curiosity seeking satiation—she didn't know what to call it.

The music from the feast and the bustle of the camp intruded on their interlude. Consumed with getting to know the man, she wished for more time together. Again, her stomach filled with an unusual burning, but this time the sensation dipped between her legs, awakening an exquisite heat she'd never experienced.

"I must get back to the feast. Your father and the other guests are waiting." He held out his hand to her. "Shall we?"

Roxana spied his gold royal seal ring. To touch the king in such a way was against the most sacred laws of her culture, yet this one was inviting it without the slightest hint of concern.

"No, Great King. I'm sorry." The words tumbled from her lips before she could stop them. "It has been a long night. I will return to my camp."

"Very well. I understand." He snapped his fingers at a guard behind him. "This soldier will see you safely to your tent. I will say good night."

Roxana bowed. "Thank you, Great King."

Before she rose, he'd already walked away, followed by his bodyguard. She politely smiled to the soldier beside her.

Desperate for the sanctuary of her family tent, she started down the path for home. Her mind reeled with thoughts of Alexander and their brief time together. Part of her wanted to hate him for what he'd done to her family and people—he was a Greek and an enemy—but another part hoped to see the fascinating man again.

What is wrong with me?

Chapter Six

Alexander entered the noisy banquet tent, and the aroma of sweat, meat, and wine displeased him. His intoxicated soldiers, laughing too loud, had broken into their bawdy songs, making him long for the relaxing company of the girl.

She'd gotten under his skin; he couldn't deny it. Mistresses he had taken to his bed had nothing on the enchanting creature. There was something about her he wanted to possess.

He arrived at the head table and smiled at Oxyartes. He noticed the man's other children and mother had already retired, leaving only the men in the tent to drink away the night.

"You were gone quite a while," Hephaestion's familiar voice buzzed in his left ear. "Everything turn out all right?"

"I'm fine." Alexander snapped up his goblet, resenting being stuck in the tent with his drunk men.

"I was talking about the girl. What's the matter with you?" The tall Greek sat back on his pillows and smiled. "Oh, I see. Did she refuse your attentions or was she unacceptable to bed?"

He peered into his wine. Thoughts of bedding the girl had plagued him from the moment he'd seen her dance, but after speaking with her, he found her mind as equally captivating as her body.

He debated what to do about her. Then the shadow of Oxyartes loomed over his right shoulder.

"I hope you did not find my daughter too distasteful, Great King. She's young and very stubborn. I've indulged her too much, but perhaps her husband will tame her wild streak, eh?"

The man's talk of marrying her off irritated him. How could such an alluring woman be understood by any ordinary man? She needed someone exceptional, someone able to allow her free spirit to grow.

"You've gone quiet." Hephaestion eased closer. "What are you thinking? You get moody when you overthink things."

He ran his fingers over the rim of his goblet. "Perhaps I'm moody for another reason." He set his goblet down and faced his host. "Oxyartes, I found your daughter to be a delight. I congratulate you on raising such a fine woman. She has spirit and brains and …"

Silence engulfed the tent as men gazed up at their table, straining to hear the king's praise.

"What are you doing?" Hephaestion pressed.

Alexander's face reddened as he considered his next move. He would anger his men, but he would also shock them. That was the key to dealing with his enemies on the battlefield, and much of what he learned in war translated to life.

"I wish to ask your permission for Roxana's hand in marriage."

The angry thumping of goblets on tables carried across the tent. His men stared in disbelief as a hush hovered in the air.

Oxyartes nervously surveyed the contingent of Greeks. "Great King, did you say marriage?"

"Yes." Alexander grinned at Hephaestion. "I'm going to marry Roxana."

The light from several oil lamps flickered as their thick smoke created sooty designs on the side of the tent. Alexander sat at his desk, scrolls and wax tablets lay in disarray before him, but he couldn't concentrate on any of them. The girl had choked off his interest in work.

Below his desk, a hulking brown dog with matted hair excitedly wagged his thick tail.

"I thought I would find you up." Hephaestion's head popped in the entrance to his study. "Hello, Peritas." He went up to the dog and pet its head.

Alexander picked up a scroll. "One cannot be king, run an empire, and sleep. About time you got here. Help me with these letters."

Hephaestion pulled a wooden stool out from the other side of the desk. After he sat, he inspected the modestly furnished tent.

"It's a wonder how a man who rules Greece and Persia lives so simply when all those around him lived so well."

"Makes it easier to pack." He unwrapped his scroll.

Hephaestion frowned and picked up the nearest scroll. "I don't remember this being in my job description, Alexander."

"Hence the title, the other Alexander." The king chuckled while never lowering his scroll. "You know I could never get through all of this work without you. Besides, you're better at writing letters than I."

"That's because I have the patience to sit down and compose a letter, whereas you only have patience for battle."

The two sat reading until Alexander couldn't stand it anymore and broke the peace.

"When are you going to let me have it?"

Hephaestion put down his scroll. "Have what?"

Alexander lowered his scroll and feigned an indulgent smile. "The lecture. You know, the ones you always give me when I don't do something expected of me."

Hephaestion shrugged. "I wasn't going to do anything of the kind."

Alexander tossed his scroll onto the desk, annoyed. "Oh? Somehow I don't believe this was supposed to be just a friendly chat."

Hephaestion hesitated, smashing his lips together. "Could you have at least told me about your intentions to marry this girl before you proposed to her father?" He cut his hand across the desk. "I mean, really, Alexander, to marry a girl with no family connections, no royal blood, and a barbarian at that. I would completely understand if you bedded her, but marriage?"

He regretted how the only man he trusted couldn't see her uniqueness. "I take it you don't approve."

"Approve?" Hephaestion stood. "Alexander, you've got a whole army of generals with beautiful daughters. Greek daughters, who would be a hell of a lot easier for these men to stomach than this baron's half-breed. You have insulted your generals and your men. What if this girl gives birth to a son? Are your Greek generals to bow before a barbarian king?"

He reined in his anger. "The child will be half mine. Half-Greek."

"In all the years I've known you I've never seen you do anything quite this impulsive. No, I take that back. You're famous for this. But marriage? To a non-royal, half-breed Persian girl? This exceeds even the burning of Persepolis." Hephaestion smacked the desk. "I know you're eccentric, but do you have to let every one of your men know just how eccentric you can be?"

Alexander took in Hephaestion's angry grimace. Of all the people he knew, this man was the only one who spoke the truth, but how could he explain his actions when they didn't make any sense to him, either? He wanted the girl, and like so many other times in his life, he'd decided to take something without considering the consequences. But would there be any consequences? He doubted it.

"You don't want me to marry her? Even if it could help settle affairs in this region? Or have you forgotten the two years of rough fighting we have suffered through in this part of the world? A political marriage could help quell a lot of ruffled feathers. Oxyartes could come in handy."

"I don't care who you marry. You know that." Hephaestion arched over the desk. "But think of your men. You're a Greek king. A king must have an heir ... a Greek heir. No matter how divine you think yourself today, my friend, eventually you will die, and then who is to run this vast empire we have worked so hard to build?"

Alexander folded his arms, shaking his head. "That's why I'm marrying this girl. Sogdiana and Bactria will be settled. I will have an heir, and the empire will have a future under a Greek and Persian king. It's the only way any of the lands we have conquered will continue. The two different cultures must be melded as one. My son with Roxana will do that."

"What's wrong with Darius's daughter, the young Stateira, for such a liaison? When you left her at Susa with instructions for her to learn Greek, you gave her family your assurances you intended to marry her."

"And so I shall." Alexander raised his voice, growing frustrated. "Stateira will be a marriage of state. Roxana is different."

Hephaestion glowered at him. "Different how? She's a woman, and they're all the same when you take them to bed."

Alexander slouched on his stool, drained. He'd spent his entire life fighting for people to understand his dreams, his visions. Here he was King of Persia and Greece, and he still had to explain himself, even to those who knew him best.

"All my life I've been told I need to marry. My generals begged me to marry before I even set foot in Persia. My mother marched enough women in front of me to build an army. Every satrap, king, and prince I've ever met has paraded sisters, wives, and daughters before me for marriage. I want to choose my wife. For once, I want to select a woman, not because she's good for the army or my empire, or for Macedon, but because she's good for me. Can you understand that?"

His friend stood back, arching a single eyebrow at him. "Are you telling me Roxana inflames your desire?"

"You know me better than that," Alexander grumbled and sifted through the pile of scrolls. "It's not about sex. I want a child from a woman worthy of being the mother of kings. Roxana is such a woman."

"Have you forgotten Barsine? Your mistress. She carries your child. You found her attractive enough. Why didn't you marry her? Her father comes from noble Persian blood and was an old friend of your father."

"She doesn't have … I don't know, something this girl has. 'She moves a goddess, and she looks a queen,' like the line from *The Iliad*. No, it's more than that. She has spirit, fire, and a mind of her own. She's like—"

"Like Olympias," Hephaestion injected.

A burn flared in his stomach at the mention of his mother. "Roxana is nothing like her." He selected a scroll and held it up to him. "See here. She has sent another of her letters demanding I get rid of Antipater as regent. Mother is never satisfied with anything. The gods know how my father tried to please her, and since his death, the unpleasant task of appeasing Olympias has fallen on me." He slammed the scroll on the desk. "That woman charges great payment for her nine months' rent."

Hephaestion sat on his stool. "Yes, I must agree. Your mother is a bitch."

Alexander picked up another scroll and threw it at Hephaestion's head. But the general was too fast for him and ducked before it could touch him.

They chuckled, and for Alexander, it was like when they were boys, running around the palace at Pella and pretending to be their heroes, Achilles and Patroclus.

"So, the generals are angry." Alexander's mood turned sullen. "Is that what concerns you?"

Hephaestion batted around a few scrolls. "They're angry today, but they're generals. Give them a battle and the whole mess will be forgotten."

"And you ... are you angry?"

"Never with you." Hephaestion smiled, and the tension brought on by their disagreement lifted. "Marry the beauty, have a hundred mixed-bloods for sons. I don't care as long as you're happy."

"Will you stand beside me at the ceremony? I would like you at my side." Alexander suspected the gesture would appeal to Hephaestion's need to be placed above the others.

Hephaestion's brilliant smile told him the ruse had worked.

"I would be honored to be your second."

A kick of satisfaction reinforced his confidence in his powers of persuasion. His father had taught him from an early age to know every weakness and strength of an army and a man. Alexander used both to his advantage on and off the battlefield.

He tapped a finger on the desk, considering his next request. "I would very much like it if you and the girl could be friends. Like Patroclus befriended Briseis for Achilles."

"Not that damned book again." Hephaestion groaned.

Alexander chuckled, relieved they had resolved the matter for the time being. "I just want all the people I love to get along."

Hephaestion cringed as he stood from his stool. "You never asked me to love your mother."

Alexander could almost hear Olympias in his head, chastising his choice of friends. "That's because Mother doesn't like you. She thinks you're a bad influence on me."

"And I am." Hephaestion went around the desk. "I let you get your way too much of the time." He kissed Alexander on top of the head.

Heartened, Alexander grinned. "That's why I'm king. So I can always have my way."

"Good night," Hephaestion called as he walked to the front of the tent. "Get some sleep. You'll need your strength for your wedding night."

Alexander let out a long breath. There was one general he'd convinced; the others would not be so easy. He could almost picture the exhausting arguments ahead of him, but it would all be worth it once he claimed the girl as his. Their brief encounter left him hungry for more of her.

Hephaestion stuck his head back in the room, interrupting his visions of Roxana. "You do know what to do with a virgin, don't you?"

Alexander laughed, letting off some steam, and threw another scroll at Hephaestion's head.

"Better than you."

CHAPTER SEVEN

E arly morning light filtered through the tent as Roxana stretched and opened her eyes. The warm rush of the previous night's excursion at the stable came to her. She tucked the blanket under her chin, recalling her stolen moments with the king.

Yasmin barged into her sleeping quarters. "Tell me what happened with you and the king. The entire camp is buzzing about it."

This was all she needed.

"Father is going to kill me for running out of the banquet like that."

"And Grandmother is going to kill you for turning your back on the king." Yasmin got comfortable on her cot. "What got into you last night?"

She sat up next to her sister and swung her legs over the edge. "It was the dancing, the smell of the food, all those Greeks, and when the king spoke to me, I … All I could think of doing was getting out of that banquet tent."

"When he went after you, every mouth in the place fell open." Yasmin nudged her with her shoulder. "What was he like?"

Roxana recalled his musical laugh, how his hair had shimmered in the torchlight, the way he'd cooed to the horses, and how he'd looked at her.

"He was nice. Not at all like a king. At least, not the way Father described the Great King Darius." She glanced at her sister's keen face. "He took me to his stables and introduced me to his horse."

Yasmin grinned. "What else?"

Roxana suspected she wanted lurid details. "That was it. He said he had to go back to the feast and then had one of his guards escort me here."

"That can't be it." Yasmin's face fell. "He didn't try to kiss you, to touch you. He didn't even try to take you back to his tent and have his way with you."

"Yasmin!" She scowled at her sister. "I wouldn't have done such a thing. That would have shamed our family."

Yasmin folded her arms, sulking. "If you ask me, that's what Father had in mind last night. Dressing you in gold was to make sure all eyes would be on you. You were paraded in front of the Greeks for one purpose and one purpose only."

She wrinkled her nose. "What is that supposed to mean?"

Yasmin tossed up her hand. "Don't you listen to the rumors around the camp?"

"No, I don't listen at tents like you."

"Well, it's said that Alexander—"

Atimexis, a whirlwind of black, dashed into Roxana's quarters.

"We have to get you ready." Atimexis grabbed for a comb on a trunk next to Roxana's cot. "Get out of those bedclothes. Your father is waiting for you."

Roxana swallowed hard. The punishment she'd feared seemed imminent. Perhaps there was still a way to redeem herself, to make amends to her father and grandmother.

"About last night—"

"Last night was a blessing for you and this family." The older woman put the comb through Roxana's long brown hair. "You did the right thing walking out on the king."

Yasmin stood up, her eyes wide with astonishment. "You were going to kill her last night. I heard you."

Atimexis let go of Roxana's hair and calmly folded her hands. "That was before her father gave away her hand in marriage."

What? The walls of her tent closed in around Roxana. She grabbed her chest as the air got thin.

Had she heard right? Perhaps it was a mistake. Before she could ask Atimexis to repeat what she'd said, Yasmin let out a triumphant scream.

Atimexis had her by the shoulders, holding her upright, but the tent still spun around her.

"Isn't it wonderful, Roxana? You're going to marry."

The exuberance in her grandmother's voice roused her from her stupor.

Still in her nightgown, Roxana tossed aside the curtains dividing the large tent into rooms.

"You must wait!" the old woman called behind her.

She frantically searched for her father, desperate for the truth.

She found him reading scrolls and giving orders to his scribe, who sat holding a wax tablet on the floor of his office.

"How dare you?" She stood at the entrance, her hands on her hips, ready to hurtle herself across his desk. "You marrying me off? Are you trading me to the Greeks like you did Histanes?"

Oxyartes stood from his desk. "Silence!" He snapped his fingers at his scribe.

The hunchbacked older man quickly gathered up his tablets and scurried from the room.

Oxyartes came around from his desk. "I have not traded you, as you so crudely put it. And I have not betrayed you." He clapped his hands sounding as exuberant as his mother. "Never in all my life would I have dreamed of such a match for you."

It was true. Her heart broke, fracturing into a thousand pieces. How had everything turned so bad, so quickly? Yesterday, she had been listening to her grandmother complain about her two left feet, and today she was to be given in marriage to some stranger.

Tears gathered in her eyes. "I don't want to marry. I want to stay here with you."

The joy on her father's face dissipated and his lips thinned into a pained grimace behind his black beard. He pulled a stool out from his desk and placed it in front of her.

"Roxana, sit."

She meekly took her seat, all the fight she'd entered the small office with withered away.

"You can't live with me all of your life." He rested his hand on her shoulder, giving her a reassuring squeeze. "You must go out into the world. Make your own family, and to do that you must marry. This man wishes to set you above all the girls in Persia. You will be his first wife because he has no others. Do you understand what a great honor this is?"

A tear stained her cheek, and she slapped it away. "I only understand I will be taken away from my home and my family and given to a man who will probably strangle me in my bed."

"Your family will never leave you, little star," he said, switching to Greek. "You will always be in our hearts. And your husband will never hurt you. He cares for you very much."

Roxana's determination returned. For the first time in her life, she planned to disobey her father.

"I will not marry." She wiped her runny nose on her nightgown sleeve. "You can't make me."

Oxyartes grabbed her by the shoulders and shook her. "I've already consented to this match. You will not embarrass this family or me by refusing. Do you know what could happen to us if you anger this man?"

She pushed him away and jumped to her feet. "What will happen to me if I marry? What will become of me?"

Oxyartes raised his hand, about to strike, and then he froze.

Roxana couldn't believe it when he dropped to his knees on the brown mat covering the ground.

Slowly, she turned to the entrance to see what had made her father cower. There, with Hephaestion at his side, Alexander waited. A small man with wax tablets in his arms stood behind them.

Alexander's gaze swept over her sheer nightgown and then like a consuming fire, the magnetism he radiated overtook her, making everyone else in the room disappear.

"I thought we were to discuss the details of the dowry this morning." Alexander came up to her. "Is this a bad time?"

"Dowry?" she asked without bowing to him. "I'm marrying you?"

"Roxana!" Oxyartes howled in Persian from the ground. "Remember yourself."

She should have been embarrassed, greeting the king in her nightgown, but she was too astonished to care. Had Alexander asked for her hand? The first question to pop into her head was why? What would a king want with her?

Alexander turned to Hephaestion. "Why don't you take Oxyartes on a tour of our camp? Perhaps you can show him how we drill our men."

"Of course, Alexander." Hephaestion waited for Oxyartes to rise from the floor and come to his side.

Once her father and the scribe hurried out of the tent, escorted by Hephaestion, Roxana feared to be alone with the king. Saying no to marriage with anyone else, she could stomach, but she wasn't sure she had the courage to say no to him.

Alexander walked past her and casually inspected her father's desk. He tossed the scrolls around.

"I take it your father didn't tell you I asked for your hand last night."

She held her head up high. "Why me?"

He rested his hip on the desk and folded his arms. His face was a mask of calm, which she found more disturbing than his penetrating eyes.

"Is there something in particular about me you don't like? Have I displeased you in some way?"

Beads of sweat broke out on her upper lip, despite the cold air in the tent seeping through her thin nightgown. How did she tell a king she did not wish to marry him without putting her life and the lives of her family in jeopardy?

"I'm honored by your proposal, my king. But I have no wish to marry you or any man. I do not wish to become ..."

"A wife?" Alexander picked up a rock her father used as a paperweight.

"A pawn," she corrected in a strong voice. "I don't want to be used to please the fancy of a king."

He dropped the rock on the desk. The loud *bam* sent a ripple of fear through her. She fully expected him to walk out of the tent and call for his guards to arrest her but he didn't. He sat back, his gaze sweeping up and down her figure.

"What am I to do with you?"

She folded her arms over her breasts, unnerved by his intrusive stare. "Are you going to arrest me?"

The slightest smile spread across his lips. "For what? Speaking your mind? Short-lived is a king who arrests his subjects for telling the truth."

A glimmer of hope sparked to life in her heart. "So, I don't have to marry you?"

"There's the problem. You may not want me, but I want you." He got up and walked toward her. "As king over this land, I have the right to take you ... forcefully, if need be. Any time I want, for as long as I want. Then I could walk away without any regrets and leave you and your family in shame."

Her stomach heaved at the idea of crushing her father and ruining her sisters' chances at marriage, but something else he had said disturbed her. *I want you.*

He closed the distance between them. The funny burning she'd experienced in her belly the night before reignited. The tingling awakened in her toes and a warm rush of heat spread between her legs.

"Fortunately for you, I do not violate the chastity of my subjects." He knitted his brow as he stood over her. "Roxana, you're a beautiful woman, and many men will want you and promise you great things. But I am the king." He lowered his head to her. "And I can give you everything you desire."

Heat billowed off his skin, and his intoxicating fragrance tempted her. Roxana struggled to find the words to argue with him, to send him on his way, but her resolve cracked. An unfamiliar urge rose from her deepest reaches, begging her to consider his offer.

"I desire to stay with my family, my king." Her voice came out tremulous, something she'd not expected. "To remain with my people."

"You won't be alone. Your brother, Histanes, will be coming with us. And then you will have me—your husband."

She shuddered at the word. "What is a husband but a man who has bought himself a wife and considers her no better than the livestock in his barn? I have no wish to be a wife or have you as a husband."

"Ah, but I can promise you palaces for homes and not barns." He chuckled, stirring her anger. "And I do not treat any of the women I care for as livestock. Ask my mistresses."

"Maybe I will!"

Roxana wanted to get away and tried to go around him, but he blocked her at every turn, reminding her of a stubborn lion refusing to give up the chase.

He reached for her wrist, pulling her next to him. "I could show you the world. You will see great wonders as my wife."

She fought his grip. "I was under the impression wives of kings only saw the inside of a palace. If I marry you, that's all I will ever see of the world."

"Marry me, and I promise everywhere I go, you will go."

An inkling of interest took hold, and she stopped struggling. To travel the world would give her a sense of freedom, the kind she'd always dreamed of, but at what cost? She took in his handsome face, unruly hair, and extraordinary eyes. Would living as his wife be so bad?

Alexander let her go. He sighed and marched to the desk. He stood with his back to her for a moment, and then faced her.

"Do you not wish prosperity for your family, for your father? Being related to the king by marriage, your father will be held in high esteem by many people. Your family will be protected."

She rubbed her wrist, still feeling his grip. Why couldn't the man take no for an answer?

"My family will be protected as long as you are king. Kings change so quickly in this part of the world. Only a short while ago, Darius was king. What happens when there is another Alexander?"

He sat on the desk. "By the gods, you've got spirit. You remind me of the women from Macedonia. Strong, tough, brave, and very outspoken." He snickered. "Debate me all you like, Roxana, but I must have you. What will it take for you to agree to be my wife?"

Roxana was taken aback by the question.

"I don't want anything from you. I only want to stay with my family. Where I am loved and feel safe."

"But I will love you. I will take care of you." He rose from the desk and edged closer. "I will keep you safe in my arms at night."

Part of her wanted to give in, but another part was afraid.

"If I marry you, I will lose my freedom. I will not be able to ride my father's horse or speak my mind because I will be your wife and become invisible. Can you understand that, my king?"

Alexander cupped her cheek and her insides melted at his touch. He was so gentle, so unlike what Yasmin had prepared her for.

"I promise I will give you your freedom. You can ride my horse and always speak your mind with me. And if the day comes when you feel I have reneged on my promise, you can return to your family." His lips hovered inches above hers. "Marry me, Roxana. Be my wife. Be my little star."

Her heart danced as he spoke, beseeching her to accept, but could she trust such a feeling? Only the gods knew for sure. Her resistance all but gone as he caressed her cheek, Roxana knew she would marry him. What choice did she have? He was Alexander, with a will stronger than her own, he would wear her down in the end. Why not give up now and accept her fate?

Unable to put words in her dry mouth, Roxana nodded.

Alexander tilted away from her. "I take it that means yes?"

"Yes." She fixed her attention on the reed mat below her feet. "Yes, I will marry you."

"Good. I'll inform your father. We'll marry as soon as possible." He put his hand under her chin and lifted her head. "I will keep my promises to you."

She defiantly removed his hand. "I hope so."

He grinned and then headed for the curtain.

He came to a sudden halt and glanced back at her. "And I promise you have nothing to fear. There will be no other kings replacing me. There will be no more Alexanders." Then he stepped through the curtain and disappeared.

CHAPTER EIGHT

Alexander stood at the front of the giant tent made of tightly woven sheep's wool and fidgeted with the gold belt on his tunic. He admired the garlands of flowers strung along the back, remembering how he had taken the tent from Darius's caravan after the Battle of Issus. He rarely found a reason to haul the monstrosity out from the baggage train, but here he was, doing the unthinkable beneath the raised canopy—taking a Persian bride.

Torchlight fluttered outside, casting wriggling shadows across the tent walls while hundreds of oil lamps burned around him. In the distance, the bawdy songs of inebriated soldiers added to the sweat dotting his upper lip.

What has she done to me?

He adjusted the purple cloak over his left shoulder, feeling more nervous than he did before going into battle. Maybe he should have taken the girl as a mistress and bypassed all the ceremony, but there was something about her he wanted to possess. Marriage was the only way to guarantee she would never belong to anyone but him.

Hephaestion shifted next to him. "You sure you want to do this?"

Alexander scanned his generals, attired in their best armor. The usually rowdy men sat stoically behind rows of tables, their wine goblets untouched. Their dour faces ignited his fury.

"They look like they're about to eat the bride."

"What did you expect?" Hephaestion nudged him with his elbow. "They see her as a captive barbarian. Give them time."

Alexander longed for some wine to settle his nerves. "Achilles married a captive lady, too. Briseis. I bet he didn't get any crap from his generals."

Hephaestion chuckled under his breath. "So this is to explain your reason for marrying her? You're imitating Achilles again?"

"Not intentionally." Alexander pulled at the neck of his tunic collar. "I never met a woman I wanted to marry before. Bed, sure. But this girl I want around me, by my side, for as long as the gods allow." He glared at his sour-faced generals. "They think this is a political alliance, but this is a love match."

"A love match? Perhaps for you." Hephaestion rocked on his toes, something he did when bored. "One day, you will have to tell me how you conned the little nymph into marrying you. I thought she sounded pretty damned adamant when we walked into her father's tent that morning."

Alexander smiled as he remembered the meeting. "I debated her on why she should marry me. In the end, I won like I always do."

"That's all well and good for politicians and generals, but this is a sixteen-year-old virgin." Hephaestion frowned at him. "You will not win her heart through debate."

He dropped his head, blindsided by the comment. He had not thought of the girl's heart. Winning her hand had been his biggest battle. Once married, he figured she would love him in time, but what if she didn't? He'd lived through his parents' bitter marriage to know he never wanted one of his own.

The flaps at the other end of the tent rustled and Roxana entered, escorted by her father. When Alexander saw her in her bridal attire, his mouth went dry.

White linen as thin as gauze shaped the curves of her breasts and slim hips while a shimmering sheer veil hid her features. Gold decorated her wrists and neck, and when she walked, the little gold bells wrapped around her ankles tinkled. Even her shoes were gold. Her long hair, piled atop her head, had a garland of white flowers woven through it, and as she approached, a heavenly scent came with her.

The ethereal creature reminded him of an Egyptian goddess he'd seen painted on the walls of the palace in Memphis. Whatever reservations he'd harbored about marrying the girl faded away. And when her green eyes flashed at him through the gossamer fabric hiding her beautiful face, he knew he would never regret this day for as long as he lived.

"I take it back," Hephaestion mumbled as the girl walked toward them. "I would have married her if you hadn't."

The tent fell silent when the bride came to a stop in front of her groom. She stepped beside him, and Alexander took her hand from her father.

She trembled, but then stopped after he gave her hand a reassuring squeeze. He pushed her bridal veil aside, and his breath stilled when he saw her face.

With delicate features, a small nose, sleek high cheekbones, a smooth brow, and exquisitely carved jaw, she was the most beautiful creature he'd ever seen.

He tilted toward her and whispered, "You are Aphrodite, Roxana. A jewel among the stars."

Despite the eyes of the guests, the decorum of the ceremony, and the surreal nature of what was happening, Alexander remained acutely aware of the woman by his side. The touch of her hand, her warmth, and the hint of jasmine on her skin soothed his restlessness. Why did she have such a hold over him?

The wedding bread served on a gold ceremonial plate had been arranged on the table in front of the couple. Oxyartes placed a small gold knife by the bread, as was the custom of his people, and waited for Alexander to cut the loaf and symbolically seal the marriage.

But as Alexander glimpsed the puny knife, he knew he needed something grander to make a statement at his wedding, something consistent with a king. He reached for his jewel-encrusted scabbard and withdrew his decorative sword. With one quick stroke, he sliced the bread in two.

Cheers broke out among the local people in the tent, and slowly the disgruntled generals joined in.

Alexander picked up one half of the loaf and fed it to his bride, smiling as she bit off a piece and chewed.

Then Roxana picked up her half and offered it to him. He observed her eyes as he ate the bread, entranced by the way they danced in the light.

The musicians struck up a lively tune as the family of the bride crowded around the table to congratulate the couple.

Oxyartes took Alexander's hand. "She's my greatest treasure, dear king. Treat her well."

The ceremony concluded, and while the servers brought out the food for the wedding feast, Alexander wiped beads of sweat off his brow.

"I need a drink."

Hephaestion laughed and slapped his back. "Not too much, my friend. You still have your wedding night ahead of you."

After the toasts were made, the wine consumed, and the wedding cake devoured, Roxana's grandmother whisked her away to prepare her for the wedding bed. While escorted from the tent, the intoxicated Macedonian crowd directed jokes at Alexander, bringing a warmth to her cheeks. She was grateful her grandmother didn't understand a word of Greek, but she did, and their taunts cut her to the bone.

She hadn't realized until then the animosity her marriage to the king had created among his men. The references to his barbarian bride hurt most of all. They were the barbarians in her country, not her. And if his men were so antagonistic toward her and her people, why was the king taking her as his wife? It seemed better for him to take her to his bed, and then leave her behind when his army moved on. More uncertain than ever about her position with the king, she hurried from the tent, not wanting to hear any more.

Once in the night air, she breathed in a few deep breaths, thankful for the reprieve. The drunk men, the ceremony, even the endless toasts proposed by her father, had worn her down. The only highlight during the whole evening had been the moment Alexander had taken her hand. But there was still more to come, and she wasn't sure she was ready.

"Your father had a bridal tent erected for you next to the king's tent," Atimexis told her as they traveled along the small path. "I've had the biggest bed I could find set up in it and used our best family linens."

Roxanne spotted brightly colored flower petals leading to a tent decorated in red and yellow ribbons. She realized what it was.

The ceremony, which once seemed impossible, now dimmed in comparison to the challenge of her wedding night. Was she supposed to feel sick to her stomach over the prospect of sleeping with a man? She knew what to expect, she'd listen to Yasmin enough in her life, but no one had prepared her for what to do or say when laying with a man for the first time.

Atimexis grabbed her arm. "Come. We don't have much time before the men escort your new husband to the bridal tent."

Husband? The word sounded odd to her. With the slice of his sword, she'd become his—in body anyway. Her heart and soul, she vowed to keep for herself.

Once inside the tent, the heady perfume of flower petals scattered about the floor accosted her.

"By all that is sacred, what were they thinking?" Atimexis brushed a mass of petals to the side with her foot. "Men should never be left to prepare a bridal chamber. The fools always overdo it." She hooked her arm around Roxana's waist. "We must get you undressed."

Roxana wished Yasmin had accompanied her, but her father had insisted that her grandmother tend to her alone.

More flower petals covered the floor of the bedchamber. The massive ebony bed in the center sat atop a small platform and boasted an array of white pillows. The piece of furniture didn't appear menacing, but to her, it felt like a huge mountain.

After Atimexis closed the curtains partitioning the bedroom from the front of the tent, she came alongside Roxana.

"Are you afraid?"

Roxana wasn't sure how to respond. They had never spoken of the intimacies between a man and woman.

"Should I be?"

Atimexis smashed her lips together, accentuating the wrinkles around them. "There are some things I should explain to you." She knelt, untying Roxana's gold shoes. "You are now a wife, and as a wife, you must endure your husband's attention. Tonight, he will come to you, and he will not intentionally mean to, but he will hurt you." She blushed while helping Roxana step out of the shoes. "Not a bad hurt. You are a virgin, and as a girl who has never known a man ... Well, when you are first with a man, there may be some pain ... when he enters you ... as a man."

Roxana stooped down. "It's all right. I know about sex. I grew up in a barn. Watched the ewes and rams every spring, and if that wasn't enough, I had Yasmin for a sister. I know what is about to happen."

Atimexis let out a relieved sigh and climbed from her knees. "When I was escorted to my bridal bed, I was a mess. I knew what was going to happen and I was terrified. You're much braver than I was."

She suddenly felt closer to her grandmother. Atimexis was no longer the sinister old woman who plotted her doom, Roxana saw her in a whole new light.

"Thank you, Grandmother."

Men singing and shouting outside the tent reminded Roxana of what was ahead. With an assertive nod, she reached for the ties on her dress.

"It's time for me to prepare for my husband."

Alexander tossed open the bridal tent flap. His sandals smooshed the flower petals as he stepped inside. The band of men who had accompanied him moved away and their cheery voices faded. He relaxed a little, rolling back his shoulders, glad the formal part of the evening had concluded. He wanted time alone with his wife.

He made his way across the short reception area to the red curtain. The weeks of preparation for the wedding, and the few moments he had spent with her had only added to his anticipation for this night.

With one sweep of his hand, he forced the curtain aside, and then he saw her.

Seated on the end of a great black bed in only a sheer pink nightdress, she had her hands folded in her lap, and her eyes downcast. The swell of her breasts and the paleness of her skin enticed him.

Her hair hung around her shoulders and down her back without any pins, barrettes or ribbons for him to remove. That was good; he wanted to feel the silkiness of it in his hands as he held her. He had dreamed of it almost every night since the first time he'd seen her.

He removed the diadem from his head. "Roxana."

When she looked up and smiled, Alexander let the crown slip from his fingers and fall to the floor.

"Yes, my king."

Alexander moved closer to the bed. He could feel the tension between them ease.

"From now on, you must call me Alexander."

"If that is what you wish, Alexander."

It was the first time he had heard her say his name. Having it spoken from those red lips was the closest Alexander had ever felt to standing shoulder to shoulder with the gods.

She stood and walked up to him, her slim hips swinging beneath her nightgown, stirring his desire. Without the slightest hint of fear, she helped him ease the cloak from around his shoulders. When she knelt to remove his sandals, he stopped her.

"I can do it. You're my wife now. Your hands are not to be soiled with such duties."

"Ah, I see." Roxana went back to the bed and sat. "Are you going to tell me exactly what my duties are as your wife?"

Alexander feared they had already gotten off to a bad start. "That's not what I meant."

"I'm sorry." Roxana's eyes burned into him. "Not my duties, then my station. What I am to be to you … or are we talking about my worth? What's the going rate for wives these days?"

"You're angry." Alexander sat down on the bed next to her. "What has happened? What has upset you?"

"Your men forget I understand their Greek. Tonight, I have heard many different reasons given for this marriage. It was called a peace treaty by some, a Persian alliance by others, and one man suggested my dowry was a means to pay for your armies. I even heard myself called the captive bride. So which am I, Alexander? What reason would you give for marrying me?"

Alexander stroked a lock of her hair, amazed at the softness. "Never listen to the silly banter of drunken soldiers." He traced the outline of her chin and jaw with his fingertips. "I have married you because it pleases me. The rest will come with time."

She could barely register a word he said as he caressed her. The butterflies in her stomach took wing and settled between her legs, creating a deep ache.

She swallowed hard, and her resolve caved, but her apprehension of what was to come mounted. "What else will come with time?"

"Love." He told her as his fingers grazed her neck. "Some married couples find love; others do not. I'm hoping we're one of the lucky ones."

Her heart raced, sounding like a drum in her ears.

"I wouldn't know anything about love."

His hand settled over the top of her sheer nightgown. "Ah, but tonight you will know love." He touched his lips to hers ever so lightly. "Tonight, you will know me."

He kissed her again, harder than before. The strange sensation roused a sweet, white fire in Roxana's belly. Was this what Yasmin had spoken of, the desire she'd overheard couples sharing in the privacy of their tents?

His lips traveled down her throat as she eased her head back, lost in his tempting kisses.

He pushed her down on the bed as he slid her gown off her right shoulder. He eased the nightdress from around her, working it farther and farther down until, before she knew it, she lay naked beneath him.

How did that happen?

She wanted to cover herself, but he was her husband. Even so, being naked with a man, a man she hardly knew, let alone a king, set her nerves quivering. She stiffened in his arms at a complete loss of what to do next.

Is it supposed to be this awkward?

He must have sensed her embarrassment because he pulled away. He sat up and rubbed his hand over his chin as his gaze swept over her body.

"Have they explained to you about—?"

"I know about sex." She tried to relax. "I'm just not sure what to do."

He nuzzled her neck as he wrapped his arms around her. "Do what you feel."

That didn't help her at all. What she felt like doing was running away, but since that wasn't a possibility, she closed her eyes and tried to picture something she enjoyed, like riding her father's horse in the fields.

When his fingertips found her nipples, a shot of heat traveled down to her groin. He pinched her right nipple, and she bit her lip, trying not to groan. The sensations skipping across her body were both wonderful and terrifying.

How does anyone enjoy this?

"I promise I will be gentle," he murmured in her ear.

Roxana thought she would explode as his hands traveled over the hills and valleys of her body. He kissed her neck and teased her with little nips until his mouth settled over her left breast. She arched her back as his teeth tormented her nipple, and then she felt his rough, callused hands skim over her flat belly and come to rest between her thighs.

The caresses and kissing stopped. She opened her eyes to see Alexander leaning over her as he struggled to remove his tunic and undergarments. He got his head stuck in his tunic, and it brought an unexpected giggle to her lips.

He laughed with her as he threw his clothes to the floor.

Her breath caught in her throat. She'd encountered nude men before, but never one like him.

His chest was smooth, unlike the hairy Persian men she had seen growing up. He had thick muscles across his chest, shoulders, and arms. And the smell of him, like clover in spring, was not the sweaty, musky scent of other men. Then she noticed the scars. White gouges and long lines were everywhere—on his shoulders, about his neck, down his arms, along his calf, and even around his ankles.

She touched a nasty white scar on his chest, the heat from his skin warming her fingers. "What have you been through?"

He glanced down at her hand. "I'm a soldier. These are marks of war. I've no part of my body without them, at least in the front."

She'd never seen the body of a soldier. The ones she knew lived in their camp, but they had never been in battle. This was something she never expected to see on anyone.

"But so many? Do they hurt?"

His disarming grin amused her. "Not at this particular moment."

He kissed her again, and she forgot about the scars, their wedding, and even the soldiers who had ridiculed her. His kiss wiped away every thought. This is what the poets meant when they spoke of the bliss of passion. She reached hungrily for him.

He climbed on top of her, slowly working his hands down to her hips.

"Open your legs for me, Roxana."

She obeyed, and when his fingers dipped into her, she flinched. It felt so strange.

He stroked her. She rocked her head back, amazed. Yasmin had never told her about the fire in her belly, the tingling of her skin, and the indescribable hunger awakened in her soul. Her sister's attempts to describe sex now seemed woefully inadequate.

His fingers ran through her hair, and she reciprocated, liking the softness of his wild mane. He didn't use oil like Persian men. His seductive essence tantalized her nose as she breathed in his skin. The light color, the softness, the feel of his muscles underneath, all added to her excitement as her hands roamed his back and chest.

"Slip your arms around me," he instructed in a soft tone.

She reached around his broad back and held on to him as she buried her head in his chest. Roxana wasn't sure what to expect, but she was no longer afraid.

"Are you ready?"

She nodded and closed her eyes, guessing the worst was yet to come.

He lifted up her hips, readied her, and kissed her shoulder tenderly as he drove himself into her.

A sharp pain radiated up her groin and she wanted to cry out. Instead, she held on to him and squeezed her eyes shut as he moved inside her.

By the gods, no one had prepared her for the intimacy of the act. She didn't think anyone could describe it. The discomfort was still there, but not as sharp, and she flinched as he eased deeper, keeping her eyes closed and refusing to shed a tear.

He pulled back and dove into her again. It burned more than hurt. She tensed, wondering how much longer it would last. She snuck a peek at his face, only to find him watching her. Caught in the act, she buried her head in his chest.

When he groaned and went still, she became a little concerned.

Is that supposed to happen?

He lay on top of her, breathing hard, as warm liquid oozed between her legs and spread on the sheet.

Alexander sat up and lifted her head to him. "Was it so bad?"

At a loss for words, she stared blankly at him, her cheeks burning.

He chuckled at her reaction. "I'm your husband, Roxana. This is what husbands and wives do on their wedding nights."

She took in a deep breath, trying to settle down. "I know. I didn't realize it would be so … uncomfortable."

"Next time, I promise, it will be better. The first time is always bad for women. From now on, we can enjoy each other."

"Enjoy? I don't understand."

He outlined her full red lips with his finger. "You will, little star." Alexander rolled away from her and immediately grabbed the sheet. "Move over a bit. I'm going to get rid of this. I refuse to sleep on a wet sheet all night."

She shimmied to the side and waited as he whisked the now blood-stained sheet from the bed and threw it to the floor.

The sight of the red spot added to her humiliation. It announced to everyone what she had endured.

"There. The old crones will have their prize to display tomorrow." He climbed back into the bed and pulled her into his arms. "Now we are truly man and wife."

She nestled against him, relieved the worst was behind her. "Yes, my king."

"Alexander," he corrected.

She kissed his chest and sighed. "Yes, my Alexander."

CHAPTER NINE

Roxana cringed at the bridal sheet strewn across the side of the wedding feast tent for all the camp to see. Alexander sat at the head table next to her, enjoying their first breakfast together. The tent, alive with laughter and the aroma of roasting lamb, was not the same as the previous evening. His Greek generals nursed their wine but refrained from their hurtful comments. She guessed he must have warned them at some point to hold their tongues and not upset her.

He clasped her hand and listened attentively, but she didn't say much while she picked at her food. She wasn't hungry after their night together.

Sometimes she looked at him, amazed he had chosen her as a wife. After all the battles, all the years of trekking across the vast continent of Persia, and he'd never married. What could he have possibly seen in her?

He occasionally glanced at Hephaestion on his right, sitting at a discreet distance. Everyone in camp talked about their relationship and she'd seen them together regularly. Did he approve of Alexander marrying her, or had he, like the other generals, considered her a barbarian bride?

While they lifted their goblets in yet another toast by her father, a messenger appeared before the king's table.

"Hephaestion." Alexander waved the messenger forward. "Be a good friend and entertain Roxana while I see to this."

She gulped, not sure if she was ready to speak with the general. What if he disliked her, or worse, ignored her completely?

Hephaestion took Alexander's seat. "You've made Alexander very happy."

"You should know, General. After all, you're my husband's closest friend."

He turned to her, wielding a boyish smile, which added to the playful glint to his eyes. "It's a lie. We hate each other terribly. It's all an act for the sake of the men."

Roxana observed her husband, who stood reading a scroll on the other side of the tent. She yearned to learn more about him so she could be of some use to him as a wife. Her father had always professed, to know a man, you must first know his friends. She'd never understood what he meant until she studied the general sitting beside her.

"He relies on you a great deal, doesn't he?"

"We rely on each other." Hephaestion's gaze stayed on Alexander. "Always have, ever since we were boys back in Macedonia."

There was something else she needed to understand—his country. "Do you miss your homeland?"

His smile faltered. "No. Wherever Alexander is, is home enough for me."

Roxana searched for some way to get him to open up to her. "You admire the king a great deal, don't you?"

"Of course. We've been through much together."

"I would like to know what you and my husband have experienced. I want to learn about Alexander's country and his life. Perhaps, General, you could help me to understand the king better so I may be a dutiful wife."

"I'm delighted to see the Lady Roxana is as wise as she is beautiful." He dipped his head to her. "I would be honored to help you, but only if you call me Hephaestion. *General* is a title used by a soldier, not a friend."

Roxana was relieved to hear him use the word *friend*. She would need more of them in the future.

"Thank you, Hephaestion. We both know how happy that will make the king."

He glided his fingertips over the smooth surface of the table. "Alexander's happiness must always be our utmost concern."

The comment confused her. "What about your happiness?"

"When my king is happy, I am happy."

Alexander approached, his frown accentuating the crease in his brow. He handed Hephaestion a scroll.

"The Baron Chorienes and some other chieftains are holding out on another great rock, farther east of here in the territory of the Paraetacians."

"Another rock?" Hephaestion stood, reading the scroll. "How many of these things are there in this country?"

Roxana chuckled. "Too many to count."

Alexander snapped up his goblet from the table. "Pass the word on to the other generals. We need to pack camp."

Hephaestion came around from behind the table, nodded to the king, and quickly walked out of the tent.

A sinking feeling settled in her stomach. *Will I go with him? Or will I be packed off to a palace somewhere?*

"How long before the camp moves on?"

"A week, maybe two." Alexander took his place at the table beside her. "I have some things to attend to before I leave this region. It should give you plenty of time to say goodbye to your family and be ready to travel."

She'd forgotten about leaving her sisters and father. How could she go on without them? But as her husband took a deep swallow of his wine, her distress eased. She no longer belonged to her father; she belonged to Alexander.

"And will I go everywhere you go? Even to war?"

He set his goblet aside. "I know the Persian custom is for a royal wife to remain at the palace in Susa, but I'm not a Persian king. I'm a Greek general with an army to lead. You're my wife, and I will want you with me whenever possible." He leaned in closer to her. "Besides, I promised to show you the world."

Roxana gave him a warm smile. "I would also like to remain with my husband, whenever possible."

He took her hand and squeezed it. "Good. I have my attendant picking out servants for you as we speak. He will see to your accommodations. And I have a surprise for you."

She relished the feel of his hand on hers. "What surprise?"

He raised her hand to his lips. "Something I know you will love."

The breakfast feast concluded, Alexander took Roxana for a tour of the Macedonian camp. Men were busy packing supplies and water, sharpening weapons, and gathering into large groups for marching. Along the way, she noted how every man casually interacted with their king and never bowed. The two guards following them were a constant reminder of the dangerous world in which she now found herself.

They arrived at the royal stables. Alexander enthusiastically led her down a row of stalls until they came to a beautiful dark chestnut mare. With a white blaze on her face and three white socks, she was short, stocky, and stood quietly in her stall as the other horses around her whinnied and pawed at the ground.

Alexander flourished his hand over the mild-mannered horse. "This is your surprise. She's yours."

Roxana stared in disbelief at the serene creature. It was something she'd always wanted but had been told she could not have because she was a woman.

"I've never owned a horse before."

"I'm assured she's very gentle." Alexander patted the horse's neck. "I can't have you riding around on those wild ponies you're used to anymore. You're a king's wife, and when you're with child, this horse will take good care of you."

Perhaps being married to the man would turn out better than expected.

Not caring who saw them, she threw her arms about the king's neck and kissed him on the mouth. "Thank you."

"I thought you would like her." He unwound her arms. "But I have even more surprises for you."

She patted her new mare's nose. "The horse is enough."

He took her hand and pulled her away from the stall. "Come. I will show you to your new home."

They soon arrived in the women's camp. Located behind the mass of army tents, it was where the wives, mistresses, and female attendants who followed the men resided. Children flitted through the dirt paths as women sat huddled over open fires, cooking or mending clothes. To the side of the main camp were the larger tents used to house the women of rank.

Alexander stopped in front of the biggest tent in the camp. "This is yours. It's made of the very best sheep's wool, not goat's hair like the others. You will live here when we make camp. There's a smaller one packed up for you to use during quick marches, and when there are palaces to sleep in, you will be given the best rooms." He held the flap open for her while two members of the of king's guard took up their station at the entrance.

Amazed at his generosity, Roxana stepped inside. Fresh cut jasmine flowers adorned the side table. Had the king requested them?

It was already furnished with some of her things—her cedar chest and her dressing table—the long Persian dining table, chairs, and statues of strange gods she'd never seen before.

"I had Bagoas pick out a few items from the treasure wagons for you," he explained as he followed her around the tent.

She turned to him, curiosity nipping at her heels. "Bagoas?"

"One of my attendants. He's Persian, served under Darius, and has excellent taste. I'm sure you will run into him sooner or later."

She'd never heard a servant praised so, especially by a king. She made sure to remember the name.

Alexander walked ahead of her, casually inspecting the contents of the tent. He touched everything and tested the chairs around her dining table. He might have been a king, but there were moments he acted more like an exuberant boy.

They stepped through the dividing curtain to the back of the tent, where their black wedding bed had been fitted with fresh white-linen sheets and stuffed with pillows.

"Here is where we shall enjoy ourselves." Alexander walked up to the bed and tossed aside a few pillows.

Roxana bashfully lowered her head. A million memories of their night came rushing back to her.

"Oh, no, my wife. None of that." He flung his arms around her, lifting her from the ground. "You're no longer an innocent virgin."

He kissed her. This time she wasn't nervous about being with him. Their day together, and all his gifts, only added to her desire for him. She'd once believed she would never want a man, but she had never met a man like him.

He guided her to the bed, plying kisses along her neck while nimbly unclasping the gold brooch on the right shoulder of her long, pleated dress. Roxana giggled when the jewelry fell to the floor, and his eager hands lifted the pale blue fabric over her head. She got caught up in it and remembered his struggle with his clothing the night before. Her chuckle grew into a full belly laugh. No longer afraid of what would come, she anticipated his caress, his scent, and the feel of his arms.

Her clothes discarded, she climbed onto the bed, enjoying his lustful gaze. Never taking his eyes off her, he threw his purple cloak to the floor and stepped out of his chiton.

"This time you will enjoy yourself, Roxana."

Before she could blink, he was on top of her, showing none of the restraint from the night before. His hands were more demanding as they fondled her breasts, his lips more fervent as they kissed her nipples.

How could his touch elicit such ecstasy? What surprised her most was how desirous she was to be with him again. Instead of fearing what was about to happen, she craved it.

He kneeled between her legs, and her reservations briefly resurfaced. She didn't want to suffer that pain again.

"Relax," he murmured. "It will be better."

When he thrust into her, there was no pain, only a brief soreness, and she winced. Then everything changed.

It started as a warm tingle in her belly rising steadily upward. Her every thought was drawn to the sensation of him moving in and out.

His arms tightened around her, he tucked his head into her neck, and then he slammed into her. Roxana tensed as the warm tingles turned into a ribbon of fire. She gripped his shoulders and threw her head back, gasping with need.

Yasmin never mentioned this part!

Just as she found a rhythm with him, meeting his hips in time with hers, Alexander groaned and relaxed on top of her.

They lay together for a while saying nothing. When he finally moved, Alexander wrapped her in his arms and played with a lock of her hair.

"Was it better this time?"

Better? She'd never expected it to feel so good. "Yes, Alexander."

He dragged his finger along her hip. "You must tell me the truth."

She sighed, still uncomfortable with revealing her thoughts to a man other than her father. "It was better. It was very pleasing."

He chuckled into her hair. "That's what lovers do. Please each other."

How did he know that? "Have you had many lovers?"

"What an odd question for a wife to ask of her husband."

She sat up, leaning on his chest. "Am I wrong to ask?"

"I would think most women don't wish to know such things."

She jutted out her chin. "I'm not most women."

"No, you most certainly are not." He tapped the tip of her nose. "Yes, there have been other women. Back in Greece, there was a woman named Campaspe. I gave her to an artist I hired once … Apelles, that was his name. And here, in Persia, there's a woman named Barsine. I was with her before we met. She's pregnant with my child. When we pull out, she will go with us. Does that bother you?"

She regretted asking about his lovers. A pregnant mistress? How could she compete with her?

"Do you care for this Barsine?"

"There was never love between us." He reclined back on the bed. "What other questions do you have for me?"

She had a thousand of them but didn't know where to begin, but then one question surfaced, intriguing her more than the rest.

"What is battle like?"

He raised his head, his expression muddled. "I've never had a woman ask me about battle before."

She traced a white scar on his shoulder, wanting to understand him better. "My father told me some stories about it, but my grandmother made him stop, saying it would give me nightmares. I've often wondered about it. I was hoping you could explain it to me, about why men like it so."

He tucked a tendril of hair behind her ear. "Men love battle because it's a time to prove themselves, to show the gods their worth as a hero among men like the great Achilles. I remember the first time I fought in a real battle against the Thracian Maedi. My father was fighting another war and left me as regent. I'd never been so terrified and excited in my life. Although, after the battle, I was changed."

Engrossed, she edged forward, resting against his chest. "How so?"

"There are so many things." He inhaled a deep breath. "The stench of it— blood mixed with dirt, smoke mixed with incense from the offerings and the burning of the dead. The exhilarating exhaustion after you've wielded a sword all day and chased down men. Then there are the sounds of screaming, moaning, yelling, and banging metal. One can never describe battle; you can only experience it."

She examined his scarred chest and imagined all the things he must have witnessed, the men he'd killed, and those he'd lost. The faces of the soldiers in his camps came to her; their devotion to him, and the way they interacted with their king.

"There's something I don't understand." She curled into him. "Why don't your men show you respect?"

He sat up, furrowing his brow. "My men respect me."

She rested her hand on his chest, hoping to soften her words with a caress.

"Perhaps, but in Persia, all men bow before the king. But all of your men, from your generals to your foot soldiers, they greet you the same way—with a word or a nod. Should they not bow before their Great King as they would a god?"

He tensed under her hand, and the mood between them changed. Had she said the wrong thing?

Alexander took her hand from his chest and held it. "To the Greek, worshipping a man as a god is not tolerated. I must accept such divine honors from the people I conquer, but I must also be careful not to insult my Greek subjects. It's a precarious position I hold. I was born a mortal, subject to death, and I must remain cognizant of that. To act as a god would endanger my soul."

She didn't understand. He was king; shouldn't his subjects do as he demanded? "Your men must at least honor you as a king. To us Persians, their behavior is, at times, confusing."

He played with her fingers. "My men have been painfully slow to adapt to the customs of others, much to my regret. Perhaps you're right. Maybe a change is in order." He kissed her hand, let her go, and rolled over. "I have much to do." He got out of the bed and picked up his clothes.

Troubled by his sudden desire to go, Roxana scooted to the edge of the bed, gripping the sheet. "Have I done something wrong?"

His tunic halfway over his chest, he glanced at her, a puzzled wrinkle on his thick brow. "No, of course not. Why do you ask?"

"You're leaving."

He reached for his cloak and sandals. "I'm a king and a general. I have an army to see to and a battle to plan. How would it look for me to sleep the afternoon away in your arms?" And with that, he marched out of the tent.

She sat on her bed at a complete loss of how to interpret his behavior. Maybe this was a glimpse of how life would be with Alexander. He was not hers to lock away but belonged to an army, and to the many different nations he'd conquered. But she still had questions about him, his life, and the other women who had come before her.

She climbed from the bed and quickly dressed. There was only one person she knew who could get the answers she needed—her sister, Yasmin.

Outside, she took the path back to the Persian section of the camp. Along the way, she passed children playing and women cooking in the bright afternoon sun. Suddenly, every face in the camp became a former mistress to the king.

What is happening to me?

Once among her people, she relaxed, bolstered by the sounds of her language, the fragrance of cinnamon and turmeric dishes cooking on open fires, and somewhere, the gentle strains of a well-known song played on a flute. The calmer atmosphere soothed her after the noise and bustle of the Greek camps.

She searched the mass of tents until she recognized a familiar ponytail of long hair.

"Yasmin?"

When her sister turned, she put her finger to her lips. Roxana heard the frenzied grunts of a man and a woman inside the tent next to them.

"Is that how you and the king sound?" Yasmin whispered.

Roxana grabbed her hand and pulled her away, more angry than embarrassed.

Back on the path winding around each of the tents, she let her sister go. "You need to stop doing that. Grandmother will take a strap to you if she ever finds out."

Yasmin smugly folded her arms while eyeing her sister. "How was your wedding night?"

She should have known that would be her sister's first question. She rubbed her hand over her chin, unsure of how much to tell her.

"It wasn't as bad as I thought it could be. Especially after listening to you all of these years."

"Did it hurt?" Yasmin's eyes twinkled with curiosity.

Roxana took in the other tents. "I'm not going to give you any details." She urged her to a large patch of grass, antsy to be out of earshot.

Yasmin frowned when they came to a stop. "I was counting on you to give me a firsthand account of what to expect."

Roxana wanted to share something to prepare her but knew no retelling would do it justice. "I think you will find out soon enough. And listening at the tents will not help you, trust me."

Yasmin cocked her head, seeming satisfied. "What's he like?"

Roxana's frustration grew. "Yasmin, please."

"I'm just wondering because according to the rumors about the camp, my dear sister, you're not the only one your husband has been sleeping with."

Roxana paused, glad Yasmin had broached the reason for her visit without coaxing. "What have you heard?"

Yasmin inspected her nails in a cagey manner. "Have you seen your husband's attendant, Bagoas. Many say they are lovers." Her sister smirked. "And then there are the rumors about that mistress of his."

This was why her husband praised his attendant. She'd heard stories about how the men preferred male lovers to women, but she'd never suspected Alexander of such affairs. Knowing others were competing for his affections incited her insecurity. What if he grew tired of her?

She wrung her hands, worried for her future. "His mistress is named Barsine. He told me she is with child—his child."

Yasmin raised her eyebrows. "But he didn't tell you about Bagoas? The eunuch. The man—more like *boy* if you ask me—who attends to the king during his bath. The whole camp is talking about it. He was loved by Darius, they say, and now by Alexander." Yasmin clasped her sister's forearm. "I didn't tell you this to hurt you. I'm telling you to be careful. This Bagoas is very skilled at getting rid of people who are in his way. Just watch your back. You're living in a whole new world. From now on, you must learn to listen at the tents. Keep up with what's going on around you. Talk to servants and make friends anywhere you can. One day, you might need to protect yourself from people like Bagoas."

Roxana shook her head, frowning. "I'm not you. How can I dare listen—"

Yasmin's grip tightened on her arm. "It wasn't long ago, Darius was king of all Persia. Now he's dead—killed by his men. What's to become of his family, his children? You need to plan ahead in case something happens to your husband."

Roxana patted her sister's hand, the disquiet in her heart building with every passing breath. "I never considered the ramifications of being married to a king. I will pay attention to such intrigues in the future."

"Oh, Roxana," Yasmin sighed, hugging her. "I'm afraid from now on our life will be filled with little else."

CHAPTER TEN

A strange sound woke Roxana from her sleep. She sat up in her black bed as an eerie mist floated above the ground. Moonlight punched through the small holes in her tent roof, casting streams of light into her room.

A shuffling noise made her grab the sheets and pull them up to her throat, afraid an intruder had entered her tent.

"I was watching you sleep." Alexander moved into a beam of moonlight. "You're like a little girl when you sleep."

In a red Persian robe and matching peaked cap, he reminded her of her father. "Why are you dressed like that?"

"To remind the men that I am a Greek and Persian king."

A large dog with matted brown fur moved out from behind him. She'd seen the creature before, trailing behind Alexander as he walked the Greek camps.

"Who is this?"

He patted the creature's side, the hollow sound resonating through the tent. "Peritas, my loyal companion, and the only person I don't seem to piss off these days."

She got up from the bed and went to the dog, holding out her hand. She'd always wanted one, but her father had adamantly refused, claiming they were unclean.

A soft tongue licked her hand, and a cold nose nuzzled her. She rubbed his face and ears, feeling his coarse coat.

"He likes you." Alexander observed her petting the dog. "He doesn't let many pet him. Which shows he's an excellent judge of character, unlike me."

The circles under his eyes disturbed her. "What's wrong?"

He directed Peritas to a corner of the tent. "I came from meeting with my generals about Chorienes and his great rock. After listening to their bickering, I just wanted some peace with you."

Generals fighting in front of their king didn't sit well with her. "What were they arguing about?"

Alexander led her to the bed. "Any number of things. They fight constantly when in the same room. They only stop when I make them. I fear the day I'm not around to control them. They will destroy each other."

That any general would disagree with his king was beyond comprehension.

"Then why not order them to stop fighting? You're their king."

"They're first my friends. Most I have known since boyhood. They have followed me, have believed in me, even if they haven't always agreed with me. I can't order them and risk losing them because I can't rule this country or run this army without them." He let go of her hand. "And then there's Greece. Despite being a king, I still have enemies back home who speak ill of me and can harm me. My rule is not absolute. The only thing keeping me king of anything is my army."

She sat on the bed, a sense of foreboding enveloping her. "What will your enemies say in Greece when they discover you have taken a Persian bride?"

He took off his red cap. "The same thing my generals say—I've become too Persianized."

Persianized. The word circled her like a vulture ready to feed. She lowered her gaze, her stomach shrinking with fear.

"And what would your enemies do if we had a son? Would he be a barbarian king or a Greek one?"

He tossed the hat aside. "He will be my son and heir to my throne. That's what I will make them see."

Despite the defiance in his voice and the steadfast determination on his face, she doubted his words. The hate between her people and the Greeks had lasted for over two hundred years. Could one child wipe it out in a day?

He let the robe fall from his shoulders to the floor. "I'm working hard to unify our two cultures by blending our armies and showing my men by example how to embrace the Persian culture."

She froze. Was that what was she was to him? A gesture of unification?

"What is it? You've gone quiet."

Roxana rubbed her temples, her mind spinning. "I didn't realize it would be like this, being married to a king."

He lifted her chin. "I hope one day you will forgive me for marrying you. I wonder now if I was wrong to make you mine. The long campaigns, the time we shall spend apart, the brutal travel, the disease, bad food, bugs, battle, and death— it's tough on seasoned veterans, but you ... Perhaps I should have ignored my impulse to have you and left you for another man."

She coiled a curl of his hair around her finger and detected the wine on his lips.

"But you didn't, and here I am."

He frowned, teeming with frustration. "You know nothing about my world. There are so many things you must learn about my enemies and my friends."

The scope of her strange reality startled her. She'd never seen the stage behind the king, the other characters in his play. Alexander had blinded her, and now the scope of new life overwhelmed her.

"Then teach me." She placed her hand over his. "I want to know who I can trust."

"Trust?" He chuckled and stepped back from the bed. "Trust no one except Hephaestion. He's my truest friend and will always protect you."

"What about your generals? Can I trust them?"

He rubbed his hand across his chin, seeming to debate the question. "They don't see you as I do. To them, you're Persian."

A bitter taste filled her mouth. "Then tell me how not to appear Persian in their eyes?"

He clasped her shoulders. "You get to know them. Win them over as you have won me. If anything were to happen to me … If you were left alone with my heir, you would have to go to my generals to help secure my son's throne." His grip tightened. "Do you understand what I'm saying?"

She did understand, and the idea of being left behind with his child in a world where his generals would determine her fate terrified her. What kind of dangerous game had she stumbled into? How could she hope to survive?

"Tell me about your men. Who should I know?"

His long sigh carried in the air. "Craterus would be my next pick after Hephaestion. He was loyal to my father and is to me. Get to know him better. He can help you. Ptolemy is loud, stubborn, and wants desperately to be tied to my family. He craves to be a king in his own right, but he's a solid man and loyal. Perdiccas is the smarter of my men—cunning, a brilliant general and politician; he's tough but fair. Lysimachus is another of my childhood friends from the court at Pella. He's the quiet one, but loyal, and a shrewd general. He wasn't pleased about our marriage, so be careful with him." He took a breath. "The others? Seleucus is difficult, an infantryman with opinions and ambition; mind yourself around him. Then there's Antigonus The One-Eyed. Keep clear of him. He dislikes women and has a taste for power. He'll take advantage of you."

She put her hand to her forehead, swimming with the names, remembering each one as if her life depended on it.

"If these men are your friends, then what about your enemies?"

He sat down next to her. "The list is very long, I'm afraid. There are many here in Persia and back in Greece."

"Like who?"

"The foremost one in my mind right now is Callisthenes. I'll introduce you to him soon. He's here as a historian for this expedition, sent by his uncle and my old tutor, Aristotle, but he's a troublemaker. I believe Aristotle sent Callisthenes to report back to him on my interactions with the Persians. The old man always railed against your people when I was his student, but I never gave any credence to his ramblings."

She gripped the edge of the bed, panic-stricken. If all his men felt as this

Aristotle, what chance did she have as his wife?

He nuzzled her cheek. "Being married to a king isn't going to be easy for you. You must stay sharp around my generals and my men. You have a good mind, Roxana, use it to help you inside my court. Look for deception at every turn, and keep those who are loyal to you close, but your enemies closer."

She had never dealt with deceitful people. *How do I tell my enemies from my friends?*

"I will do as you ask. But I still don't understand how your men will not abide by your decisions or respect your word as king. What's the point of being a king if you're not treated like one?"

"I've been thinking about what you said. Maybe I should do something to make my men bow to me. Prove to them and the Persians I'm king of this land. Might improve things around here."

The apprehension clawing at her insides forced her to stand. "You said Greek men would never bow to another man."

"If I demand it, they will bow to me."

His dark voice rattled her. She'd never heard him speak so harshly.

"Won't making such demands anger them? Make them turn against you?" She slid his sword belt from around his waist and set it to the floor.

"Perhaps if I turn it into a ceremony of some kind. Something done in front of your people to shame them into bowing before me."

Shame? She guessed the contentious generals Alexander struggled to control wouldn't be pleased with his tactics.

"Are you sure a ceremony will make it easier for your Greek men to accept this?"

"I am. Once we have put Chorienes to peace, I will prepare a special banquet for my men to show me the proper respect." He stood and eased his chiton over his head. "I'll have Hephaestion make the arrangements. He's the only one I trust to do as I ask. He understands better than anyone."

The slight cut across her heart, but she didn't let it show. She would never share his confidence like his generals, or his comradery like his army, or understand his wars. She would have to be content with whatever he had left to give her.

She gazed into his bloodshot eyes. "I'm glad he's there for you."

"You're not jealous of him? My mother was always jealous of him."

The tension in his voice piqued her curiosity and spoke volumes about how to proceed. To maintain his affections, she vowed never to speak ill about the ones he cared for. She would have to keep her emotions hidden, even from him.

"I'm your wife. I'm content with that. I can never be jealous of someone who loves you and watches over you in ways I never can."

He kissed her forehead. "Thank you, little star."

She'd made the right choice. Soon they would be on the road, leaving Alexander her only protector. She needed to keep him happy, no matter how much it hurt.

His kisses caressed her cheek and slipped down to her neck while he tugged at her nightgown. He pulled her onto the bed with him. The tearing of fabric briefly filled the tent until she found herself naked and pinned beneath him.

His strength surprised her. Gone was the gentle lover. He was different tonight, more forceful, but she wasn't afraid. She no longer wished for him to be a considerate husband. Roxana was ready for something more.

"I want you to understand me." He lifted her head to meet his and hungrily kissed her.

Her lips trembled at first, but then an overwhelming longing took over. When she passionately kissed him, he jerked away.

"I want you to know me—all of me."

His arms went around her, and he nibbled the soft nape of her neck. She raked her nails down his back, urging him on.

She felt she would scream when his rough hands parted her legs, and his fingers pushed deep inside her.

"I can't wait." He lifted her butt off the bed.

He drove into her in one forceful thrust, moving deeper than ever before. The slapping of their hips together, their panting, and soft groans permeated the tent.

Her muscles tensed, and her only thoughts were of the tingling building between her legs. Then a cascade of heat overtook her. She arched, and a scream escaped from her lips. Caught in a climax of light and sensation, she forgot everything around her. Suddenly, she went limp, spent of energy as Alexander grunted above her. He bit into her shoulder and, he too, went still.

She lay covered in a thin film of sweat and drenched with satisfaction. When he opened his eyes and saw her resting peacefully beneath him, he kissed her cheek.

"Did I hurt you?" He rolled off her and touched the red marks on one side of her neck. "I had too much wine and got carried away. I'm sorry."

"No, don't be sorry." She removed his hand from her neck and gently kissed his fingers. "I'm starting to enjoy myself."

"I was beginning to wonder."

Roxana cuddled against his thick chest, remembering what he had said to her. "I want to know you, Alexander. All of you."

He hugged her, sighing into her hair. "Then we best start at the beginning. The place where I grew up is quite beautiful. Pella. You shall see it one day when we take our sons there."

She relished the way his voice rattled around in his chest like thunder.

"And you will meet my mother, Olympias, and perhaps one day my sister, Cleopatra. She lives in Epirus now and is married to the king, my uncle. You'll like Cleopatra. She's the funny one and a good bit like our father. When we were kids, Cleopatra and I would sneak out of the palace and hunt for light bugs. That was until the time Mother caught us …"

He went on, telling her about his family, his friends, and where he grew up.

She listened, enchanted by the sound of his voice and content in the knowledge that she was finally getting to know her king.

CHAPTER ELEVEN

Alexander's baggage train, comprised of women and children, loaded belongings into wagons, onto the backs of oxen, horses, and mules. The call of animals, the clanking of pots, and rolling of wheels carried across the valley below the great rock Roxana had once called home.

The confusion of where to go amid the chaos frayed her nerves. Everyone seemed to have a duty, but she just stood to the side while her newly assigned servants packed up two large wagons made to accommodate her, her tent, furniture, and bed. Once everything was on board, she was ushered to a second wagon by her new maid, Morella. She had a seat on a pile of pillows next to a window cut into the wagon's canvas.

Slowly, her cart followed the rest of the baggage train. Her family's tent grew smaller in the distance. She tried not to cry and entertained herself with the crowds of women and children surrounding her. Some walked, carrying large packs on their backs, while others rode horses or sat in open carts. Horses, goats, sheep, and a few oxen were herded between groups, keeping the animals from bolting. The organization needed for such relocation astounded her. How had Alexander moved so many people and animals across Persia like this?

The rising heat of the spring sun shortened the tempers of the women in the long caravan. Here and there, fights broke out. Children cried, and horses whinnied. Afternoon slowly crept to evening, and by nightfall, the camp halted, not far behind the men.

After checking in with the stable master and looking in on Hera, her little mare, she would stroll beneath the stars, winding her way through the wagons and tents of the women, hoping to stretch her legs from the tedious journey. Children scrambled to get out of her way. Women preparing the evening meals ignored her, a few smiled, and many whispered as she walked past, but no one spoke to her.

While wandering through the camp, she picked up the women's frenzied Greek murmurings. The gossip they shared at her expense racked her heart. Tales of the king's former mistresses, his adoration for his handsome general, and the eunuch who shared his bed while his wife traveled alone had become the preferred topic of conversation. She never let on she understood their language—never gave them the satisfaction of seeing her cry. The sense of isolation gathered like a storm in her heart. Here she was, wife to the king, but instead of bringing her adoration, it only created pain.

All around her, the air was alive with a flurry of spices. Fires crackled, and the far-off strains of harps and flutes accompanied her back to her wagon. The happy banter of families compounded her loneliness. She longed for her family. There was no Yasmin to dream with, no Irania to tease, and no Father to hold her while she wept. For the first time in her life, Roxana felt utterly alone.

It took days of achingly slow travel for the army and its followers to reach the base of the mighty rock of Chorienes. The impressive structure was a virtual eagle's nest, surrounded by cliffs and almost inaccessible. Compared to her previous high mountain retreat, the formidable rock formation was daunting.

While the army engineers erected her lavish tent, Roxana dutifully waited in her wagon. The first time she'd seen the tent go up, it had been entertaining; the second time, interesting. Now the entire affair had become tedious.

She climbed from her wagon and paced the dusty ground, anxious for her servants to put her furniture and belongings inside. She was about to inquire why it was taking so long when she noticed a pretty Persian woman coming toward her.

"You're the king's little star, am I right?"

Her Greek common, she had long hair, a vibrant shade of brown, and haughtily carried herself, much like a spoiled cat. Her features were plain, except for her flat nose, but she wore a long peplos, or Greek women's tunic, trimmed in gold, and colorful cloak, which clung to her sizable baby bump.

"You speak Greek." Roxana decided her light hazel eyes were dull and unimpressive.

"I'm Barsine, my lady." She dipped her head. "Congratulations on your marriage. Alexander is a fine man."

Roxana shuddered at the name. She raised her head, holding in any hint of her surprise. "Thank you, Barsine."

Roxana swore her eyes seared her skin, or was that the midday sun? She struggled to find any inkling as to what could have sparked Alexander's interest. Barsine was no beauty, and she was far from graceful.

"My baby is due soon." Barsine held her protruding belly. "I hope for a son."

"Is this your first child?" Roxana asked, betting she had birthed a few bastards already.

"My third, but the king's first." She bowed again with more pride than respect.

"Yes, but who ever really knows how many bastards a king fathers." What was keeping her servants from finishing her tent? She needed to get away from the distasteful woman.

"Oh, Alexander has fathered no other children. Of that I'm sure." Barsine scrutinized Roxana like a meat vendor sizing up a prized goat. "He has no real interest in women or babies."

An old fat cow of a woman with no teeth and even less hair appeared from behind Barsine and bowed deeply to Roxana. She spoke with a thick Greek accent, apologizing for the disturbance. Then she grabbed Barsine's arm and dragged her away.

A nudge of satisfaction careened through her as the protesting Barsine got shooed to the side of the camp designated for the generals' mistresses and nobility. But the encounter left Roxana with a bad taste in her mouth. How dare the woman be so brazen? She strived to rise above petty annoyances, and not put on any emotional display, lest she make the king look bad, but how could such a vile creature be his mistress?

If she's the best he had to choose from, no wonder he married me.

"That's her mother," a deep voice said to Roxana's left.

Hephaestion had his back resting against her wagon while his red stallion waited next to him, pawing the ground. Dust covered his leather greaves and sandals. His curly brown hair was matted and sweaty.

"Alexander asked me to check on you." He eased up to her, coaxing his stallion along with him. "He wanted to make sure you were all right after such a long time on the road."

"Tell the king I'm well. Will you be checking on Barsine as well?"

He chuckled and wiped his eye. "No. She will not bother you again. Alexander told her to stay away from you, but no can ever predict the mind of a woman."

"It seems Alexander can." The shouts of servants, the slam of wagons, and whinny of horses rose around her. She turned to the general. "Do we always travel like this?"

"I'm afraid so. This is the way of military life. We spend more time on the road than in battle."

A petite woman with upswept dirty blonde hair, a pug nose, and dressed as a servant came up to her.

"We've finished setting up your quarters, my lady."

Roxana smiled at her new attendant. "Thank you, Morella."

She shielded her eyes from the blinding sun and raised her head to the general. "Perhaps you would like some refreshment before you return to the king."

He collected the reins of his horse. "Thank you, but no. I have much to do with the army."

A measure of disappointment settled over her. She would have enjoyed some company. "Of course. The battle."

He turned away and with one quick swing, landed atop his stallion's back.

"I'll let Alexander know you've settled in. He was worried about you."

Roxana peered up at the handsome man, appreciating his attempt to appease her, but not believing a word. "Does Alexander worry about people? I think not."

He angled over his horse's neck to hide his words. "I assure you he does worry about those he loves."

Those he loves? The comment awakened the pain her short journey had inflicted.

"The women's camp is filled with stories of his liaisons, past and present. I have no doubt he worries about all of them."

Hephaestion gazed at the hurried unpacking around him. "There are more untruths circulating through the camps than facts. Alexander ignores them, so should you. He married you, Roxana, not the others. Remember that."

But why me?

In the space of several days, she'd been inundated with tales about his former lovers, abandoned in a baggage train, met his pregnant mistress, and now her husband's second had come to check on her while he remained too busy. She doubted Alexander treated his beloved Bucephalus the same way.

She kept her anger stifled behind her serene smile. "Thank Alexander for his concern, and for yours, General."

Hephaestion tapped the flanks of his horse and took off toward the army camp.

Dust kicked up as he cantered away, and Roxana's loneliness returned. But this time it was sprinkled with a decent helping of anger.

"If the gods are kind, I'll soon have a baby to fill my hours, and I won't need the king," she murmured, heading into her tent. "Please, let the gods be so kind."

CHAPTER TWELVE

ephaestion crisscrossed through groups of men unpacking horses and wagons. He dodged soldiers and acknowledged many of the faces he recognized from battle. Then he spied the gold pike atop Alexander's tent shimmering in the late afternoon sun.

He rushed past the sentries at the tent entrance to find Alexander at his war table with a few of his generals seated around him. Peritas was also at the meeting, lying in his usual spot at Alexander's feet.

Alexander pointed out strategic locations on the large map spread across the table. His sunburned nose, face, and arms made Hephaestion smile. Alexander repeatedly refused to wear a hat to protect his fair skin from the strong Persian sun.

Still stubborn.

Alexander spotted him, and Hephaestion caught the hint of distress in his eyes. He pondered what minor catastrophe had befallen the army. While the dog's tail tapped the floor in greeting, Hephaestion cautiously approached the table.

Ptolemy slammed his fist against the map. "Are you out of your mind?"

"Hear me out." Alexander rested a steady hand on Ptolemy's thick arm. "I want to tell you about—"

General Perdiccas stood, flashing his dark eyes at Alexander. "I think we have gone far enough."

Alexander patiently smiled, and Hephaestion could see the irritation brimming in his features.

"I would think that too, if I were you, Perdiccas. But I am Alexander, and I say we go on."

Hephaestion's bitter rival, Craterus, sneered at him. "I suppose you already know about this?"

Hephaestion reached under the table and gave Peritas a quick rub behind the ears, trying to remember Alexander's repeated warning about playing nice with Craterus.

"Know about what?"

"Alexander is thinking of going to India!" Ptolemy roared.

Hephaestion snickered under his breath. He always did this—threw out wild notions which the army had to execute. He loved the man, but at times he questioned if his genius masked his insanity.

Without giving away a hint about his thoughts, Hephaestion removed his cloak and discarded it on a nearby bench. "When do we go?"

"What do you mean, when do we go?" Craterus pressed his fat lips together.

"For the gods' sake, Hephaestion, will you stop and think this through seriously for once?"

The comment made him toss all Alexander's warnings aside. "That's your problem, Craterus." Hephaestion took his usual seat on Alexander's right. "You're always too serious."

"Stop it, both of you." Alexander raised his voice and glared at Hephaestion. "We all know Darius was never able to control his governors so far east. India has great influence over them. If we want to maintain the eastern part of this empire, we need to consider a campaign in India."

"Alexander, what about the men?" Perdiccas, always the composed one, rested his hands on the table. "Some of these veterans have been with you since you first crossed the Hellespont. They may want to go home instead of moving farther from it."

"The men will go where we tell them," a red-faced Ptolemy shouted loud enough for the entire camp to hear. "You're always trying to create a problem where none exists, Perdiccas. You would drive Zeus mad."

The crusty general, Antigonus, rolled his one eye at the two men. "Here we go again."

Perdiccas's cheeks took on a rosy hue. "It's called planning. Maybe you should try it some time."

Ptolemy jumped from his stool, his hand on the hilt of his short sword.

"I need you two to concentrate on the battle, not killing each other. Such behavior would anger the gods … and me." Alexander waited while Ptolemy resumed his seat. "We could even be just a few months away from the endless stream of ocean at the world's end. Imagine that; to stand at the end of the world."

"Alexander, we have to be practical." The rugged Seleucus, head of the infantry and smallest of the close-knit generals, inspected the map with his sharp brown eyes. "What about supplies and water? At least when we set off for Persia, we knew what we were up against. But this? There are too many unknowns."

"It is better to live with courage and die leaving an everlasting fame." Alexander grinned. "That is what India can give us."

Hephaestion hid his smirk behind his hand. Sometimes the man was insufferable.

"Well, it's giving me a pain in my ass." Ptolemy relaxed his weighty bulk on his stool.

"Do we have to think about it now?" Lysimachus, the quieter of the generals, spoke out.

The stocky man with the rugged face never said anything in their meetings other than, "Good morning," which always bugged Hephaestion. Alexander liked men who shared their opinions, not brooders.

The recalcitrant general stood. "I've got to get the men ready to tackle this rock. I can't plan one battle and think about India, too."

There was a murmuring of assent around the table.

"We'll be heading back into Bactria after we're done here." Alexander tapped a corner of the map. "The governors in that region need to be reminded I am king. After we get things settled there, we'll talk more about India. Go and prepare the men."

All the generals, except Hephaestion, slowly made their way from the war table, mumbling amongst themselves.

He waited for Alexander's chief officers to exit the tent before he spoke.

"I thought you would like to know your bride is settled in."

Alexander kept his attention on the map. "Is she?"

Furious at his disregard for the girl, Hephaestion swept the map off the table.

"She's your wife and in a new world with no one around her she recognizes. She's not in this campaign for the booty or the everlasting fame. She's in it for you."

Alexander sat back, not showing a glimmer of concern. "I'll go and see her tomorrow if it bothers you so much." He tapped a finger on the table, grimacing. "I still have to write to Mother about my marriage. Want to help me?"

"Absolutely not. She's your mother—thank the gods."

Alexander rested his elbows on the table, cradling his head. "She's going to faint when I tell her I've married. All the daughters of wealthy, royal Macedonian families she insisted I meet, and I take a Persian bride who's nothing more than a chieftain's daughter."

"Why don't you write to her and tell her you've married a Persian and are going on to India?" Hephaestion went around the table and took a seat across from him. "If we're lucky, the shock might just kill her." Once in his seat, he dropped his head. "There's something else."

Alexander took in a steadying breath. "Go on."

He fingered a small gouge in the old wooden table. "Our old friend Callisthenes has been spending a great deal of time with some members of your king's guard. I know you allowed him to tutor the pages, but it's raising some concerns among the generals."

Alexander knitted his brows. "What kind of concerns?"

"Some of the pages have confided in me. They say there's a rift developing among them. It seems your historian is fanning the flames. You know how he likes to cause trouble for you."

Alexander drummed his fingers on the table, imitating Hephaestion.

"I've noticed he and a few of my guards spending a great deal of time together lately. Probably filling their heads with how I don't exemplify the Greek ideal. More like I don't exemplify Aristotle's ideal."

Hephaestion folded his hands, glad to see him interested in the problem. Sometimes he was hard to pin down on a topic.

"I can have him questioned if you like."

"Aristotle will hear of it, and I don't need him badmouthing me in Greece." Alexander stopped drumming and closed his hand into a fist. "Let's see what he does. Make sure he's watched and report back if you hear anything else."

Hephaestion stood, ready to get men on the situation.

Alexander glanced up. "Next time you feel the need to check on my wife, let me know. I can send gifts with you to make her happy,"

Hephaestion sneered at his empty gesture. "She doesn't want gifts. She wants you."

Alexander pounded the table. "I can't please her and an army. And in my life, the army will always come first. She must understand that."

"Then spend time with her and teach her about your life." Hephaestion went to the tent entrance. "You need to win her loyalty and trust. Otherwise, you will end up with a hurtful marriage like your parents."

Alexander rubbed his face. "A battle is easier to plan than the seduction of a woman."

His confusion amused him. "You've already seduced her. Now you have to win her heart." He darted out of the tent before Alexander asked him how.

Even the gods can't help you there.

Her first night beneath the stars next to the rock of Chorienes, Roxana stood at the entrance to her tent enjoying the last vestiges of cool air before the oppressive heat of summer arrived. Laughter and singing surrounded her and the aroma of cooking food made her empty tummy rumble.

She'd refused the dinner of peaches, Persian cheese, and dates, too depressed to eat. She'd hoped her husband would check on her, but as the stars popped out in the dark sky, she resigned herself to another night alone in her big bed.

"Are you sure I can't offer you something, my lady?" Morella appeared next to her, holding a goblet of wine.

Grateful, Roxana accepted the heavy metal cup. "The wine is perfect. Thank you."

"My mother always said wine on an empty stomach wasn't good for any woman. It keeps babies away."

Roxana ran her finger over the rim of her goblet. "Yes, but when there's no man around to have babies with, the wine helps pass the nights."

"I was married once." Morella's slight smile held a hint of sadness in it. "He died at Gaugamela. We'd only been married for two years. Our son died soon after him."

The sorrow of war and the devastation Alexander and his men brought hit home for her. "I can't fathom how difficult it must be for you to serve the wife of the man who took your husband from you."

Morella searched the night sky. "War touches everyone sooner or later. If you ask me, the losers in war are lucky. We know what awaits the winners."

A woman covered in a pleated red peplos sauntered by the entrance. Her face hidden behind a sheer white veil, she scurried down the dirt path leading away from the women's camp.

Goblet in hand, Roxana stepped outside, curious.

Half hidden by the shadows, the graceful creature ventured to the thin stretch of land separating the men from the women's camp. With a quick look each way, the woman scampered across the darkened strip of ground to the gathering of tents on the other side. Her figure disappeared behind a campfire billowing plumes of black smoke into the sky. Soon, the laughter of men drifted past.

"Where is she going?"

Morella came outside, modestly covering her head with her brown shawl. "The men's camp, probably to see her man, or to see several men. Who knows with these Greeks."

Other women appeared, crossing the boundary between the two camps as the light from torches lit their way. With keen interest, Roxana observed the activity.

"Does this happen often?"

Morella took her elbow. "The king is said to frown on such fraternizing between the camps, but the morals of these Greeks are as loose as their tongues. The more I'm around them, the less I trust them." She guided Roxana back to her tent. "I'm amazed one man can lead them."

"What else do you know about the Greeks, Morella?"

"What more is there to know, my lady?"

Roxana formulated a plan. A way to glean knowledge about the unruly Greeks, and perhaps find a way to see her husband.

"Morella, go to my bedroom and fetch my thickest shawl, and find one for yourself as well." She handed her servant her goblet of wine.

Morella took the drink, her face scrunched in confusion. "Why?"

Roxana grinned. "Because tonight, we're going to become like the Trojan Horse."

Cocooned beneath a mountain of woolen fabric—Morella had insisted she cover up completely—Roxana could barely see out the slit over her eyes. The material was hard to breathe through, but she was sure no one would recognize her. Refusing to listen to reason, she led her disguised servant along the thin path winding toward the barrier dividing the camps.

Excitement streamed through her when they crossed the dark space. Morella held her hand, squeezing too hard and hurting her fingers. Soon, the sounds of the Greek men moving about rose around her. Then they made it to the line of torches next to the first of the men's tents.

She stopped, debating which way to go as a wisp of smoke from the campfires drifted between them.

"You're never to let go of my hand. Do you understand, my lady?"

Roxana rolled her eyes at her maid. "There's nothing to fear. They won't hurt us."

Morella fiddled with the fabric over her face. "You're innocent, child. You don't know the ways of men, these men especially. You're married to a king. You've never known the common soldier."

Ignoring her warning, Roxana led her between two tents set close together. Staying in the shadows, she peeked around the side of the tent on her right. Two men rose from a campfire a few feet away.

Still in their chitons, covered in dirt and sweat stains, they came toward her.

"When he's done in the north, we'll turn back for home," a soldier with a boyish face said. "He can't keep us in this country forever."

"Are you daft?" The soldier next to him slapped his back. "The king likes it here. Now with that cow of a wife of his, he'll probably stick around and spit out barbarian brats to run roughshod over us. We all know he only married her to lock up her father's support. We wouldn't have the supplies to camp before this rock without his grain and gold."

They walked past, not paying attention to her or her servant. Roxana found the comparison to a cow funny. She'd never been called that before.

"What are they saying?" Morella asked.

Roxana put her finger to her lips and stepped closer to the campfire where other men sat on logs, drinking from clay cups.

"I hear he bathes every night with the boy." A fat man with an eye patch and a scar down his left cheek chewed on a wedge of meat. "Can you believe that? With that fine piece of ass waiting for him in the next camp."

Morella nudged Roxana to move along, but she held her ground.

"He never keeps the women long. Just like his old man." A veteran with scars along his thick arms and chest sat with his chiton gathered around his hips. "Philip liked the boys, too."

"But this boy is Persian and dangerous from what I hear." A third soldier nursed a clay cup in a hand missing a few fingers. "Seems a shame to toss aside a perfectly good woman, even if she is a barbarian."

Her grasp tightened on Morella's hand.

"What is it, my lady?"

"Let's just hope she doesn't end up pregnant like the last bitch he bedded." The one-eyed man tossed a bone into the fire. "Bad enough we're gonna have them in our ranks. I don't want the bastards ruling over me."

"The king needs to get out of his Persian mood." The veteran with numerous scars stood. "The boy I can tolerate because he keeps him from the girl. Even his Persian outfits are good for a laugh, but let's hope that's where this influence ends." He went to a wineskin hanging on a stick close to the fire. "I don't want to become one of these ass-kissing barbarians. I want to get home to Greece and spend my booty on my family and my land."

"You're hurting my hand." Morella pried her fingers free from Roxana's grip.

One of the men spotted them.

"What you got hidden under all them clothes?" The soldier with scars grabbed his crotch and rocked his hips. "Why don't you take them off and give me a little tonight?"

Morella gasped and yanked her away.

They ran through the tents and back across the divide as the roar of laughter died behind them. They didn't stop until they were inside Roxana's tent.

Morella wrestled with the flaps, tying them closed before she faced her charge.

"Do you see what I mean? What in the blazes were you thinking? We can never do that again. If the king knew you—"

"The king will never know." Roxana unwound the black shawl from around her head. "I will never tell him."

She dropped the wrap and freed herself of the others Morella had bundled around her. The night's excursions had given her a great deal to consider.

"You were right, Morella." She went to the curtain dividing her bedroom from the front of the tent. "The Greeks can't be trusted."

CHAPTER THIRTEEN

The heat of summer spread across the valley below the rock of Chorienes. Pale blue flowers stained with morning dew grew along the edges of Roxana's tent as Alexander stood outside the entrance, inspecting the structure.

Fresh from his morning prayers and sacrifice to the gods, he nervously tugged at the neck of his crisp white tunic as his guards waited behind him. It had been two weeks since they had made camp beneath the great rock and matters of war and state had kept him away. He feared her reaction when she saw him.

"Are you going in, my king?"

Oxyartes walked up to his side, the gold thread in his fluted Phrygian hat of royalty sparkled in the sun.

Alexander studied his oiled black beard and prominent nose, seeing little of his wife in his face. "She will be pleased to see you."

"Then let us go in and surprise her."

Feeling pressured to put on a good show, Alexander shoved the flap aside and bounded into the tent unannounced.

But the small reception area was empty.

"Where is she?"

"Don't tell me you have lost her already, Great King."

Alexander was about to say something when a pug-nosed woman with an armload of bedlinens rushed in.

She saw the two men and dropped to her knees. The linens went toppling to the ground, and then she babbled something in Persian.

Alexander impatiently turned to Oxyartes. "What's she saying?"

"Her name is Morella, your wife's attendant. She's begging your forgiveness and asking that you not beat her for not having your wife's chambers cleaned earlier. She says she was sick this morning and—"

Alexander raised his hand, stopping the lengthy translation. "Ask her where my wife is."

Oxyartes barked something in Persian to the woman on the floor.

She replied without looking up.

"She says she was gone this morning, very early. She leaves early every morning." Oxyartes frowned, his eyes shrinking with skepticism. "Your wife never tells any of them where she's going. Only that she was dressed as a man."

Why was she sneaking out of her tent? Did she not realize how dangerous that could be?

"Ask her what my wife has been up to. What does she mean by dressed as a man?"

Oxyartes raised his hands, begging for Alexander's indulgence. "Dressed as a Persian man … in trousers, my king." An amused twinkle shone in his dark eyes. "Perhaps I can be of some assistance since I've known my daughter much longer than you. There's only one place Roxana would go this early in the morning. Where are your stables?"

Followed by the king's guard, the two men maneuvered the numerous trails cutting through the women's camp to the outskirts of the men's camp. A makeshift stable, build of tent canvas and wood beams came into view.

Once at the edge of the paddocks, Alexander scoured the surrounding fields bursting with brilliant yellow and white flowers.

A short distance away, next to a clump of fir trees, a single rider exercised a small dark chestnut with three white socks. Baggy clothing hid the rider's figure, but the long brown hair flowing behind her was unmistakable.

Roxana put Hera through several turns at a canter while Oxyartes came alongside him.

"She's an excellent rider. You taught her well."

"I did not teach her." Oxyartes placed his hand on his chest, catching his breath. "Tasia, Roxana's mother, taught the girl to ride before she could walk. When the gods took her, I was devastated, but I had Roxana. Tasia lives on in her."

"Father!" came from across the field.

The horse galloped straight at them. Before Hera had even come to a stop, Roxana swung off her back and ran straight into her father's arms, leaving Alexander to gather the horse's reins.

He admired their closeness. He could never have greeted his mother or father in such a manner. Philip would have scolded him for showing too much emotion, and Olympias would have reminded him of his station.

No wonder my wife dislikes me.

"What are you doing here?" Roxana asked, not letting go.

Oxyartes was the first to pull back. "I've just arrived. I'm here to negotiate with Chorienes. To see if we can get him to surrender before winter sets in. Considering the astounding activity of your husband's army, I'm sure he will come to his senses very soon."

Alexander patted the mare's neck. "Yes, we've been working day and night to fill a ravine we found around the rock. My forces are getting close to the top. That's why I've not been able to come and see you." He dropped his voice, hoping to sound menacing. "Why did you not leave word with your maid you were riding? Someone should know where you are at all times, little star. The camps are dangerous for a woman alone."

Roxana gave him a cold, hard stare. "You promised me my freedom. Allowing me to ride Hera when I want is part of our bargain."

"And I will keep my promise. As long as you remember you're the wife of a king and a target just like me."

Her stubbornness reminded him of the day he'd walked into her father's tent and found her refusing to marry. He'd hoped their nights together had tempered her spirit.

Apparently, I have a lot to learn about women.

Oxyartes darted his gaze from Alexander to his daughter. "I bring news from home. Yasmin is to be married to a captain in my army. Irania is well."

Alexander handed her the reins. "We will speak after you have visited with your father."

"No, Great King." Oxyartes stopped him from turning away. "I can meet with Roxana later."

"You two have catching up to do." He gave her one last glance, aching to make things right again between them. "We will talk later, my wife."

He set out for the men's camp.

Hephaestion's warnings about spending more time with her came back to taunt him. He angrily swatted at a tall stalk of weeds by his hand.

I hate it when he's right.

Once Alexander left, Oxyartes shot a disgruntled scowl at his daughter. "What are you doing? You should never challenge your husband so."

While Alexander's figure grew smaller against the morning sky, her anger poured out of her. "I haven't set eyes on the man for two weeks. He has sent me no messages, no word on where he is or what he's doing, and when he sees me, all he can do is attack me."

Her father's eyes bulged, and his mouth fell open. "What did you expect? The man every night in your bed? He is King of Persia."

"Why did you marry me off to him? Did you think I would be happy being ignored? To be forgotten amid a sea of other lovers and only remembered as a passing fancy?" She bit her trembling lower lip, not wanting to cry in front of him. "In the camps, I am called the neglected wife. Do you have any idea how that feels, Father?" Fed up, she turned and led her horse back to the barn.

"What do you want me to do?" Oxyartes shouted, following her. "I can't tell the king to spend time with you. It's not my place."

Roxana spun around to him. "I never asked you to do anything!"

"Why do you talk to me in such a way?" His voice broke, sounding tormented. "I thought you would be happy with Alexander."

"Happy?" she shouted, dropping her reins. Hera shied away. "Did it ever occur to you the wife of a king is not a wife but a thing? I'm just something to be packed away with his treasure. It's like I don't exist anymore."

Oxyartes's cheeks turned red. "You are a woman! This is your place. You have no voice. You have no rights. You must accept a man can do what he likes, whenever he likes, and you have no say."

Hearing her father trample every freedom she hoped to have finally released her tears. The emptiness in her soul created a suffocating tightness in her chest. The pain reminded her of the agony she'd experienced the moment her mother had died.

Oxyartes wrapped his arms around her, cooing softly. "No, my love. You mustn't cry. You are so different from other women, Roxana. What makes you different is also what the king admires most about you—your fire." He kissed the top of her head. "Don't blame Alexander if he can't spend more time with you. You must learn to support him, to listen to him, and help him in any way you can. And never be angry or jealous of those who take him away from you. Be there for him, and he will be there for you."

She stopped crying as his words sank in. She sniffled, and then wiped her nose on her sleeve. "I thought my only job was to make sons."

"A wife bears children, yes." He wiped a tear from her cheek. "But a wife can be so much more for her husband. She can listen, help, give advice, speak her mind, and always tell her husband the truth."

"Did my mother do those things for you?"

"Tasia did all those things for me, and she made me a better man because of them." He tapped her nose. "That is what you must do for Alexander. Be there for him, even if he cannot always be there for you."

She sighed, feeling better, but still troubled. "That doesn't sound very fair."

"Love never is, my daughter. It's neither fair nor impartial. It simply is."

"This isn't love, Father. It's politics."

He grabbed her arm and squeezed his fingers into her flesh. "The king has never seen this as a political match. You brought no lands, no wealth, no armies with your dowry. He took you from a remote corner of Sogdiana and made you his wife. He loves you and you, I think, love him."

Roxana shirked off his hand and went to collect her horse. "I don't love the king. I can never love him." She tugged the mare away from the grass and toward the stable, anxious to end their conversation.

Oxyartes chuckled, his happy laugh following her.

"Oh yes, you do, Roxana," he called, making her clench the reins. "Only a man

you love could make you feel so miserable."

An early wicked winter wind descended from the nearby mountains. The unusual cold surprised many in the camps. Rumors about the unexpectedly long and tough campaign with Chorienes and the dwindling food supplies floated around the women's section, but Roxana paid little heed. All she registered was Alexander had not come to see her. Her head reasoned he was busy with his army, but her heart had another excuse. An excuse the whisperings of her servants only helped to reinforce.

On a frigid evening, when the half-moon beamed down on the formidable rock, Roxana dismissed Morella and the rest of her servants, fed up with their loose tongues. She did not wish to overhear any more about the bastard son born to Barsine or how Bagoas stayed in the king's tent at night, keeping him warm during his campaign.

On her stool in front of her brazier, she combed her hair and occupied herself with trivial matters—anything to keep her thoughts from Alexander. She hummed a simple melody her mother had taught her.

"You're alone." His familiar voice came from the curtained entrance to her bedroom.

Roxana stopped humming, undone by his presence, but didn't turn to greet him.

"You're angry with me." Alexander came up to her. "I've stayed away for too long, I know, but the siege became arduous. You should have seen what my army and engineers did. The causeway they built adjacent to the rock was quite impressive."

The mention of his army made her throw her silver comb onto her dressing table. The *clink* echoed in her tent.

She found the nerve to raise her head to him. Gold fabric glistened back at her.

"It was taken from a caravan coming from India. It's called silk." He held out the precious material to her. "I brought it for you to wear at my banquet tomorrow night."

She caressed the cloth as her heart broke all over again. "Should you be having a banquet with the food stores running so low?"

A fleeting look of dismay marred his features. "Haven't you heard the news? The siege is over. The banquet is to celebrate the peace your father negotiated. Chorienes is distributing needed provisions to the camps from his vast supply on the rock. He even gave me this cloth to give to you."

She folded her arms, widening her eyes at his question. "No, I haven't heard. All the news I get is about the king and his Persian boy."

He dropped the material and arched over her, gripping the sides of her stool and circling her with his powerful arms. "What have you heard?"

His menacing voice frightened her, and she recoiled. "They say the king's poor wife has been abandoned for a eunuch. Once loved by Darius, he—" She clamped her mouth shut, afraid to go on.

He shoved back from her and ran his hand through his wavy hair. "I would advise you to come to me if you ever hear gossip that upsets you. I will tell you the truth. A wound by the sword is much easier to bear than a wound from gossip. You must not listen to fools, only me."

She got up and gave him a mocking bow. "I'll do that next time I doubt the validity of what I hear, my king."

He stood in front of her, his lips pulled back in a sneer. "I've had horses easier to tame than you."

She'd heard enough about the pain men inflicted when they beat their wives, but she could not let fear silence her.

"I'm sure you spent more time breaking them than you have ever spent with me!"

"Is that what this is about?" Alexander's voice thundered around her. "You're angry with me because you feel you have been ignored."

"Feel I have been ignored?" She met his obstinate gaze with her own. "I haven't seen you in weeks. The only news I get about you is when I overhear my servants. You have sent me no messages, no news if you are well or hurt, or sending me away."

Alexander balled his hands into fists. "I will have your servants replaced in the morning. There will be no more tongues wagging around you, I promise." He made his way toward the entrance.

Suddenly she didn't want him to go. Her anger retreated like a flock of birds turning as one in the sky, and she wished nothing more than to have him hold her. Why? How could a man who infuriated her so weaken her resolve against him?

"There's no use getting rid of the servants," she said when he yanked aside the curtain. "It's not only the servants who talk. You can't silence the whole camp. You may be the king of the land, but you don't have power over the minds of men or women."

He stopped and relaxed his hands before glancing back at her. "I will not have my wife the subject of idle gossip."

Roxana stooped and gathered up the lovely gold fabric. "Gossip I can live with. I have always lived with, but it's not the gossip that hurts." She carried it to the bed. "What hurts is knowing that I'm not what you want." She set the material down and ran her fingers over the delicate material. "I'm sure such a beautiful cloth will make a fine outfit for your banquet."

He approached the bed. "Roxana, I only wish to make you happy."

She moved the silk aside and sat. "I would have been happy left in my family's camp."

"That would not have made me happy." He lifted her chin. "You're what I want, what I've always wanted in a woman."

She retreated from his touch. "What's so special about me?"

He knelt before her, placing his hands on her knees and gazing up at her with a warmth she had not seen since their wedding day.

"When you first danced for me, I fell in love with the way you moved, how you carried yourself. But the moment that made me want you was when you walked out on me. I knew then you had courage, and to be the wife of a king, you will need a great deal of it." He sat next to her. "Did you know coming to Persia was my father's plan? Philip wanted this more than anything. After he was assassinated, it became my plan. So much of being a king is doing what others want, being what they expect. Part of those expectations will be marrying other wives. I know what watching your husband take others to his bed can do. My mother went through it. It made her bitter and created a great divide between my parents which lasted most of my life. I swore I would never do the same to my wife, but when I became king, I knew I couldn't keep that vow. I need sons to live on after me, and political marriages to seal pacts, acquire armies, and attain land. I wondered if I would ever find a woman strong enough, brave enough, loving enough to be able to stick by me as king, and grow old with me long after my other wives have left. That's what I see in you. I did not marry you for my kingdom, my alliance with Persia, my army, my generals, or even my mother. I married you for me."

The walls around her heart built up by weeks of loneliness and anger crumbled. She never envisioned being any man's passion.

"I think I understand a little better now." She gripped his hand, squeezing it tight. "I never expected love in a marriage, but to be the woman you chose is some consolation."

He kissed her forehead. "I don't know love as a husband, only as a king and a general. Armies don't love you until you prove yourself. Generals don't love you until you lead them in victory. And the people, they will never love you until they can trust you are a good and wise ruler. You have to win love, earn it through deeds. I hope that will happen to us. Once we prove ourselves, endure a few battles, and learn to trust, we will find love."

She rested her head against his chest, comforted by his words. "I don't know if I have the strength for any more battles with you."

He laughed into her hair. "I agree. I hate arguing with women. My father used to say, 'An angry woman is a dangerous woman.' How right he was."

"What else did your father say?"

Alexander turned her face to his. "He said, 'with women actions always speak louder than words.'"

Roxana wrinkled her brow. "What did he mean by that?"

He pushed her down on the bed. "I'll show you."

The moon was already high in the sky, creating ribbons of light around her bed. She lay snuggled next to him, with her head tucked into his right shoulder. Her glossy locks spread out on the pillow beneath her as she ran her hand gently over the ruddy skin on his chest. The contentment streaming through him was something he'd not known with another woman. Why had this beauty bewitched him so? Even her frenzied lovemaking had surprised him. It seemed with every time he took her to bed, her hunger for him became more fervent.

"I met Barsine the first day when we made camp here," she said, raising her head.

"Really?" Alexander imagined the two women coming to blows. "And who won?"

"Hephaestion came to the rescue." Roxana hesitated. "I heard about your son's birth."

He dropped his head back on the pillow, wishing she hadn't mentioned the boy. "He's to be named Heracles. She and the boy will be leaving for Pergamum when the child is old enough."

She rested her elbow on his chest, jabbing it into his firm muscles. "She wasn't what I pictured for you."

He winced, figuring she meant to hurt him. "What were you picturing for me, or should I even ask?"

"I thought she would be younger." She scrunched her eyebrows together. "She has to be older than you."

"She's a few years older." He remembered Barsine's quick wit and how she never tired in bed. "We grew up together in Macedonia. Her father was a friend of my father's. After her husband was killed at the Battle of Issus, she was captured with the family of Darius."

"What about Bagoas?"

Alexander sat up, confounded. He'd never expected her to mention his name, and that she had angered him immensely.

"It's not proper for a wife to talk about such things."

"Why not?" She put her face closer to his, a challenging lilt in her voice. "I understand you will have other lovers, but I can deal with it better if we talk about it. I'm not a woman who accepts things without questioning. You should know that about me by now."

Her eyes burned into his.

Alexander's gut twisted into something akin to the Gordian Knot. *Why does she have such a power over me?*

He gripped her arms, aroused by her boldness. "There are times when I think I have mastered you, satiated my desire for you, and then you look at me, confront me, and it's like the first time we met." He kissed her neck, intoxicated by the hint of jasmine on her skin.

"Does this mean we're not going to talk about him?"

He lifted her and playfully spanked her bottom. "I'm done talking."

Alexander gave in to the temptation of her, hopelessly confounded by the softness of her skin and sweet taste of her lips. There were a thousand other things he had to do, but he could not tear himself away. In the morning, he would return to his duties as king. Tonight, he would enjoy being hers.

CHAPTER FOURTEEN

Inside a circle of torches, a massive fire pit had three goats turning on a spit. The air saturated with paprika and orange flower tickled Roxana's nose, while the short table in front of her held an array of gold plates, silver goblets, and jugs of honey water and heady Persian wine. She sat back on her pile of pillows and glanced at the twinkling stars, enamored with the clear night sky the gods offered for Alexander's celebration feast.

The guests, seated according to rank, had Roxana and her father immediately to the right of the table occupied by Alexander, Hephaestion, and Chorienes. Several high-ranking members of the Macedonian army were also there, dressed in their best armor, along with a large contingent of Persian nobles.

Roxana was aware of the eyes of both Greeks and Persians on her, but she only hoped to attract one man's attention with her sparkling gold outfit.

"The king hasn't been able to keep his eyes off you." Her father lifted his goblet. "I take it things are better between you."

"We've come to an understanding." Roxana reached for the wine and drank heartily.

"Do not drink so much, little star," her father advised. "You're not used to this heavy wine. Add more water, so you don't get drunk."

When she lowered her goblet, Hephaestion appeared in front of her table. In a bronze cuirass made to mimic the perfect male form and purple cloak, he cut a dashing figure. She could see why she'd thought him the king when they had first met; he looked the part.

"Baron Oxyartes, Chorienes and Alexander wish for you to join them at the king's table. If you don't mind, I will entertain the king's wife while you talk business with the king."

Oxyartes quickly went to his son-in-law. When he arrived at Alexander's table, he graciously bowed and joined in the men's conversation.

Hephaestion took a seat on the pillows. "The king keeps sneaking peeks at you. It's quite entertaining. I've never seen Alexander so smitten."

Roxana set her goblet down. "I find it hard to believe the king could be smitten with anyone."

"Oh, he can be. He may profess to be a true son of the god Zeus, but he's as human as any man." Hephaestion rapped his knuckle on their wooden table. "Alexander told me for the next banquet he will have chairs placed behind the tables instead of pillows, as per the Persian custom." He picked up the jug of water and added it to her half-full goblet. "Isn't that exciting?"

"Hephaestion, why are you sitting next to me and not the king?"

He shifted about, getting comfortable. "I've heard the rumors flying around the camps, and I came to give you some advice. To belong to Alexander requires you to separate your heart from your head. What he fancies today, he will not tomorrow. He's not a man to be tied down in one place for too long, or to one person for that matter. Not that his favor will ever wane; he needs to be free. That's the key to him—to keep him, you have to set him free."

An unsettling feeling rose from her stomach. "Any reason you're giving me all this goodly advice?"

"He does not wish to hurt you. Unfortunately, there are others who care nothing about hurting you and who desire to turn you against the king by spreading untrue rumors about him." Hephaestion's eyes traveled across the room.

Roxana followed his gaze to a short, stocky man with dark curly hair standing several feet away from the king's table. In a wrinkled chiton and a purple cloak, he kept his head down, listening to a young soldier of the king's guard next to him. She could make out the curve of his weak jaw and his sunken cheekbones. He looked up, and his black eyes connected with hers.

"His name is Callisthenes. His uncle is our old tutor, Aristotle. He serves Alexander as a historian but is more like an avid troublemaker. Some of his talents lean to creating malicious gossip to hurt the king. Gossip centered around a young eunuch who attends the king's bath." Hephaestion dropped his head and admired the table setting. "Have you heard of him?"

Her distressing feeling transformed into a gnawing. "Yes, I've heard of Bagoas."

"Don't believe everything you hear." He drummed his fingers on the table. "I know more about what you're going through than you can realize. Gossip about my relationship with the king has haunted me for years, but only Alexander and I know the truth. Alexander's enemies use his friendships against him, and servants like Bagoas offer a rich cache of hurtful innuendo to smear the king's image."

She smirked at him. "But are the rumors true?"

His heavy sigh told her they were. She lifted her goblet to her lips, yearning for the taste of wine.

"You're his wife, and you will bear his children. You will be the mother of kings. That, in itself, is the best revenge for gossip, whether it is true or not."

A dull pounding began behind her right eye. Her father had been right; the wine was too strong for her.

She spied her husband's table. Her father and a fat, bearded man—who must have been Chorienes—laughed together. Suddenly, Alexander smiled at her, and all her pain disappeared like mist in the morning sun.

"Thank you, Hephaestion. I appreciate your kind words and advice."

"I said nothing, dear lady. I merely came to the aid of a beautiful woman."

After Hephaestion strolled back to Alexander's table, the officials, generals, and men of Alexander's court became a hodgepodge of faces, all hiding an array of lies and deceits. How could she tell the enemies from the friends, and who could she count on to help her negotiate the perils of court life? Her attention focused on Hephaestion as he exchanged a few words with her father. She understood Alexander's reliance on him. Of all the men in the room, his face was the most trustworthy.

Her father resumed his seat at her table, tucking his red robe about him as a big grin peeked out from behind his black beard.

"You won't believe it, dear daughter, but the king has just told me." Oxyartes became engrossed by something happening down from their table.

A group of Persian officials walked solemnly from the other side of the gathering. Their long robes dragged the ground as they approached the king, their heads bowed and their eyes hidden.

The first man stopped in front of Alexander's table and bent at the waist, almost touching the ground.

"I praise you mighty king and show my respect to your throne."

Alexander came out from behind his table, his cuirass shimmering in the torchlight.

He gripped the man's shoulder, seeming grateful for the acknowledgment.

Roxana didn't understand what was happening. "Father, why are those Persian officials bowing at the king's table?"

"They're Chorienes's men. He's having them pay homage to the king." Oxyartes lowered his voice. "The king plans to have his Greek generals bow to him in a ceremony of acceptance before the Persian court."

Her heart climbed in her throat. She'd advocated Alexander to have his men pay him respect and suggested the ceremony, but after living in the Greek camps and listening to their vicious gossip, she had a better understanding of their stubbornness, anger, and their refusal to kneel.

This might not be a good idea.

After the Persian officials resumed their seats, Roxana's grip tightened on her goblet, nervous about what would happen next.

Hephaestion rose and also bowed low before the king. He then stepped up to Alexander and kissed his cheek. When he turned back to the banquet guests, he stared directly at the Macedonian generals.

"Now is the time for all our countrymen to honor our King of Persia. Come and bow to your king."

A heavy silence descended over the gathering.

The furious Macedonian generals glared at Hephaestion.

Her father whispered in her ear, "Why aren't his men coming forward to bow to the king?"

Roxana feared for her safety and her husband's. She kept an eye on the tables of Macedonians across the fire from her, waiting for the hiss of swords drawn from their sheaths.

"Greeks do not bow," she said in Persian. "And by asking them to, Alexander may have gone too far."

She waited, her chest burning because she was afraid to take a breath in case the world came crashing down around her.

Hephaestion strolled to the table of Greek commanders seated to the right of Alexander. He searched the line of men, challenging them with his eyes.

"Will you not honor your king, gentlemen?"

Not a single man rose. She scoured the perimeter of torches, hunting for the fastest means of escape.

Then, with much moaning and grumbling, the Macedonians stood from their tables. She relaxed her hand on her goblet, letting it slip down the stem. Thank the gods, his men had given in to his request.

A line of burly Macedonian generals in their shiny armor, formed in front of the king's table. Their disgruntled faces taut with indignation would have meant nothing to her before her marriage, but after spending time with their king, she sensed danger.

Each of the generals received a kiss from the king. One by one, officers from the army came before Alexander; even the black-eyed Callisthenes joined them. When he knelt before Alexander, the king became engrossed by something Hephaestion whispered to him, ignoring his historian.

Roxana knew the brush off was meant to make a point and she expected the thickly built man to confront the king. Instead, Callisthenes shrugged his broad shoulders and turned to the Macedonian men seated at their tables.

"So I go back to my place poorer one kiss."

The Macedonians roared with laughter, except for one. Alexander stood, his face red and his eyes simmering with his displeasure.

"It's all very exciting, isn't it, daughter?"

Roxana's attention remained riveted on her husband, uncertainty prickling her skin. "What is?"

"Chorienes and Alexander have struck a great bargain." Her father rolled back on his pillows. "Chorienes has offered to provide the entire army for two months so you can go to India."

"India? But what of the men?" Her trip to the camps still fresh in her mind, she knew there would be resistance. "They might want to go home, not farther east?"

Her father twirled the tip of his oiled beard, arrogance seeping from every pore. "They will go wherever the mighty Alexander leads them."

She didn't share her father's confidence. After tonight's festivities spread throughout the camps, she wondered how much more his men would take before they refused to go farther and headed home to Greece.

The wine he'd consumed at the banquet wore off as Alexander finished his walk in the chilly night from his tent and stood outside the entrance to hers. He glanced up at the starry sky, wondering if the gods still smiled down on him. Lately, his burdens seemed heavier than in the past. Maybe it was age, or perhaps it was her tugging at his heart, but his world had become so much more than the thrill of battle.

Alexander ordered the guards to wait and walked inside. The reception area was dark, all the oil lamps out. He stumbled around with only shards of fading torchlight creeping into the tent to guide him. When he ran into the curtain dividing the rooms, he tore at it, desperate to get to her.

In her bedroom, the light was better. She stirred on the bed and sat up, rubbing her eyes.

"Why are you here so late? The sun will be up soon."

She tossed aside her blanket and walked up to him. The sway of her slim hips beneath her nightgown made him smile.

"I could not take my eyes off you all night. I wanted to go to you, but ..."

"What a cruel world we live in." She rested her hand on his chest. "Where husbands and wives have to sit apart at a party. Do you think things will ever change?"

He marveled at her lips. "Women have no place with men. Until that changes, little else will."

"One day women will surprise men and rule the world."

"Perhaps they already do."

He touched the hollow at the base of her neck, where he drew the faintest circles. Then his hands were on her shoulders, working the flimsy fabric of her nightgown down her arms.

"What happened tonight at the banquet may make your Greek soldiers angry. Are you—?"

Alexander's kiss smothered her words.

He roughly wrestled the nightdress from around her, but she didn't protest. Instead, she held his face and gazed into his eyes.

"You're different. What's wrong?"

"Nothing's wrong. I haven't been able to stop thinking about you." He rested his forehead against hers. "I can't stop wanting you. I've never known that before with anyone."

She combed her hand through his hair, her touch driving him mad. He longed to remember a time when she didn't occupy his thoughts but he couldn't. He'd always wanted her. Before they had met, he'd dreamed of having a woman filled with her fire.

"What has changed?" She took his hand. "I'm the same woman I was yesterday."

He let her lead him to the black bed. "Tonight, when I saw you sitting with Hephaestion wrapped in gold and looking like a goddess, it was the first time I realized I love you."

She stopped and cocked her head. "You love me?"

He sat on the bed and pulled her into his arms. "I've loved a horse, a dog, but never a woman."

He sensed her resistance. It was as if she didn't know what to say. He wished he knew what she was thinking, but she was as perplexing to him as the gods.

"Usually when a man declares his love for a woman, she says something about how she feels."

She slid her arms around his neck. "I don't know how to say—"

His kiss cut her off. He didn't want to hear her say anything but she loved him. He would never accept anything else. He could wait to hear those words from her, but he would hear them.

Alexander had conquered kingdoms and won great battles with his mind and his patience. He would use the same tools to win her, even if it took a lifetime.

He kissed her cheek and lowered his mouth to her ear. "No more talk, my wife." He lifted her into the bed with him. "There's been enough words between us tonight."

CHAPTER FIFTEEN

From the entrance of her tent, Roxana admired the green leaves popping up on the winter-weary trees scattered around the women's camp. The calls of goats, sheep, and horses drifted by as they grazed on the fresh shoots of grass. The lush essence of spring tantalized her after the long, cold winter.

A burst of activity erupted as women gathered supplies for the coming march to the province of Bactria. With the great rock won, and an alliance secured with Chorienes, it was time to move on.

The heavy stomp of soldiers approaching from the men's camp sped up her heart.

The king is coming.

She dashed into her tent and exchanged her dark woolen cloak for a bright green one. At the copper mirror, she pinched her pale cheeks and smoothed her hair, wanting to be her best.

The soldiers stopped outside her tent, and she went to her reception area to receive her husband. But Alexander didn't march through her doorway— Hephaestion did.

The sight of his dusty bronze cuirass and greaves set off an avalanche of anguish.

He came up to her, circles rimming his expressive brown eyes.

"I've brought members of the king's guard to keep watch over you day and night. Alexander's orders."

She clasped her throat, fearing the worst. "Has something happened to the king?"

A wide-eyed Morella stumbled in from the back, carrying a wooden chest. "My lady, I've found—"

She nearly dropped the trunk when she saw Hephaestion.

"Morella, please wait outside," she said in Persian.

Her maid set down the chest and hurried to the door.

Hephaestion took Roxana's elbow. "No harm has come to the king, but a plot to assassinate him has been uncovered." He led her from the tent entrance to the back of the reception area, lowering his voice. "The news has sent the generals and much of the army into a frenzy. An attack on the king is an attack on them."

Roxana didn't understand the Greeks at times. An army of followers who would rush to defend a king they would not bow to didn't make any sense. Then again, much of what the Greeks did was a mystery to her.

Hephaestion's lips twisted in an uncharacteristic grimace. "Five pages from the king's guard were going to kill Alexander as he slept last night. Fortunately, he was out drinking all night with a few of the other generals and me. He never returned to his tent. The conspirators got anxious when their plan failed. One of them leaked the details of the assassination attempt to another member of the guard, who went directly to the king." He took a breath before adding, "We believe Callisthenes is the instigator."

"Callisthenes?" Roxana cringed. "Is this because of what happened at the banquet?"

"Callisthenes has caused problems for Alexander in the past. I just never believed he was stupid enough to attempt to assassinate the king."

A chill embraced her as the shadow of a sentry, carrying a long spear, moved outside her tent. "If the attempt was on the king, why do I need protection?"

"The plot was hatched after your wedding to the king. Callisthenes wanted revenge for Alexander's taking a Persian for a wife instead of a Greek."

The news made her dizzy. She yearned to reach for a piece of furniture to steady herself but feared appearing weak. The animosity between the Greeks and Persians confronted her every day but she'd never imagined such hatred would drive one of Alexander's men to murder. Her husband's warning of the courage needed to be a king's wife resonated with her.

"What about the pages who plotted to kill Alexander? What will happen to them?"

He clutched the hilt of his sheathed sword. "They will be tried and then executed by stoning. As for Callisthenes, I don't know what Alexander has planned for him, but whatever his fate, I fear it will create more enemies for Alexander back in Greece. They will not take kindly to the killing of Aristotle's nephew."

Roxana took in Hephaestion's perfect profile. "Can you stop his death?"

Hephaestion offered a sad smile, highlighting the despair in his eyes. "To let him live would invite other attempts. Alexander comes from a long line of assassinated kings and knows he needs to set an example for others wishing to destroy him."

What would happen to her if her husband ended up on the wrong side of an assassin's blade?

"The guards are to go everywhere with you from now on. Even when you go off riding Hera in the morning." The insistence in his voice seemed out of character for the even-tempered general.

A weight settled on her shoulders.

So much for my freedom.

Hephaestion turned toward the tent entrance. "Welcome to the life of a Macedonian king. From now on, you will always be watched. I can't have anything happen to Alexander's greatest treasure."

After he left the tent, Roxana closed her eyes and silently cursed her fate. She didn't know what was worse—being the wife of a king or being the Persian wife of a Greek. It would seem each scenario had dangerous disadvantages. She just wasn't sure which one was going to get her killed.

A vibrant green blanketed the landscape of trees and fields along the rut-covered road heading to Bactra—the largest city in the Bactrian province. Roxana ached to climb from her seat in her hot wagon and stretch her legs and relieve her aching back in the shade of the nearby trees. The summer sun was high by the time the stone walls of the city became visible. The promise of a cool palace with floors, ceilings, a private room and bath after months in her tent sounded like a dream come true.

The rolling hills outside the city walls became cluttered with men from Alexander's army setting up camp, erecting tents, and building paddocks for their animals. The rest of the long procession slowly entered the thick timber city gates as anxious residents stood by, glaring with disapproval.

Dirty-faced children hugged wide-eyed parents as her wagon rolled past. She knew their anxiety, had experienced the same fear when Alexander's army had settled in her homeland. She wished she could reassure them, but would they listen? She was a Persian married to a Greek—she had no place with her people or with Alexander's. She was adrift on an ocean of animosity, and the only harbor she had was her husband's arms.

Inside the city walls, horses, wagons, and men jumbled together. Sentries charged with providing housing for the army shouted for men and women to spread out to different quarters of the town. She, along with the mistresses of Alexander's generals, was shown to the best residence in the area, the palace of the former satrap.

The corridors of the small mud brick palace had dreary depictions of Persian soldiers pillaging, and destroying towns. The floors were mud brick as well but painted with colorful floral displays, and the ceilings covered with blue like the sky. The contradiction astounded her.

In her rooms in the women's quarters, bright blues, reds, and yellows were used to recreate scenes of birds on the walls. Even the furniture had bird themes. There were benches shaped like doves and a bed designed to resemble a giant black swan on the water. Thankful to be out of the elements, she collapsed on a chair and kicked off her dusty brown leather shoes.

"Do you think they will have any hot water, Morella? I'd love a bath."

Morella lifted an armful of clothes from one of Roxana's trunks. "I'll get you hot water, my lady, if I have to whip a few of the lazy old crows around here to do it." She set the garments on the bed. "Already had a few words with some of the staff. You wouldn't believe what I found out." She picked up Roxana's shoes. "That fat old cow, Barsine, and her bastard boy are here. Her servant girl told me the king wanted his infant son to stay in the palace." Morella turned her inquisitive gaze to Roxana.

She didn't give an inkling of a reaction. "The king is very kind."

"You're much nicer than I would be." With a snort, Morella went back to her trunk. "I would have given the woman a what for, I tell you. You know, I heard from the assistant architect, whose brother is an attendant of General Ptolemy's, that Barsine had shared the general's bed for a while, but he got tired of her and gave her to Alexander. Can you imagine? And then the old crone goes and gets a son off the king." Her servant blushed. "I'm sorry, my lady. I didn't mean to offend. My mother always told me my mouth would get me in trouble one day. She said I spent too much time listening at tents and around doors."

Something Yasmin had once told her came to mind. Roxana explored her maid's honey-colored skin and her deep-set brown eyes. Morella's skill for collecting information could prove useful.

"Morella?" Roxana got up. "Can you … I mean, do you know a lot of people in the camps?"

"Well, everybody eventually knows everybody, ma'am. We all run into each other often enough. It's sort of like a traveling city."

"Could you find out things for me? I could pay you."

Morella's eyes grew, and a grin spread across her small mouth. "What you need to know, ma'am?" Morella giggled. "I can find out anything."

A *whoosh* carried across the reception area as the doors to Roxana's rooms flew open.

Two members of the king's guard entered. Roxana was about to ask the reason for the intrusion when a sunburned Alexander strutted inside.

"Ah, there you are," he called when he saw her.

Her heart sped up at the sight of his pink face and peeling nose.

Morella immediately fell to the floor, kneeling before the king.

"Tell her to leave." Alexander nodded to Morella. "I want to talk to you."

Roxana told Morella in Persian she would no longer be needed.

Her servant got up and backed out of the room. The two guards waited patiently at the black doors for her to withdraw, then quickly closed them.

"You really should learn some Persian, Alexander," Roxana scolded in Greek as she walked toward the ebony swan bed, which was big enough to sleep three.

He came up to her, tossing aside his peaked red Persian cap. "Don't have time. Besides, what would all the interpreters I have working for me do?" He undid his belt while inspecting the bird motifs on the walls. "Do you like your rooms? Best in the house. Better than mine. Cooler than mine, too, in this dreadful summer heat."

He dropped the leather belt. The scabbard of his sword rattled when it hit the floor.

"Yes, I like my rooms, but after so many months in a tent, anything is a luxury."

With a leering grin, he eased the Persian coat from around her shoulders and pitched it to the side.

She could guess why he had come to visit. Not that she was complaining, she just wished they could talk a little before they made love. She had so many things she wanted to know about him.

"It's the middle of the day, Alexander. Don't you have advisors to be advised by or someone important to meet?"

He arched over her, resting his hands on the bed. "I have all kinds of men to meet. I have to revamp the Bactrian government while I'm here and get ready for India. Right now, all I want to do is talk to my wife." He hungrily kissed her.

She eased back from him. "Who are these people you keep waiting so you can talk to me?"

"Ugh!" He groaned. "Who cares? Ministers, advisors, generals … I've even been told I've got a king coming to see me from India. He wants to assist me with my campaign. We can discuss it later." He eagerly tugged at his long Persian tunic.

"When it comes to being with a woman, our chitons are easier," he mumbled, struggling with the heavy material.

"Maybe you should try Persian pants." Roxana unpinned her pleated dress and dropped it to the floor next to his pile of clothes. "They're very comfortable."

Alexander picked her up in his strong arms. "I leave those for you to wear."

He scooted her up the bed. After he set her on the black sheets, Alexander gazed past her naked body to the headboard.

"Oh, that won't do." He wrinkled his brow at the black swan head curved over the bed. "I can't make love to you in this thing. I'll feel like I'm going to be swallowed by a large duck."

Roxana glanced up at the bird's head. "I think it's supposed to be a swan."

"Looks like a mad giant goose." He grabbed her hand and pulled her off the black sheets. "Reminds me of the geese I used to chase around the palace grounds at Pella when I was a boy. One bit me right on the ass once." He wheeled around, trying to get a peek of his firm backside. "I still have the scar."

Roxana laughed, entertained by this playful side. "Another war wound?"

"Yes, the only battle I ever lost." He smiled, giving her a glimpse of the little boy within. "Don't tell anyone you know of my defeat. It could ruin me."

She pictured him as a precocious child, running amuck in his family's palace.

Would their son be the same way?

"I'll wager you were a real torment to your mother."

He frowned. "More like the other way around. Mother was a torment to me. Still is in many ways."

"What about your father?" Roxana asked as he led her from the bed to their pile of clothes on the floor.

"Sons are different with fathers than daughters. Can't have been all that fun for the old man to see me and know I was waiting in the wings to replace him." He sat on the pile of clothes. "It wasn't like he was going to retire. He was king and the only way a king gets to quit is to die."

The thought of losing him awakened a horrible, sickly feeling. They'd only been married for such a short time, but already, she couldn't comprehend life without him.

Is this love?

She didn't believe so. Roxana chalked up the rush of emotion to her situation, and the dire turn of events his death would bring.

She reclined next to him. "Will you see your son the same way? As your replacement?"

He gathered her in his arms. "My father and I were never on the best of terms even when we got along." He kissed her shoulder. "I would have to get to know my son before I could decide."

Roxana nibbled her way along his neck to his ear. "Then we'd better get started on your son and heir, so you two can have lots of time together."

CHAPTER SIXTEEN

A king named Taxiles arrived at the palace. Said to rule over everything west of the Hydaspes River, he brought soldiers, attendants, and twenty-five painted elephants, which caused quite a stir in the camp—particularly in the stables, where the whinnying of horses kept Roxana up most nights.

Numerous banquets were held across the city to welcome the new king, and Roxana attended every one. She wore a new, stunning outfit to each event. In gold, silver, rich fabrics of purple and red, she dazzled Alexander, intent on attracting his attention. She might have won his love but keeping it required a whole different set of tactics.

After another formal banquet at the palace, Alexander invited her and Hephaestion to his rooms—something he'd never done before. Perhaps this was progress? He was no longer coming to her rooms; she was going to his.

When his guards pushed open the doors to his chamber, the aroma of spicy incense burned her eyes. Done in black stone, with red paintings of Persian gods and men readying for war on the walls, it had none of the airiness of her quarters.

"I think Taxiles's visit offers a wealth of information of what lies ahead for us in India," Alexander said to Hephaestion as they walked inside.

In his billowing Persian tunic, coat, and gold Greek diadem, Alexander appeared to be a confusing blend of cultures. Hephaestion also wore a Persian coat and a long tunic, matching the king, but to Roxana, the outfit looked better on him.

Hephaestion followed her into his reception room. "The trunks of ivory, silk, and those strange gems called rubies piled high in the main hall of the palace have excited the men for India."

Alexander dropped his red and gold Persian coat to the ground as she went to inspect one of the portraits on his walls.

A chariot, complete with fire-breathing horses pulling a sword-wielding Persian in brightly colored apparel, had her mesmerized.

"Roxana," Alexander called to her. "Come, sit."

The thick, heavy furniture contrasted with everything Roxana knew about her husband's simple tastes. She went to a high table with chairs and had a seat next to Alexander.

An attractive young male servant poured three goblets of the sweetest Bactrian wine. After serving the drinks, the same man rescued the king's coat from the floor.

"The riches in India will make us wealthy men." Alexander lifted his goblet.

In a corner of the room, Peritas attentively minded his master. The dog and the form-fitting yellow peplos she wore to impress her husband made her uncomfortable.

"What do you think, Roxana?"

Alexander's question pulled her attention from the dog. "India seems like it will be quite an adventure."

Hephaestion struggled with his coat, attempting to get comfortable in a chair across from her. "With Taxiles on our side, and the new Persian recruits swelling our ranks, we might just take all of India."

"Persian recruits?" she demanded.

"Yes, I'm getting recruits from all the new territories." Alexander scooted closer to her. "You made me realize I need to build a more cohesive empire."

His admission left her awestruck, but she also suspected the men would blame her influence for his actions. Instead of warning him, she stuck with the topic of India, not wanting to ruin his jovial mood.

"What else do you know of India? Other than what Taxiles has told you."

"Not very much," Hephaestion admitted. "We only have stories about the exotic plants and animals. We know a little about the religion there, called ... What is it, Alexander?"

"Buddhism. They practice this rite where they make the wives climb on the funeral pyre with their husband's body. Then they are burned alive, joining the husband in the afterlife or some such rot. Can you imagine that?"

Roxana didn't like the sound of it. "What about if the wife dies? Does the husband climb on her funeral pyre?"

Both Alexander and Hephaestion burst into boyish laughter.

"You wouldn't follow the old man onto the funeral pyre?" Hephaestion asked.

"No." The idea horrified her. "Why, would you?"

"Of course. I am Patroclus."

Roxana put down her goblet, ashamed of drinking so much. "I've heard this name before. Who is it?"

Alexander peered into his wine. "Patroclus and Achilles were heroes from a famous Greek story about Troy."

"Ah, yes." Roxana smiled, recognizing the tale. "The one with the horse that hid the soldiers inside it. My mother taught me some of your Greek legends. But not about this Achilles and Patro ..."

"Patroclus," Alexander enunciated. "The legend goes that Achilles and Patroclus were the deepest of friends and vowed to die for each other. I'm descended from Achilles, on my mother's side. I feel my life has paralleled his in many ways. I even have his shield. It was a gift from the people in a village near old Troy."

"You hope it's his shield." Hephaestion sat back, grinning. "They probably produce dozens of shields belonging to Achilles every month in that village for the tourists."

Alexander gave his friend a dirty look. "It's all in a book called *The Iliad*. I'll get you a copy and someone to read it to you."

"I read Greek." Roxana felt the eyes of both men on her. "My mother taught me that, too."

Hephaestion banged his goblet on the table. "You're unique, Roxana, even among Greek women. If you want to understand why the twisted heap of bones you're married to does the things he does, read *The Iliad*. He sleeps with the copy Aristotle gave him under his pillow."

She made a mental note to track down a copy of the book. Any insight into her husband would be worthwhile.

"Yes, it's true." Alexander drained the dregs from his goblet. "I consider it a handbook in the art of war. I keep it close by, always. That and a knife."

After the incident with his guards, she understood why.

"If our king ever slept, then he might need a knife under his pillow." Hephaestion bowed his head to Roxana. "I'm sure you may have already noticed our king rarely sleeps."

Without thinking, she proclaimed, "He sleeps with me."

Alexander and Hephaestion roared with laughter.

Roxana, realizing her mistake, turned a bright shade of crimson. "Forgive me. I've had too much wine. I should not have spoken so." She lowered her head.

"Don't be silly, Roxana." Her husband raised her chin. "I have no secrets from Hephaestion and neither should you. After all, he too is Alexander."

The comment gave her pause. "The day I met Hephaestion, one of your generals … Ptolemy said the same thing." Roxana scrutinized the two men. "What does that mean?"

Alexander set his goblet aside. "It takes a lot to keep this operation going. More than one man. Alexander is really two men or more, depending on how you look at it. Everything I am, I am because of the people around me. Aristotle once said together Hephaestion and I make the perfect king. He's the planner, and I'm the man of action. He supports me, keeps all of my secrets, and anticipates my needs. We're the same man really, but not the same." He turned his head slightly as he observed his wife. "Does that make any sense?"

The black doors to Alexander's rooms opened. Ptolemy walked in unannounced.

He strolled up to the table. "What's she doing in here? It's bad luck to have a woman in the king's chambers."

The rudeness of the man astonished her.

"I asked Roxana to join Hephaestion and me for a nightcap." Alexander arched one eyebrow at the cantankerous general. "There's no harm in that. Is there?"

"Never seen you bring women to your quarters before." He furrowed his brow. "I need to talk to you, alone."

Alexander motioned to his wife. "Hephaestion, bring Roxana back to the harem for me."

Sad their time together had come to an end, Roxana rose from her chair.

While Hephaestion accompanied her to the chamber doors, she glimpsed the brown dog asleep in the corner. She envied the dog being able to stay with Alexander day and night.

Two soldiers stepped behind her in the corridor, ready to escort her back to her rooms.

"You must forgive Ptolemy." Hephaestion closed Alexander's doors. "He's a bit rough around the edges."

Roxana came alongside the elegant Greek as the two walked down the hall to the women's section of the palace.

"I want to thank you for allowing me to sit with you and the king during your meeting."

"Thank Alexander." Hephaestion strolled beside her, letting her set the pace. "He wanted you to join us tonight so you would not feel ignored."

Roxana swallowed a nervous lump in her throat. "He told you about that?"

"You weren't listening back there. Alexander tells me everything. He wants to make you happy, Roxana. Making people happy pleases him."

A thread of doubt swept through her. "I want to please Alexander, but I'm still not sure I can."

"The key to pleasing Alexander is simple. To him, there's nothing more important than being loved. By his men, his people, and even those he conquers. For him, to be loved is to be honored, and that pleases him very much."

They entered the women's quarters of the palace, her mind on fire with all she'd learned. She wanted to please Alexander, but could she ever love him? Part of her would always consider him the Greek king who had captured her homeland and changed her life forever. She doubted if even the gods were powerful enough to sway her resolute heart.

"Perdiccas is an ass." Ptolemy sat next to Alexander, his hand around Roxana's half-empty goblet. "The men are fine with going to India. Did you see their faces when King Taxiles brought those painted elephants through the city gates? Bloody amazing that was."

Alexander chuckled at his old friend, glad he'd convinced him. He would need his support for the long march into India.

Hephaestion closed the doors on the sentries stationed outside. "Still bitching about Perdiccas, Ptolemy?"

"Just as much as you complain about Craterus." Ptolemy flashed him a snide grin. "I'll let the men know about your plans. We'll make ready for the split at the Cophen River."

Alexander got up and went to the serving table, wanting more wine. The infighting amongst his generals had gotten out of hand. He would have to do something about it before his campaign into India.

"I'll meet with the generals at first light. I want to make sure everyone is settled with the new Persian recruits before we push off for the Caucasus Mountains."

Ptolemy's scowl told Alexander he wasn't happy about the Persian recruits mingling with the Greeks.

Without saying another word, Ptolemy walked out of his chambers.

Ptolemy was loyal and also shrewd, but he knew not to create waves. He needed more generals backing his plans rather than fighting them.

He retrieved a wine jug and carried it back to the table. The *thump* of heavy doors closing reverberated through the room.

"What do you think?"

Hephaestion eased into his chair. "You don't have to ask me. I will do it."

Alexander poured himself more wine. "When we were at Mieza, Aristotle used to go on and on about the inferiority of women." He put the jug aside. "I always agreed with him until I met Roxana." He resumed his seat, already missing her smile and her perfume. How would he survive the months ahead without her? "I want you to take her with you when you go with Taxiles. She will be safer with you through the Khyber Pass than with me in the mountainous regions."

Hephaestion sighed. "Along with the rest of the baggage train, the mercenary cavalry, and half the Companion Cavalry."

"You will take Perdiccas with you. It would be good for the men and my head if I separated you from Craterus and Ptolemy from Perdiccas." He sipped his wine, wanting to dull his sense of desire for her. "I need you and Perdiccas to secure a bridgehead at the Indus River and gather supplies for the crossing. When we meet up at the town of Ohind, we can regroup the army and make ready to enter into the Punjab region. King Porus lives there. He's the arch rival of King Taxiles."

"What will you be doing while I babysit your wife, Perdiccas, and half the army?"

Alexander ran his thumb over the smooth surface of the goblet's rim, wondering why Persian cups were so superior to the Greek's. "King Taxiles tells me the mountain people where we're going are resistant to foreigners, and ruthless fighters." Alexander smiled. "Perhaps I shall find something to do while I'm up there."

"Just don't get yourself killed. I'm not quite ready to throw myself on that funeral pyre just yet."

The doors to the king's apartment slowly creaked open. A slim figure glided inside, holding a white towel. His long, black hair was pulled back with a white ribbon; his black eyes were downcast. The sinewy man padded to the king's gold bathtub at the far end of the room.

Alexander took in his fluid movements, comparing them to his wife's. She was the more graceful, and the more compelling, even if the eunuch possessed a certain charm.

"I guess it's time for your bath." Hephaestion stood. "I should retire."

The deadpan expression on Hephaestion's face bothered him. How long had it been since he'd sat with his oldest and dearest friend and talked—yesterday, a month ago, or a year ago, he couldn't remember. But tonight, he wanted to spend time with him before the long separation ahead.

"I won't be needing you anymore tonight, Bagoas." Alexander gave a dismissive flick of his hand, keeping his eyes on his general.

Bagoas bowed low and scurried across the room to the doors.

Once the boy was gone, Hephaestion slumped into his chair.

"That thing hates me."

Alexander put down his drink. "That thing is a damned fine attendant and a rather handy little spy when the need arises."

With an aggravated hitch in his voice, Hephaestion asked, "Will he go with you when we split up at Cophen River?"

He folded his hands, keeping up his blank expression. "Yes."

Hephaestion let go a long breath, flaring his nostrils. Something he usually did when he was thinking or perturbed.

"I will see you in the morning."

"Don't go. Sit." Alexander motioned to his chair.

"I see no reason to stay."

"You don't need a reason to stay." Alexander pushed a goblet toward him. "You never have, and you never will."

CHAPTER SEVENTEEN

Her wagon jostled and shimmied, navigating the bumpy road, while the crisp air from the Caucasus Mountains kept her nestled beneath blankets. The view from her wagon window offered lush vistas of densely treed forests against the rising backdrop of the jagged white mountains ahead. But every time she took in the immense, slow-moving baggage train around her, she debated if such a traveling city could follow the army through the harsh mountain passes.

Their ranks had swelled since leaving Bactra. Persian troops joining Alexander's army added to the length of the baggage train. Unfortunately, the petty fights common in the women's camp escalated, usually along cultural lines, but what did she care? Her people didn't acknowledge her because she'd married a Greek, and the Greeks continued to avoid her because she belonged to the king.

At night, when the campfires roared and the smoke hung over the wagons, Roxana, accompanied by her two guards, checked on her only friend in the camp, Hera. The calm horse was the one living soul in whom she could confide her troubles—the main one being her empty womb.

Since they spent more time apart than together, she doubted if she would ever be able to bear the king any children. If that wasn't bad enough, her misery was dealt another blow when she encountered Barsine and her son.

"No signs of stirring yet in your belly, eh, little star?" Barsine caught up to Roxana's wagon one day as the camp moved toward the Cophen River.

"I had heard you gave birth to a healthy little bastard boy, Barsine." Roxana gazed out her window to the woman walking alongside. "How happy you must be." She noticed the sleeping child cradled in a sling around Barsine's chest.

"And I've heard the king never visits his Persian wife, but only spends his time with his Persian boy." Barsine laughed, showing a large gap where her two front teeth used to be. "How happy you must be, dear lady."

A guard walking next to Roxana's wagon shooed Barsine away with his long spear. The fat cow scrambled back to her place with the other mistresses and whores of Alexander's generals.

Her wagon moved on, and Roxana held her head up high, refusing to give the women more fodder for their gossip. She was the wife of a king, even if she felt like nothing more than another treasure the mighty Alexander had collected.

An antsy Alexander settled into his unfinished palace rooms in the newly built city of Kapisa. Before picking up an open wax tablet on his desk, he frowned at a half-done mural of red lions and green griffins on his walls. Then, noise from his open window took him away from his work.

Crammed with men, women, and children, the streets outside his palace rooms were a hotbed of reunions and goodbyes. To appease his army, he had relaxed the rules for the strict demarcation between the camps.

At the far end of the town, three massive timber gates allowed easy access to the numerous caravans crossing the Khyber Pass and heading for the trade routes cutting into India. To his right, the Cophen River, a rushing mass of dark water flowed past a small harbor.

The city was the perfect launching point for his grand campaign into India.

But the throngs of people coming together outside his window lifted his mood more than the fighting ahead—Persians and Greeks, sharing in a happy celebration. It was the last time many families would be together before Hephaestion left with the baggage train to travel the safer Peshawar Road through the Khyber Pass.

The plans for impending separation drove him back to his desk, but his loneliness enveloped him like a thick blanket.

Will she miss me when I leave?

He shrugged off the question and went back to the latest tallies of supplies needed for the long trek, but after reviewing the figures twice, he put the tablet down. He couldn't stop thinking about her.

He'd avoided visiting Roxana's rooms, wanting to wait to break the news of their long separation. He also didn't want to see her indifference when he told her of their extended time apart. She knew his feelings for her, but did she have any regard for him?

The more he dwelt on the subject, the greater his agitation. He had to know before he left if there was any hope of love from her.

Alexander set out from his rooms, his king's guard right behind him.

Light streamed through the window along the corridor. He ran his fingers through the tendrils of sunshine stretching toward the gray stone floor as he walked the last few steps to her rooms.

He entered the wooden doors to her chamber unannounced.

She sat on a bench by one of the windows, the copy of *The Iliad* he'd given her in her hands. Her back to him, she didn't hear his light footfalls across the tiled floor. Mesmerized by the way her lips moved as she sounded out every word, he admired the curve of her small chin and the way her hair shimmered in the sunlight.

"I will send you more books. I always carry a large trunk of them with me."

When she turned, a sinking feeling overtook him. She didn't look pleased.

The book placed on the side of the bench, she rose to greet him. "I didn't hear you, my king." She bowed, keeping her distance.

"I'm glad you like to read." Uncomfortable with the formality between them, Alexander held his arms out to her. "It has been a while since we've seen each other, little star. Come, let me feel my arms around you."

She turned her back on him and made her way to the carved bed, decorated with lions. Once she had a seat, Roxana glared at him.

He dropped his arms. "You're angry. What is it this time? Have I ignored you yet again? Or you have heard some nasty rumor about me? Or can it be something else, perhaps?"

"How long will you be gone?" Her tone was flat and emotionless.

By keeping her lodged in the palace, he'd hoped to spare her from the news sweeping through the camps about the coming separation.

Sighing, Alexander approached the bed. "I didn't want you to find out about the campaign until I was ready to tell you, but the gossips beat me to it. I should have told you sooner. Forgive me."

Her face remained impassive. Like a statue sculpted by a master, she displayed tremendous beauty, but no heart.

"When will the army pull out?"

He traced the regal outline of her jaw, memorizing every inch of her. "Tomorrow."

Roxana stood and dropped her outer coat to the floor. "Then I will do my duty."

Her words cut him to the bone, worse than the deepest gash from a sword.

He clasped her arms, pinning them to her sides. "That's not why I came. I wanted to talk to you, to spend time with you. Do you think the only reason I visit is to make love to you?" He let her go, upset he couldn't find the words to tell her how hurt he felt.

She coolly collected her coat and eased it around her shoulders.

"Why must everything be like the siege of Troy with you?" His strained voice echoed throughout her rooms. "I have conquered great lands, won major battles, built an empire, but still I can't win one morsel of emotion from you. Why is that, Roxana?"

The glint of astonishment shone from her eyes. "I have married you, shared your bed, traveled with your army, been ridiculed when you take other lovers, and stood by as your mistress bears your son. And you still feel you have not conquered me? What must I do ...? Prostrate before you, Great King?"

"It's you who have conquered me!" Alexander threw his arms around her. "Why is it I can have strangers praise me, have my soldiers adore me, and make foreign kings bow before me, but I've never heard you say you love me. Tomorrow I leave for a long and dangerous campaign. Do you have no kind words for me?

Nothing for me to carry with me when I'm gone?"

She squirmed, attempting to free herself. "Is that what you need to hear, Alexander? My declaration of love? So you can feel like you have won me?"

Blinded by his anger, he picked her up, carried her to the bed, and threw her on the blanket. In an instant, he was on top of her, holding her down as he tugged at her coat.

"I've never had to beg anyone for love, Roxana. It has always been given freely to me. But with you ...? If I die on this campaign, my one regret will be never hearing how you feel about me."

She stiffened beneath him. His fury quickly dissolved. He let her go and rolled to the side of the bed.

"With you, I lose control, and that's something I never wish to do." He sat up, wiping his brow with a shaky hand.

He could not let this go on. How long would it be before the sickness she awakened in him carried over to his ability to lead his men? Best to cut ties before it went too far.

"Perhaps you should return to your family instead of going on with the baggage train. I can arrange for you to receive a large amount of gold to ensure your comfort. You will remain my wife for whatever benefit it will bring you, but I promise never to visit you again."

He was about to climb from the bed when she gripped his arm.

"I do not wish to return to my family. I want to remain with the baggage train."

Hardening his resolve, he removed her hand from his arm. "I will do whatever you wish. I want only for your happiness, Roxana."

No longer lifeless, her eyes radiated warmth, and a slow smile graced her lips.

"Then do not die, Alexander. I can only be happy as long as I'm with you."

Alexander buried his face in her jasmine-scented hair. "Does this mean you will miss me just a little?"

She leaned back, cradling his head. "I've fought against my feelings for you. I didn't want to let the great Greek warrior king take away my last possession—my heart. But my walls are not as sturdy as the cities you have bested. I care for you, deeply. Is it love? I don't know, but I am sure of one thing—I never want to live without you."

He put his arms around her, elated, relieved, and for the first time certain she would declare her love for him one day.

"You have given this soldier all he needs to carry into battle—you."

Alexander kissed her, thanking the gods for whatever strange magic she held over him. For one night, the army and all his problems could keep. He planned on savoring each kiss and every caress as if it were his last.

CHAPTER EIGHTEEN

"I see you've had your nose in a book. Just like Alexander."

Hephaestion entered Roxana's small traveling tent. She was relieved to see the general and welcomed his visit. The month since leaving the army at the Cophen River had been hard for her and the other women. The bleak snow-covered trails and treacherous terrain of the Khyber Pass compounded their sagging morale.

He took the book from her and curiously gleaned the text. "How are you coming along?"

She warmed her hands on the brazier by her feet as the bitter wind pummeled her flimsy tent. "Reading Greek was always more difficult for me than speaking it, but I'm making headway."

Morella appeared at the tent doorway. "Can I get the general anything?"

She was about to interpret for Hephaestion when he said, "Wine with water and some dates."

Roxana viewed the general in a whole new light. "You speak Persian? I never realized."

He handed back her book. "We've been in this country a long time. Some things rub off."

She placed it in her lap. "They have not rubbed off on Alexander."

"He always has so much to do. He puts off things he feels he can attend to later. Like learning Persian."

She pictured her husband's smile, his laugh, his face as he slept in her bed.

"Have you heard anything from him?"

Hephaestion stretched for the grate filled with kindling. "He has engaged some of the tribes in the local hill lands of Bajaur. Fierce fighting, he writes, but he is well."

She welcomed any news, even second-hand. "I'm glad."

Hephaestion rubbed his hands together, appearing uncharacteristically nervous.

To Roxana, he always seemed the opposite of her husband—level-headed, calm, and never prone to anger or nerves.

"He asked about you. Wanted to know how you're doing."

"I'm fine, Hephaestion." She peered down at her book as a shadow settled over her heart. "And no, I'm not with child. I can guess that's the king's primary reason for him asking you to visit me."

"You misunderstood me, Roxana." A deep line settled over his smooth brow. "I'm not asking whether you carry the king's child. I'm asking how you are. How you are getting along now that he's gone?"

Worry for her husband tightened her chest. How did the wives and lovers traveling with her stand the constant ache in their hearts and restless nights? But Hephaestion didn't need to hear an army wife's woes. What he'd probably seen and experienced on the battlefield was worse than any suffering caused by long separations.

"I've learned to keep busy. I have my reading, and I also sew and weave a little. My maid, Morella, has taught me. She says it's below my station, but it helps to occupy my mind."

"It's hard to love a man you share with the world, don't you think?"

She could not help but grin. Was there anything the two men didn't discuss?

"If you're trying to get me to tell you how I feel—" A realization hit her. "He told you to ask me, didn't he?"

"No ... not exactly. Alexander writes to me and in every letter, he asks about you. What you are doing, if you are well. It wouldn't hurt you to drop him a letter to let him know how you are."

Roxana fumbled with her book. "I never thought of writing to him. I assumed he would be too busy with matters of war."

"Alexander would never be too busy for a letter from you." Hephaestion's eyes glistened in the firelight. "I've been the middleman when Alexander negotiates treaties, deals with his army, his generals, but I have never had to run back and forth between Alexander and his wife. So, for my sanity and his, write to him. He wants to hear from you."

Morella came inside and took a tray of dates and a jug of wine to a table. After a quick bow to Roxana and the general, the blushing woman scampered out of the tent.

Hephaestion strode to the table and filled a goblet with wine.

To Roxana, the man with the sharp features and uncanny eyes was a friend, but also a stranger. Perhaps getting to know the person her husband relied on for all things would give her some insights into the king.

"Tell me about yourself, Hephaestion. I feel I've known you so long, but so little. How did you meet my husband?"

After selecting a date, he went to a stool across from her bench.

"My father brought me to court at Pella when I was six, to be educated with the king's son under the tutelage of Leonidas." He set his goblet on the ground.

"You knew Alexander's parents?"

"Too well." He popped the date into his mouth. "Philip pushed Alexander hard, and Olympias hated him for it. But Philip knew he had to prepare his son for war and politics. He also wanted the Greeks to accept Alexander as a Greek king."

She pulled her coat closer, bothered by the relentless cold. "But he's Greek. How could other Greeks not accept him?"

"Even Greeks are prejudiced against their kind." He chased down his date with some wine. "Alexander is Macedonian, and to the Greeks of Athens, he's a barbarian. Alexander could stand at the right hand of Zeus and still Athens would not be impressed. Many speak out against him. One man, Demosthenes, has become a thorn in the king's side."

The disrespect of his soldiers suddenly made sense to her. Greeks had never learned to value a king.

"I find it hard to believe a man can speak out against the king and still live."

"It's our way." Hephaestion propped his goblet on his knee. "Where we come from, men can speak out against anything they wish."

"And do Greek women have the same right?" The words angrily tumbled out before she could stop them.

She waited for his heated response, but he just gaped at her.

"I find it mind-boggling how men can discuss, debate, and fight for equality, but it never occurred to them that maybe women might like a chance at it, too. You've never known the true worth of your opinion until you have had it disregarded not because of what you said, but because of your sex." She wistfully smiled, amused by the irony of her plight. "Women bear men from their bodies, but those same bodies can never be considered equal."

"You should visit Egypt. Their women have much more equality there. They're nothing like Persians."

The mention of the exotic land she'd heard about from travelers and read in books enticed her.

"You've been there? What was it like? Did you see the pyramids, the Sphinx, the great city of the dead?"

His eyebrows rose at her enthusiasm. "We didn't get to see many of the famous buildings, but Egypt does have a captivating culture. Ptolemy always swears he's going to retire there." He snickered. "We saw a good bit of the land though when we rode across the desert to visit the Oracle at Siwa."

"What were you doing there?"

"Alexander wanted to ask the God Ammon a question. He's always doing that—asking the gods for their approval. After all he's done, all the land he's conquered, sometimes he's still insecure about his place in history."

The insight surprised her. "What did he ask the god?"

He rolled his eyes. "What he always asks? 'Will I die leaving an everlasting fame?' It's all he thinks about."

She took in the general's disgruntled countenance. "You make it sound like you don't approve."

"No, that's not it. I want him to stop obsessing about a future he can't control and start living a life he can. You have to be a man first before you can be a legend. But for him, they are one in the same."

A burst of wind thrashed against her tent, interrupting her thoughts. "Do you have any other stories of your adventures with the king?"

He took his goblet to the serving table. "It's late. We will be pulling out at first light." He went to the tent entrance and then hesitated. "But I can call again and share some more of our exploits."

"I would like that very much."

After he ventured out into the bitter night, Roxana hugged herself.

Perhaps the journey wouldn't be so tedious after all.

CHAPTER NINETEEN

The winds turned colder. High drifts of snow made the going slow for Roxana and the other women. Patches of ice along the narrow pass proved daunting for the wagons. She found the days and nights of bitter weather debilitating.

On a night when the caravan had stopped to rest, Roxana sat huddled around her brazier when Morella brought her disheartening news with her dinner.

"Word at the food wagon is children are falling sick everywhere, my lady."

Roxana eyed her plate of dried goat and bread. "What are their maladies?"

Morella warmed her hands. "Coughing, chills, some have terrible rashes, a few have died already. Burned in pyres next to the road. So sad."

Roxana put her plate aside, a sense of urgency sweeping through her. "Do you know where these children are?"

"The sick wagon. With the others, of course." Morella kept her gaze on the fire. "They have a midwife tending to them, but what do they know of caring for children. The doctors appointed to our camp have been too busy treating the ailing soldiers traveling with us to visit the children."

Roxana went to her cot and tossed a thick woolen blanket around her shoulders. "Show me where the sick wagon is."

"No, you can't go there. The wife of the king must not endanger—"

She silenced the stout woman by placing a hand on her shoulder. "I may be wife to the king, but I'm also a healer. I might be able to help."

Morella grudgingly nodded. "I may not agree with you, but I won't stop you. Nothing breaks my heart more than a sick child."

"Me, either." She pulled the blanket snug. "Now, show me this wagon."

The night was clear, but the air burned her skin. She covered her face as best she could as she left her tent, her guards fell in step behind her.

The brutal wind cut through her, and her thin leather shoes did nothing to keep out the snow and wet. But Roxana wasn't deterred. She could not turn a blind eye to suffering—even Greek suffering.

The covered wagon was set far away from the tents, for fear of the disease spreading to the rest of the camp. Blankets had been tossed over the top to provide some protection from the cold while a massive fire burned beside it. Horses secured to a pile of stacked rocks not far from the wagon stirred when she and Morella approached.

The pitiful sounds of coughing and crying awakened memories of her mother's demise. She twisted her fingers, anxious she might not be able to offer any asistance.

May the gods give me strength.

They reached the back steps of the wagon and halted when a figure climbed out. A woman as round as she was tall, wearing the apron of a physician, wheezed as she maneuvered down the steps. There were deep lines around her mouth and dark eyes. The shawl covering her head offered a peek of gray hair, and her lips pulled back in a toothless sneer the moment she spotted Roxana.

"What you doin' here? This is no place for the king's Persian wife."

Roxana bristled against the insult but stood her ground. "I came to check on the children," she asserted in Greek. "I can help. My mother trained me as a healer."

"Healer?" The craggy woman laughed and went to the fire, a bowl of dirty linens in her hands. "You know nothing of healing, girl. Go back to your tent and let these souls die in peace."

Roxana wasn't about to leave. She had confronted tougher opponents than the old woman and gotten her way.

"What are their symptoms?"

The woman pitched the linens into the fire. The flames flashed as the strips were consumed, sending sparks into the air.

"They have the wet cough. All of them. It hits the young ones, and the weak when there's too much cold and dampness. Most of these will be gone in a few days." She wiped the long sleeve of her black wool dress over her brow. "But there will be more to replace them. There always is."

Encouraged, Roxana moved closer. "What are you giving them? What treatment?"

The older woman's hostile features softened. "There's no treatment for wet lung, child, except to get them out of the cold, which will not happen for weeks, or so General Perdiccas tells me."

"Can I see them? Listen to their chests?" Roxana crept closer. "There might be some remedies you could try. Things to help lessen the coughing."

The tough old woman put her hands on her hips, her eyes teeming with aggravation. "Have you ever seen someone with wet lung, tended to them, cured them?"

Roxana's courage faltered. "My mother died of it, and I tended her the last weeks of her life. Have I cured anyone? No. But what harm can come from letting me try?"

The woman chuckled, and her protruding belly shook. "What harm? These are Greek children. They don't need your kind caring for them. Go to the other side of the camp and tend to the sick barbarians if you want to help."

She was about to climb the steps when Roxana reached for her arm. "The king will hear of how you've treated me. I'll be sure to mention it when I speak to him again."

The lines between her brows deepened. "All right. Come inside. But don't say I didn't warn you. If the mothers in the camp find out you were here, you'll regret it. Your Alexander's chosen, my lady, not theirs."

Roxana took her words as a challenge. If she could convince his people of her honorable intentions, maybe she had a chance of convincing his generals as well. Any step to prove herself to the Greeks, and appear less Persian in their eyes, she had to take.

She left Morella to wait outside and entered the wagon.

The caustic stench of feces, urine, and decay stung her eyes, and she covered her nose with her blanket. The only light came from hanging oil lamps, whose black smoke stained the canvas of the wagon. Wooden buckets for waste and vomit cluttered a central aisle, along with others filled with water frozen into solid chunks of ice. Spread out on either side of the narrow aisle, over twenty children, ranging from toddlers to those on the cusp of adulthood, lay lethargic on filthy, stained mats with nothing more than rags to keep them warm. Pale, sweaty faces with sunken eyes stared back at her. Bones poked out beneath skin not covered from the cold, and there was not a grieving mother or grandmother in sight. The pitiful creatures had been left to die alone.

Her heart clamored for justice. Guilt inundated her for not knowing such a heinous place existed, and not stepping in sooner to help.

"Where are the food bowls? The water? They're starving."

The older woman grunted. "Food is for the living. It's common in the camps for the sick to starve. It's the humane thing to do."

"Humane?" Roxana shouted with outrage. "But they need more food, not less. How else can they fight to gain their strength back?"

The bulky woman deftly negotiated between two children and went to a young boy. With dark curly hair, he lay motionless, his open mouth gaping upward, his eyes dull.

She checked his breath, listened to his chest, and then pulled his blanket over his eyes.

"Damn, and I thought he might pull through. I birthed him and his sister. She died last week. His father doesn't know yet. He's with the king fighting in the north." She stood and sighed. "What a horrible reunion he will have with his wife."

Roxana's sorrow quickly turned to rage. The desolate faces of the sick fed her anger.

She went to the child next to her, a young girl with matted yellow hair and the prettiest blue eyes. She knelt and examined the little one's face, the color of her gums, her fingernails, and then bent her head to her chest, straining to hear her breathing.

The ragged sound meant the sickness in her lungs had progressed to a dangerous point.

"What treatments have you given them?"

The old woman came up to her. "Some porridge and water. Willow bark to ease their pain when I can get it. The camp doctors don't like giving their limited supply of medicines to children."

Roxana glared at her, horrified. "And you call me a barbarian?"

"The strong are the ones given every chance to survive in your world and mine." The old woman gazed around the wagon. "I could argue all I want with the generals for more supplies, but no one would listen to me." She rubbed her hand across her brow. "Greek or Persian, women have no voice."

"I will get you everything you need." Roxana climbed to her feet, eager to get to work. "Linens, blankets, food, and medicine. They will need Elecampane to ease their breathing and help clear the lungs." She faced the crone. "Where do I find these things?"

The exuberant laugh answering her was unexpected. "You have to get a requisition order from General Perdiccas or General Hephaestion. But they've already denied me, twice."

With a steadfast obstinacy burning in her stomach, Roxana gathered the blanket around her shoulders.

"Well, they won't deny me."

With Morella and her guards trailing behind her, Roxana set out across the camp, intent on finding the generals. She didn't even feel the cold anymore; her anger kept her warm.

"How will you get them to agree with you?" Morella asked as they trudged through the snow. "These are generals, not the king. Your beauty may not sway them."

"I don't need my beauty to reason with men. I've been using my mind for that all my life."

Despite her frozen hands and numb toes, she never wavered from her mission. When she arrived at a large tent set up at the far side of the camp, two soldiers greeted her with stern faces.

The *clank* of spears crossing in front of her barred her way into the tent, sparking her indignation.

"I demand to speak to General Hephaestion."

The soldier to the left regarded her as if she were nothing more than an insect.

"He's not here. He's with the scouts checking the pass ahead. He'll be back in the morning."

The children she'd seen did not have that long. She had to push on. "Then let me speak to General Perdiccas."

The spears remained in front of her face. She balled her fists, about to demand they announce her to the general when the tent flap rustled open.

General Perdiccas appeared. She remembered having seen him with Alexander in the past. With reddish-brown hair tinged gray, and a thick middle, he stood before her wrapped in a robe and scowling behind his brown beard.

"My lady? What is it?"

His voice was far from welcoming, and she found the way his small dark eyes swept up and down her figure quite rude.

She lowered the blanket from her head. "I must speak with you about the conditions in the camp. Particularly the sick children. I've just come from their—"

"No one cares about sick children!" He ran his hand through his hair and mumbled something she couldn't make out. "Go back to your tent before you catch your death. Your husband will be furious with me if I let you die."

She'd been shoved aside and made to feel worthless ever since she'd arrived at the camps, but she wasn't going to allow it anymore. She was the king's wife and would damn well use her title to get something done or die trying.

Roxana put her foot partially in his tent, letting him know she had no intention of leaving. "My husband would not be pleased to hear you let others die on your watch, General. Especially, other Greeks," she added with a cocky half-smile.

The scathing rebuke in his eyes told her she'd pushed too hard, but she didn't care.

"Let's not discuss this here." Perdiccas waved her inside.

She entered his tent, grateful for the plume of warmth greeting her from his brazier. His quarters reeked of his musky scent blended with the pungent odors of olive oil and old leather. The welcoming flames of his fire called to her, but she stayed back. Her discomfort seemed inconsequential after the plight of the children.

Perdiccas retrieved a goblet of wine from a table next to a small stool. She quickly scanned his tent, drawn to his vast collection of armor set up in the corner and the cot close to the fire.

"Greeks—men, women, and children—die every day in the camps, Lady Roxana. I can do nothing to save them." He took his goblet back to his stool and sat. "Neither can Alexander."

"But you can help the sick, help those suffering have some comfort. Food, blankets, medicine—surely, you can spare that."

He sighed, his broad shoulders flexing under his red robe. "I can't spare the supplies. If you haven't noticed, we're in the middle of the Khyber Pass. There's nothing to eat, very little to use for firewood, and we're weeks from arriving at Ohind to meet up with the army. I have to be frugal for the strong in our group to survive."

"But isn't the duty of the strong to also provide for the weak?" Her adamancy fueled her resolve to make the man see reason. "Aren't contingencies taken into account when you planned for this excursion? When my father placed our family atop the great rock, he sent up twice the expected number of rations. If he, a mere chieftain and not a skilled general such as yourself, can have such foresight, then do you expect me to believe you don't have double the supplies for our party?"

"What do you think would happen to our extra rations if everyone in the camp found out a wagon full of sick children got their portion of food, medicine, and clothes? How long would we last after riots broke out, and gangs charged the supply wagons?" He put his goblet on the table. "There's a reason we keep supplies limited during desperate situations. It maintains control, something vital to getting our party out of these mountains."

She took a step closer, debating her next move. She'd listened to her father as he met with his men, had learned from him, tried to replicate his course of action when haggling with her sisters, brothers, and grandmother. "There is always an angle," he had once said. "You just have to find it." Then, a flash of insight came to her.

"This is not an army." She kept her tone even, masking her intent. "Women do not think like men. They will lie, cheat, steal, and kill for a child. You will find a woman protecting a child to be more ferocious than the most seasoned veteran of battle. And when you push women too far, they will revolt to save their children. How many more children have to die before you wake up with a knife at your throat?"

His eyes bulged. "Women can't fight and are no threat to my soldiers. They can be controlled easier than an army."

Roxana regrouped, coming up with another tactic. "And what if the men in the army learn their sons and daughters died because you refused them supplies?"

Perdiccas stood, chuckling. "You are tenacious. I will give you that."

"What if it was your child, General? Would you refuse me then?" The amusement left his eyes, and a cloud of doubt darkened them. "I'm not asking for much, just enough to see to the comfort and care of the sick. After all the women in these camps have been through, you owe them this kindness. They may not fight your wars, but they live with them, carry each loss on and off the battlefield just as you do."

He tipped his head, studying her.

Her fingers throbbed as the feeling came back to them, but she didn't lower her head, determined to not back down from her position.

A grin peeked out from beneath his beard. "You may go with one of my men to gather what you need from the supply wagons, but let's keep this between us. If anyone asks, you stole it. If Hephaestion or your husband ever find out I let a woman talk me out of extra supplies, I'll never hear the end of it."

She wanted to dance about the tent, ecstatic she'd convinced the man to help her.

"I promise it will be our secret. Thank you, General Perdiccas."

"You better call me Perdiccas from now on. General seems too formal for co-conspirators." He took her elbow and guided her to the tent entrance.

"Then you must call me Roxana, if we are to work together again."

Perdiccas opened the tent flap for her. "I hope not. Negotiating with you once is quite enough for me."

CHAPTER TWENTY

Roxana and the long baggage train finally reached the outer limits of the small town of Ohind—a modest settlement without high walls, and only a few stone buildings set amid a hodgepodge of wooden huts. Her wagon ended up in one of the lush green fields around the town. The return of color to the landscape was a welcomed sight. And when the townspeople brought fresh supplies of grain, livestock, and wine to their camp—paid for by the generous King Taxiles—she suspected the worst of their adventure had ended.

It was her first encounter with the Indian people, and despite the language barrier, everyone seemed to get their meaning across. They didn't have much; that was obvious by the state of their clothes and the shacks they lived in, but they were a kind and happy people. She hoped their warm reception would be a harbinger of things to come.

Her large tent pitched next to a small stream, Roxana supervised several attendants as they set up her things and unpacked her trunks.

While she waited for the servants to finish, she raised her closed eyes to the sun and thought of her husband's imminent arrival. Picturing their first embrace, first kiss, and their first night together after months apart, sent a tingle of excitement through her.

"My lady?"

Someone tugged on the skirt of her heavy Persian coat.

At her feet, a little girl with yellow hair and beautiful blue eyes held up a bouquet of early spring wildflowers.

"My mommy told me to give these to you and say thank you."

Roxana took the bouquet and was about to kneel to greet the child when she took off, disappearing behind a maze of camp followers.

"They heard what you did," Morella said in Persian behind her. "About the food and medicine for the sick. The whole camp has been talking of little else for weeks."

Roxana remembered the child's bright eyes. "I saw her. She was one of the sick in that horrid wagon."

Morella came alongside her. "Yes, her mother and I chat at the food wagon."

Roxana cast a questioning glance at her maid.

Morella winked at her. "Gossip can work both ways, my lady. It can tear a person down or build them up. I prefer spreading the latter." Her maid waddled to her wagon.

Roxana lifted the flowers to her nose, inhaling their fragrance. Perhaps she'd broached a bridge with the women in the camp, and would no longer be seen as Alexander's Persian bride, but as one of them—a woman, waiting for her husband to return from battle.

Shades of red, pink, and yellow bloomed in the fields around Roxana's tent as spring took over India. Blue skies drenched with sunlight called to her after weeks of nothing but snow, ice, rocks, and mud. She spent her days in the fields, relishing the warm air, riding Hera through the high grass, or gathering herbs and medicinal plants with Morella.

"I think this is beneath you," her maid complained as they meandered through a sloping meadow by a mountain stream.

Roxana glimpsed her guards resting beneath the canopy of a few leafy banyan trees. "I never want the camp to run out of supplies needed for the sick." She folded a bunch of chamomile flowers in her apron. "Even if I have to gather it myself."

Morella swatted at a bug. "But you're the wife of the king? Order some servants to gather your supplies."

Roxana gazed out at the vast field, invigorated. "I prefer to get it myself. Besides, I need to stay busy until the king returns."

Morella rested her hand on her hip, smirking. "I heard a servant say to the blacksmith, who overhead from the supply wagon master, who was told by Perdiccas, that Alexander is headed back. He's coming across the great plateau toward Ohind. The large dust cloud trailing behind his army has been spotted by many in the camp. He should arrive any time now." She stretched her back. "Perhaps you should be in your tent, making yourself beautiful for your husband, and get out of this hot sun."

Roxana pictured Alexander fresh from his expedition and up to his elbows in generals, officials, and dignitaries.

"Even if he returns, it might be a while before he gets to me. He will have others to see."

Morella wiped her hands on her apron. "That doesn't bother you?"

"No, not anymore. Because I know he will come to me eventually. He will find me, and I will wait."

Morella snickered. "Boy, have you changed."

"Yes, I have. I've discovered quite a bit about myself while he's been away. The absence was good for me. I could be someone other than the king's wife. I realized if I'm going to be apart from my husband for extended periods, I'd better make a life for myself."

Thundering hooves rose in the valley. Roxana shaded her eyes to investigate the commotion. In the distance, a band of horses galloped toward the camp.

"Someone's in a hurry." Morella squinted, observing their frantic pace. "Must be important news for one of the generals."

Roxana lost interest. "Come, we need more of this Indian ginseng plant. I've read it can do wonders for the sick."

Morella groaned. "Yes, my lady."

They went farther into the meadow, following the bend in the small stream as Roxana combed through plants and patches of high grass for anything she could use to treat the sick.

"Who's that?" Morella asked, staring across the meadow.

Her guards jumped to attention, grabbing for their spears.

A single rider on a dark horse came barreling toward them.

The afternoon sun blocked Roxana's ability to make out the messenger. Then other riders appeared. They paced their horses to catch up to the man in front.

Where was the group headed in such a hurry? There was nothing around her but meadow. The town of Ohind lay in the opposite direction.

Then another reason came to mind—a dark and sinister terror seized her. Had something happened to her husband? Were the messengers coming to tell her Alexander was dead?

Roxana's knees buckled, and she stumbled.

"My lady!" Morella grabbed for her hand. "What is it?"

Grief robbed her of her ability to speak.

The soldiers with her walked ahead to greet the party, but she couldn't move.

A strange play of light caught her eye. The way the sun glistened on the reddish hair of the first rider sparked a memory.

"Alexander?"

"I guess he needed to see his wife before all those other men," Morella whispered and let her go.

He rode up to her on a dark bay with a white slash across his nose. His chiton had splashes of mud across the chest.

His horse came to a halt in front of her, kicking up flecks of grass.

"I come to see you first thing, and where do I find you ..." He swung off his horse. "Picking flowers."

A contingent of the cavalry officers arrived and the warm welcome she'd hoped for dissolved behind the expected protocol afforded a king. She lowered her eyes.

"Welcome home, my husband." She dipped her head. "I thought you would be busy with your generals when you returned."

He took the last few steps up to her. "And I thought you said you didn't want to be ignored."

Roxana's laughter tumbled out. The weeks of loneliness and agonizing over his safety slipped away.

"I've missed you, my wife. Did you miss me?" The heat of his breath on her cheek stirred a dormant fire inside her. "Tell me you missed me. Please, Roxana."

She touched his chapped lips and the raw, sunburned skin on his cheeks.

"Yes, Alexander. I missed you. I missed you terribly."

Alexander tossed his arms around her, picked her up, and spun her around. He laughed with her, and when he put her on the ground, he kissed her.

She pulled away, mindful of the eyes on them, and then a healing red scar on his right arm distracted her.

"Was the fighting hard?"

"We had a successful campaign in the hilly regions of Swat and Nysaea, as well as victorious battles in the valleys of Bazira and Ora."

The names meant nothing to her—all she could think about were the ugly marks on his body. She wanted to erase them, blot them out, so there was no reminder of what he'd endured.

"You need a salve for your skin."

"My skin is fine." He lifted her chin, peering into her eyes. "I can't stay."

Before the long absence, she would have become upset about his leaving so soon after his arrival, but he had come to her first, and that was enough.

"I understand."

"Seeing you will make the rest of my day tolerable." His lips caressed her brow, sending a tingle to her toes. "I'll come to you later tonight after I've finished with my generals."

She backed away, yearning for the sun to set and the stars to show themselves.

"I will be waiting."

Roxana awoke to find Alexander sleeping naked next to her. In the early morning light, his battered body amazed her. How could he look so wretched but still feel so wonderful?

He stirred and opened his eyes to find her smiling down on him.

"That's something I've been longing to see for some time now. I have missed your smile, little star."

She nestled next to him. "So have I. When you left, you took my smile with you."

He held her in his arms. "Ah, I don't agree. There was still enough of it left to charm Hephaestion."

"Hephaestion and I spent a great deal of time talking, mostly about you. I like him. I can see why you depend on him so."

"What did you do to the chilly Perdiccas? It takes more than a pretty smile to make that stingy man part with his camp supplies."

"Who told you?" She sat up, mystified he'd received any word of the affair.

"Hephaestion. He met me at the road leading into the city and gave me a report about the bridges I instructed him to build, the scouts sent to the Punjab to spy on King Porus's forces, and how you found your skills as a healer and a negotiator while I was away." He lips caressed her ear. "Very impressive."

She hesitated, unsure of what to make of his comment. "You're not angry?"

He lay back in the bed. "Not at all. I've informed Perdiccas when we venture into India, whatever you require, you're to receive."

Emboldened, Roxana decided to ask the question that had been bothering her. "Why are we going to conquer India? You're already Great King over Persia. Isn't Persia enough for you?"

A frown darkened his features. "My father asked me a similar question once. It was the day he gave me Bucephalus. He told me I would have to find a kingdom big enough for my ambition. So, that's what I'm doing."

"When will you have enough?" She stretched across his chest. "Or will you just go on fighting until you're too old to raise a sword?"

"It's never a question of having enough. It's a question of pleasing the gods. To have great worth, to be the best—this is the ideal to a Greek man." He combed his fingers through her hair. "I am a king; therefore, I must strive harder than other men. I want to emulate the feats of the great warriors who have gone before me like in *The Iliad*. Only then will I please the gods."

She touched his lips, troubled by his compulsion. "You have already surpassed what any other man has ever done, Alexander. Why go on?"

"To make sure that no man can repeat what I have done. So there can be no more Alexanders."

A chill enveloped her as she rested her head against him. While the steady beat of his heart dulled her fears, images of a life lived in tents and foreign palaces consumed her. Was a nomad's existence the price she had to pay for belonging to such a restless man?

"Are you ever going to settle down and rule this great land you've conquered?"

Alexander lifted her head. "What are you talking about? I am ruling it."

"I mean ruling it from a palace or a city, instead of a tent in the middle of a jungle." She poked his chest, hoping to encourage him to consider the idea. "You could give us a home, and your men some peace."

"Perhaps one day. When I have grown too old to lift a sword, we will have a palace. Until then, my enemies require I remain a mobile king."

She stuck out her lower lip in a sulky pout, frustrated by his answer. "Why not do to them what you did to Callisthenes?"

"Callisthenes was not an honorable way to deal with an enemy. He died in his prison cell. When Aristotle finds out, he will not be happy. Neither will the Greeks back in Athens."

She didn't like the brooding tone in his voice. He no longer sounded happy like before.

"But when you take India, won't that appease them?"

"I hope so. I hate to think of returning to Greece only to be confronted with war instead of victory."

What did she know of Greece? Not much. She pictured going there with Alexander but facing his countrymen scared her. The camps had given her a taste of the reception she would receive.

"Do you plan to rule this kingdom from your homeland in Greece?"

He traced her lips with his finger. "You ask too many questions, wife."

The tingling in her belly reawakened. She kissed his finger, impatient to have him again. "Then find a way to keep me from asking more, my husband."

He wrapped her in his arms. "I'm sure I can come up with something."

CHAPTER TWENTY-ONE

The relentless spring rains inundated the land along the Hydaspes River as the baggage train and army traveled to join Alexander's ally King Taxiles. Everything turned to mud, and Roxana feared for the welfare of their caravan as they trudged through ankle-deep trails.

After the army pitched camp at an appointed meeting place along the river, Roxana and the rest of the baggage train set up on a patch of ground far to the rear of the men.

Standing at the entrance to her tent, she spied the groves of trees and the broad swath of land between the two camps. "Why have they put us all the way back here? I don't like being kept at such a distance."

"It's to protect us from the forces waiting to confront the king's men on the opposite bank of the river." Morella encouraged Roxana back inside. "It's whispered King Porus has two hundred elephants trained for battle. Horses hate elephants. So how does the king beat them?"

The news added to her edginess. She went to a bench set up in the corner just as the rain picked up again.

"Alexander will figure it out. He always does." She rubbed the back of her neck, wanting relief from the constant tension plaguing her. "He didn't get this far without being an excellent general."

"Are you still feeling ill?" Morella asked.

"I can't shake this. Everything I eat tastes off. Perhaps it's the fever everyone is coming down with."

"The camp doctors think it's because of all the wet." Morella paused when the patter of raindrops grew louder. "I heard a steward to General Craterus told a guard in the women's camp, who let it slip to one of the cooks, that the generals are concerned about getting the cavalry and men across the swollen river."

Unable to sit still, she got up and went to the serving table. "Alexander's generals will come up with a plan to defeat the forces of this King Porus." She lifted a goblet and a jug of wine, hoping the alcohol would soothe her.

Morella approached the table, wringing her hands. "I've also heard the men have lost faith in this campaign into India. Many of the wives and mistresses talk about how their men want to leave this terrible place."

Roxana poured the dark liquid with a shaky hand. "Everyone is fed up with the constant rain. Fires can't stay lit, food isn't getting cooked, and I've ruined two of my best dresses slogging through the mud." She ran her thumb along the stem of her cup. "Today, one woman told me the gods have abandoned us in this wretched country. Do you think that's true?"

"Nah." Morella smiled. "The gods would never abandon your king."

Roxana took her goblet to the tent entrance, hoping to get rid of the suffocating stuffiness and humidity.

She shoved aside the flap and sighed wondering if she would ever feel dry again. Then something appeared in the corner of the doorway.

Snake! It was a green-scaled, yellow-bellied creature with long, forked tongue.

She screamed and dropped her wine, stumbling backward.

Morella dashed up to her, and when she spotted the snake, pushed Roxana out of the way.

She removed her shawl and swung at the serpent, cursing in Persian.

Roxana stood to the side, cringing as the yellow-eyed vermin dropped to the ground and slithered outside.

"They're everywhere!" Morella slapped the flap closed. "Many have suffered snake bites in the camps. Snake charmers roam the grounds searching for them."

"Well, they missed that one!" Roxana rubbed her hands along her arms. "How much longer will we be in this ungodly place?"

Morella scooped up her goblet. "Until the battle is won."

Roxana doubted their ordeal would end there. She'd seen the way Alexander talked about war and suspected he would pursue it as long as he had breath.

Morella patted her arm. "You should rest, my lady. You're very pale."

Roxana turned for the back of her tent. "If we don't get out of this country soon, I will go mad."

A cacophony of neighing horses, war horns, shouting men, and swords clanging on shields woke Roxana from a fitful sleep. She bolted upright and caught the edges of the morning sun creeping over the eastern portion of her tent.

"What in the name of all the gods?"

She tossed the covers aside, glanced down, and took in the added height of her bed. All of her furniture was set on blocks to keep it out of the mud. While bent over the side of her bed, she also checked the floor for snakes.

Satisfied, she was about to climb down when Morella pushed the curtain divider aside.

"What is that racket?" she asked.

"The battle has started, my lady." She spoke over the din. "General Perdiccas has issued an order for all the women in the camp to prepare bandages for the wounded, mix ointments, and offer prayers to the gods for victory."

Roxana stood, feeling woozy. "Well, at least when the battle is over, we might be on the road again and away from this place."

Then as fast as the noise of men, horses, horns, and the pounding of shields started, it stopped.

Roxana waited for the commotion to begin again.

Thunder rumbled in the distance.

"More rain?" Roxana sat on her bed, disgusted. "Does it ever end?"

Her maid reached for her robe. "I heard one of the other servants say that it's the monsoon season in this land. The rain can go on for weeks and weeks."

"Rain and war." Roxana snickered. "I'm sure Alexander is in his glory."

After almost five days of the intermittent cries of men, call of horns, and drum of shields, Roxana received the first formal word on the victory from one of the many messengers employed by the king.

"From the king. He wishes for me to express that the army has won a great victory. There's to be a celebration tonight in the feasting tent for King Porus and his new treaty with the King Alexander. Your husband also wishes for you to attend the banquet ... covered in gold. He wanted me to emphasize in gold, my lady."

Roxana smiled, pleased by the request. "Tell the king I will happily join the celebration of his glorious victory. I look forward to hearing about the battle."

The messenger bowed and trudged out of her tent and into the relentless rain.

Giddy at the prospect of seeing Alexander, she glimpsed her muddy feet and Persian trousers. How would she get to the feasting tent without being covered in muck?

"Morella!"

The servant came rushing up to her side. "What is it, my lady?"

Roxana held her head up, glowing with happiness. "Get my best gold outfit from the chests and order a litter bearer. Tonight, I dine with the king."

With mud up to their ankles, her litter bearers slogged through a winding path leading past tents sagging with the weight of rain. Soldiers huddled beneath any bit of shelter shared wine sacks distributed to celebrate the great feast. For one night, she hoped, everyone could enjoy a respite from their deplorable conditions.

While she made her way along a torchlit path to the massive tent, the clouds parted, allowing slivers of moonlight to accompany her. Roxana took it as a sign from the gods that her life would soon change.

After being carried by one of her guards from her litter to the sloppy tent entrance, she adjusted the sheer gold fabric around her hips. It was the same Alexander had given her to dine with King Taxiles. Her fingers trembled at the prospect of seeing her husband. She hoped they would have a few minutes alone together; she needed to speak with him.

Her head held high, she stepped out from the shadows and entered the banquet area. The aroma of succulent food tempted her, but then a wave of nausea rose.

A hush descended over the tent as she moved into the light from the torches. She ignored Alexander's generals, suited in their best armor, and the Persian men in their thick robes and fluted hats. The only face she longed to see was her husband's.

At the head of the tent, Alexander's table, trimmed with bouquets of red and yellow flowers, stood apart from the rest. He was there, beaming as she glided across the mats. Roxana searched his features for scars, red marks, and bruises, but he appeared unscathed.

She moved closer, feeling the weight of his eyes taking in her every curve. His gaze filled her with such happiness. She longed to run to him, fling her arms around him and whisper her surprise, but she had to wait. At the table, she cordially bowed. Alexander stood and took her hand, the torchlight glistening on his ceremonial cuirass.

When he squeezed her hand, her happiness lifted her spirit and washed away every care. When had everything changed between them? A month ago, yesterday, she could not pinpoint when he had become her world, but he had, and she was glad for it.

Alexander turned to a very fat gentleman attired in a stunning gold embroidered robe. Two gaunt men in loincloths helped pull the obese man up from his pillows. A bandage around his right shoulder and side poked out from beneath his clothes as he got to his feet.

Alexander brought her around the table. "My dear friend, King Porus, this is my wife, Roxana."

An interpreter translated for the king.

Porus bowed to Roxana. He turned to his interpreter and spoke in a very brisk manner.

"He says you have a beautiful wife and asks if you would like another," the gangly young interpreter related.

Alexander smiled graciously. "Thank you, my friend, but I have all I need in the way of wives, for the time being."

"Very wise answer, Alexander," she muttered under her breath.

"It's the truth." He escorted her to her table.

She cocked an eyebrow. "For the time being?"

He raised her hand to his lips. "For always."

After she took her seat on an array of red pillows, Alexander filled her goblet with wine.

"Was the battle hard fought?" She nodded to Porus. "He's injured."

"Porus's elephant tossed him into a tree, but he suffered more losses than we did. Elephants trampled most of his men after we confused them with our continuous noise. His sons were less fortunate. They met their demise at the end of a sword."

His cool reappraisal of the bloodshed stunned her. Where was the caring man who had just given her such endearments?

"The way you describe battle frightens me. It's like you're reading from a book. There's no emotion in your voice."

He tossed his head to the side, unflustered. "Why should there be. It's war. Men die, armies fall, and a winner is proclaimed."

A pang of discomfort rose from her chest. "Do you ever think of those you've killed?"

His eyes changed. Like the curtain of night closing over the day, darkness crowded their gray light, and a coldness emanated from his being.

"There is no need to revisit the dead."

It was the first taste she had of the warrior. He had stayed away during their times together. Only the caring Alexander, the gentle king, had come to her, but this man was different. This was the ruthless killer she'd heard whispers about in the camp, and he scared her.

"I see," she finally got out.

"Alexander was extremely brave," Hephaestion called from the king's table. "He gallantly rode up and down river banks, even challenged elephants, and when he finally captured the king, he was very gracious. He won Porus over, and now they're best friends."

Alexander scolded Hephaestion with a playful smirk. "You exaggerate."

Her husband resumed his seat next to Porus and Roxana studied the way he chatted with the injured king, smiled, and laughed when the interpreter passed on something funny. She never realized the many sides to him, but they were now coming to light. She thought ahead to the news she had to share, and what Alexander would say. She ran her hand over her belly, hoping he would be pleased.

Perdiccas, a few tables down, raised his goblet to her.

Ptolemy, seated next to Perdiccas, furrowed his brow at the exchange.

"You have your work cut out for you with Ptolemy." Hephaestion slid in next to her. "Women come very low on his list of priorities. He admires strength. Perhaps you should go hunting with us some time. Show us some of your skills."

Hiding a sly smile, she reached for the goblet. "It may be some time before I can join your hunt, General. It seems the gods have other plans for me."

An old, wrinkled man, wearing a coat of dirty, rumpled linen, came to the king's table. He gave a toothless smile and bowed his bald head.

Alexander stood and greeted the old man warmly, embracing him as a friend.

Roxana pointed her gold goblet at the newcomer. "Who's that?"

"Calanus," Hephaestion told her. "He's a Buddhist. Alexander asked him to join us. They've been discussing religion."

A Macedonian guard walked up to the king and whispered in his ear. Alexander listened attentively, then his happy expression vanished.

He raced out of the tent without a word to anyone.

Roxana waited, her heart pounding, as Hephaestion listened to the guard's message, and then his eyes found her.

He rushed back to her table. "I have to go."

Roxana got up, aching with unease. "What is it?"

He lowered his voice, coming closer. "His horse, Bucephalus, is dying."

She had to go to him. He would be devastated and needed someone to share his pain.

"I want to be with him."

He passed an eye over her outfit. "You're not attired for the stables, my lady."

"Take me with you, General. That was not a request."

He clasped her hand and guided her out of the tent.

They jogged most of the way, sloshing through mud and puddles littering the path to the stables. She didn't care about her ruined clothes; all she could think of was her husband's sorrow.

By the time she arrived at the stables, Alexander was already inside the horse's stall, sitting on the wet hay and cradling the elegant black creature's head in his lap.

She covered her mouth, not wanting to cry out as he spoke softly to the animal, tears rolling down his cheeks. Guards, physicians, and grooms looked on, moved by the king's anguish. The Greeks acted so tough on the outside, but she suspected they were just as kind-hearted as Persians.

The regal black horse struggled, his breathing slowed. She ached to go to her husband but knew from experience his grief, like a stone sinking to the bottom of a pond, needed to settle. Only then would he crave the warmth and comfort of others.

The quiet in the stall shattered when Bucephalus let out a groan and went still. Alexander kept on, holding his horse and murmuring to him.

It was Hephaestion who finally coaxed Alexander away from the lifeless beast. He escorted a dazed king from the stables.

Roxana stayed behind, wanting one last goodbye with the stallion her husband had adored. She trekked across the wet hay as a handful of men left the stall. Alone with the mighty Bucephalus, she stooped down and caressed his gray nose.

She remembered the day she'd won the animal's affection and the way Alexander had been with him. So many memories came back to her of their first meeting. Then someone tugged at her elbow.

Hephaestion helped her from the stall floor. "I need you to stay with him. He wants me to see to Bucephalus, but I don't want him to be alone right now." He accompanied her from the stall to the muddy path outside the stables. "While I'm busy, you must sit with him. Keep him company."

They maneuvered the slippery trail, and Roxana wiped the tears from her eyes. "No." He stayed her hand. "Let him know you grieve, too. It will help him."

When the gold pike from the top of the king's tent rose before her, she halted in the mud, not sure if she was the right one to console him.

"Perhaps someone who has known him longer, remembers Bucephalus better, should be with him."

Hephaestion urged her ahead. "His men may have known him longer, but you know him better. You've seen a side of him few of us will ever encounter." Hephaestion helped her to the entrance of the large tent. "I will return when I can." He spun around and headed back to the path.

Roxana walked past the guards, wiping the stains from her clothes. Mud squished in her gold shoes as she stepped through the doorway to his reception area. She'd never seen the inside of his tent, having spent her nights with him in her bed.

His meager possessions appalled her. There wasn't much furniture, only a table, a few stools, statues of his gods, and a small brazier to warm the damp nights. She tiptoed along until she stumbled into his private quarters.

He did enjoy some luxury in his sleeping area. A massive bed, rumored to have once belonged to King Darius, sat on blocks above the wet ground. Made of the deepest red cedar, it had carvings of Persian griffins above the head and giant claws for feet. The only other grand item, his gold tub decorated with forest creatures, stood off to the side. On a rack next to the tub were his various suits of armor, helmets, swords, and shields. She reached out to touch the three white feathers on his helmet when something in the corner moved.

He sat on a wooden stool next to a table piled high with scrolls, wax tablets, and maps. He had his face in his hands, and at his feet was his brown dog.

The animal's black eyes watched as she drew near. He didn't growl or bare his teeth. She held out her hand to him, praying he remembered her.

Roxana came alongside her husband. "Alexander, I'm so sorry. I know what he meant to you."

He raised his head, appearing lost for a moment. When his arms went around her waist, he tucked his head into the curve of her neck.

She melted at his touch, relieved he had embraced her and not sent her away.

The dog, sensing Roxana was there to help, wagged his tail.

"You understand, don't you?" His voice was almost childlike with grief.

"When I was a little girl, my mother gave me a pony. Kushia—that's what I called her. She was my best friend and the only person who knew all my hopes, dreams, and secrets. Then my mother died. The next day, Kushia was gone. My grandmother gave her to a farmer outside of the village. I've never forgotten Kushia." She kissed his lips tenderly. "Bucephalus has been the one you have shared everything with, too."

Alexander pulled away, wiping his hand over his eyes. "The first time I did anything significant in my life was the first day I rode him. My father doubted I could handle the horse since his trainers had failed to calm him. But I proved my father wrong. Ever since then, I've never been apart from Bucephalus."

"Except for the time he was captured," Roxana reminded him, glad to see his sorrow retreating.

"Yes, except for then … and now." He cleared his throat, regaining his composure. "I must pay him tribute. I shall build him a shrine."

Roxana peered into her husband's brilliant eyes. "You must do more than that. Build him a city."

Alexander's face lifted, and then he kissed her hard on the lips.

She held on to him, wanting to share so much more with him, but tempering her excitement for when the time was right.

The rustle of someone entering the private chamber made Alexander arch away from her.

A slender man—almost a boy—with a towel folded over his arm slinked across the floor. He had black eyes, lined with coal, long, glossy black hair pulled from his face, and high cheekbones carved into his pale skin. His lips had an odd shade of red—red ochre or natural she could not decide. The makeup, the towel on his arm— she realized who the painted attendant was in her husband's tent.

"I won't need you tonight, Bagoas." Alexander glanced back at his wife. "Have you ever bathed with a man?" He raised his eyebrows playfully.

Roxana demurely dropped her head. However, she kept it raised enough to catch Bagoas slinking out of the room.

Alexander picked her up and stood holding her in his arms as her feet dangled above the ground. The gesture made her forget all about Bagoas. She giggled as he spun her around.

He set her down, still holding her close. "We will share my bath and make plans for my beloved Bucephalus."

Her desire to share her news blossomed in her chest. He needed something hopeful, something to direct his sights to the future and not the past.

Roxana patted his chest, a proud smile on her lips. "You have to be careful with me from now on."

He nuzzled her nose. "Careful with you? Since when? You're as tough as any one of my generals."

She took his hand and placed it on her flat belly. "You must be careful with *us*. I am with child."

He stood before her without a hint of anything in his stoic features. She panicked, afraid her news had been too much at such a time. But then he cupped her face, and the most tender regard lit up his eyes.

"The gods granted me a taste of the honey-sweet fruit in the Elysian Fields when they gave me you."

She wrinkled her nose. "What is that?"

"The place where we Greeks believe the righteous and heroic go after they die." He touched his forehead to hers.

His explanation stirred her apprehension. "Will I be allowed to join you there? Or will your gods frown on it?"

"They wouldn't dare." He pecked her cheek. "It will never be Heaven for me without you."

CHAPTER TWENTY-TWO

The reprieve from the rain didn't last. Soon the clouds, thunder, and endless hours of steady drops plinking on tent roofs returned, but Roxana didn't notice. Her bliss blotted out the mud, saggy tents, and chaos created by the constant deluge. She'd found happiness as Alexander included her in every aspect of his daily affairs.

She attended morning prayers and sacrifices to his gods, often queasy as the priests read the auspices from the intestines of dead birds. After a quick stroll around the camps to check on the latest problems, they would eat breakfast together and Alexander—never one tempted by spicy, rich foods—would try to tease her with sumptuous dishes.

"You must eat, Roxana." He had a servant parade several trays of sweetmeats and honey cakes before her as they ate in his tent one morning. "I want you as fat as a stuffed goose."

Roxana sampled every dish he had prepared for her. Her morning sickness made it agony, but she ate. The king's ardent attention was worth any discomfort. Pleasing him had become all she wanted, no matter the cost.

"Why does morning sickness happen?" he asked as she put a honey cake aside, turning green at the smell. "I've read some physicians recommend special herbs for the discomfort. I will have them prepared for you, and you must try each one separately. Tell me which one works for you so I can keep a log. We can use the information for your next pregnancy."

"Next pregnancy?" She pushed her plate of food away. "I'm not sure I'll survive this one."

He put his hands on her growing belly, grinning with pride.

She never believed a child could make a couple grow so close. Her father had never acted so when her younger stepsiblings were born. She debated if it was a Greek thing or something innate to Alexander's curious nature.

"I can't wait to see how big your belly gets."

The excitement in his voice resonated with her. She wanted to remember it always.

"A big belly means it's a boy. We have to monitor how active the child is. Active babies in the womb are healthy babies, or so I was told."

In addition to observing Alexander's usual activities, Roxana got to take part in planning the funeral rights for all the men who had fallen at the Battle of Hydaspes. Alexander even decided to give his army a month off to celebrate the victory in the fertile plains of King Porus's territories.

The king ordered traditional Greek games to lift the spirits of his damp men, and all the artists, actors, and poets traveling with the camp had to stage elaborate productions. Alexander took her with him as he helped to oversee the staging of plays, music, and poetry readings. She soon came to understand Alexander had a weakness for such events, making her admire him all the more.

What amazed Roxana most about her husband was how he laid the foundations of his two new cities by the Hydaspes River. One called Nicaea to commemorate his victory at the site, and the other Alexandria Bucephala in remembrance of his faithful companion. The detail he took in planning marketplaces and residential areas showed her a whole new side to his fascinating mind. It seemed there was nothing her husband couldn't do.

His energy astounded her, too. She'd never been privy to his every moment, but now she understood his stamina was endless. He never seemed to tire when he met with engineers and builders for hours at a time. Roxana, on the other hand, had less vitality with every passing day. She frequently dozed during her husband's many city planning meetings.

The games briefly lifted everyone's spirits, but as the mud rose and the rain fell, Roxana found it hard to find any joy in their soggy situation. Many of the army veterans griped about the wool and linen padding for their armor becoming moldy and rotten. The only replacement was the flimsy cotton available in the land. Called "Indian rags" by the men, they claimed it offered little protection from chafing. All around her, metal rusted, leather mildewed, horses became lame with thrush and sore hooves, and everyone complained about the mosquitos, loss of sleep, and poor living conditions.

Roxana often wondered how the Indian people survived in such a land, but they seemed to adapt to everything in stride. Their resilience amazed her at times, as did their poverty. Their clothes always drab, they were thin and shared vital necessities with their animals just as they did with their children. Their customs made no sense to her, but the few interactions she'd had with the locals left her homesick for her Persian ways.

The sour mood of the army became a growing concern among the generals. One evening, Alexander called an assembly of his Macedonian commanders in his massive feasting tent to discuss his plans for their future. He also insisted she attend so he could announce the birth of his child, hoping it would cheer his army.

Roxana stood to the side with Hephaestion and Ptolemy as Alexander climbed on a table in the front of the tent to be seen by all. She was nervous about her first formal meeting with the heads of respected families and leaders from his army. Most of the men she'd greeted during her tours of the camps with Alexander, but the scarred, worn, and exhausted faces staring back at her now held a mixture of curiosity and resentment. After all this time, was she still his Persian wife?

"I want you to know that India is ours, conquered by our hands. All her wealth and glory belong to you," Alexander announced, calling the meeting to order.

The murmurs of the men shut out the sound of the rain beating down on their tent.

"I believe we will soon see the edge of the Endless Ocean at the end of the world and the end of our vast empire. An empire that we will hold for many years to come and will pass on to our sons." He turned to Roxana. "An empire I will leave to my sons. The child the Lady Roxana carries will help us to continue onward into the future."

Some of the men mumbled, others broke out in a loud fit of cheering, a few applauded, and some glowered at her, saying nothing at all.

The varied reactions troubled her. Would her child be received with the same mixed response? Even if it was a boy?

"To reach the Endless Ocean, to make sure our empire is secured, I want to build a fleet to sail down the Hydaspes to the Indus, and eventually out into the Endless Ocean. We will need large ships to carry our army, which will require most of our men to help with the logging and building." Alexander waited as a rumbling of assent went around the tent. "I know the weather has disheartened us, but new armor and recruits are on their way from Thrace. I want to know you men support this endeavor. I want to know we will go on and conquer the world together."

A loud roar of cheering overwhelmed Roxana. The men rushed forward to touch their king. Alexander willingly obliged them by shaking hands and hugging those he knew from years of battle.

With his men he was different. She understood he was their leader, their conqueror, their general, their military genius. But with her, Alexander was a man. She might have fed his passion, but his army fed his soul. Through the feats he accomplished with them, he would live on in the hearts of men until the end of time.

Following the meeting, Alexander's mood changed. He became irritated and snapped more at his generals and servants, something Roxana had never seen him do. Still devoted to his constant preparations during the day, he kept his nights for her.

Roxana relished their time together but knew it would soon end. She had come to accept, with Alexander, nothing ever lasted very long.

"I have to head east," he told her one night as they lay naked in each other's arms.

"I know. I can tell you're ready to move on to the next battle."

"I want you to stay here." He kissed her cheek. "I'm leaving my most trusted general, Craterus, with some of the army to oversee the building of my new fleet and continue with the construction of Nicaea and Bucephala. I need to separate him and Hephaestion for a time. I'm getting tired of their petty arguments. It's hurting morale."

She steadied her voice, not wanting it to crack when she spoke. "How long will you be gone?"

"Until I've secured the areas east of here. Porus has a few rivals we have to subdue. I will safeguard routes along the way to keep the lines of communication open, so you can write to me and tell me how big you're getting." He patted the small swelling of her belly. "Are you angry with me?"

She sat up, shaking her head. She could never contain him, never set boundaries for him. He was Alexander—he had to explore and conquer.

"You're a warrior and will always need to go. After watching you for weeks with your men, I realize that now." She gazed into his eyes, her heart breaking at the idea of being apart. "Will you be back for the birth?"

He eased up on his elbows, a hopeful smile on his lips. "I will try. If I'm not, you are to name him Alexander, all right?"

"What if it's a girl?"

"Olympias, after my mother." He chuckled. "She will love that."

"Are you sure she'll be happy about her grandchild?" Roxana remembered the men's faces at the assembly meeting. "My half-Persian child?"

He gripped her shoulders, his mouth turned downward. "Of course, she will be happy. My mother may send me piles of letters complaining about everything I do, but I know she will be glad I married. Being a grandmother is what she's always wanted."

Her fears about his men subsided. If his mother approved, maybe his men would in time.

"I look forward to meeting her one day."

Alexander rested his hand behind his head. "I hope you're not too disappointed. She's a formidable woman, but also a difficult one to read. Tough as nails, but she has a soft spot, even if it's buried beneath a mountain of dung."

She playfully slapped his arm. "You shouldn't say such things about your mother."

"I will let you make up your mind about her when you two meet. I'll make sure I'm away on a long campaign when that happens."

Roxana eased back down and rested her head against his chest. She listened to the beating of his heart and his breath moving in and out. How many more long campaigns would there be? And what happened if he didn't survive? She couldn't envision a life without him, but her concerns were no longer just hers.

"If something happens to you and Hephaestion, what becomes of the baby and me?"

The lines on his brow deepened as he raised his eyes to the ceiling, the light tapping of rain filling the silence.

"Craterus is my second-in-command while I'm gone. He will wait for the child to be born and if it's a boy, he will be my heir. The generals will keep my empire safe for him." He played with a tendril of her hair. "And if it's a girl, and as beautiful as you, she will be a princess sought by kings."

Another disturbing thought settled over her. "But then who will run your empire?"

Her hair slipped from his fingers. "There's a man back in Macedon named Antipater. He's my regent while I'm away from Greece. He's tough, resourceful, and my generals respect him. He will know what to do." He pulled her close. "But I will come back, little star. I will always come back."

Throughout the long months of Alexander's sojourn into the eastern parts of India, Roxana sat at her little desk in her tent while listening to the never-ending rain and wrote to her husband. Though she was convinced her letters, filled with the trials of her increasing girth, her sleepless nights, and his growing cities and burgeoning fleet, probably bored him, she sent them anyway.

Alexander's correspondence contained descriptions of swollen rivers, deadly battles, unusual plants and animals, and always of the continuous rain. The letters made her feel closer to him. And with each one, she hoped there would be news of his return, but as time went on, there wasn't, and it nagged at her.

How far would he go? And would he ever want to come back?

To stay busy, she would take her guards and visit the river's edge to check on the progress of the boat builders. Ships in various stages of construction—from frames with stretched wood between two end posts to those with boards rising from the hull to finished vessels with masts loaded with sails—lined the newly constructed harbor. The flurry of activity and the fragrance of freshly cut wood kept her mind off her swollen feet, aching back, and empty heart.

Occasionally, she would run into General Craterus supervising the men. The no-nonsense man with long arms, a thick beard, and a deep, gravelly voice first came across as suspicious of Roxana's presence at the docks. His reception was chilly, and their conversations strained, with most of the general's answers being monosyllabic. But with time, and a great deal of smiling on Roxana's part, the crusty Macedonian and the king's wife soon found a common interest—Alexander.

"Never known a man who could dissect an army like Alexander," Craterus said one day as they strolled along the shoreline.

He'd come to check on the work crews made up of soldiers assigned to build Alexander's fleet. The sun ventured out from the clouds above, and many of the men stopped to take in the welcome sight.

She endeavored to keep up with the general in the thick sand. "Why do you think he's so good at it?"

"He had Philip for a father. Damned fine general he was."

She took in the frenzy of activity around them. Everywhere men unloaded timber from carts, shaped planks for the ships, worked on platforms along half-finished vessels, or high atop the decks of nearly completed boats. The constant banging of hammers echoed around them.

Craterus stopped at a workman's table. "Philip had the same knack as Alexander with an army. He could pick out its strengths and weaknesses in no time." He snapped up a nog or wooden treenail. "But he had his faults. All the years of watching his father at Pella, Alexander vowed never to repeat Philip's mistakes. Probably why the king strived to become the personification of self-control. His father, on the other hand, used to say Alexander was full of himself."

She browsed an array of tools as snapshots of Alexander's self-control came to her—his strict diet, his religious devotion, his disciplined body, and mind.

"Did you know Philip?"

"Served under him, I did." He gave her a warm smile. "Liked the old man immensely. He had a wicked sense of humor. Made Alexander what he is today. He taught him to be a leader, to inspire men—a true general. In some ways, Alexander reminds me of Philip, but then there's a great deal of Olympias in him, too." He tossed the nog back on the table. "Now there's a difficult woman."

The mention of Alexander's mother piqued her curiosity. "Alexander often speaks of her. What's she like?"

They traveled along the sandy beach as the general collected his thoughts.

"Devout; prays to the gods incessantly. She's also emotionally volatile and has a nasty temper when provoked. Everyone at the palace preferred to stay away from her. Including Philip."

"And Alexander?" Roxana added, keeping up. "I get the sense he wants to stay away from her as long as he can."

"I sometimes wonder if she's the reason we've stayed in Persia so long. She can be cold, petty, and ruthless." Craterus kicked up the sand. "She even scolds him frequently in his letters about how generous he is to his friends. She's afraid he will make all of us kings and leave nothing for himself."

"Alexander has told me about her letters. But still, she must love him a great deal."

"Oh yes, without a doubt." He waved to a group of soldiers on the deck of a ship. "Olympias is, shall we say, an overly devoted mother. For her, Alexander has always been the world." He shrugged, glancing back at Roxana. "She's a follower of Dionysus—our god of wine and revelry—and any follower of that god tends to be overly dramatic and emotional."

Roxana rubbed her abdomen, feeling the child move. "One day I hope to meet her. So she can visit with her grandchild."

The slight rise of his upper lip gave her an inkling of his contempt for her mother-in-law.

"Be prepared. She'll be nothing like you expect." His caustic warning carried across the dock. "Just remember she adores her son, and none of us are good enough for him. Me and the others have suffered through many of her tongue lashings, and you will too, I'm afraid. Always remember, it's Alexander we must please. May the gods help us if the day ever comes when we must bow to Olympias." He wiped his face with his hands. "I pray I'm long gone if that ever happens."

CHAPTER TWENTY-THREE

The receding rains of the monsoon season gave way to the chilly winds of winter across the valley. Tents billowed in the strong gusts and the change of season brought relief to everyone in the camps, except Roxana.

The child grew bigger by the day, and pressed on her lower back, making every position uncomfortable. Her only relief was the letters from her husband, but one day they stopped coming.

"Is the king well, General?" she asked Craterus when she sought him out along the walls of the booming cities of Nicaea and Bucephala. "I've received no letters from him lately."

The general watched a group of men raising a gate along the wall.

"He's fine, my lady. Just busy. He writes he'll be home soon."

The general's deadpan voice did little to reassure her. Without her husband's correspondence, she had no hints as to what he was feeling or thinking. It was as if he'd shut himself off from her. Had he stopped loving her? What could have happened?

A few days later, Craterus sent her word that lookouts on the newly built walls had spotted the long, winding column of the king's army. Her heart soared.

Escorted by Morella and her guards, she forced her swollen body through the mud and up a steep set of steps, to one of the highest points of the wall to view the approaching army. The sight of the endless line of men, horses, carts, and wagons crossing the Hydaspes River filled her with joy. Women around her cheered, but no one was happier to see the army than Roxana. With the birth of her baby approaching, she longed more than ever for her husband.

Soldiers entered the city gates, and the celebrations began. Wine, food, and dancing filled the paths throughout the camp. Roxana trudged back to her tent through the slop, getting bits of information of the campaign and its difficulties.

"We refused to go any farther," one pocked-face soldier said as he entered the women's camp.

"The army rebelled against the king," a toothless crone cried out as she came to a turn in the path.

And before she sighted her tent at the top of a slight hill, another woman hugged her children and said, "We're going home—back to Greece."

The rumblings alarmed her, but she regarded such chatter as hearsay. Camp followers were known for embellishing any story they picked up, but in the back of her mind, her concern continued. It was as if the winds of change had swept over their world.

"What is it?" Morella asked.

She inspected the battered tents around her. A light rain tumbled from the dark clouds above.

"I'm not sure, but I intend to find out."

Later that night, Roxana paced the floor of her tent, listening to the drum of rain as she recalled everything she'd heard. She waited like a penned-up mare, craving to be set loose, for some word from her husband. She didn't expect much, a note or a messenger asking about her well-being. Surely the king would want to know the health of his child.

"You should sit," Morella scolded from her stool. "Too much walking isn't good for the baby. Rest. He will come to you."

But Roxana was done waiting for the king to come to her. She would have to go to him.

"Morella, get my coat."

With her guards plodding behind her, and her maid shielding her from the rain with a shawl, Roxana marched through the thick crowds of people, drunk with wine and celebration. She maneuvered past campfires and eyed the pyramids of shields, spears, and swords created by the soldiers to keep their weapons safe from the rain. She drew closer to the walls of the new cities. Torchlights twinkling on the king's gold pike guided her across the boggy ground.

She reached Alexander's tent. Two soldiers from the king's guard stood at attention, their crossed spears blocking her way.

"Is the king inside?"

"He's in a meeting with General Hephaestion," the shorter guard told her while keeping an eye on the camp behind her. "I don't know if he would want to see you."

The impertinence in his voice angered her. "Get him. Now!"

The taller guard flinched when she raised her voice and disappeared into the tent, leaving her in the cold drizzle.

Hephaestion came flying out the tent doorway, sporting a scowl.

"By the gods, man!" He took her arm. "You don't leave the king's wife out in the rain!" Hephaestion guided a drenched Roxana into the tent, leaving Morella with the sentries.

He snapped his fingers at a servant waiting inside. "Get more wood for the king's fire and get the Lady Roxana a towel."

The servant retreated to the back of the tent.

Roxana relaxed, happy to see Hephaestion. "Are you well?"

His smile was the same warm, generous one she remembered. "I'm good and very glad to see you."

The servant reappeared with a dry towel, which Roxana gratefully accepted. She patted her damp face and hands.

"I need you to come with me." His voice sounded uncharacteristically serious.

"What's going on?" She gripped the towel to her chest. "I keep hearing things in the camp."

He put his index finger to his lips and guided her into the back of Alexander's tent.

In his sleeping area, only a small lamp was lit in the corner. It took her eyes a few moments to adjust, but he was there, sitting with his face in his hands, leaning against his wooden desk.

"Alexander?" Hephaestion pushed her forward. "You have a visitor."

He raised his head, and the heavy lines carved into his pale face shocked her. Even in the faint light, she could see his red eyes.

He stood and held out his arms to her. "Roxana."

She waddled toward him.

"Look at you!" Alexander put his hands on her abdomen. "Is he moving about much?"

"All the time." Roxana kissed her husband's brow, relief washing over her. "He's never still. Like his father."

He took her face in his hands and kissed her tenderly. "I got your letters." He guided her to his empty stool.

After she sat, she stared at the two men. "Tell me what's going on. Why did you stop writing to me?"

Hephaestion rolled his eyes as if he were sick of discussing the matter.

Alexander, on the other hand, paced in front of her.

"When we reached the banks of the Hyphasis River, the army refused to go any farther. The men wanted to go home. Even the generals turned against me. What was I to do?" Rage saturated his voice. "After all the things we've been through together, they had no stomach to go on. Can you believe it?"

"Were you there?" she asked Hephaestion.

"No, I went off with Porus to settle some business in his provinces. Alexander wanted some new cities founded, so he sent me."

Roxana remained calm, hoping it would rub off on Alexander. "Did you talk to them?"

"I gave a brilliant speech. I talked of treasure, pleasing the gods, and the honor of further victories." Alexander stopped pacing. "After that, I withdrew to my tent, refusing to talk to anyone, but they would not relent. Finally, on the third day, I had the auspices read. Even the gods had turned against me. I had games and twelve huge altars built. Then we headed back." His broad shoulders sagged as if the vital force of life had left him.

"I met up with him on the way here." Hephaestion folded his arms, appearing glum. "That's when I heard what happened."

"They have taken away my destiny, my immortality." Alexander paced some more, his face a deeper shade of crimson. "How can I achieve greatness if my men aren't willing to take part in my deeds?"

"The destiny of your men is not your destiny, Alexander," Hephaestion argued. "You're a man beyond limits, but your men are not. They want to go home, see their wives, children, and homeland again. Enjoy the riches they've won. Eight years is a long time to be on a campaign."

"I will never forgive them," Alexander angrily spat out.

"You cannot lead the unwilling," Hephaestion declared in a raised voice. "Without the heart for battle, armies whither, men die. Wars are lost that way. Besides, your luck could not hold out forever."

Alexander faced his friend, his eyes brimming with defeat. "My luck has finally left me. What am I to do without it, Hephaestion?"

A pang of jealousy shot across Roxana's heart, something she'd sworn she would never feel for his devoted friend. It seemed he knew Alexander better, and in a way she would never comprehend. She shoved the upsetting feelings aside. She needed to help her husband, and the only way to do that was to redirect his focus.

Roxana struggled to her feet, keeping her face stern. "What are your plans?"

"My plans? Roxana, have you been listening to—"

"You can't go any farther east, but there's still a lot of this damned wet country for you to explore." She turned to Hephaestion, seeking support. "You have a fleet ready and waiting to take you down the Hydaspes. Are you still interested?"

Her husband sulked, not saying anything, but the anger in his eyes evaporated.

"As far as I can see, nothing has changed here except for your direction." She rested her hands behind her sore back, knowing she was getting through to him. "You're greater than this, Alexander. You're above these things."

Alexander smiled and the deep lines on his face melted away.

"She's right." Hephaestion grinned. "You are Achilles."

"Yes, I am. We'd better get started on that new direction." Alexander strutted out of his quarters and yelled at the guards to call his generals.

Hephaestion turned to her. "I wondered how long it would take you to come."

She went back to her stool, aching to sit. "You could have sent me a message ahead of time, telling me what happened."

"I couldn't take the chance. Scrolls get read, and messengers gossip. And I couldn't come and get you without leaving him. I've been cooped up with him for almost ten days. His depression has been bad, worst I've ever seen. I needed your help. He needed your help."

She took in the dark circles under his eyes and realized his nights had been far more uncomfortable than hers. "You're a true friend, Hephaestion."

"I'm his friend ... and yours. How much longer do you have?"

Her hand rubbed over her round bump. "A little over a month, I think. I hope."

"Have you made the preparations for your confinement?"

"Morella, my attendant, is seeing to everything. I've retained one of the best midwives in the camp."

"I'll have Philip, the court physician, made ready for you."

She smirked. "What do you expect the court physician to know about birthing children? I thought that was women's work."

"Not when the woman is the wife of the king." He lowered his head to her. "Nothing must happen to you ... he won't survive it."

Alexander stepped into the room. He observed the two of them standing in the shadows.

"Why is it so dark in here? Let's get these lamps lit, so I can take a good look at my wife." He knelt at her side, putting his arms around her.

Her joy overflowed. He would be on hand for the birth. She hoped the rebellion of his men would send them back to Persia and civilization. Perhaps they could settle down in a palace, and he could rule his kingdom. It seemed feasible, but knowing Alexander, she doubted his restless spirit would ever allow it.

And that, more than the impending birth of her child, made her anxious for what lay ahead.

CHAPTER TWENTY-FOUR

On a chilly morning just as the sun broke out behind a low cover of gray clouds, Roxana sat bundled in her wagon on the shore as Alexander's giant fleet of two hundred boats—including the eighty newly constructed thirty-oared galleys—made ready to sail down the Hydaspes River.

Assigned to go with Hephaestion, most of the army, the elephants, and the baggage train were headed to the palace of Alexander's ally, King Sopeithes. Roxana wished she could be at her husband's side on the lead vessel as he poured libations into the river with a golden bowl, asking Heracles, Ammon, and a slew of other gods to bless their journey.

Trumpets sounded the signal for departure. The oars of the galleys lowered, the sails of the other ships ran up the main masts, and the shouts of men to "make way" carried in the air.

The roar of people on the shore cheered, mixed with the whinnies of horses packed on the decks of several of the bigger barges. Tribes of Indians came out to greet the boats as they sailed along. They chanted, tossed flowers in the water, and their holy men, adorned in mere rags, raised their heads to the heavens, calling on their gods to keep the fleet safe.

"I've never seen such a sight." Morella watched the mass of boats heading down river. "How do they manage so many ships at once not bumping into each other?"

Roxana tucked the blanket around her. "Alexander's admiral of the fleet, Nearchus of Crete, is in charge of coordinating the entire affair. He's hired every Egyptian, Phoenician, Cypriot, and Indian he could find to man the oars. He believes they have a better knowledge of ships than the average Macedonian soldier."

"Your husband certainly sets out to impress the gods." Morella came around to her side in the wagon, fluffing her pillows. "I'm sure he will come up with something just as momentous to announce the birth of his child."

She smiled and promised to one day tell her child about their father's wondrous feat—the day he sailed down the Hydaspes after conquering India, Persia, and the rest of the known world.

The ride along the bumpy road tormented Roxana's aching back. It also initiated a funny pain in her belly. The green landscape filled with monkeys and colorful birds, and her assortment of books, did little to entertain her on the three-day journey.

Late in the afternoon, when her wagon pulled into the palace complex, Roxana could not have been happier at the prospect of having a roof over her head, if only for one night. Morella helped her out of the wagon. Then she bent over as a sharp pain cut through her.

"Are you all right, my lady?"

Roxana didn't want to alarm anyone. "It's just my back."

"No wonder riding around in this wagon." Morella offered her a hand, and Roxana gratefully took it. "You should be in bed."

Roxana never revealed her discomfort to the other women around her. She remained ever vigilant of her behavior, not wanting anything to reflect poorly on Alexander.

She put her weight on Morella as the servants of King Sopeithes showed her through lavish corridors decorated in gold leaf and inlaid with gemstones. Sweat poured from her brow, and her heartbeat pounded in her ears. Her pains were early.

Not now! Not here!

Once she reached the carved ivory doors to her quarters, she dropped to her knees.

"My lady!"

Morella ordered the servants carrying her trunks to help get Roxana to her feet.

She gripped her maid's shoulders, gritting her teeth as fire rocked through her. "Get word to General Hephaestion. The baby is coming."

Hephaestion paced the thick planks of the pier, still wearing his stained tunic from the day before, stubble on his unshaved face. He waited for the first sign of white sails, barges, and galley ships on the river as the orange sun rose over the jungle of trees.

The yellow rays were stretched over the water by the time the king's ship docked. Alexander stood on the deck, the short, stocky figure of his admiral Nearchus next to him.

When the ship's ropes dropped to the dock attendants, Alexander spotted Hephaestion. He shouted to lower the gangplank.

He hurried off his ship and ran up to him.

"What is it?"

Hephaestion lowered his voice to keep the news from the others around them. "Roxana's pains have started."

The color drained from Alexander's face. "She has another month to go."

"Yes, the baby's early." He clenched his hands, hating to be the bearer of such troubling news. "I have Philip with her now, as well as the midwives. They said it could take some time. This means we can't leave tomorrow like you planned."

"Then we wait." Alexander scrubbed his face with his hands. "We'll hold the fleet and the armies here until the child comes. I'll not have my son born in the back of a wagon."

Hephaestion was thankful. Getting Alexander, a man who hated postponing anything, to change his mind was often very difficult.

"I'm sure your wife will appreciate the gesture."

Alexander held his wrist. "Don't let anything happen to her. I know women are made for such things, but she's so fragile. I can't lose her."

Hephaestion patted his shoulder, attempting to comfort him. "She's strong."

"But there are always dangers." He turned to the water, hiding his face. "I'll get the priests started on reading the auspices and making sacrifices for a safe delivery."

Hephaestion understood his fear. It was his as well. He would be devastated if they lost Roxana.

"Of course, you will want to see your son or daughter as soon as they arrive, right?"

Alexander arched his back and showed his profile. "Hard to believe I'm going to be a father."

Hephaestion put an arm around his shoulder. "I've got wine back in my rooms at the palace. We should drink and wait for news of your child."

"Yes. I could use a drink." Alexander wiped his brow. "Several, as a matter of fact."

Hephaestion chuckled. "This is a side of you I've never seen before: the expectant father."

Roxana sat naked on an ebony-carved birthing stool with her legs splayed apart over a round hole cut into the center of the seat. Morella supported her back as a fire roared in a mudbrick hearth next to her. On the wall in front of her, a female goddess holding babies and standing on a cat was meant to ease her pain. When another contraction gripped her, slicing through her insides like a hot knife, she suspected the goddess was a sham. She cursed and bit down on the moist towel placed in her mouth.

Why had no one told her it would hurt like this?

Terrified, sweaty, and her muscles quivering with fatigue, she had not slept a wink all night. Water had gushed from between her legs well before dawn, but still, the baby had not come. She'd never wished harder in her life for her mother to be at her side. She would have accepted her grandmother—any familiar face would do.

Most of all, she wanted Alexander. One moment in his arms would give her the strength to go on.

Another spasm erupted in the small of her gut and roared up her belly.

"That's good." Morella wiped her face. "You're doing so well."

She focused on her attendant while she rode through her agony. Right behind her maid, Philip, the court physician kept a watchful eye on her progress. Being naked in front of a man other than her husband added to the humiliation of having her legs spread open, showing every part of her to everyone in the room.

"They're coming closer," a squat, round woman said in Greek from the side of the chair.

Philip glimpsed the fading light from the window. "It's almost evening. If the child doesn't come soon, I will have to cut her to help the baby along. I have the king's authority to do whatever is needed."

Cut! Roxana almost spat the towel out of her mouth, ready to run from the room.

The fat woman laughed. "No need for your knives. I will get the baby out of her. You know nothing about babies, Physician."

Another tornado of pain swept through Roxana. She bit down hard on the towel while whimpering. The fat midwife jabbed her fingers in between Roxana's legs, adding to her shame and agony.

She gave Roxana a toothless grin. "There's the head, my lady. Your child is about to be born." The midwife went to the front of the stool and squatted. "Now you must listen to me."

Another hard contraction hit, sending a blazing fire into the very pit of her groin. She clenched her fists, trying not to scream.

"Yes, yes, a big one there." The fat woman cupped Roxana's face, demanding her attention. "The time is coming when you must push this baby out."

Roxana relaxed, exhausted, as the discomfort eased. Out of the corner of her eye, she could see the doctor respectfully facing the wall. Then another pang came on her.

"That's it." The midwife scurried to take up a position between her legs. "I need you to push, bear down in your bottom, and help the child out."

Roxana tried her best. She grunted as the sharp cramps cut through her, the sweat pouring from her. Morella dutifully stood by her side, giving her hand encouraging pats, but all she could think about was the pain.

"Ah there, the head is here." The midwife's face lit up. "Good. On the next cramp, push again and don't stop."

Roxana did as she was told until the pain turned her inside out. Her groin was an inferno and when her suffering became so excruciating she could no longer stand it, she let go a long, piercing scream.

Alexander paced in Hephaestion's rooms. Depictions of strange snakes with two heads and dragons on the walls didn't help his nerves. Neither had the wine. Usually, wine calmed him; tonight, nothing worked.

He wanted to go to her, check on her progress but knew better than to show up in a birthing room—it was bad luck for the mother and child. He was too superstitious to risk angering the gods. So, he paced and prayed, harder than he had in his life.

How had his father endured such matters? Then again, his children had been born at the palace at Pella, not in the jungles of India. For the first time, he regretted bringing Roxana along. She'd been such a joy, become so important to him, he'd never considered sending her away. What would he do if she didn't survive?

Through the window looking out on the river, he caught the top of the sun setting below the water. Imagine the sunsets he would have seen standing at the shores of the Endless Ocean. He'd almost made it. The disappointment still stung every day.

Footfalls in the corridor chased away his lost dream. He headed for the chamber doors.

Hephaestion came in, but he wasn't alone. The court physician, Philip, was with him. Neither man smiled, and Alexander's heart sank.

"What is it?" He charged the men. "Tell me!"

Philip stepped forward. "It was a boy, my king. He was stillborn."

Crushed, Alexander gripped his shoulder. "And Roxana? Is she …?"

"She's fine." Philip hooked his hand on his white physician's cloak. "She can have more children. Nothing to worry about there."

Alexander sneered, not hiding his disgust for the physician. "Leave me."

Philip gave Hephaestion a fretful glance and then quickly left the room.

Alexander turned away, trembling. His nails dug into his palms as he pictured the pain his wife had endured—what she still endured.

"Did you see her? How is she?"

Hephaestion rested a hand on his shoulder. "How do you think she is?"

Part of him wanted to take a moment and grieve for the child. Alexander had never pictured himself as a father, but after she had told him of her pregnancy, he'd thought of nothing else. The child had died. His son had died. He believed only the gods knew the reason why they did such things. After keeping him from reaching the end of the world, the death of his son seemed a cruel judgment.

"Where is she?"

Hephaestion guided him to the door. "I'll take you to her."

In a bed of teak and ivory, freshly cleaned, with new linens around her, Roxana faced a window, letting streams of moonlight trickle across the black floor. No lamps burned, no attendants were in her room. She had even sent Morella away. All she had was the moonlight, and portraits of elephants and peacocks to keep her company.

The throbbing in her groin turned into a dull ache, but the pain in her heart hurt more than the worst of her labor. She had lost the child.

I failed him. Like his army, like his enemies, I let him down.

Alexander would send her away. She would return to her father, or worse, be sent to live in a palace. And why not? Losing the baby was her fault. She had done something wrong, and the gods had punished her for it.

The doors to her bedroom opened, and light from the outer chamber filtered in, casting shadows on the wall. Believing it was Morella coming to check on her, she didn't utter a sound, hoping her silence would send the woman on her way.

"Roxana?"

His voice brought tears to her eyes.

Roxana rolled over, afraid to look at him. Her shoulders shook as she resisted her urge to cry.

The light from the doors remained, and on the walls, his shadow grew smaller as he approached the bed. She covered her mouth, not wanting to cry out, but the sting of her tears made it impossible to remain silent.

"I came to see you." The side of her bed dipped. "The physician told me about our son. He said you were very brave."

"I'm sorry," she murmured into her pillow. "I'm sorry I lost him."

He gently turned her, coaxing her to face him.

His hair a tousled mess and his eyes red and raw with emotion, he reminded her of the time when his beloved horse had died.

"You did not lose him." Alexander swept the hair from her cheeks. "Why the gods let some children live and some die is a secret they will never share with us. Just like men on a battlefield, you can never tell their intentions, but we must abide by them."

She sniffled and wiped her nose with the sleeve of her nightdress. "You don't blame me?"

He crawled into the bed with her. "How can I ever blame you? You are my treasure." His arms went around her, and she relaxed against him. "I blame myself for dragging you to India with me, for not sending you someplace safe to have the baby. But I'm selfish. I want you with me always."

His words opened the dam in her heart, holding back all the emotions she refused to acknowledge.

"He was so beautiful," she said as the tears blinded her. "I saw him. He had ten fingers and ten toes. I wanted him so much, but they took him away from me." She sobbed against him.

"Shhh." He held her close, kissing her salty cheeks. "There will be more babies. You will see." He rocked her in his arms. "One day we will have another Alexander, I promise."

The future was a black pit, empty of the hope for other children, or a day when her pain would ease. Roxana only yearned to hold the baby she had lost. In her husband's arms, she cried away her heartache as his tender words and sweet caresses continued through the night, attempting to conquer her sorrow.

CHAPTER TWENTY-FIVE

"**M**y lady, you must eat."

Morella hovered over her with a plate of roasted lamb and sweet cakes—what she had craved when pregnant. But the reminder only made her retreat into her mound of blankets piled in the corner of her wagon.

"The king is worried about you." Morella tucked a loose lock of Roxana's hair from her braid behind her ear. "He gave express orders for you to have anything you wanted from the food wagons while we're on the road, and if it was not on there, to get it for you, no matter what."

Two days after the loss of her baby, Roxana was once again traveling with the baggage train. Her husband had stayed with her until news of a tribe preparing their cities for battle reached him. The prospect of war had roused Alexander from his sorrow, but not her.

"Where's my husband?" she asked, turning her nose up at the plate.

"With the fleet. We're to meet up with him in a few days." Morella put the plate to the side. "The maid to General Ptolemy's mistress reported the king is planning for a great battle when we arrive."

Another battle. How very Alexander.

The numbness enveloping her made it hard to consider anything other than her heartache. Thinking about where they headed or who her husband met in battle required too much effort. All she wanted to do was forget.

"Morella, bring me wine."

"No, you must eat." Morella squatted in front of her, a mother's concern in her brown puppylike eyes. "I know how you feel. I've been there." She brushed her finger across her cheek. "But drinking away the days will not help. Losing a child is the most painful sorrow a heart can endure. When I lost my boy, I didn't want to go on, but I did, and it brought me to you." She held Roxana's hand. "You have a husband who loves you, and there will be more babies. More life to bring into the world. You must think of what will be."

The words rang hollow. She wanted her dead baby, not the promise of another.

Roxana yanked her hand away. "Bring me wine."

With a resigned sigh, Morella stood and went to the back of the wagon.

Roxana rested her head against her pillows as the rocking of the wagon reminded her of the way Alexander lay in bed with her, holding her, and telling her how much he loved her. It had been the only thing keeping her from slipping below the surface of a black ocean, never to return.

"You must eat something, my lady."

Morella repeated the words to her morning, noon, and night as the baggage train and army continued through the dense green lands filled with exotic animals and strange tribes.

Roxana refused any food, only taking unwatered wine whenever she could. Her physical wounds healed quickly and the soreness of the birth was almost gone, but her melancholy remained.

"Come, my lady," Morella said to a tipsy Roxana. "The attendants have set up your big tent."

While Morella helped Roxana to her tent, she inspected the lush forest surrounding her. "Where are we?"

"Only the gods know. We have stopped so the king can subdue a fierce Indian tribe." Morella eased her onto a bench in her reception area.

Roxana rubbed her head, attempting to stimulate her foggy mind. "Maybe I'm just a woman, but it seems to me all these battles tend to run together."

Morella draped a shawl around her shoulders. "Yes, your husband does have a fondness for war."

She had learned a great deal about her husband during their time together, and even more from those who knew him best, but many things about him remained a mystery. His nature, his proclivity for war, his drive—where had they come from? She might never know.

"Is she up?" a familiar deep voice called in Persian from the tent entrance.

Hephaestion's brisk gait made Roxana smile. His exuberance was as contagious as it was heartwarming. With his thick curly hair matted from his helmet and his face stained with the local mud, he reminded her of a playful child more than a busy general.

"I'm awake, Hephaestion ... barely." Roxana tried to raise her head. "You must give me your secret for your endless amount of energy. I'm in dire need of it."

When Hephaestion looked at her, his face fell. He turned to Morella.

"Has she eaten?" he asked in Persian.

Morella shook her head. "Not a bite in days."

Hephaestion knelt before Roxana's bench. "This won't do, Roxana," he gently reprimanded, switching back to Greek. "Alexander is mad with worry about you. He doesn't want this. He sent me to check on you."

Her vision cleared as she took in his faint smile. "Where is he?"

"Making final preparations before we attack the Mallian Indians. Then he plans to press on down the river." He gripped her hand. "You must take care of yourself for Alexander. He does not want to see you weak."

"Why is everything we are, everything we do, for him, Hephaestion?"

"Because he is all that matters to both of us. He needs us to be strong, so he can be strong. So please, little star, you must eat."

She found the courage to ask the questions haunting her since leaving the palace. "What did they do with my son? Did someone make sure he was cleaned and anointed before they sent him to the gods? I must know."

Hephaestion took a deep breath, letting it out slowly. "Alexander prepared the child and built a small pyre for him at the river's edge. I was with him. It was just the two of us. That was all he wanted. We stayed with the pyre until it was nothing but ash."

Roxana pictured her son's funeral pyre gleaming in the night, wishing she could have been there, but knowing the anguish would have been too great. Alexander and his closest friend attending to the baby reassured her. Her arms still ached for her son, and she doubted it would ever fade, but that the child had known something of his father's love before being sent to the gods comforted her.

"Thank you for telling me."

His gaze narrowed. "Promise me you will try to eat."

She nodded, not sure if she could keep her promise, but not wanting him to add to his troubles on the eve of battle.

He touched her cheek. "I have to get back."

"When does this battle begin?"

He got to his feet. "In a few days."

Roxana retreated to her bed. She slept fitfully as the camp around her bustled with activity. The clatter of armor, the shouts, and cries all woke her at different times. She would listen to the intrusion, shake her head, and return to her slumber.

Morella encouraged her to sit at a table and eat. A parade of sweet cakes, exotic fruits, vegetables cooked in stews, bread with cheese, and small portions of lamb appeared before her. She took a few bites of the food to pacify her maid and sipped most of the wine served. Roxana never stayed up for long and soon sought the comfort of her black bed, embracing the visions that came when she closed her eyes.

She was happiest in her dreams. There she was a mother, holding her son, rocking him, and feeling complete. Then the visions took on a different tone. Her child disappeared, and Alexander replaced him, snuggling with her in their black bed, laughing with her under a tree, watching the stars together. But as day blurred into night and she lost track of time, the nightmares took over.

People ran throughout the camp, shouting, crying, calling for the gods to save someone, but she could never tell who. Right when she went to question a faceless stranger in her dream, they would disappear.

Anxious to discover the cause of everyone's distress, she went from one person to the next. Fog floated above the ground. The camp became dark, filled with shadows her lamp could never chase away. A sense of foreboding overtook her. She feared someone she knew had been harmed but could never learn who. She dashed from tent to tent, screaming for someone to talk to her. Then, a child came up to her. The same young blonde girl with big blue eyes she had helped.

She held up a bouquet of blood red flowers. "You have to come now, my lady."

"What is it?" Roxana gripped her skinny arms. "What has happened? Why is everyone crying?"

The girl tipped her head, reminding her of Alexander. Then her face changed. The child became her husband.

"Wake up, Roxana. I'm dead," he said in a booming voice.

Gasping, Roxana sat up. Where was she? The tent around her was familiar. It was her tent. She was safe. It was just a dream.

It seemed so real.

She pulled at her damp nightgown and swung her legs over the bed.

The faint cries of women rose around her.

She stood up, her legs shaky, but the high-pitched cry of grief made her forget her weakness.

Prayers to the gods, both in Persian and Greek, circled her tent.

"Why has this happened?" one woman cried out.

The lamentations of men mingled with the sharp, piercing scream of women. "The king is dead!"

Roxana wiggled into the black baggy long tunic—the one Morella had begged her for days to wear. Her ears pricked, straining for confirmation.

Morella barged into her room. Tears had turned her brown eyes red.

"Oh, my lady," she called, half weeping. "The news is all over the camp. The king is dead."

She stood, unable to move or breath. Her Alexander? It had to be a hoax, a lie created by the enemy. She grabbed for Morella's hand.

"When did this happen?"

Morella held on to her. "At the battle with the Mallain's they say. No one knows for sure. There are so many stories flying about."

A shred of hope presented itself. Alexander had once advised her to never believe what she heard about him.

"Come to me if you ever hear gossip that upsets you. I will tell you the truth."

Without a word to Morella, she dashed out of her tent. Once outside, the world assaulted her senses. The brightness of the sky, the loud voices in her ears, the heat on her skin, the aroma of smoke and food cooking besieged her. Being so far removed from the land of the living since her son's death had made her visceral reaction all the more painful. She didn't stop to adjust—she ignored the demands of her guards and took off running.

She struggled to move at first, almost as if she had forgotten how to use her legs, but her fear gave her wings. Alexander couldn't be dead. The gods would not be so cruel as to take her baby and her husband within weeks of each other.

Roxana passed wailing women pouring dirt over their heads. Despair pressed against her heart, begging like a demon to be let it in.

Time slowed as she ran desperate to reach the king's tent. Her dream came back to her, and she fought to suppress the gut-wrenching agony bubbling below her resolve.

She spied the glint of gold from the pike atop Alexander's tent when she reached the edge of the men's camp. All around her, soldiers sat in the dirt, cradling their swords and helmets with tears streaming down their cheeks. People kept shouting, "The king is dead, the king is dead," but Roxana refused to crumble.

She had to push her way through men and horses before she reached Alexander's tent. At the entrance, his guards wept, but she stayed strong. Until she saw her husband's corpse, she would never be convinced.

"Is he here?" she yelled at the younger of the two men.

The bright-faced boy attempted to get the words out but couldn't. He just sagged against his spear as pandemonium erupted around her.

Horses bolted from their masters, sending piles of shields and swords clattering to the ground. The animals tore down the trail between tents, coming right at her.

Hands caught her as she almost fell against the tent to get out of the way of the beasts. She expected to see one of her husband's sentries, but her eyes widened when Bagoas appeared.

He helped her to her feet. "The king is at the front lines, my lady. The generals have him there."

She wanted to find out if he was alive or dead. Every fiber of her being yearned to be with him and she would kill anyone who tried to stop her.

She gripped the man's slender arms and shouted, "I have to see him!"

Roxana fully expected Bagoas to back away, terrified by her outburst but instead, he took her hand.

"I will take you to him."

She prayed to every god she knew, Persian and Greek, as Bagoas led her out of the base camp and deep into the hostile Indian jungle. Her only thoughts were of seeing Alexander again. To touch him, breathe in the sweetness of his skin, stroke his unruly hair—all the things she had done a thousand times before.

On the slender dirt path beaten into the dense brush, men in armor, horses pulling small carts loaded with weapons, and archers carrying quivers full of arrows surrounded them. Roxana kept a hold of the eunuch's hand, terrified she would get trampled, but not willing to stop.

"They seek revenge for the king," Bagoas explained, keeping pace with her. "They will kill everyone now."

Hate coursed through her like fire. "I hope every last one of them dies. I wish I could be there to see it."

The thick jungle path opened on to a field. Spread out on the green grass lay long rows of wounded men covered with mud, blood, and flies. Most had limbs missing, or eyes taken out by arrows. Others had gaping wounds to their heads, spurting vital fluid or guts dangling from slashes along their bellies. Hundreds writhed, screamed, called out for loved ones while staining the grass with their cruor. Attendants in filthy long white tunics, saturated with crimson and mud, ran from man to man, assessing their wounds and doing what they could. The stench of blood, feces, dirt, and fear hit her, but Roxana didn't register it. She avidly searched the men on the ground for her husband, sickened less by the sight of them, and more by the belief her husband might be among them.

"Where will I find the king in this?"

Bagoas pointed across the field to a tent. "He's there, my lady."

Weakness overtook her legs again as Bagoas continued on, negotiating the disfigured bodies until they reached the large tent. Trepidation flooded her. Could she do this? Face seeing her Alexander dead or mutilated like the men she had passed in the grass?

A nervous trembling settled in her hands as she stood next to stacks of swords, shields, and spears outside of the entrance. She batted the tent flap aside and marched inside, only to run smack into a wall of teary-eyed men.

She wanted to scream for them to move. He was her husband, and she deserved to be with him, not them. About to shoulder her way past the blockade of men, Bagoas touched her.

"He's not dead," he whispered. "But he needs your care. Help him."

With that, he disappeared into the crowds huddled around the entrance. At first, she wanted to cry, to weep with relief, but then her anger flared. Why hadn't someone come to her, spared her the torture she'd just endured.

Never mind that. Alexander needs you.

A swell of strength filled her, something she had not possessed since … Roxana took a deep breath, awake for the very first time since the death of her son.

With the determination of a mother bear, she shoved the men out of the way. They yielded, and when she broke through their ranks, she halted, gutted by what lay before her.

Pale as snow, smeared with blood, and lying naked on a shield across a makeshift table was her Alexander. A large wound in his right upper chest gurgled with a mixture of blood and air. Around the table, his generals remained transfixed, attuned to their king's every breath. They didn't notice when she walked into their midst.

She slowly eased up to him and touched his icy cheek. He lay very still as if a sacrifice to the gods. Roxana refused to give in to her desire to cry out. Instead, she stood there, controlling her panic and caressing his cheek.

"Alexander, I'm here."

His eyes fluttered, and for an instant, she glimpsed their brilliant gray, but then it was gone.

A hand settled on her right shoulder and gave her a squeeze. "He passed out right after Perdiccas removed the arrow barb from his chest," Hephaestion said behind her. "I would have sent word ..." His voice dwindled to an unintelligible whisper.

Roxana didn't face him. She curled her fists at his disregard for her feelings. Later, when she had helped the king, she would throttle the man for putting her through such agony. How could these idiots be such brilliant generals, but have no regard for anyone who didn't wield a sword or ride off into battle?

Focusing on her husband, she lowered her eyes to the wound. The air and blood made bubbles when he breathed. Bright red blood still flowed from it, trickling down his chest. The more she examined his injury, the calmer she became. This was something she knew how to do—heal. She could use her skills to help him.

I must stop the bleeding first. He's lost too much blood.

"I need spider webs!" She turned to the generals gathered behind her. "I need you to send men out into the jungle and get me spider webs from the trees, not the ground, so I can stop this bleeding. Then I'll need clean linens and wine—"

"I'm in charge of the king's care," a voice interrupted from the back of the row of generals.

Philip, the court physician who had stood by and done nothing during the birth of her son, stepped out from behind the men. "I know what is needed here, not you."

Hephaestion came forward. "This is the king's wife. She has every right to care for her husband."

Roxana didn't need Hephaestion to help her. She would stand up for herself. "I assure you, I'm trained in the care of wounds and have read—"

"Who trained you?" Philip demanded, halting in front of her.

"My mother taught me everything I—"

"You're a woman, and you have just passed a child. Therefore, you're unclean and should not tend the king."

The generals standing behind the doctor had their glassy eyes riveted to the rise and fall of Alexander's chest. They didn't speak up for her or defend her. Their reaction awakened a lifetime of injustice, a hundred conversations where she hadn't mattered because of her sex. The fury each encounter stoked rose until an inferno blazed in her soul. She'd had enough!

The sinewy physician gave her a tolerant smile. "I think it would be best for the king if you—"

Before he could finish, Roxana cocked back her arm and punched the haughty man right in the nose.

Now that felt good!

Hephaestion's mouth fell open and the other generals awakened from their stupor.

Philip bent over, grabbing his nose as a faint trickle of blood flowed between his fingers.

"Get me the things I asked for, now!" she shouted at the men. "And get this ass out of here before I have him beheaded!"

Hephaestion spun around. "You heard her! Move!"

Generals bounced off each other as they quickly fled the tent. Perdiccas grabbed the stunned physician and escorted him outside with the others. Ptolemy and Hephaestion were the only men brave enough to approach her.

"By the gods, I've never heard a woman talk like that!" Ptolemy's raucous voice broke the tense mood lingering in the tent. "I doubt the men will ever cross you again." His gaze drifted to the king. "Can you help him?"

She rubbed her sore hand, going through a list in her head. "Just get me spider webs ... and some honey."

"If I have to collect it myself, you shall have everything you need." The burly general hurried outside.

Roxana sorted through a pile of clean linens next to Alexander. "I need wine."

Hephaestion jogged across the tent to a refreshment table set up by the entrance.

"Why wine, Roxana?" Hephaestion passed her a jug of warm wine.

She poured the wine over the clean linens. "Wine can clean a wound as well as intoxicate."

"What about the honey?"

She dabbed the wine around the gaping hole in Alexander's chest, checking out the edges and measuring the size. "After I stop the bleeding with the cobwebs, the honey will keep the wound from turning putrid." She glanced back at Hephaestion. "I should have punched you along with that stupid physician for not sending for me right away."

He ran his hand over his chin, wincing. "We thought we were doing the best for him. I realize now we were wrong."

With her husband safely in her care, her nerves settled and her reason returned. "Tell me what happened at the battle. Everything that happened."

Hephaestion stood by as her nimble hands tended to the king. "He led his men up one of the city walls, encouraging them to fight. Recklessly, he didn't wait for the men to join him before he jumped down from the wall and into the city by himself. The Indians went after him. By the time any of the men could get to him, he'd been shot. The arrow went through his breastplate. The men carried him back on his shield." Hephaestion's shoulders shook, and his eyes glistened. "Damned shield of Achilles. He always carried it with him into battle. Where was the blasted thing when he needed it to protect him from that arrow?"

His voice broke, and he turned away from her. She'd never heard him so upset. It reminded her there were others who loved Alexander, others who wanted the best for him.

Something touched her hand, and when she looked down, Alexander's fingers were on hers.

"I'm not leaving you," she whispered. "I'm not going to let you die."

His eyes never opened, but his fingers stayed on hers. The small gesture meant everything to her.

Hephaestion clasped her shoulder. "I believe the king has a new physician."

She kept an eye on the rise and fall of her husband's chest. "But will the general's let me stay with him day and night?"

"These men admire strength, Roxana. And you just showed them a boatload of it."

Chapter Twenty-Six

The light coming through the tent doorway faded to dark, and the generals left her to tend to Alexander. Roxana kept vigil at her husband's bedside with only a servant to assist her. She packed his wound with the ample supply of cobwebs, honey, and linen bandages Ptolemy had brought.

She spoke to him while she worked, not sure if he heard her, but it made her feel better. News from the camps, her travels in the baggage train, her long sleep after the death of their son, her heartache, and her dreams. Anything that came to mind she shared, so he would know she was there.

While he slept, she wiped the sweat from his brow, memorizing every detail of his face. When had it happened? When had he stolen her heart? She didn't know, but here she was, deeply in love with a man she'd once deemed her enemy.

By morning, her spirits rose as a faint hint of color brightened his cheeks and the bleeding in his chest stopped completely. Confident he would survive, she sent one of her guards to search for Hephaestion and give him the news.

Exhausted but happy, she sat on her stool by the makeshift bed she had put together for him, thanking the gods for keeping her husband alive and giving her the chance to embrace her love for her king.

On the second day, Alexander was awake, weak but able to talk. His wound, bandaged and packed with honey, still concerned Roxana. It would need time to heal, and the king would require lots of rest in the process—something she suspected he would never do.

She sat on a stool in a corner of the tent, rolling clean bandages, as he listened to his generals gathered around him, updating him on the battle. She wasn't happy about all the activity but knowing Alexander, she couldn't keep him away from his men for too long.

"The other Mallian towns in the territory have surrendered. They're afraid of what we might do to them." Ptolemy arched over the foot of his bed, sporting a smug grin. "After you were hurt, the men went mad. They killed the entire town—women, children—everyone." He scowled. "You scared the crap out of us. It was a stupid thing to do, Alexander."

"I know," was all he whispered.

Her eyes found his across the tent. He'd grown paler during the visit. She got up to chase the generals from the tent when Hephaestion came up to her.

"She's been here the entire time. She refused to let anyone else care for you."

"Refused?" Ptolemy chortled, walking up next to Hephaestion. "She punched that idiot doctor of yours in the nose. Damned man wouldn't lift a finger to help you. Your wife ordered us all about like a seasoned field commander. She was brilliant."

Roxana smiled as she listened to Ptolemy retell the story of how Philip's nose had bled and bled. When he got to the part about how she'd sent them in search of cobwebs and honey, Alexander lost his fight against his fatigue and closed his eyes.

She shooed the men from the tent, insisting the king needed to rest.

"He's much better, Roxana," General Craterus told her on the way out.

"Keep up the good work," Perdiccas encouraged, patting her shoulder as if she was one of his soldiers.

The leaders of Alexander's army walked across the blood-soaked grass outside the tent, laughing amongst themselves. Their confidence in her had broken down a barrier. She sensed she'd earned their respect in some small way. Roxana hoped it meant she was no longer the despised Persian bride, but one of them—a Companion to the king.

The next day, he took small amounts of broth, and his voice grew stronger. She propped him up on several pillows while he listened to his generals confer about plans for the rest of the campaign. She stuck close to him, keeping a watchful eye. Now and then, he would turn to her and smile.

That smile was all she needed to keep going. She occasionally nodded off on her stool while his generals went on about supplies and the shape of the men. To stay awake, she would roll bandages or check his dressing, anything to stay close to him. She'd become terrified of being out of his sight in case something happened.

"I'll keep the men busy while you recover." Ptolemy's boisterous voice filled the tent. "They've been brooding around the camp, waiting for you to appear. No matter what we say, they don't believe us. Discipline has suffered a bit because of their concern."

Alexander pointed to his work table at the far end of the tent. Hephaestion went to the table, picked up a wax-inlaid wooden tablet and stylus, and brought them back to the king.

The other generals didn't seem to notice the silent communication between the two men, but Roxana did.

"Write this down," Alexander ordered in a raspy voice. "I am alive and well. No force of the enemy has taken my life or my spirit. The gods have protected me as they have protected you. We will soon be on the move again, and I will be standing in front leading the way." He paused and winced as he moved in his bed. "Have that read throughout the camps. Make sure all the men know it's my word."

Hephaestion tucked the tablet under his arm. "I'll get your secretary, Eumenes, started on this. I'll be back soon." With a knowing smile to Roxana, he headed out.

Ptolemy patted his leg. "Then we will leave you to your rest, Alexander." He turned to her. "You've done well."

The other generals acknowledged her with a nod or a smile as they filed past and followed Ptolemy.

She went to Alexander's bedside, invigorated by the small victory. Roxana adjusted the bandage on his chest, checking it for blood.

He placed his hand over hers. "Did you punch my physician in the nose?"

"I know what you're going to say, 'It wasn't the proper thing for a king's wife to do.'"

"Perhaps not, but you've earned the respect of my men because of it. And that pleases me."

A small red patch blossomed on his white bandage.

"Alexander, don't talk anymore. You're bleeding again."

"Did your mother teach you to …?" He touched his dressing.

"Yes, she had to. I was very accident prone as a child. Even broke my arm falling out of a tree."

Alexander tried to laugh, but then grimaced and paled.

She agonized over his pain, wishing she could do more. Feeling helpless was akin to torture for her.

"Rest now. You need to save your strength."

While she rearranged his pillows, Alexander tenderly kissed her cheek.

"You will be my physician from now on, my love. I promise you will be notified first thing when I need you."

Roxana helped him back on his pillows, shaking her head. "I hope you never need me again. I may not survive it."

He caressed her cheek. "You should rest. You're so pale. You've not fully recovered from childbirth."

"Being with you is more important. And it's helped me. This made me realize what matters most—you."

He repositioned himself, smiling happily. "Could it be that I've conquered the unconquerable?"

She gazed into his brilliant eyes, contentment filling her heart. "Women are never conquered, my king. They're simply awed by the gift of love."

Not even three days later, Roxana became infuriated when four of Alexander's guard carried him from his tent to an open gold litter stuffed with pillows. She feared for his wound with all the jostling.

"I will be safe on a ship, my love," he explained, holding on to her hand. "I will journey to the junction where the three rivers meet and flow into the mighty Indus. The majority of my troops are camped there."

She jogged alongside, frightened for his health. "You're not well enough to do this!"

He let her go. "I can never be seen as a weak king. A weak king is a dead king."

"You're injured, not weak," she argued. "The men will understand."

Alexander held his right side and gave her a faint smile. "The men must see me, Roxana, and I must see them."

She stayed back while the escort carrying his litter set out across the field. She stomped her foot, frustrated he'd ignored her instructions.

Is anyone going to ask me what I think?

Determined not to let him out of her sight, she stayed close to him, keeping a wary eye on his breathing and bandage.

At the army camp, men came out in droves to see Alexander. They lined the narrow path to the river and cheered, rushed the guard around him, and called to their king.

The display astounded her. She kept checking on him, bothered by his constant waving and the rocking motion of the litter, but he seemed to thrive on the attention. He became more animated with every step closer to the dock. The love of his men uplifted him. Their adoration was better than any tonic she could administer.

She waited on the shore as Alexander was taken on board one of the tall, thirty-oared ships. His soldiers positioned him on a gold couch set below a great awning so everyone lining the riverbank could see him.

"Come." Hephaestion appeared, holding out a set of reins. "We'll meet his ship."

Her beloved Hera waited next to the general's red roan, Thunder.

He swung up on his horse's back. "His tent has been set up at the junction in the river. Once he's off the ship, you can tend to him."

They rode along the shore, dotted with a few trees. Men clogged the beaches and breaks in the tree line along the way, waving as the ship went past. Most of the soldiers were thin, sick, many were sunburned, and they all had a dazed look in their eyes—one that came from too much fighting.

Roxana's distress intensified when the awning over Alexander unfurled, exposing the very pale king to the hot Indian sun.

This is too much!

Well-wishers crowded his ship as it docked, forcing Roxana back. His litter was carefully brought down a gangplank, but when his guards reached the sandy shore, they halted.

To her astonishment, a horse arrived for Alexander. He mounted the animal and rode through the crowds to his tent. Men touched him, threw flowers, and wept. Roxana rode behind him, getting angrier and angrier at his foolishness. After he dismounted, he gave a wave to his troops and walked unassisted into his tent.

An exasperated Roxana darted inside after him. She found him gasping for breath.

"Alexander, are you mad?" She scrambled to his side.

Hephaestion joined her and put his arm around Alexander's shoulders, supporting his weight. They got him settled on his bed, and Roxana ripped away his loose tunic anxious to check the state of his wound.

A blossoming red spot appeared on his bandage. When Alexander coughed, a droplet of blood trickled from the side of his mouth. A swell of cold fear settled over her.

"Do you mind telling me what the point of all this was?"

Alexander's eyes shifted to Hephaestion.

Hephaestion grinned as if reading the king's thoughts. "The men needed it. So did Alexander."

CHAPTER TWENTY-SEVEN

Frail and emotionally drained from weeks of tending to her injured husband, Roxana continued with the baggage train under the command of General Craterus. They took the open road along the Indus River. Fertile valleys of lush fruit trees, colorful birds, and cool breezes made the journey pleasant and gave her time to think. She'd endured a great deal, and the young woman she had been—naive, unsure, and nervous—had disappeared. Her suffering had given her strength, deepening her relationship with the king and gaining the confidence of his generals. She no longer worried about being ignored.

When Alexander left with his fleet and army, rushing off to confront treacherous tribes and one stubborn king named Musicanus, she didn't despair at another separation. Alexander had not healed, but she didn't argue when he decided to go. He needed his men and war to recover completely.

After months on the road, and numerous letters from her husband about the many skirmishes he encountered, the baggage train met up with the fleet and army at the town of Patala. There the palace of another defeated king waited. Roxana reveled in the idea of having a room with four walls and a floor. She also longed for a bit of privacy—something hard to come by in the camps.

A veteran of the baggage train, she'd become familiar with the frenzy of settling into a new location. Soldiers directed the separate camps to predetermined fields outside the palace gates with a clear demarcation between the men and women along a small stream. Shouts arose as women often haggled over which bit of land to call their own. Her wagon, along with others belonging to the generals' women, received an escort out of the campsite and to the palace gates.

Roxana passed families unhitching oxen and horses from carts and wagons as they unloaded tents, cooking utensils, bedding, and furniture. Pens for horses, oxen, sheep, and goats, hastily went up. Children ran amid the grassy fields, and soldiers crossed the stream to hunt the row after row of wagons and tents for loved ones. The process never failed to amaze her, and with each new settlement, the number of people mushroomed. The army and baggage train together exceeded the biggest city in Persia.

On the way to the palace, her wagon drove by a small harbor, where a few ships unloaded horses, weapons, soldiers, and trunks of belongings onto the pier. Most of the vessels sat anchored in the river.

Everywhere the noise of a myriad of voices, animals, wagons rolling, and armor clashing blotted out her thoughts. Closer to the palace, the rickety wood and mud-brick homes of the small town jutted against the thick walls. But despite their pitiful circumstances, the Indians along the way came out to greet her, giving the only thing they had to show their respect—flowers.

Once settled in the best rooms, by order of the king, she marveled at the blue stone floors and her diamond-embedded ceiling, meant to twinkle in the lamplight, or so claimed the steward who showed her to the chamber.

A cook arrived, pushing a tray of aromatic dishes, asking her to choose a favorite. A seamstress brought yards of silk fabrics in a rainbow of colors to make her new clothes. A bath attendant filled a stone pool at the rear of her colossal bedroom with hot water and showed her a selection of twenty different scented oils. Gardeners delivered vases of fragrant flowers while her palace maid placed the softest linen sheets on a silver-inlaid bed big enough to sleep five.

The activity baffled her. When her husband appeared at her door later that evening, she discovered the reason for her pampering.

"Do you like the accommodations?" He strolled up and pulled her into his arms. "I told the king to make sure you had the best of everything."

"This was all your doing? It's too much."

"Nonsense." He kissed her forehead. "You deserve it."

She patted his chest and noticed the lump of his bandage. "I want to check on how you're healing."

Alexander took her hand and led her to the bed. "I'm agreeing to this because you won't enjoy yourself with me until you do."

He lifted his tunic over his head, tossed it to the bed, and sat, smiling up at her.

Roxana touched the dark circles under his eyes, convinced he'd pushed himself too hard on the latest campaign. "You need to eat more meat. Your blood is still too thin."

"I will eat more meat, if you will." He playfully slapped her behind. "How am I going to get you pregnant again if you don't pick up some weight?"

She untied the ends of his bandage. "I don't think you have the strength to get me pregnant."

Roxana unwound the bandage from around his chest, thankful he had stuck to her instructions on how to dress his wound—she'd even made sure Hephaestion knew how to do it. The hole from the arrow remained, but the new pink skin along the edges encouraged her. At times when he took a deep breath, Roxana could tell the injury pained him. Would it cause him more problems in the future? The question kept her up at night.

He held her face in his hands. "I'm fine, my wife."

She frowned at him. "You're still weak and the wound could—"

His lips silenced her, kissing away the reprimand she was about to inflict. His arms went around her and pressed into her back, holding her close.

Roxana gave into him, happily, greedily. It had been so long since she'd felt desire, she had almost forgotten the pleasure of it.

His lips skirted her cheek and chin, and when he wrenched the Greek cloak from her shoulders, letting it fall to the floor, she giggled. The anguish of the past left her as his kisses slid down the curve of her neck, and when he had found the tender, fleshy part at the base, he bit down hard.

"I have missed the feel of you next to me, Roxana."

She caressed his scarred and battered body. She had missed him, too.

Impatient to be with him, Roxana removed her peplos and shoes, leaving them piled on the floor beneath her feet.

Alexander tossed his arms around her pale, thin body and pulled her onto the soft sheets.

She combed her hands through his wild mane as white heat exploded in her belly. He kissed her chest, her breasts, and then he positioned her beneath him.

"Will you still want me when I'm too old and broken to lift a sword?"

"I will always want you." She traced her fingers along the scar on his left cheek. "And I will always love you."

"You love me? I began to lose faith I would ever hear those words from you." He settled next to her, grinning. "When did you know?"

She sighed, relieved she'd finally told him. "The night after you were shot with the arrow. I suspected for a while, but then I was sure. I'm hopelessly in love with you."

He tickled her sides. "And you only decided to tell me now?"

She held his hands to make him stop. "You've been busy."

His lips came closer to hers. "Took you long enough."

When he kissed her again, she wrapped her arms around him, thankful they had returned to this. They had beaten despair, injury, loss, and distance to find each other again.

He wasn't the same man who had made love to her on their wedding night, but he was the man she loved. Roxana would take him scarred, battered, broken, or sunburned because, for her, living without Alexander, wasn't any life at all.

She lay next to him in her fancy silver bed, warily attuned to the rise and fall of his chest. She observed his fitful sleep as shadows crawled across the wall and eventually disappeared into the darkness. His brow furrowed and his mouth frowned as if he were arguing with the gods in his dreams. When he finally stirred, she marveled at the brightness of his eyes.

"Have we spent the whole afternoon in bed?"

Roxana snuggled next to him, grateful for the time together. "We needed the rest."

"I want you to do something for me." He kissed her forehead. "I want you to take better care of yourself ... while I'm away."

"Away? But you just arrived." She sat up, suspicious of what he had in mind. "If you're leaving, where am I going?"

He left her question hanging in the air while he got comfortable on the bed.

"I'm sending you with Hephaestion and most of the older veterans in the army to set out for the north road toward Carmania." He adjusted his pillow. "We're heading back to Persia and, eventually, Babylon. But first I must go south with Nearchus and the fleet along the river. There are still some Indian tribes yet to be subdued, and—"

"No! If you want to send me away, I can live with that, but take Hephaestion with you."

He raised his eyebrows. "You're not angry about me leaving again?"

How could she explain her feelings? She'd stopped caring about the distance between them the moment she knew she loved him.

"I'm not angry. I'm frightened. The only comfort I will have while you're gone is knowing Hephaestion will be looking after you. He should go with you, not me." She climbed out of bed and picked up her clothes.

"Who is the king here?" He followed her. "You don't give me orders, Roxana."

She planted her feet, clasping her garments, ready to fight to change his mind. "It's about time somebody did."

Alexander stood in front of her, staring at her naked body. He took a deep breath and regained his composure.

"What would you have me do?"

The question stunned her. In the past, he would never have asked her opinion. It was a turning point in their relationship. He had stopped to consider her feelings instead of ignoring them.

"Send me off with Craterus or Perdiccas but keep Hephaestion with you." Clutching her clothes to her chest, she raised her head. "If he is with you, I know you will be safe."

Roxana waited for him to debate her, insisting she was a woman and knew nothing of war, or laugh at her suggestion. But he didn't. Alexander stood calmly before her, considering her proposal.

"All right. I will take Hephaestion with me." He came up to her and eased his arm around the small of her back. "I like it when you speak your mind." With his other hand, he took her clothes and dropped them to the floor. "It shows me your fire."

"Fire?" She fidgeted. "My grandmother used to call it insolence."

He pulled her to him. "That's because she didn't understand you."

"Do you understand me, Alexander?"

"No, but I'm trying, little star. Maybe one day we will understand each other."

She slid her arms around his neck, happy to feel so close to him. "When we are old and gray, perhaps."

"There are times when I want nothing more than to grow old with you, but then I think the gods may have other plans for me."

A cold breeze caressed her skin, and she trembled.

"What are you saying? Do you plan on going before me, leaving me at the mercy of your generals?"

His mouth closed in on hers. "I seem to remember you handled my generals pretty well when I almost died."

She touched the still healing wound on his chest, then her mind suddenly clouded with black thoughts about her husband's destiny. "I dread to think what would have happened to your empire, your army, to me if you had died that day."

"Yes, there will be great funeral games after I'm gone." He held her tighter. "But I'm here with you now, and we have a lot more life ahead of us."

But the shroud of darkness settling over her heart would not leave. Even as Alexander coaxed her back to the bed, she feared what lay ahead—for both of them.

"You wanted to see me?"

Hephaestion strolled into the reception area Alexander used as an office in his palace rooms. He sat on his stool, holding a letter while a slew of dispatches covered his desk, waiting for replies. He picked up the hint of lavender on his friend's clothes.

"Where are you off to? Meeting a woman in the camps?"

Peritas trotted across the floor and sniffed Hephaestion's hand, begging for attention.

He stroked the old dog behind the ears.

"They have hot water in this place and bathtubs the size of your ships. I'm just taking full advantage of the luxury before it's back to tent life and smelling like a pig."

Alexander glimpsed the letter in his hand and frowned. "Mother sends her regards."

"What does she blame me for now?"

He slapped the letter on the desk, wishing he'd never opened it. "My marriage to a mere baron's daughter when I'm the King of Persia. She's convinced it was all your doing." Alexander sat back, sizing up his friend's smirk. "When Mother's mad at me she always blames someone else. You just happened to be handy this time." He picked up another letter and waved it in the air, the weight of his responsibilities eating at him. "Antipater writes she's trying the patience of the court, and his too, I suspect. He complains she's interfering with matters of state again and asks me to speak with her."

Hephaestion folded his arms. "If we put Roxana and your mother in a fighting pit together, who would you put money on?"

Alexander rubbed his face, tired of being pulled in so many directions. "That's something I never wish to see—my mother and my wife in the same room."

Hephaestion grinned. "What is it? You never let Olympias's tirades bother you before."

He hesitated, not sure how to approach his dilemma. "I have a problem. I want to please my wife, but I also do not wish to upset you."

"Ah, I see. Roxana isn't happy. Let me guess, she wants me with you and not leading the baggage train into Carmania with Perdiccas."

Alexander chuckled, astounded by Hephaestion's powers of perception. He always seemed to pick up on his thoughts. Even after all their years together, he still found it astonishing.

"How did you know?"

"Before we went off to deal with Musicanus, she begged me to stick close to you. I promised her I would. She said I was the only one she trusted to make sure you were safe."

Alexander pressed his lips together, not pleased with his predicament. "And you're the only person I trust to look out for her. She isn't strong enough yet. She's in need of a friend while I'm gone on this long campaign." He drummed his fingers on the desk, at a loss. "What to do?"

Hephaestion rested his hands over Alexander's, putting a stop to his tapping. "The decision isn't hard. We both make your wife happy."

Alexander chuckled. "Never believed I would alter my plans to please a woman, let alone a wife."

"Pleasing a wife is not the same as pleasing a mother—your mother especially." Hephaestion squeezed his hand. "I'm glad you're finally listening to Roxana. She's a smart woman who knows what's best for you."

He held on to his hand, unsure of what he would do without his friend. Advisor general, tactician, administrator—he depended on him for so much.

"I hope you're not upset with me."

Hephaestion countered the suggestion with an affable grin. "There's nothing to be upset about. If she wants me to go, fine. If you want me to go, fine. Now Craterus, he may have some objections."

Alexander selected another scroll from his pile. "Craterus always has objections."

"Should I go tell Craterus or will you?"

"No, definitely not you." Alexander cracked open the seal on the scroll, glad one problem, of the several hundred he had, was resolved. "I will handle it."

"Give Olympias my best when you write to her." Hephaestion ambled toward the doors. "Tell her I'm sending her a selection of every poisonous snake in India to keep her warm in bed at night. That should make her happy."

Roxana stood by her palace window overlooking the pool stocked with orange fish. Morella shouted in the background, supervising the palace servants as they went through the arduous task of packing up her belongings for the long journey back to Babylon. She thought of her son, like she did a thousand times a day. Who would he favor? Her or Alexander.

A blackbird outside her window settled on the branch of a nearby tree, its enormous wings drawing her attention. She envied the creature as it preened its feathers. Free to fly where it wanted, unencumbered by trunks, wagons, servants, or even a horse.

How many times had she packed up her worldly possessions? Ten, a hundred— she'd lost count. But this packing bothered her more than the others because she feared her life with the king would soon change. Babylon was the capital of Persia, and site of the royal court. She would have duties there, formalities, and protocols to observe, slicing away more of her precious freedom. On the road, she was like the rest of the women she'd come to know in the camp; in Babylon, she would be the king's wife and cut off from the world.

While servants ran to and fro carrying trunks and boxes, Alexander and Hephaestion strolled into her palace rooms.

"Roxana?"

His voice sent a warm tingle to her toes. Would that ever change? She hoped not.

Alexander, with Hephaestion at his side, stood in the middle of the reception area, a sea of servants on the ground at their feet.

He looked good—rested, a hint of color in his cheeks, and not out of breath. It gave her confidence he would survive the fighting ahead, but the man at his side gave her more reassurance for her husband's well-being. With Hephaestion sticking close, Alexander would get the best of care.

"Alexander, what a surprise. And Hephaestion. This is an unexpected pleasure."

Alexander held out his hand. "I thought we should come and say goodbye before we go off to the boats."

She took his hand, an inkling of foreboding running through her like it always did with her husband lately.

"You've never seen me off before. Is there—"

She stopped in mid-sentence and let go of his hand as she spied the men and women scattered on the floor. Roxana was acutely aware of the many curious ears around her. Whatever moment she shared with her husband during their last parting, she didn't want it all over the camps the next day.

She ordered the servants to clear the room.

Clothes were left strewn over open trunks still half-packed with her belongings. Furniture sat crowded into a corner, still in need of sorting for her wagons.

Morella was the last out of the room. When her doors closed, Alexander held out his hand to her.

"I brought you something."

The large silver coin mystified her. Her husband usually did things in a big way, especially his gifts. This seemed out of character.

"What, no more gold necklaces, ruby encrusted slippers, pearl earrings? Now I'm only to receive coins?"

Hephaestion strolled over to one of her open trunks. "Yes, he thought it might be easier to pack that way."

Alexander flourished the coin. "This is my silver decadrachm commemorating my battle at the Hydaspes with Porus. I just got them in. I wanted to bring you one to show you." He handed her the coin. "What do you think?"

Her fingertips tingled as she turned the piece over. On the front was the image of a man on a horse carrying a long Macedonian spear, fighting against a retreating elephant and rider.

"That's me on Bucephalus. The man on the elephant is Porus."

Hephaestion snickered. "Just in case you didn't happen to remember who we were fighting at the Hydaspes."

She clutched the coin to her breast. Of all the gifts she'd received from the king, this would be the most precious to her because it pictured him on his beloved horse.

"It's wonderful. It's the first thing you have given me with your portrait on it."

Alexander frowned, making his eyes appear more menacing. "I never thought. I'll get Lysippus, my royal court sculptor, to get you a bust or some such thing to carry with you. He's the only artist worthy enough to represent me." Alexander elbowed his friend. "See? It told you she'd like it."

Rolling his eyes, Hephaestion stepped closer to Roxana. "That's my cue to leave. I just tagged along to say goodbye." He kissed her cheek. "Gain some weight and don't worry."

"Hephaestion," she called as he proceeded to the doors, her heart rising in her throat. "Take care."

"I will take care of both of us." He quietly closed the heavy doors behind him.

The silence in the room consumed her. How is it she could share so much with a man, have so much to say, but when he was about to set off, possibly never to return, words failed her.

Alexander shattered her discomfort when he put his arms around her. "He wanted to see you off. He's grown quite fond of you."

"I've grown quite fond of him. He's a good man and a good friend."

He touched her forehead with his. "I want you to heed his advice. Gain some weight, and I don't want you worrying about me. You're only to be concerned about yourself." He kissed her forehead. "Understood?"

A tightness seized her throat. Why was this goodbye so much harder than the hundreds they had shared? Perhaps because this time, there were no more walls between them. He had brought down the last of her defenses.

"I'll try to do as you say, husband." She patted his firm chest. "But you are ordered to look after yourself, too. No more feats of bravery. Come back to me without any more holes."

"Now that I have my orders, it's time for me to go."

He kissed her lips, and she held him close, wanting their embrace to last a little longer.

"I'll see you in Carmania, little star."

After throwing open her doors with all the gusto of a warrior, he headed into the sunlit corridor, his unruly hair bouncing on his shoulders as he went.

She memorized every nuance as he strode away, savoring their parting. When he was gone, her heart became like an anchor, sinking to her depths. Would it ever get easier? She doubted it.

Roxana examined the silver coin in her hand, admiring the crude impression of the king. She traced his face with her finger, already finding fault with the likeness, but she didn't care. At least, she could carry him with her from now on.

She closed her fist around the coin and placed it over her heart. "I pray to all the gods, Greek and Persian, keep him safe, so he can return to me."

CHAPTER TWENTY-EIGHT

The long, meandering caravan of weary army veterans, women, children, and animals headed along the bumpy road to the north. The promise of the crisp air offered in the southern portion of the Hindu Kush would be a welcomed break from the summer heat. Frequent stops were made to meet with Persian officials and deal with the numerous problems plaguing their excursion—broken supply wagons, runaway horses, blocked portions of the road, and hazardous weather.

Roxana's apprehension for her husband hounded her during the achingly slow journey. To combat it, she spent her days reading, writing him letters, sewing, but mostly sleeping. The monotony of the scenery, endless cliffs alongside the road, drove her to catch up on the sleep she'd surrendered during Alexander's recovery. Large meals of sweet cakes, lamb, Persian cheese, and bread also helped to encourage her growing affinity for long afternoon naps.

After she noticed her clothes were too snug, she combated her boredom by riding Hera alongside her wagon.

"You should be in this wagon," Morella scolded on a beautiful afternoon as the mountain breeze nipped her face. "It isn't proper for you to be riding alongside your wagon with your guards."

Roxana wanted to laugh at her maid's sense of decorum. After everything she'd been through, what did it matter if she spent some well-deserved time with her neglected Hera.

"I'm the wife of the king, Morella." She winked. "I can do as I please."

Physically, she was the woman she'd been before her pregnancy, but the girl who had married a king at the base of the Sogdiana Rock was gone forever. Her sorrow had reshaped her, making her wiser, braver, and more anxious about the future than ever before. Would it get easier? She didn't have an answer, but as long as Alexander kept writing her letters, she could survive.

But a few weeks after she regained her strength, his letters stopped. Desperation for news about her husband kept her from sleeping and eating. The weight she'd gained slipped away, and her lack of sleep made her numb inside. She sought out General Craterus on more than one occasion, asking if he had any word, but the upbeat man claimed everything was fine. She didn't believe him.

Her only respite was on her little mare's back, riding her through the mountain passes. She would enjoy the sun on her face and try not to think of her husband. It never did any good.

One chilly autumn afternoon as they halted to gather supplies from a nearby town, she exercised Hera next to a clear blue lake and received an unexpected visitor—General Craterus.

He jogged up to her horse, waving a letter. "Roxana, I have news of the king."

Her fingers shook so hard she couldn't hold her reins. She got off Hera, wanting to run to Craterus, but her legs barely held her upright as the sickening swell of fear took over her senses. She wanted to ask what he'd discovered, but her voice dried up.

He reached her and pressed his lips together. "I've just learned the governors who were supposed to be sending the king supplies as he crossed the Gedrosian Desert failed to do so. The king has been lost in the desert for some time now without food or water. You must prepare yourself. This desert is an inhospitable place and an army of men trapped without supplies might perish without a trace."

She bent over, feeling sick and let go of her reins. Hera stayed by her as if sensing her anguish.

"Is he dead?"

Craterus helped her to stand. "I honestly don't know. But we must hurry the caravan on to Carmania to get any news. The governors who withheld supplies are being arrested as we speak. The first group of the traitors will be brought before me in a few days. They will travel with us to Carmania. After this mess is finished, we will decide what to do with them."

She wanted to see the treacherous governors burn for their injustice. How could they turn on their king?

"How long before we reach Carmania?"

"Another thirty to forty days. Don't give up on him, Roxana. Alexander will be in Carmania when we arrive. He has the strength of a thousand lions. He will survive."

She found her reins while Craterus headed back to the camps. The numbness created by weeks without his letters spread into every crevice of her heart. The general's words gave her some hope, but not much.

How much longer will his strength last? How long before the last of those thousand lions have left him?

The thirty-five days of hard marching to the fertile farming territory of Carmania tortured Roxana. Not only was the trip arduous, but the uncertainty over her husband's fate took its toll. Her face thinned, her limbs withered away, but her hope for the safety of Alexander and his men never left her.

Fields of grain, vineyards, and paddocks filled with livestock hugged the road as they crept on toward the capital, Gulshkird. The abundance surrounding Roxana did little to offset her despair. Many of the women in the camp had the same overpowering sense of hopelessness as their wagons trudged ahead.

But news of the plight of the army in the Gedrosian Desert came when they neared the capital.

Morella climbed into the wagon, waving her arms one morning as Roxana prepared for another day on the road.

"My lady, he's alive. The king's alive."

Roxana yearned to believe her but the women's camp had swirled with rumors of the army since they had first arrived in the region. She didn't trust any of them.

She contained her excitement. "What did you hear?"

Morella smiled gleefully. "I was collecting water from one of the water wagons, and I overheard a cook say she was told by the lady's maid of Perdiccas's mistress, he received news the other day of the king's arrival in Gulshkird. He's alive and waiting for you."

Incensed Perdiccas had not come to her, but also skeptical, Roxana quickly finished dressing and went in search of her horse.

"Is it true?" she asked after riding ahead to join Perdiccas at the front of the long caravan.

"What are you doing up here?" Perdiccas's eyes seared into her. "Women are to remain in the rear of the procession."

Her patience shattered. "Tell me the news!"

Perdiccas ordered the soldiers riding beside him to fall back.

She encouraged Hera closer to his proud black stallion.

"He's alive. That's all I know." He kept his voice low as he checked around them. "They made it out of the desert, but it cost us twelve thousand good men."

She closed her eyes and pulled Hera up, horrified by the loss, but also exhilarated. Alexander was alive.

"He will be in Gulshkird when we get there," Perdiccas told her. "Put on some weight and make yourself presentable."

Her heart bursting, she turned Hera and headed back to the end of the long procession to resume her place with the women and treasure wagons.

Her husband had survived, and she could start living again.

A long twenty-five days later, the band of wagons, men, women, and children reached the gates of the market town of Gulshkird. The thick walls, sentry posts, shops, busy market center, and crowds of Persian inhabitants took some getting used to. After two years in India, the sound of her native language, aroma of familiar foods, and colorful clothing of her people felt like a warm embrace after a very long winter.

The sumptuous palace of the former local governor sat on a rise in the center of the thriving city. He'd paid for his treachery with his head, and now Roxana resided in his wife's rooms adorned with lapis lazuli-studded walls. With a private fountain, a grove of orange trees outside her garden door, and an inground pool, the accommodations impressed her. But where was the king?

After she settled in, Roxana sent Morella in search of her husband.

While palace servants worked around her, she paced the white marble floors of her luxurious suite of rooms, anticipating Morella's return.

"I found him," Morella breathlessly said as soon as she burst through the doors. "His rooms are on the far side of the palace. He hasn't received any visitors since returning from the desert. He wants no one to see him. Only General Hephaestion sits with him."

From her experiences in India, she knew why Alexander kept away—he was distraught.

Roxana ran from her rooms. She ignored Morella's insistence she change from her travel clothes or at least send a messenger to her husband first. But that wasn't her way. After the weeks she'd spent on the road, sick with fear, plagued by nightmares about his well-being, she had to see him.

Once outside the harem walls, Roxana ventured down the mosaic-tiled floor to the king's quarters, escorted by her ever-present protectors. At every sentry point along the way, the soldiers bowed their heads and let her pass.

Directed to a pair of gold leaf doors, she approached the two guards—boys, really—who stood at attention with their hands clutching their long Macedonian spears.

"I wish to see the king."

The taller of the two young men looked her over. "I have to announce you, my lady."

Roxana held his arm as he was about to step inside the open door. "I'll announce myself."

The flabbergasted sentinels didn't stop her when she entered the rooms. Roxana wanted to see her husband, and no one could get in her way.

The reception room was dark. Drawn curtains shut out the day, and only a single oil lamp burned on a stand. She could barely make out the décor, but as she scanned the walls, a growling griffin surprised her.

A hand grabbed her elbow, and she nearly jumped out of her skin.

Hephaestion stepped into the faint light, half his face left in shadows. Something was off about him.

"Hephaestion! You scared me to death."

She dragged him closer to the lamp.

Roxana swallowed hard when his entire face warmed in the light. Sickly thin, his skin was dry, cracked, and peeling from too much sun and wind. His clothes, always neatly pressed and form-fitting hung loosely on his frame. The familiar spark of mischief in his eyes was gone.

Sickened at the sight of him, she gripped his bony forearm. "What's happened to you?"

"The desert is a ruthless mistress." His voice was raspy and faint. "Sixty days in her care just about destroyed me."

She touched the wisps of gray in his hair. "I've heard stories, but I want the truth from you."

He went around her and leaned his back against the wall. "The omens were bad from the start. First, Peritas died as we traveled down the Indus, and then we hit the Gedrosian Desert. I've never in all my time during our campaigns suffered as we suffered in that blasted place."

She crept closer, her unease burning a hole in her stomach. "And Alexander?"

Hephaestion took a long breath. "He blames himself for the disaster. He's been in mourning for his men since our return." He rested a hand on her shoulder. "How well you look. Back to your old self. That will please him." His gaze rose to the inner chamber doors at the end of the rectangular room. "Go to him. He needs to see you. It will help him."

Without a second glance, she left Hephaestion and headed for Alexander's inner chambers.

Inside the doors, smoke from oil lamps hung thick in the air while shards of light snuck through the heavy curtains. Scattered about the floor were Alexander's trunks and boxes, filled with books and letters. Next to the window, his wooden desk. A massive bed of carved elephants sat at the end of the long room, but he was not in it. Then the creak of a chair came from a darkened corner.

"I'm afraid you will not like what you see, Roxana."

Alexander's voice was coarser than she remembered, but the sound of him sent a torrent of euphoria rushing through her.

She cautiously approached, craving just a glimpse of him. "You're alive. That's all that matters."

His contemptuous snicker circled the bedroom. "Alive? That is open to debate."

She wanted to offer him comfort, some encouragement after his ordeal. "You're here with me and whatever happened is behind you."

"It will never be behind me."

The bitterness in his voice sounded like it had risen from the depths of his desolated soul.

She crept close, yearning to hold him to her, and take away his misery.

"Tell me what happened to you. Let me understand, let me share your burden."

His hands came into the light, rough, cracked and bleeding in spots. Their grating sound repulsed her as he rubbed them together.

"It was my idea to go across the desert. Cyrus the Great had tried and failed. I thought with the fleet close for supplies we would fare well, but we lost track of the boats early on."

He coughed, and the ragged sound vexed her.

"The pack animals were the first to be killed off when our supplies dried up. Then the wagons and carts broke down in the deep sand. That meant the sick and wounded had to be left behind because there was no way to transport them. We could not worry about individuals; we had to save—" His voice broke.

She came around to the front of him. Tears welled as she pictured men left dying in the sands. How it must have destroyed him to leave them. He lived for his men.

He shifted on his stool. "We lost hundreds a day to heatstroke and starvation, and at night when we marched, many of the men fell asleep in their tracks. When we finally found a small stream in the desert, we rejoiced. Some of the men drank too much water and got sick. And then the rains came …" He sat forward on his stool, putting his head in his hands.

She could make out the outline of his wavy hair and ached to run her fingers through it.

He kept his head down as he went on. "Our small stream swelled into a raging river. Men, horses, weapons, and some of the women and children who had joined us were swept away. Even my tent and belongings were lost."

Roxana stood before him; his figure hunched in front of her, hiding his face. He reminded her of the beggars she'd seen in India. Men whose hunger had taken away their sanity, they knelt in front of her wagon or passing soldiers asking to be fed or killed.

With a tentative hand, he fingered her dress. "The heat and sand became overwhelming. Our horses grew weak, and all the men had to walk. And when we lost all hope, I rode ahead with a small group of men to scout out the area." A raspy breath escaped his lips. "That was when I was most afraid. Wondering if I would live or die. But then we made it to the sea and dug wells for water. When my belly was full of water, I realized what I had done. I'd killed my men."

She touched his extended hand. His rough, dry skin felt like the sands of the desert he had left behind.

"You must not think that way. You did everything you could for your men."

"There's still no word from the fleet and General Nearchus. If I have …" He raised his head, grasping her hand. "I felt certain I would never see you again. But you're here." He moved into the light. "You're more beautiful than even my memories of you."

She tensed as the breadth of his suffering manifested. The slim rays of light from the curtained windows caught his sunken eyes, the red and peeling skin on his face, his swollen and cracked lips, the hollow curve beneath his protruding cheekbones, and the streaks of gray in his wavy mane.

"My Alexander." She tossed her arms around him, the cut of his bones pressing into her. "You're here, and that's all that matters to me."

Chapter Twenty-Nine

For the next three days, the sun rose and fell, but Roxana doggedly remained in the king's rooms, caring for her husband's debilitated body and mind. She prepared oat baths for his skin, fed him his meals when his blistered hands could not hold his food, listened to his numerous stories of the march through the desert, read dispatches to him when his eyes could not focus, and slept in a chair by his bed, listening to his mumblings during his troubled dreams.

Exhausted, but not about to leave him, she prayed to the gods for something to lift his spirits.

Salvation came when on a rainy afternoon Hephaestion dashed into his chambers, waving a scroll.

"Alexander, great news. The fleet arrived a few days ago at the nearby port of Hormozia. They're all safe."

Roxana went up to her husband, thrilled they'd discovered his missing ships.

Alexander lifted her from the floor, spinning her around. "We must have feasts and games for the reunion of the men, the Indian campaign, and the march through the Gedrosian Desert." He put her down. "Go back to your rooms, order new clothes for the feasts, so you can outshine everyone as you always do."

She took in the red remaining in his eyes. "I should stay. You're not quite—"

"I will be fine for a few hours with Hephaestion." He kissed her forehead. "We have business to discuss."

She headed with her guards back to her chambers, hankering for a bath and a change of clothes.

"Ah, Morella," she said as she entered the doors to her suites. "Quickly, a hot bath, so I may return to the king. And send the dressmaker to me. I'll need new outfits made for the feasts the king is planning."

Roxana sensed something off about her maid's lackluster smile.

"What is it?"

Morella shut the doors after checking the corridor outside. She came up to Roxana, tight-lipped and wringing her hands.

"While you've been with the king, rumors have been flying around the palace about the Macedonian and Persian officials executed for their part in the Gedrosian disaster. Many at court are afraid. They say that eunuch has a strong influence over the king, and more Persian blood will flow."

Roxana kicked off her shoes. "No one influences Alexander but Alexander, but I can see why the Persian officials are upset. The king has been plagued with disloyal officials and governors ever since he left India. It would not take much to make him see guilt where perhaps none exists."

"Then is the gossip about the eunuch true, my lady? That he's a malicious deceiver, who wants revenge on those who wronged him in the court of Darius?"

"Not in my experience. He was kind to me when Alexander was injured. He could have ignored me, but he didn't."

Morella went to Roxana's dressing closet. "Ah, but you're the king's wife. To anger you, he would anger the king. He's not stupid. He knows whose ass to kiss."

She chuckled at her maid's coarse language. "You don't think I should trust him?"

"Not as far as you can throw him." Morella retrieved her blue robe. "Maybe the king's wife should try and offset the whisperings of his eunuch. I know the Persians in the palace would sleep easier at night if they believed it was your influence, and not that boy's, which steered the king down the right path."

Roxana followed her maid across her bedroom, impressed. "I might not always agree with what the king does, but I'm not sure I could talk him out of something once he made up his mind."

Morella set the robe over the back of a nearby chair. "You should try. It doesn't take much weight to tip the scales of justice from the wisdom of a king to the ravings of a tyrant."

Tyrant? She'd never thought of the king as anything other than just, but she'd only seen one side of him—the husband and lover.

Perhaps it was time to take more of an interest in her husband's affairs.

On the last day of the games, an exhausted Roxana relaxed with a book at her dining table. A breeze from her gardens brought in hints of orange blossom from her grove of trees, and even though it was winter, the birds still regaled her with their sweet songs. In the distance, the roar of the crowds at the amphitheater wafted in and out.

Morella entered her private chamber and set a tray of dates and wine at her table. The way her maid hovered, Roxana guessed she'd discovered a juicy piece of news. Morella always hovered when she had gossip.

"The harem quarters are buzzing, my lady." Morella set the dates on the table in front of her, a slight frown on her lips.

She selected a date, curious what could make her usually chipper maid so glum. "What is it? Are the women still angry they couldn't attend the games? I know it's a silly Greek tradition, but we all must observe—"

"It's not that." Morella twisted her fingers. "This might upset you."

She popped the date in her mouth and set down her book, more than intrigued.

"Go on."

Morella folded her hands, keeping her gaze on the floor. "The king judged a dancing contest among the men today. One of the men dancing was that eunuch."

Roxana sat back. "And?"

"The young man won the competition." Morella nervously cleared her throat. "And when he went to collect his laurel crown for the victory, the king kissed him."

Her first instinct, to disregard the event as an overrated rumor, quickly gave way to her concern for how the kiss would be interpreted by his men. In particular, those generals she'd worked very hard to win over.

"Was I wrong to tell you?" Morella asked.

Roxana wiped the sticky residue of the date from her fingers. "No. I'm glad you told me."

Did she rise above the whispers of the woman sure to accompany her in the corridors of the palace? Or did she do something, like confront the king?

How could loving a man bring so much pain and so much joy? Perhaps she needed some time to formulate a plan for the public reaction sure to come from the event. Putting some distance between her and the king might guarantee she would handle the situation rationally when they did meet again.

"Morella, put the outfit I was going to wear to the banquet tonight back in the trunk. I won't be attending."

"Should I send word to the king?"

She plucked another date from her tray. "No. I'm sure he won't mind."

The rays of the late afternoon sun crept through Roxana's bedroom window and spread across the marble floor. She sat on a bench, reading from a book of poems by a Greek named Pindar, enjoying her solitude.

From the outer reception area came the heavy footfalls of someone entering her rooms. She set aside her book. She'd been waiting for him to come to her, just not as quickly as this.

"Ah, there you are."

Alexander entered her room in a wrinkled tunic with a purple cloak haphazardly tossed over his left shoulder. He shut the decoratively carved doors to her bedroom and strolled toward her bench, a perplexed line between his brows.

"You weren't at the feast I gave last night for those Persian officials from Gedrosia. I thought you would be there."

She stood, hiding any hint of her inner turmoil. "I didn't know you wanted me there." She went around him, letting the long trail of her green silk dress follow her.

"You've been at every banquet I've given. I just thought you would be at that one." He followed her to a table filled with jugs of wine and honey water. "I've gotten so used to looking over and seeing you by my side, when you weren't there, it was rather disconcerting."

He coughed, which by itself was nothing, but the distress in his eyes worried her. It let her know the pain from the arrow wound had never left him—not that he would admit it.

She ran her hand across his brow, sweeping away a few wisps of gray hair—all that remained of his time in the Gedrosian desert. "You need rest."

"Never mind that." He took her in his arms. "Why weren't you at the dinner last night?"

She put a wall around her heart, wanting to speak her mind without letting her emotions take away her impulse.

"Your kiss is the reason why I didn't attend the party. Everyone is talking about it."

His lips thinned into an angry line. "I've told you before to ignore the malicious talk in the camps and come to me when you have questions."

His cold tone made her pull away. "I don't have any questions, only concerns."

"It was just a kiss. He won the dance contest, and the men were egging me on to kiss him, so I did. There's nothing more to it."

His words did not ease her pain. "Do you know what many are saying about him? About his influence over you?" She dropped her voice, accentuating her frustration. "Persians and Macedonians fear he will convince you to put more men to death. If you aren't careful, Bagoas will divide your officials. You've already had one mutiny. Do you want another?"

He tossed up his hands, the flush of anger on his cheeks. "You're exaggerating. You know nothing of politics or the aspirations of the ambitious men around me fighting to gain my favor. They will spread whatever lies they need to get ahead. Do not concern yourself with such matters, Roxana." He wiped his hand across the reddish stubble on his chin. "You're starting to sound like my mother."

The comparison hurt. The last thing she wanted was to be like the woman who drove him to exasperation.

She bowed her head, afraid she had made a mistake. "I'm sorry. I will not bring it up again."

His arms eased around her but did little to offset her disappointment. "I didn't mean to upset you. What I wouldn't give to run away from the meddlers, my ambitious officials, the court, and the dreary business of my empire to have some alone time with you."

Still upset over his dismissal of her concerns, she attempted to wiggle out of his embrace.

"You can't run away from your duty."

He refused to let her go. "Your happiness is more important to me than my duty. While I'm gone, I want you to promise whatever chatter you hear, you will know it has nothing to do with my feelings for you."

She sagged against him, weary of the constant packing and unpacking. "Where are you going?"

"I have to take a quick trip up to Pasargadae to check on the renovations I ordered for the tomb of Cyrus the Great." He let her go and returned to her refreshment table. "It will be just the Companion Cavalry, Perdiccas, some infantry, and a few of the elephant corps. We will be roughing it, so I will be sending you and the rest of the army, along with my scandal-loving court officials, with Hephaestion."

She raised her brows. "And will your bath attendant be joining you?"

"He will if you mention him one more time." He smirked and sniffed a jug of wine. "After I finish in Pasargadae, I will be heading to Persepolis."

Her concern about Bagoas dwindled at the mention of the former capital of King Darius. Everyone in Persia had heard what Alexander had done to the ceremonial capital and architectural showcase along the Pulvar River.

"My father used to tell me of the ancient tapestries, priceless treasures, statues of the gods, and countless belongings of the royal family housed at Persepolis. He cried the day he heard you burned it to the ground." She faced her husband, trying to fathom the reason for destroying so much history. "Why did you burn it, Alexander?"

"It seemed the thing to do at the time. We'd been drinking, quite a lot." He selected a goblet from her table. "Someone got the crazy notion to burn the city up, send it to the gods or some such nonsense. The things one does under the influence of wine can seldom be explained. I'm sorry I did such a reckless thing now."

His motivations for such a heartless deed revolved in her head. Had it been a drunken action, an impulsive one, or was there another reason? One she feared more than the others.

"Are you sure you didn't burn the city up to show your hate ... no, not hate, but maybe dislike for Persians."

"I don't dislike Persians, not at all. I married you, didn't I? Burning the palace had nothing to do with my feelings."

"Then if the palace is destroyed, why are you going back there?"

He snapped up the jug of wine. "Calanus, the Indian philosopher who travels with us, asked to see it." His face grew sober as he poured his drink. "He's been growing weaker since he joined our group in India. He's asked me to build him a pyre in Persepolis, so he can climb on top of it, and I can send him off to his next life."

She stared at him in open-mouthed astonishment. "A pyre? Do you mean burn him alive? Like what those husbands do to their wives? You can't be serious."

He put down the jug, frowning. "I refused at first, but it's what he wants. I must make sure he's seen off properly to please the gods." He sipped his wine.

She rubbed her arms, horrified by the image of such a monstrous death. "Do you think he will do it?"

Alexander set his goblet on the table. "He's a brave old man. I admire his seeing to his end with such dignity. What puzzles me is how he has said goodbye to many of my men and officers here in Carmania but insists he will not bid me farewell when the time comes."

The light in her window faded to dusk, and a chill washed over the room. "Why would he refuse you after all you've done for him?"

With a toss of his head, Alexander stepped up to her. "Because he says he will see me in Babylon soon enough."

The cold disappeared when his arms settled around her. "What is that supposed to mean?"

"Calanus believes every soul is reborn in a new body. I think he will be reborn in Babylon." He kissed her lips. "As our son."

A ribbon of panic wound its way around her heart and cinched so tight she couldn't breathe. "Perhaps he meant something else. Some misfortune you haven't considered."

"What's the matter with you this evening? First, you fear my bath attendant is plotting against me, and now you see doom in the dying words of a tired old man. This isn't like you."

She rested her head against him, wanting the reassurance of his warmth. "I'm sorry. Perhaps all the banquets and intrigue have tired me."

"Then we will stay here tonight and lock the doors." He nuzzled her cheek. "If we can't run away, then maybe we can steal a few hours for ourselves. It will be our last night together until I see you again in Susa."

She dreaded another long journey in the baggage train. "And why are we going to Susa and not staying here?"

"The royal palace of the king is there. I have meetings with officials and important duties I've long neglected."

Roxana noted the sadness in his voice. "Which duties?"

He tightened his arms around her. "Do you ever tire of questions, wife?"

"No. Do you ever tire of being king?"

He sighed and lowered his lips to hers. "Only when it keeps me from you."

CHAPTER THIRTY

Once Roxana's wagon stopped at the steps of the towering white stone palace in Susa, servants rushed out to greet her. The rectangular pools of bright blue water and gardens of towering citrus trees at the entrance took her breath away.

If this is the outside ...

Whisked along the arched white granite halls of the harem, she passed door after door bejeweled with pearls, sapphires, and amethysts.

The lavish decorations disappeared when the palace servants led her down another, smaller corridor. Her enthusiasm for the opulent accommodations faded when she arrived at an unadorned pair of wooden doors.

Inside was a narrow sitting area with no adjoining garden. The accommodations baffled her. This was reputed to be the most magnificent palace in Persia next to Babylon, so why was she given such paltry rooms?

"This is certainly a step down." Morella peered out the window to a minuscule pool of water.

The furnishings were modest, and the few decorative tiles set in the walls had swirls painted into them, but nothing of the caliber she had seen in the halls. The bed, made of cedar, had a lumpy mattress and barely enough room to sleep one comfortably.

Roxana decided she would sort out the arrangements with Alexander when he arrived. It must have been a mistake.

"I'd say this was built for a lesser wife or even a concubine." Morella collected one of Roxana's trunks the palace servants had brought in.

She scanned her trunks and sighed, not eager to unpack. "I've been living in my wagon and traveling tent for almost two weeks and any bed, no matter how small, has got to feel better than my hard cot."

Morella squinted, glancing back at the doors. "But who is in those fancy rooms we passed in the hall?"

Roxana glimpsed her maid's perplexed profile and chuckled. "I'm sure you will find out soon enough."

The beams of the morning sunlight trickled through the window in Roxana's dreary rooms on her second day in the palace. She sat at her rickety dining table, in a chair with a saggy seat and waited for Morella to return from the kitchens with her meal.

Once unpacked, the room appeared even smaller. The furniture she brought with her cluttered the black floors of her sitting area while trunks, waiting for servants to put them away, lay piled outside her bedroom door.

"The kitchens here are a gossip haven," Morella announced, coming through her chamber doors with a tray in her hands. "I found out the reason why we have such bad rooms."

Roxana eyed the cheese and fresh peaches on the tray. "What is their excuse for sticking the king's wife in rooms no bigger than my tent?"

"The family of Darius is here." Morella set the tray on the table. "A few daughters, and a prince of the former king. Plus, cousins, nieces, and nephews. Even the family of the former king, Artaxerxes, is here. Not much of them though. Some daughters and some nieces." Morella's eyes popped open. "Oh, I almost forgot about the old woman. Darius's mother, the great Sisygambis—she's here, too."

Why would Alexander come to a place filled with the family of the king he'd usurped? To her, it seemed odd.

"With all those people living in the place, I guess we shouldn't complain. We're lucky to have a room."

The raised voices of men came from the outer hall.

Roxana hesitated, not sure what to expect. Then the doors to her rooms burst open.

"Hello, Roxana." Alexander strolled in, followed by the elegant figure of Hephaestion.

Morella dropped to her knees.

Roxana stood, her heart thumping with happiness. He looked well, rested, and she wished to run to him and toss her arms around him, but she would have to wait until they were alone.

"Morella, fetch some wine for the king and general."

Her maid kept her head bowed until she shut the outer doors.

The corners of Alexander's mouth edged downward. "Sorry about the accommodations. It's only for a short time."

She didn't care. All that mattered was he had come to her. "I'm comfortable, Alexander." She turned to Hephaestion, greeting him with a smile. "It's good to see you again, General."

"Oh, you must congratulate Hephaestion. I've made him my chiliarch, or vizier. He's officially my second-in-command now." Alexander patted Hephaestion's shoulder.

A weight lifted from her heart. Should anything happen to Alexander, she knew Hephaestion, as his second, would secure her future and her children would be safe.

"It's a well-deserved honor, but you've always been Alexander's second, for you too are Alexander."

"Thank you." Hephaestion held out his closed hand to her. "I brought you a small gift. Something I saw and I thought you might enjoy." He opened his hand to reveal a long gold necklace cut to resemble thick rope.

That he had thought of her touched Roxana deeply. It was the first time he'd presented her with any gift, and on such a momentous day, made it all the more precious. She felt closer to the king and his friend than ever before.

She took the necklace, caressed the intricate detail, and marveled at the weight of it.

"It's beautiful. I shall treasure it always."

Hephaestion cleared his throat. "If you will excuse me. The other Alexander wants to be alone with you." He quickly left the room, closing the doors with a loud smack.

"Is something wrong?" Roxana faced her husband. "He seems out of sorts."

Alexander ducked to the side, avoiding her gaze. "Yes, ah ... perhaps he's nervous about his impending marriage."

Her husband's sheepish reaction added to her growing apprehension.

"Marriage? To whom?"

"Hephaestion is going to marry the daughter of Darius, Drypetis."

She attempted to gauge his feelings, but he remained impossible to read, as he usually did when he tried to keep things from her.

"When did this happen?"

"I've ordered it." He went to her table and inspected her plate of food. "All my generals are to take Persian wives. Ptolemy, Perdiccas, Nearchus, and the rest of my generals will have wives from the family of Darius. I'm acknowledging all the marriages of my men to Persian women made during the campaign. Their children will be considered legitimate, at least here in Persia. I'm trying to tie our two worlds together—Persian and Greek."

His grin seemed sincere, but she sensed there was more.

"When are all of these marriages to take place?"

"In a few days. There will be a great feast with dancing and music. It will be a wonderful celebration and to show the unity between our two worlds to assure everyone there will be peace from now on." He selected a slice of peach from her plate and popped it into his mouth. "I'm to take a wife as well. Two wives, actually."

The disclosure hit her like a punch to the gut. The air in the room became thin and her face flushed. She tried to keep her head held high, but the pain in her heart made her stoop over.

"Wives?"

He came up to her, putting a supportive hand on her shoulder. "You knew I would marry again. It's my duty. We've discussed this."

She wriggled out from under his hand, ready to pummel him. "That was before I spent more than two years being dragged through the mud, mosquitos, grime, rivers, deserts, and living for months at a time in a tent while you went off to kill people!"

His lips pressed together in a callous grimace.

"This will not change anything between us. I'm marrying Stateira, the daughter of Darius and Parysatis, and the daughter of the former king Artaxerxes. These women will link me with both branches of the Persian royal family. I have to set an example for the men. I'm struggling to fuse my Macedonian and Persian men together, and they need to see their king married to a Persian."

"You are married to a Persian! Me, remember? Or have I just been some passing fancy because I'm not of royal blood?"

His face turned a familiar shade of crimson. "You're not a passing fancy! Far from it. You know that."

His news scraped away every last fragment of hope Hephaestion's appointment had given her.

"By marrying the daughters of kings, you will make me a secondary wife, a lesser wife, a wife of no consequence. Is that what you want?"

"Roxana, calm down. Nothing has changed between us."

Her anger descended into grief. She thought of her dead son and her family. Of all the injustices she'd experienced, this was the most excruciating. Her voice, her influence, her life became inconsequential the moment he married women of royal blood.

"What about our children, Alexander? What is to become of them?"

"They will be great men."

"They will be dead men." She shoved him away and stormed to her bedroom.

He followed her. "No one will touch them, ever."

She stopped at her table and sank against it, her legs weakening as fear replaced her fight.

"No sons of a lesser wife will ever be left alive if those daughters of kings bear you a son. Sons of lesser wives are killed. I know. I've seen it." She wiped her nose on her sleeve. "My father has no brothers. Atimexis made sure no other sons came before her own." Her voice faltered as her distress tightened her throat. "In one sweep of your hand, you have just transformed me from a wife to a threat to the Persian throne."

"Enough!" His strident voice carried throughout her rooms. "I told you some time ago who I take to my bed is my affair and not yours. I am a king, and I will have other wives. My father had seven. A king must marry and produce children. You'd best keep that in mind, my lady." He started for the doors.

Enraged, Roxana picked up the first thing she could find—a small decorative cosmetic pot—and hurled it at him.

It hit him on the back of the head.

He stopped, nursing the tender spot and then faced her.

"You will not do that again."

"Other lovers I've learned to live with, Alexander, but this ..."

She stumbled to her bed and fell across the green covers, convulsing with sobs.

Through her tears, she saw him leave her rooms, and the pain cleaving her heart apart was as potent as the moment she'd seen her dead son. The loss of the only man she had ever loved, and the betrayal of her trust, curled her into a ball. She suddenly wished she could join her baby in those promised Elysian Fields.

Alexander shut the doors to her room and rested his head against the dark wood, eviscerated by her tears. The sting of his head where the pot hit him was nothing compared to the horrible burn in his stomach. He was a dog for hurting her—he knew that—but what choice did he have?

His father had warned him never to love a woman because the pain of hurting her when he took other wives would destroy him.

He was right.

The weight of his duty kept him from returning to her rooms. She would survive it, as would he. But would she still want him, trust him, be with him again? Losing her was the one defeat he could never accept.

"So how did it go?"

Hephaestion waited with his arms folded, leaning against the wall, his lower lip fixed in a glum pout.

Alexander pushed away from the door and stiffened his back. "I don't know who it hurt more—her or me."

His friend ambled closer in his casual way. "She's been your wife without exception for over two years. Did you think she would accept your new wives without a fight? This is Roxana we're speaking of, after all."

Alexander pressed his fist to his lips, wishing he could seek the counsel of the gods.

"What would you have me do, not marry?" He punched the air, more frustrated than ever. "You were the one who reminded me when I married Roxana that I'd already declared my intention to the royal family and had to keep it. So that's what I'm doing—honoring my word."

"That was before we both got to know her." Hephaestion's voice sounded as heavy as Alexander's heart. "Now she's become a part of us, a part of you. I care for her, and do not wish to see her hurt."

"I never wished to hurt her, but I have no choice. Stateira and Parysatis will be marriages of state. Roxana was …"

"A marriage of passion," Hephaestion said, finishing his words.

"Passion, yes. She's always been that and so much more. Why else would I put her through the hell she's braved to stay with me." He wiped his face, drained of every morsel of energy. "What if she never forgives me?"

Hephaestion clapped his hand over Alexander's shoulder. "Love is forgiveness—isn't that what Calanus always said? Now you must love her more than ever to make her forgive you."

He remembered the religious man who had climbed the pyre at Persepolis and wished he could consult with him now.

"How do I do that?"

Hephaestion urged Alexander along the hallway. "I have no idea."

CHAPTER THIRTY-ONE

The strains of harps, flutes and laughter from the wedding feast floated throughout the palace and into Roxana's room. Morella kept sending concerned glances her way, but Roxana ignored her. She lay on her bed, exhausted, emotionally empty, and wishing she could go home to Bactria.

"Men are pigs." Morella angrily tugged her thread through her sewing. "All the things you've been through, and the stupid man takes more wives."

Roxana slid her legs over the side of the bed, aching for movement, but her heart wanted to stay curled up in her sheets.

"Please, Morella, talk of something else."

Her maid slammed her sewing down on her bench by the bed. "You know they're saying he's marrying General Hephaestion to Stateira's sister because Alexander wants to be the uncle to his children."

Wishing she could be alone, but at the same time thankful for the companionship, Roxana went to the window that overlooked her tawdry pool.

A burst of laughter wafted through her bedroom doors. She closed her eyes, attempting to shut out the joy the rest of the palace celebrated.

"You're not the only one unhappy, my lady." Morella came up to her. "The other generals, they say, are not too keen on these marriages. And I hear Stateira is almost as tall as her father. Darius was one of the tallest men in Persia. I wonder how the short and stocky Alexander will feel about bedding a Persian giant."

The mention of Alexander in bed with another sent her to her goblet. But the cup was empty.

She held up the silver chalice to her maid. "Morella, get me some wine."

Morella walked quickly out of the room.

Roxana sank onto her bed, still holding her goblet. She wanted to go back in time and relive the day she'd agreed to marry the king. She should have fought harder to resist Alexander, refused her father's pleas, risked everything and run away—any other outcome would have been better than this.

But you found love. Isn't that worth something?

The *clunk* of a ceramic jar on her refreshment table made her get up. She took her goblet to the table.

"Leave me."

Roxana topped her goblet off with straight wine and refrained from adding a drop of water.

"If you don't add some water to that, you'll get very sick," Morella scolded in a soft voice.

"Please, Morella. I need to be alone."

Roxana took a long sip. The bitter flavor hit her tongue. She grimaced, hoping the more wine she drank, the less she would notice the offensive taste.

Morella gave her one last sigh and left her room.

Roxana didn't care what her maid thought.

She drank deeply, almost emptying the cup with one gulp. She choked back the urge to vomit as the wine settled in her stomach. When it passed, she refilled her goblet.

The more you drink, the less you will hurt.

A bout of lightheadedness gripped her. She quickly guzzled more wine, hoping the sensation would turn to numbness.

The refrains of laughter from the wedding party continued to find their way into her room, but the wine didn't lessen her pain. It created a veil of fog to mask it.

Time would ease the constant throbbing in her heart—she'd learned that with her son—but never eliminate it entirely. Even the gods were at time's mercy because none of them, Greek or Persian, could ever stop it from moving forward.

Hephaestion negotiated the brightly painted corridors of the women's quarters on his way to Roxana's rooms. The perfume in the air was too thick for his taste, the fat eunuchs disgusted him, and the willowy women wearing sheer frocks and batting their eyelashes made him want to hurry back to the safety of the army.

The reports from her maid were not what he'd expected. He knew she was upset, but spending her days drunk in bed was not the Roxana he knew. He could forgive it when she'd lost her child, but she had not lost Alexander. Hephaestion planned to make sure she was well aware of that fact.

Her guards stiffened to attention when he approached. Hephaestion never acknowledged them and thrust the doors open, wanting the noise to announce him, not the soldiers. He was too angry to be formal.

He walked into her rooms to find her curtains drawn and a dismal darkness everywhere. The air was thick with the bitter aroma of old wine, smoke from oil lamps, and the faintest hint of jasmine.

Trunks hugged the walls of the sitting area. Her servants should have taken them to storage when she first arrived.

Shoddy organization in this place. Wish I had a week to straighten it up.

At her bedroom doors, he showed the same determination and shoved them open, letting them strike the walls as he entered.

He strolled into the room, and the darkness annoyed him. He couldn't see anything.

A loud gasp accompanied him to the window. He quickly drew back the curtain, letting in the bright morning sun.

When he spun around, he discovered her maid.

"Get your lady some food and pack her things," he barked in Persian.

The maid didn't hesitate and scurried from the bedroom, never raising her head to look at him.

He went to the bed, searching the mound of blankets for her. He debated what to do, but then he decided to throw decorum out the window. He yanked back the covers, not caring if she was naked. She had to get out of that damned bed, even if he had to drag her by the hair to do it.

"Get up!"

She lay curled on her side with her back to him, her lovely rich brown hair fanned out on the pillow. Slowly, she rolled over to him.

Her snow-white skin shocked him. Her cheeks had lost their pink hue and her lips their reddish tinge. He could barely see the green in her bloodshot eyes.

She sat up, covering her face and wincing at the light. When her eyes opened all the way, her expression switched from confused to angry.

"What do you want?"

He took her elbow and lifted her into a sitting position. "Your maid came to see me. She's says all you've done for three days is drink."

Like an old woman, pained with every movement, she grimaced as she eased her legs over the side of the bed.

"How is married life, General?"

The question siphoned away his anger. Silently berating his harsh treatment, he let go of her arm.

"You're being silly, Roxana. All the wine in the world won't help."

She struggled to lift her head, displaying a smug smirk. "How is your wife?"

He recalled the brown-eyed waif he had spent the last three days patiently indulging with attentive kisses and lots of hand-holding. She still acted terrified in his presence, but after their second night in bed together, he was thankful she'd stopped trembling when he touched her.

"Drypetis is a sweet girl, but I did not choose her. She was chosen for me."

"I'm very happy for you." Roxana stretched for her goblet on the table next to her bed.

Hephaestion snatched it away, flinging it to the floor. "Do you think, for one moment, Alexander could stop loving you because he had to marry another. This isn't about how he feels—it's his duty. He would have never agreed to marry either of those girls if he'd known you at the time."

A single teardrop landed on her wrinkled Persian dress, soiling the linen.

The sight made him close his eyes, chastising his stupidity.

"I'm sorry. Men of war are not very good when it comes to words of love. I'm sure Alexander is better at telling you his feelings than I could ever be at relaying them."

She sniffled and wiped her nose on her sleeve. "I know Alexander's feelings for me haven't changed. But the situation between us has."

"I don't see it that way."

"Before, it was only me, but now I've become a secondary wife and will have to come behind his royal wives, will have lesser rooms, smaller staff, and his time will be divided. He was all mine." She snickered. "Well, not all mine. I had to share him with the army, you, his generals, Bagoas—"

"He's still all yours." He took her hand. "You haven't spent a lifetime sharing him with the world: I have. Take a piece of advice from one who knows him better than most—he doesn't abandon those he loves. He has taken you across the world with him because he would not leave you, and he won't leave you now."

She yanked her hand out of his, a flat, empty look on her face. "I wish I could believe you.

Roxana settled back in her bed and curled on her side, ready to return to sleep.

Her stubbornness, her disregard for all his patience and understanding reignited his frustration.

He was about to walk away when the jug of water on the table next to her bed gave him an idea.

He lifted it and poured the cold water over her head.

She jumped up, screaming. "You bastard!"

He threw the empty water jug on her bed. "Now that I have your attention ... Pack your clothes and get dressed. You're coming with me."

She wiped her face. "Where?"

"Opis. Alexander has decided to take a cruise with Nearchus down the Eulaeus River to the Persian Gulf. I'm to take the army and meet him at Opis."

He strode to the bedroom doors, his mind already on all the other things he had yet to do to prepare the army to leave.

"Will the new wives be joining us?"

Her mocking tone brought him to a halt at the doorway.

"No. Stateira and Parysatis are to stay in Susa, along with my wife Drypetis." He glanced over his shoulder. "He wants you in Opis."

He had to admit, with her hair wet, her cheeks rosy, and her eyes glaring at him, she was a formidable woman.

"Get ready to move out. We leave at sunrise."

In the corridor, Morella waited just down from the sentries. She didn't grovel when their eyes met. She raised her head and came up to him.

"You spoke to her?" she said in Persian.

Morella reminded Hephaestion a great deal of the woman she served.

"I think she understands the situation now. Get her ready to travel."

"Thank you, General." She went to the doors. "I knew you would get through to her. She's as stubborn as a mule."

He chuckled as he walked away.

Just like Alexander.

CHAPTER THIRTY-TWO

Through the window in her wagon, Roxana caught glimpses of the small towns packed with merchants, soldiers, women, children, and livestock. Life teemed along the royal road to Opis, from every stone house, market square, merchant shop, or field of ripening grape vines. But she felt far removed from the world outside.

She never ventured to join the other women in the baggage train when their caravan stopped to rest. Even a few days after her drinking bout, her head hadn't fully recovered. Her heart definitely hadn't.

She spent her time thinking about the endless travel, the agony of loving Alexander, the gossip, the loss of her son, the generals, and the devastation of battle. At night in her little tent, questions about her future plagued her. Did she have a future with the king, or was the best behind them?

She hated Alexander for what he had done—putting her one step above a concubine. But then, when she admired the night sky, their times together would streak across her mind like a shooting star. He'd been honest about taking other wives and lovers. He had not abandoned her. And he had not stopped loving her, but had she stopped loving him?

By the time the baggage train reached Opis, Roxana had accepted her fate. She had no other choice. Women had no say in their lives, and the only way the wife of the king could leave her husband was to die.

Numb with hopelessness, Roxana mindlessly walked through the corridors of the beautiful white palace by the Gyndes River, blind to the tapestries on the walls or the painted dolphins on the floors.

Her rooms did awaken a spark of interest. With colorful murals of ocean creatures and sky-blue tiles from floor to ceiling, they overlooked the glistening river. Instead of gardens outside of her rooms, she had a small piece of beach all to herself.

"Now this is more like it." Morella went to the window and breathed in the fresh air. "Very nice. Better than Susa."

Roxana didn't say anything. She didn't want to discuss Susa ever again.

While Morella supervised the servants unpacking her trunks, Roxana realized how tired she'd grown of her adventures. The new names and faces she had to remember, the different customs she had to follow, and the patience she needed with each new household weighed her down. When would the travel end in a home with friends and family? Love, loss, war, and all her time on the road had finally broken her. And her gloom snuffed out the last traces of the inner fire that had won her a king.

Roxana picked at the porridge served while the morning sun streamed into her bedroom through the open window. A pounding on her doors almost made her drop the pretty glass cup of watered-wine served with her breakfast.

"Maybe it's the king?" Morella suggested.

Roxana went to her bed to collect her robe, aggravated by her maid's hopeful tone.

"The king doesn't knock, Morella."

"Is she here?" a deep voice boomed in Persian.

In a breastplate made of thick layers of linen and short chiton, a man with familiar brown eyes strolled into the center of her bedroom.

He held out his arms. "Roxana, do you not recognize your brother?"

"Histanes!" She went to him, desperate for the embrace of someone familiar. "You've grown since last I saw you."

Morella bowed and slipped out the open doors.

"I'm a man now." He gave her a quick hug and stepped back. "General Hephaestion suggested I come and see you. He says you've been upset since Alexander's weddings. Is this true?"

Hephaestion's meddling annoyed her. "The general shouldn't have asked you to come."

"But I wanted to come." Histanes poked out his chest like a proud peacock. "To bring you news of my promotion. I've been posted to a special unit of all Persian officers. Additional men are coming from all over the empire to join our ranks. They're to be trained as Macedonians. The king plans to send his old or disabled soldiers back to Greece and replace them with Persians. Word around the camps is he prefers Persian troops to his old Greek ones."

She had enough experience with Greeks to guess how they would take the news of their Persian replacements.

"What do the Greek soldiers think of this plan?"

He wiped a smudge of mud from his cuirass. "The king is to announce his decision once he returns from his trip to the ocean, but I'm sure they will get used to the idea in time. They hate all Persians, but the whispers in the camp say the king believes their attitude will change as more Persians enter his army."

The churning in her stomach intensified. "I wish I could believe that, Histanes, but I've spent more time dealing with the Greeks' dislike of Persians than you."

"Whose side are you on, Roxana? You were raised Persian, not Greek. You should be happy they're leaving our land."

She went back to her dining table, her appetite replaced by nagging suspicion.

"I'm married to a Greek king—any child I have will have to lead both Greek and Persian men. I can no longer afford to choose sides."

His abrasive chuckle cut into her. "But that was before Alexander took royal wives. Their sons will lead men; your son will be no better than me."

The reminder of her humiliation incited her fury.

Instead of chastising him, Roxana flopped into her chair.

"Take my advice, Histanes, steer clear of the gossips."

"I thought you more than—"

Hephaestion cleared his throat from her open bedroom door. "Sorry to interrupt," he said in Greek while nodding to Histanes. "I came to see if you had settled in."

An edgy friction rose between the three of them. For Roxana, it was as if she were torn between her Greek world and her Persian one.

"Thank you, General, for checking on me."

"I should get back to the camps." Histanes showed her his profile. "Good to see you, Roxana."

His mud-stained cloak flapping behind him, her stepbrother rushed past Hephaestion and into the outer chambers.

His footfalls grew fainter until the *thud* of her closing outer doors sounded. To Roxana, the sudden silence represented an ending. The last connection to her family and her Persian past had been severed. The handsome Greek general she regarded as a friend stepped into her room and her nostalgia abated.

"I overheard the tail end of your conversation and thought I should step in. I hope you're not angry with me."

"Never with you, Hephaestion." She pushed her porridge to the side and folded her hands. "My feelings for Alexander are another story."

He spied the river beyond her windows. "These marriages were a matter of state; or more to the point, marrying Stateira was to please Sisygambis. She wanted to see Alexander married to her granddaughter. He didn't want to upset the old woman, so he made a great feast of it and married all of his generals to Persian women."

"I understand. He doesn't love either woman."

He pulled out the chair across from her. "The marriages were business. Your marriage was not. He will always put you first."

"Will he? I'm not convinced of that anymore." Uncomfortable reopening old wounds, she changed the subject. "Is it true what Histanes said about Alexander sending troops home?"

"Yes, he plans to announce his intentions when he arrives the day after tomorrow ... although, half the men know already. He's sending Craterus with them."

The mention of the crusty general she had come to respect shocked her. "Craterus?"

He examined her delicate drinking glass. "Alexander will be sending him back to Macedon to take over as regent. He's ordered his current regent, Antipater, to come to Persia."

The shakeup intrigued her. What was her husband up to?

"Why the change?"

Hephaestion's nonchalant shrug did nothing to assuage her curiosity.

"Olympias fights Antipater on everything. Alexander is tired of being a go-between and having to put up with his mother's tantrums. He believes Craterus will handle her better than Antipater."

She stretched for her wine. "You make her sound like a very disagreeable woman."

"Disagreeable is a nice way of putting it." He arched an eyebrow. "I'm surprised Alexander hasn't mentioned his constant bickering with Olympias."

"No." Roxana rolled her glass in her hands. "Alexander has always spoken highly of her."

"Olympias is his mother—he loves her, but she also drives him insane. Half the time I think he's stayed so long out of Greece to get away from her. She's overly devoted to her son and continually involves herself in his affairs. Be careful with her. Many do not trust her, me included."

A chill settled over her. "I hope I never meet her."

"Don't worry." Hephaestion paused as Morella carried in a jug of wine and a tray of dates. "If I know Alexander—and I do—he will never bring you back to our homeland while she's alive. He will spend the rest of his days traveling, conquering cities, and building his empire until Olympias is laid out on her funeral pyre. Only then will he go home."

On a warm day at high tide, Alexander's thirty-oared ship arrived at the docks. Roxana took in the festivities from her balcony in the palace. Before Susa, she would have tingled with excitement to see him again; now, she had little interest in the processional parade as it wound from the docks and through the city gates.

Troops attending the parade moved out from the crowd and shouted at the king. What was said, she could not make out, but the gestures were unmistakable. The men were angry, and she could guess why. They had gotten wind of Alexander's orders for his veterans to return home and the new Persian troops sent to replace them.

The jeers and hissing carried up to her balcony as the procession made its way to the palace. Even from her vantage point, she could see Alexander's red cheeks and sense his fury.

Roxana feared the men had gone too far. *Angering a lion will only make him eager to draw blood.*

When Morella brought word of how a furious Alexander retreated to his rooms and refused to see anyone, except Hephaestion, Roxana wasn't surprised.

"Shades of the mutiny in India," she told her maid.

But Alexander would get his way in the end. He always did. It was how he had conquered the world, and her.

Early one morning, when the cries of men outside the palace walls compelled her to her bedroom window, she smirked at the scene below. Macedonian troops crowding the palace called, cried, and pleaded for Alexander to forgive them. They threw their shields, swords, and long spears to the ground, begging for him to take them back in the army.

"Seems the king's ploy to replace his Greeks with Persians has only made his men love him more," Morella said as she took in the begging soldiers.

Roxana pitied his men. Alexander had betrayed them with Persian replacements, the same way he had betrayed her with his new wives.

A great cheering came from the grounds. She stuck her head out the window to see what all the commotion was about.

Alexander appeared below, walking among the men, without his king's guard and wearing Persian clothes. He embraced every soldier, hugging them, kissing them, and shedding tears of joy. The men wept too, and some broke out in shouts, praising their king. Others collected their arms and made their way back to the camps, laughing and singing songs of victory.

Roxana ducked inside as the ruckus continued. "It would seem everyone forgives Alexander everything."

Morella rested her elbow against the ledge. "Have you forgiven him, my lady?"

"No." She went to her bed and snapped up her robe. "I can't change my stars, but I have learned to live with them."

Morella came up to the bed and helped her with her robe. "Knowing your husband, there will be banquets to celebrate this reconciliation with his men. He loves celebrating, your Greek king. You might want to start thinking about what outfit to wear."

Roxana blanched at the idea of attending any party given by the king. "If he has a banquet, I will not attend."

"Nonsense. The king would want you to be there." Morella went to a nearby trunk and lifted the lid. "You should go and look your best."

Roxana's determination reawakened as if from a long slumber. She peered out the window at the setting sun while the cheers of men still drifted into her bedroom.

"He has made my position very clear. I'm only a secondary wife. Until he orders me to his side, I will stay away."

The raucous singing of drunk men echoed throughout the palace. Spindly threads of early morning sunlight stretched toward Alexander's feet as he stood inside Roxana's bedroom. He'd left the Persian and Greek officials still drinking to his health at the banquet to celebrate his reconciliation with his troops because he couldn't stop thinking of her.

Roxana had not come to the dinner, and her face, her eyes, her giggle, and her smile had haunted him. He could not eat or even drink without her by his side.

Fed up with his longing, he decided he would confront her and demand to know why she'd abandoned him. But standing in her bedroom and watching her sleep, his courage disintegrated.

Alexander drank in her face as she lay in her bed decorated with seashells. He hated what he had done to her. The marriages had been as painful for him as they were for her. To bed two women he didn't love was uncomfortable. His nights with Stateira and Parysatis only had made him miss Roxana's arms even more.

He leaned against the wall, bathed in shadows, taking in the rise and fall of her chest. Could she ever forgive him? Did she still love him? He'd asked the same questions so many times he'd lost count.

She stirred and stretched, the sound of her movement coaxed him away from the wall. He went to the foot of her bed.

"You were not there tonight."

She sat up and when she saw Alexander, she pulled the sheets around her neck and drew her knees in tight.

"How long have you been standing there?"

"Not long." He removed the purple and white ribbons of his diadem from his head. "I was watching you sleep. You do not sleep peacefully, my wife."

She got up and reached for a long robe to cover her sheer nightgown.

"Which of us wives would you be referring to?"

He played with the ribbons of his diadem. "Is that why you didn't come to the banquet tonight? I've already told you my marriages—"

"You did not order me to go," she interrupted, tying off her robe.

Her words hurt more than the arrow that had pierced his chest. "I have to order you to be with me now, is that it?"

"I'm a lesser wife. I have to be told what you want of me. I can't imagine you would want me around all the time. That's only something a queen can presume."

His heavy cuirass suffocated him, so he yanked off his cloak and flung it to the floor. Then he pried the breastplate and backplate from his torso, snapping the ties securing it. Alexander hurled the armor against the far wall where it clanged as it came to rest.

She lifted an eyebrow. "Feel better now?"

He charged up to her, wanting to quell the rebellion in her eyes, but also wanting to take her in his arms and never let go.

"I will not beg for your company, Roxana."

Her insolent smirk didn't surprise him. He'd pushed her too far, but how to make amends?

"I will not seek your company unless I'm ordered to do so. You have left me with no other choice, my king."

If he had to play this silly game, then so be it.

"If that's the way you want it. We will be leaving for Ecbatana soon. Have your bags packed and ready to go on with me. You're ordered to keep company with me there." He stopped and took a breath, fighting to stay calm. "I'm having games to celebrate a festival to our gods. You will be at those games with me, at my side at all times." He moved in closer, the jasmine on her skin taunting him. "Is that understood?"

"Yes." She dipped her head. "I was under the impression women were not allowed at such events."

"They are now!" He balled his fists, wanting to strike something.

A sharp pain cut across his right chest, taking away his breath. The warmth drained from his limbs. He closed his eyes and swayed.

Her arms went around him. Her hair tickled his cheek.

He opened his eyes while Roxana eased him onto her bed.

"You've had too much wine, Alexander."

He wiped the sweat from his brow as he sat.

She removed her robe and poured water from her bedside jug on the fabric. Then she wiped his face.

The water replenished him, and the pain receded.

He pushed her hand away. "It's not the wine. Now and then I get a little weak, that's all."

She dropped the wet robe to the floor. "You need more rest. You can't do everything."

"I will rest at Ecbatana. It's nice there. The mountain breezes will bring some relief to this hot autumn season." He reached for her hand and raised his head to her. "I've missed you, little star."

The line of her lips softened and the coldness in her gaze retreated. The change gave him hope.

He sank into the bed, tired of always fighting to keep those he loved around him. When had that happened? His energy never faltered, but lately, he had to push harder to get through the day.

She sat next to him, holding his hand. "I thought your new Persian wives were keeping you company. I've heard princess Stateira is quite beautiful, and that Parysatis has the body of a goddess."

He frowned, running his fingers over her soft skin. "Stateira is too tall for me, and Parysatis has the face of a cow. Besides, they are not you. No one is."

Encouraged by her touch, he kissed her lips, tenderly at first, afraid she might pull away.

She trembled, but then became impatient for more. Alexander wrapped Roxana in his arms, lowering her to the bed.

"How can you defeat me with just a kiss?" she murmured into his wild hair.

"The same way you vanquish me every time you smile."

He slid the sheer fabric of her nightgown over her head. He luxuriated in the fullness of her hips and the swell of her breasts.

Roxana sat up on her elbows. "Why do you think it's this way between us?"

He chuckled and stood back from the bed. "Who can know why the gods do what they do?"

When the last of his clothes fell to the pile around his feet, he climbed on top of her.

Her hands roamed his broad back, tracing the thick muscles all the way down to his round butt.

"Will this desire ever fade?"

"Not even after my last breath has been cast to the stars." His arms tightened around her. "I will never stop wanting you."

CHAPTER THIRTY-THREE

The heat receded and the arid plains turned into crisp mountain passes as Roxana's wagon followed the baggage train and army to Ecbatana—the summer residence of the Persian kings. Clear blue lakes filled with geese and ducks accompanied her to the stone city gates, but the serenity of the land did nothing to appease her uncertainty.

She vacillated during her trip over her feelings for the king. At times, her love for him returned, and then his betrayal would once again harden her heart.

But when her wagon rolled through the city gates, she decided it best to dedicate herself to rebuilding their relationship. She also hoped the tiered gardens and scenic views from the mountain retreat would give the king time to rest.

Her rooms in the western portion of the main palace received more of the fresh mountain air than any other part of the complex. With a private garden, complete with a swan-filled pond, and six gardeners, her residence also boasted a private stable with a lush green field for Hera. Fifteen servants and three cooks were at her disposal, along with grooms and a seamstress. Ecbatana was the closest she'd come to being treated like a queen.

Roxana attended the first day of games right after her arrival. The murmurings of the crowd in the amphitheater as she took her seat next to the throne of the king brought a flutter to her belly. Alexander's reassuring squeeze on her hand calmed her, and by the time the first event—riders exhibiting their horsemanship skills—entered the arena, her nerves had left her.

That night, Roxana sat alone in her quarters, reading a book, when a light rapping came from her door.

"The king wishes to see you, my lady," her guard announced.

She tugged at the loose-fitting robe over her nightgown, checking the empty passageway outside her rooms. "Is everything all right."

The young man dipped his head. "He's with General Hephaestion and wishes for you to join them."

Before their time together at Opis, she would have slammed the door on the poor guard, but her heart had softened. Roxana had not forgotten Alexander's other marriages or forgiven him, but she'd discovered she was happier with him than without him.

Escorted by her guards, she arrived in front of the king's ebony doors carved with the winged disc of the great god Ahura Mazda. Before entering the rooms, she smoothed her gold-trimmed Persian coat, wondering if she should have worn Greek attire. She'd been so excited to see the king, she'd not taken the time to choose an appropriate outfit.

The black walls of the reception room came across as cold and decidedly masculine. Then the laughter of men, from a sitting room to the side, coaxed her deeper into the royal rooms. She peeked inside an arched doorway. Her husband sat on a couch stuffed with pillows. Across from him was Hephaestion, a silver goblet in his hands.

"We should explore the Hyrcanum Sea, as well as find out where it goes." Alexander lifted his goblet to his friend.

Hephaestion noticed Roxana at the doorway. "Ah, there she is."

Alexander patted the seat next to him. "Come sit here, my wife. I want to tell you of my plans."

Roxana sashayed across the room and took her place at his side.

"You're too drunk to talk of plans, Alexander." Hephaestion adjusted his pillows, letting his wine slosh.

"You're just as drunk as me." Alexander scowled. "And what's wrong with exploring the Hyrcanum Sea? We need to discover if there's a passage to India. It would help trade immensely. You know I'm right."

Hephaestion raised his goblet to her. "Do you see the things I have to put up with, Roxana? He's such a temperamental brat."

She broke out into a fit of giggling. She'd forgotten how much joy the two men brought her. It was like before they had crossed the Hindu Kush to India, they were happy again.

"You're like children. After everything you two have been through, I would expect a little more maturity."

A wobbly Hephaestion set his goblet on the floor and struggled to stand. "I'm too tired and too drunk to be mature."

Roxana jumped to his aid and placed a steadying hand on his arm. His skin was burning up.

"Hephaestion, you have a fever." She cupped his face. "Are you sick?"

A pang of guilt rolled through her. She was well aware Alexander had been working too hard, but she'd never acknowledged Hephaestion's fatigue. He always pushed himself as much as the king.

He removed her hands. "It's just a chill. I've had it for a few days. It will pass."

The king came over to Hephaestion's side. He felt his friend's hot cheeks.

"Let's not take any chances." He turned to Roxana. "Tell the sentries to send the physician, Glaucias, to Hephaestion's chamber."

Roxana proceeded to the ebony doors and barked her orders to the sleepy-eyed young men.

The shorter of the two sprinted away.

Back in the sitting room, Alexander had his arm around Hephaestion's waist. "I need to get him to bed. You go on back to bed, too."

She didn't want to leave them, especially not with Hephaestion being ill. What if something happened and she wasn't there?

"Let me help. Let me tend to him."

"No, I will have the physician look in on him." Alexander supported an unsteady Hephaestion as they hobbled from the room. "We've done this before, haven't we, old friend?"

"I'll be fine." Hephaestion snickered at Alexander. "I can walk myself."

"No, you can't, you'll fall."

"You're such a nanny goat, you know that, Alexander?"

They headed out the lavish doors of the king's chambers.

She waited at the doorway as the men, followed by Alexander's guards, made their way toward Hephaestion's rooms. Their laughter reassured Roxana's hopes everything would be fine, but the dread she'd felt when she'd touched Hephaestion's flushed face had not abated. If she could not be at his side to attend to him, then she would pray for his recovery. Because without him, Alexander was sure to be lost, and so would she.

The games continued the next day with contests of skill in weaponry, but Hephaestion's and Alexander's absence from the royal box at the amphitheater alarmed Roxana.

"How is your chiliarch this morning?" she asked General Perdiccas, the *ding* of swords against shields coming from the ring below.

His guarded smile hinted at his concern. "The doctor says the fever has run its course and prescribed quiet and rest. Alexander is with him, won't leave his side. He's ordered for Hephaestion to have no visitors."

"I should go and check on them."

Perdiccas clasped her hand as she rose from her chair. "Even you must stay away. The king will call when he needs you."

She resumed her seat but could not sit still.

After the morning's events ended, she retired to her rooms, desperate for any word.

But the ample supply of hearsay she'd relied on had dried up completely. She suspected Alexander had clamped down on the gossip hounds in the palace. But why didn't he want to share anything with her?

Roxana spent the night tossing in her bed. By morning, when Morella brought her breakfast tray, she feared the worst.

"I have no news." Morella set her plate of bread and cheese in front of her. "The whole palace is buzzing about the general's illness, but no one knows for sure how he is."

A knock on her chamber doors interrupted her breakfast. A member of the king's guard entered the room and bowed to her.

"The king wishes you to join him in the royal box today, my lady. He will be there."

She wanted to hug the young man.

Morella turned to her after the soldier left. "See? All that restlessness for nothing. I told you that general was tough."

The sun was bright, the air invigorating, and Roxana's spirits lifted when she sat next to the king. The ravenous eyes of the crowd focused on Alexander let her know she wasn't the only one curious about Hephaestion's health.

"How is he?"

Alexander patted her hand. "Better. The diet of broth is helping the gut, the doctor says. He is even grumbling about being hungry, which means he's on the mend. Hephaestion always starts complaining when he's feeling better."

"I'm so glad. I've been worried."

Then a roar reverberated inside the amphitheater. The start of the boy's race brought the crowd to their feet. Alexander stood and cheered as the runners made their way around the short, oval track.

A messenger arrived at Alexander's side. Roxana thought it odd the king would be disturbed in the middle of a race. The man whispered something to Alexander. The king's face fell. He bolted out of the box, his king's guard scrambling to keep up.

The crowd of spectators gasped as the king fled from the arena. No one cheered when the winning runner crossed the finish line.

Roxana confronted the messenger. "What is it?"

The fair-haired man got on his knees, clasping his hands as if pleading for his life. "It's the chiliarch, my lady. He's taken a turn for the worse. The doctor said for the king to come right away."

Roxana tore out of the royal box, tripping over chairs. She leaped down the stadium steps and ran to the palace of Ecbatana. The lump in her throat made it hard to breathe, and her tears blurred the gray stone path beneath her feet. She silently asked all the Greek and Persian gods to spare the life of the man she cared for almost as much as the king.

The moment she reached the palace walls, a horrible wailing greeted her. Akin to the cry of a tortured beast, she knew what the sound meant.

Pushing through courtiers, priests, and servants, she reached the outer doors to Hephaestion's rooms. The people gathered there had red eyes. Some sobbed, and others rested their heads against the walls to hide their shock.

In front of the beaten silver doors to the chiliarch's rooms, two guards held an older man, wearing the white cloak of a physician, on the floor.

"Spare me, my king. I didn't do anything wrong!"

The captive writhed and tried to free himself.

She attempted to go around the soldiers and a shadow moved in front of her.

"You should not see this, my lady."

Bagoas blocked the doorway.

The sight of the eunuch triggered her anger. Why was he in Hephaestion's rooms? She made a move to push past him, but he held her arm.

She was about to reprimand him for touching her when she noticed he was shaking.

"What has happened to Hephaestion?"

His blank mask told her nothing. She searched for any sign, and a horrid iciness enveloped her.

"He's dead." The eunuch's lifeless tone echoed through her. "The king has ordered his physician to be put to death." He pointed to the prisoner. "He left him to attend the games, and when he came back, the general was dead."

Dead. The word registered but not the meaning. How could the vibrant, handsome man with the affable demeanor and caring soul be dead?

A gaping emptiness opened in her chest, raw, debilitating, and excruciating. It allowed the cold surrounding her to seep inside, taking her strength. She tried to scream, but the sound stuck in her throat as the doors in front of her wavered and bent. The cold spread to her limbs, and then her legs buckled.

She fell forward, unable to stop herself.

Bagoas caught her, helping her to stay upright amid the growing number of spectators gathering outside the rooms.

"No," finally tumbled from her lips. "Not him. Not him, please not him."

Beyond the silver doors came the wretched cries of what sounded like an animal screaming in pain. The piercing noise roused her. She covered her ears, but it still got through, mirroring her grief.

Bagoas helped her to her feet and handed her to the sentries. "Get her to her rooms."

Someone carried her along a corridor. Swaths of light came and went, but the voices in her head, the images in front of her didn't feel real.

Then Morella's face appeared. Beyond her, sea creatures covered the walls.

"There, there, my lady." Morella held her, rocking as they sat on the blue floors.

The fog lifted and the reality of what had happened snapped into her head. It jolted her, and then the sorrow came like a wave crashing in from the sea.

She curled into a ball, shut her eyes, and sobbed.

"Shhh," Morella whispered, still rocking her. "We will all miss the gentle general."

Still in the outfit she'd worn to the games, Roxana sat in a chair in her reception room, a doleful Morella at her side. A haggard-looking Perdiccas and Ptolemy stood in front of her.

"Please, Roxana, you must go to him." With a bright red fuzz on his face and dark circles under his eyes, Ptolemy seemed genuinely distraught. "He's locked himself away with Hephaestion's body and has had no food or water for almost two days. Whenever any of us try to enter the room, he throws us out."

"Hephaestion's doctor has been hanged." Perdiccas exhibited the same lackluster expression she'd seen reflected at the bottom of her wine goblet. "Alexander ordered the soldiers to take the man straight out into the courtyard and hang him from the first high tree they could find."

Roxana tapped the arm of her chair, debating what to do.

"The physician deserved to die."

"It was Hephaestion who broke the doctor's diet orders." Perdiccas's voice quivered with fatigue. "He had wine and a chicken when he was only supposed to have broth. The doctor's only crime was leaving his patient to go to the games."

Ptolemy came up to her, holding out his hands. "The empire cannot come to a standstill for the death of one man, even if he was the king's second. Things must be done; business must be carried out … orders given. Without Alexander, Perdiccas and I can only do so much."

"I'm surprised at you, Ptolemy." Roxana rose from her chair, the fire in her belly igniting. "Hephaestion was your friend."

"I've lost many friends since I set foot in Persia," Ptolemy insisted in a stern tone. "I grieve each one, but in my own way."

Was his sadness any different from hers? His condescension added to her rising irritation but the two days of wine and no food muddled her head.

"What has any of this got to do with me?"

Perdiccas stepped forward, his cold gaze tearing into her. "Hephaestion told us how you dealt with Alexander after Bucephalus died and after the mutiny in India. We need your help now."

Their gall stunned her. To come to her, when Alexander had an army filled with generals he trusted, why? Then it struck her.

"You're afraid to go near him. You fear that if anyone attempts to remove Hephaestion's body, Alexander will order them killed, too."

Ptolemy stuck out his chest. "We're not afraid, just concerned. Alexander has killed men in anger before. Cleitus was one of us, and when he challenged Alexander, he was run through with a spear. We can't have that happen again. We must get some control over him, bring him back to reason. He will listen to you."

Everyone she'd met in the Greek camps had an agenda—to woo Alexander, coddle Alexander, win favor with Alexander, and now these fools feared him. Hephaestion had been the only genuine soul among them, leaving her with no one to trust.

"When Alexander married me, you and your men spoke with such malice. I was the Persian bride, ridiculed and despised because I wasn't Greek. Now you come to me to save you from the very king you thought I wasn't good enough to marry. I know why Alexander made Hephaestion his chiliarch; he was worth the lot of you." She stormed from the room, heading to her bedchamber.

Roxana listened as the generals left, closing the outer doors. She went to the window to view the mountains, her mind reeling.

Why Hephaestion? He was the glue that held them all together. How would she continue without his strength?

Strength. The word revived a memory of Hephaestion after the Gedrosian Desert. He'd told her Alexander needed her to be strong then, just like he needed it now. But did she have any fortitude left? She searched the mountaintops and knew she had to find out. No matter her despair, her fatigue, and her desire to walk away from everything, Roxana could not give up on her husband. She had to show him how to go on.

"Morella, I need to change," she shouted to the servant, who hovered close to her doorway.

"Where are you going, my lady?"

Roxana moved away from the window, her determination crawling back.

"I'm going to see the king."

CHAPTER THIRTY-FOUR

Roxana stood before the doors to Hephaestion's rooms, the afternoon heat clinging to her skin while she fought the overpowering urge to cry. The empty hall, abandoned by those fearful of the king's wrath, was quiet. She pictured a decimated Alexander on the other side of the doors, and then Hephaestion, still in the bed where he had died. Was she ready for this? What choice had the gods given her?

Her anger with those pompous, fickle, thunderbolt-wielding deciders of her fate formed a knot in the center of her chest. Where were the gods now?

Funny how they abandon us when we need them most.

But her rage propelled her forward. After two days of tears and wine, it had been her only source of energy. Bitterness had gotten her here but would not help Alexander. He needed hope, not hatred to heal.

When the sentries stationed outside the rooms opened the doors, she summoned her resolve and stepped inside.

Except for a sliver of the afternoon sun, the room was dark. The pungent odor of death wafted by. She recoiled, fighting the urge to gag, and eased inside. Through the shadows she made out a man lying on a bed, partially covered with a sheet.

A small ray of light crossed Hephaestion's face. The stench grew stronger as she neared him, but what amazed her was how peaceful he appeared. There wasn't the slightest hint of corruption on his skin.

At the bed, she touched the general's cold cheek. "Of all the people I've known, you were the kindest to me. I will always remember you, my friend." She kissed his forehead. "Until we meet again."

"'And Briseis wept over the body of the slain Patroclus. For she too had loved the best friend of Achilles.'"

His eerily calm voice came from the corner of the room.

A hint of motion drew her eye. Alexander sat on a stool not far from the bed, hunched over, his head lowered.

"He was my only true friend, too. My Patroclus."

She strained to make out his face in the darkness. "He was the first person to befriend me after I married you. The only friend I ever had in the camps. I loved him very much."

Alexander moved, and the extent of his grief became evident. He'd torn the top of his rumpled tunic, his hair was disheveled, his face had several scratch marks, and his knees displayed spots of dried blood.

"I've sat here for two days wondering why, why did the gods do this to me?

Take away my only friend, my only love. Achilles survived the pain of his friend's death, but I don't know if I can."

He sounded as if every breath gave him agony.

She slowly approached, remembering how she used to catch her father's skittish horse in the field. Mindful of every step, she kept her voice soothing and held out her hand.

"When our son died, and I shut out the world, Hephaestion came to me. He told me 'That won't do, Roxana. Alexander wouldn't want this.'" She knelt down and put her hand over his. "This won't do, Alexander. Hephaestion wouldn't want this. He would want you to go on."

His tear-stained cheeks and bloodshot eyes caught in the light.

"He was part of me. How do I go on without my other self?"

"He was part of both of us." She gripped his hand, willing her strength to him.

"But what do I do? How do I—?" His tremulous voice gave out.

She traced the scratches on his cheeks, undone by his misery, wanting to take it away, but knowing she never could. Her son had taught her grief could never be healed, and the person holding it could never let go. It was a guidepost helping to change the course of life. Whether the new road was good or bad was up to the traveler. She wanted to help Alexander find his way on this new journey just as Hephaestion had helped her.

"You will go on, Alexander. Both of us will go on. And our lives will be the richer for having had such a dear friend." She put her arm around him, encouraging him to stand.

His movements were stiff and slow, but she got him to his feet.

"We must see to his funeral." She held on to him as he shuffled closer to the bed. "I will help you."

"I've been thinking about what must be done." Alexander stretched his hand toward Hephaestion. "I want all the horse's manes and tails clipped. All ornaments are to be removed from the city walls, and all music and dramatic plays at court and in the camps are banned. Hephaestion's late regiment will bear his name, and his men will carry his image as its standard. Daily sacrifices are to be made at temples across the city, and I want architects and sculptors commissioned to design memorial shrines for him across the empire. And I will send to the oracle of Ammon at Siwa, asking for Hephaestion to be granted divine honors so he can be worshipped as a god."

"And his funeral?" she asked, resting her head against him.

"Babylon." Alexander dropped his hand to his side. "There, I plan to say my last farewell."

Roxana sipped from her elegant glass of wine as Alexander sat across from her at the ivory dining table in his rooms, picking at his plate of roast fish. He'd lost weight over the past few weeks. His cropped hair, cut to grieve his friend, made the circles around his eyes stand out and accentuated their dullness. Bothered by his appearance, she searched for a distraction.

Piles of busts and paintings of Hephaestion—either gifts from the fearful or genuinely grieved—stared back at her. All of Hephaestion's belongings, along with an assortment of swords, shields, and armor, sat stacked against the wall. The shrine gave her comfort, but also concern for Alexander's state of mind. He'd made progress the few weeks since his friend's death, but he needed more time to come to grips with his loss.

"The funeral will be after I arrive in Babylon," Alexander told her as he pushed his untouched plate to the side. "It will give Perdiccas time to escort Hephaestion's body and the rest of the baggage train to the city, and then make the necessary preparations."

"I'm sure your new chiliarch will follow your commands to the letter." She reached for her wine, preferring alcohol to the food. "How long will it be before you join me in Babylon?"

He drummed his fingers on the table, the sound filling the room.

"I have to fight the Cossaeans tribe before heading to the city. They've been causing trouble on the road between Babylon and Susa for many years, hurting supply lines. It's time someone gets rid of those brigands."

Encouraged by the fight in his voice, she smiled. "It's good to hear your spirit returning."

"I need action. When I get to Babylon, things will be better."

"When was the last time you slept?"

"I can't sleep. All I can do is think about him." He abandoned the table and went to the window. "He's there every time I close my eyes."

He stared out into the evening sky.

She'd gotten used to the long lapses of silence. Sometimes they would only last a short while, other times all day. She'd become an expert at predicting their duration by the look on his face.

Sensing this one would take a while, Roxana rose from the table and headed for the doors, anxious to leave him to his memories.

"Don't go. I want you with me tonight."

The tenderness in his voice moved her. It had been a long time since she'd heard it. It was the first intimation they had a future together. She hoped so. Since

Hephaestion's death, she wanted more with Alexander, to be as they had been before Susa. His other marriages had changed things between them, but the fragility of life made her vow not to wallow in it.

"I will do whatever you wish."

He tentatively ran his fingers along the edge of the window sill. "We used to stay up until sunrise just talking, he and I. I miss that."

She went to his side. "Then we will stay up until sunrise talking, too."

His arms went around her, and she melted into him. His embrace chased away her sadness. Hephaestion had told her how special she was to Alexander, and for the first time since marrying the king, she believed him.

Roxana nestled her head against his chest, wishing she could make him the happy man she'd first met in Sogdiana.

"Going off to battle won't be the same." He kissed her brow.

"You were separated before in battle. The times when he was with me, heading the baggage train on some long trek across the mountains. Think of him that way."

"Then it will only hurt more when I return."

"But I will be here." She ran her fingers over his short-cropped hair, missing his wavy mane. "No matter what journeys you take, at the end of every one of them, I will be waiting."

His smile was small, but it was the first one she'd seen in weeks.

He tightened his arms around her. "Then I will always come back to you."

Encouraged, she stood on her toes and pecked his lips, but before she could back away, he held her face.

The emptiness in his eyes vanished. He kissed her back, tenderly at first, but then urgency replaced his gentleness.

He abruptly pulled away. "Is it wrong for me to want you so much when I still can't stop thinking about him?"

She caressed his cheek. "Hephaestion would want you to do what makes you happy. That's all he cared about, your happiness."

"You make me happy."

Her arms went around him as the last coils of her resistance melted away. "Then he will be pleased."

He kissed her again with all the passion she remembered from their early days together, but it felt different. The heartache and trials of the past had changed them, and the compulsion of youth had given way to a burning desire more intense than she'd ever known. What they shared had grown into something reaching beyond their bodies—it had captivated their souls.

Chapter Thirty-Five

The road to Babylon was a restful one for Roxana. The late fall winds from the mountains kept her comfortable during the journey. However, by the time the caravan finally reached the city walls of Babylon, ferocious winter gales roared across the valley between the Tigris and Euphrates Rivers. The hostile gusts distressed her. It was an ill omen.

In the massive palace of Nebuchadnezzar, Roxana received six rooms, all bathed in sunlight. A wall of windows in her bedroom afforded a view of the Tigris River. Her bathroom had running water; her living room had a pond with orange fish. There was even a private monkey trained to dance and entertain her. But despite the luxury, Roxana's unease persisted.

She kept busy by exploring the wonders of the most magnificent palace in the Persian Empire. She visited the private zoo, ate in the lush rose gardens, and checked on Hera in the massive stone stables. At night, she listened to court musicians, poets, and even hosted parties for the women of the harem who had traveled with her from Ecbatana. There were many diversions, but none of them could keep her thoughts away from her increasing disquiet or her husband's impending arrival.

"You got fretful like this last time you were pregnant," Morella told her one early spring morning as she retrieved the chamber pot for a nauseous Roxana. "It's just nerves."

She sat up in her bed, waiting for her spell of sickness to pass. "What about the stories going around the palace about bad omens and sacrifices having blackened hearts?"

"Priests always see doom and gloom in every sacrifice. It's how they earn their keep." Morella gave her a motherly smile. "You lost a baby, and are scared for the health of this one. That's all."

She wanted to argue with her maid, and insist this sensation was different, but perhaps she was right. The baby growing inside her had to be the source of her jitters. What else could it be?

A month later, the blast of horns from the palace heralds announced the king's approach to the city gates.

A jubilant Roxana watched Alexander's procession through Babylon from her balcony. She thanked the gods for her husband's safe return. She would have him with her for the birth.

But her happiness melted away when the growing pyre for Hephaestion along the banks of the Tigris cast a long shade over the festivities. The massive structure loomed higher than any other building in Babylon, even the towering walls around the city. At one point, the darkness covered Alexander's golden chariot, completely blocking out the sun. The omen sent a shudder through her.

Then something Alexander had once told her came to mind.

We will meet again in Babylon.

The unsettling incident sent her inside, itching for the taste of wine. She'd hoped with his return, her worries would fade, but instead, the sense of foreboding eating at her for the past few weeks grew stronger.

"You look like you've seen a ghost," Morella said when she walked into her bedroom.

Roxana ignored the comment, afraid to mention what she'd witnessed.

"Get me some wine." She went to a bench set up by her open bedroom window. "And leave me alone for a while. I need to think."

Roxana was on her third cup of wine, with her tired feet propped on a stool, when the clatter of shields and spears came from her outer rooms.

A boisterous man's voice drifted inside. "Where is she? Where is my wife?"

Alexander walked through the cedar doors, filled with the energy she remembered from before Hephaestion's death.

She set her wine aside, eager to greet her husband.

He strutted up to her and instead of pulling her into his arms, rested his hands on her protruding abdomen.

"It's a boy. I know it. When you wrote last winter that you were with child, I knew it was a boy."

"It could be a girl, Alexander. But it moves about like before, so it must be a boy." She brushed aside a reddish-brown lock from his forehead, glad to see he had let his hair grow back after Ecbatana. "It's good to have you here."

He went to her refreshment table and poured himself a goblet of unwatered wine.

"Almost didn't make it. Damned Chaldean astrologers from the temple of Marduk tried to keep me from entering the city."

"What?" Roxana joined him at the table, disturbed by the news.

"Yes, some foolishness about bad auspices if I entered the city from the west. I was suspicious at first, but then I agreed to go around to the eastern side of the city by the Ishtar Gate, which is mostly swamp, and make my way from there. A real mess that was. Never worked out, and I had to come in the west gates anyway."

An uncomfortable twinge raced through her. "The palace priests have been reporting bad omens for months. Should we be concerned? Maybe there's something wrong with the baby."

"Roxana, don't upset yourself." He chuckled as he swirled his wine. "If I'd listened to every auger I've come across, I would never have made it out of Greece." He sipped from his goblet. "Everything will be fine. Our son will be healthy. I know it."

The change in him surprised her. "I thought you believed in omens."

"I do." He swallowed more wine. "But I've been hearing this same talk of bad omens all along the road from Susa. I've had enough of it."

A shred of jealousy replaced her dread. "You visited Susa?"

He saw her reaction, put down his goblet, and took her hand. "I stopped by on my way back from fighting the Cossaeans. I wanted to see if Drypetis was with child. She isn't. It would have been some comfort to have his child with me."

Roxana let go of his hand, his visit to Susa still bugging her.

"I sacrifice to him every day."

"As do I." He picked up his goblet. "The Oracle at Siwa sent back my reply about making him a god. They said he was to be worshipped as a divine hero. My poor Patroclus; it seems he will always be a hero and never a god. I hope his shade is at ease amid the golden flowers in the Elysian Fields."

Roxana turned from the table, her hands twisting as she debated her next question.

"Did you visit anyone else while in Susa?"

He slammed his goblet on the table. "I saw Stateira, not Parysatis."

A tightness cinched her throat. "And will the daughter of Darius be making any announcements about future heirs to the throne?"

He came up behind her and put his arms around her, nuzzling her ear. "You are my true wife. You carry my child, and you're the one I want to spend time with. And I only visited Stateira to please Sisygambis. The old woman's opinion means a lot to me."

Appeased, she pulled his arms closer. "I've been watching them build the pyre for over a month now. When will the funeral be?"

He rubbed her belly. "Before I can deal with the funeral, I have dozens of envoys here from all over the empire, including my regent, Antipater, from Macedonia. It seems the Greeks back home are giving me trouble again. And I have yet to see any representatives from Arabia. Their disrespect for the King of Persia has to be dealt with swiftly. I've already sent a naval expedition to survey the lands, so we can start planning our campaign there."

"You're going to Arabia? But you just got back." She fretted over his bloodshot eyes and pasty skin. "You need to rest, Alexander. You can't keep up this hectic pace."

He took her hand and kissed it. "I'll be fine."

She tried to gauge his mood, but since Hephaestion's death, he kept so much hidden from her.

"I sometimes wonder what you're thinking. I'm not a fool. I know Achilles did not long outlive his Patroclus. I don't wish to see your life parallel your Homeric legend. Do not drive yourself so. Even kings need to rest."

"I have plans to see to." He kissed her cheek. "I shall visit again."

He exited her apartments, taking his wine with him.

The brief meeting created more worry than she'd expected. He was troubled and restless. She sensed he was close to a breaking point, and with the baby demanding more of her energy, Roxana feared she would not be there to catch him when he finally fell apart.

"Ah, here she is."

Alexander walked up to Roxana when she entered the silver and ebony-paneled dining room. A dinner party for the arrival of the envoy from Pella was already in full swing.

Gathered around the black dinner table, set in the Persian style, Perdiccas, Ptolemy, and Nearchus sat along with another man Roxana had never seen before.

"Cassander, this is my wife, the lovely Roxana," Alexander said, taking her to the table. "Roxana, this is Antipater's son from Macedonia."

His son? But where was Antipater?

Roxana smiled at the short, ugly man with a thick beard, stocky body, and wearing a purple cloak. Something was troubling about him—perhaps the darkness in his bug-like eyes or the condescending sneer on his lips. Whatever it was, the child inside her kicked, sensing her dismay.

"Cassander, I'm pleased to meet another of the king's Companions."

"Oh, you speak Greek." Cassander stood from the table and came to her, his large eyes almost grotesque with amazement. "I had no idea Persian women were so cultured."

"Careful man," Alexander griped. "That's my wife you're speaking of, and she happens to be a Persian woman of exceptional beauty and talent."

Cassander bowed to Roxana, but his cold gaze revealed no apology. "Quite sorry, my lady." He slapped Alexander on the back. "I never realized how well you got along with these Oriental types. I mean, Father told me you were close with them, but really."

His rude comments amazed her. It was her wedding day all over again.

Alexander lowered his voice, adding weight to his harsh rebuke. "Cassander, these are my people, your people now. You will not refer to them as Orientals."

"And you?" Cassander pointed at Alexander's bright blue Persian tunic. "Don't you think you have overdone this Persian thing? To rule over them is one thing, but to dress like them is another."

"Watch your tone, boy," Perdiccas growled on the other side of Cassander.

"No, I will not watch my tone," Cassander snapped. "You seem to forget, Perdiccas, while you and Alexander were off fighting great wars and conquering the world, I was left, along with my father back in Macedonia, to tend to rustic sheepherders who know nothing about royalty. While you lived in faraway palaces, we had to put up with the cold Pella nights. While you slept in the arms of beautiful, exotic women, Antipater had to put up with the continuous whining of that old cow Olympias, who—"

Cassander never got to finish his words. Alexander picked the man up with one arm and threw him against the wall.

"You will not speak of my mother in such a manner," Alexander shouted at the cowering figure. "You owe me. Your father owes me. You remember that, boy. When I order my regent to come before me, he'd better show up and not send his stupid, foul-mouthed, ingrate of a son in his place."

Cassander stayed on the floor, trembling.

Roxana went to him and checked his head for wounds.

Ptolemy came behind her and offered the frightened Cassander his hand, helping him from the floor.

"You'd better go."

"Thank you," Cassander whispered to her. "I will remember your kindness."

A shiver shot through her. Why didn't she believe him?

Cassander scurried out of the room. The generals around the table glared critically at the king.

Ptolemy went back to his chair. "You shouldn't have done that."

"Why not?" Alexander tossed up his hands. "He insulted me, my wife, my mother, and the Persian people. What's wrong with teaching the little pig a lesson?"

"Because he's Antipater's son!" Ptolemy smashed his fist into the table. "Antipater has been your regent for ten years and has served you faithfully. You do not anger loyal men." Ptolemy wiped his sweaty brow. "I'm going to talk to him. Smooth things over." He stormed toward the silver inlaid doors.

Nearchus, who had been silent throughout the entire episode, suddenly stood. "It's an early day tomorrow, Alexander. I will retire to my chambers." He politely bowed to Roxana and followed Ptolemy out of the room.

"What is wrong with you?" Roxana asked.

"I am king around here." He held up his right fist, flashing his gold seal ring. "It's about time I knocked a few heads together to remind people who's in charge." He then marched out of the room, slamming the doors behind him.

His rash behavior frightened her. She'd seen him angry, depressed, and in deep mourning, but she had never witnessed such outrage.

"He's not been well these last few months." Perdiccas refilled his goblet, appearing unfazed by the incident. "He's been prone to wrath, just like that, in the past."

She rubbed her belly, the child's kicking causing her discomfort. "I know he has a temper, but I've never seen him do anything like this."

He lifted his goblet. "Youth isn't eternal, Roxana. When you've suffered as much as the king, you tend to pay the consequences." He sipped his wine. "I know he misses Hephaestion. We all miss Hephaestion. He was the only person who could soothe Alexander's tirades. Without him around, I fear for the king and his peace of mind."

His words upset her. She did not wish to hear anymore.

"I will go to him."

"Hopefully, you can help the king as well as his old friend did." Perdiccas never raised his gaze from his goblet. "I hope for all our sakes you can calm him."

Roxana hurried from the dining room and headed down the long corridor to the king's quarters. She replayed the scene with Cassander in her head. Alexander's reaction had been rash, but it was his hate that disturbed her. It was a side he had kept from her; a side she wished she'd never seen.

At the golden doors to his room, she gestured for his guards to allow her to pass, but they refused to admit her and barred her way.

"I want to see the king."

"He is … ah, bathing." The shorter man cleared his throat. "Perhaps I should let the king know you're here."

Bathing? Roxana didn't care. "Get out of my way."

She shoved the soldiers aside and pulled one of the massive gold doors open.

She'd only taken a few steps into the room when she ran into Alexander, who sat in a chair in the middle of his onyx-lined reception room. He raised his head and furrowed his brow when he saw her.

"What is it?"

The guards quickly shut the doors behind her.

Roxana put on her best menacing scowl. "I want to talk to you!"

The sound of water pouring filled the adjoining bedroom.

She took a few steps closer to the arched entrance and peeked inside.

Bagoas, in only a loincloth, poured hot water for Alexander's bath into his golden tub. Next to it, the enormous bed of King Darius. It was made of olive wood and reportedly taken from Greece during the great war.

The attendant stopped when he saw her.

Her flush of jealousy was cut off by a flutter from her belly as the child moved. Hephaestion's voice came alive in her mind.

You will be the mother of kings. That, in itself, is the best revenge.

He'd been right. The lithe man with his flowing black hair was no threat. He had never been one.

"Bagoas, leave me alone with my wife."

The attendant bowed and walked through the reception room without making a sound. The outer chamber doors closed and silence inundated them.

He folded his thick arms. "Why are you here?"

She paced in front of him, attempting to calm down and collect her thoughts.

"Are you on some self-destructive path, Alexander? Because what I saw tonight scared the life out of me."

"What are you talking about?"

"You told me once you don't like to lose control. So please explain to me, what did I just witness? Because you were acting like a madman."

He whacked his fist on the arm of his chair. "He insulted me!"

"So what? That's no excuse to throw the man's head against the wall. You showed me a side of you tonight I've never seen, and I don't want to see again."

Alexander slowly climbed from his chair. His movements were not those of the powerful man she'd known. He appeared stiff, almost wooden as he came toward her.

"Have you ever thought that maybe I'm tired of being gracious to idiots? I'm tired of others constantly questioning my motives and reasoning." He took a labored breath, putting his hand on his right side. "I am the king, and I'm trying to plan a campaign into Arabia, build a new harbor for our growing fleet, and run an empire. At every turn, I have people questioning me. No one questioned when I wanted to cross the Hellespont and go into Persia. 'Go Alexander,' the Greeks begged, 'make amends for what Persia did to us.'" He scowled at her. "Now everything I do needs a reason behind it, an explanation for my action. Can't I do as I wish?" He covered his head with his hands. "To go on conquering the world until I'm ready to stop."

Roxana's heart broke. Her father once told her, "Everything is simple when you're young; as you age, it gets complicated." She'd never understood what he meant until now.

She rested her hand on his hopelessly untamed hair and kissed his head. "What can I do?"

He took her hand and held it. "Stay with me. I feel so alone these days."

Steam wafted up from his tub. "I'll help you with your bath."

She went to remove his sandals, but he stayed her hands.

"On our wedding night, I told you not to soil your hands with such duties."

"What I do, I do out of love, husband, not duty."

He arched over her, studying her face. "Do you still love me, after everything I've done? Married you, dragged you across the world, and ignored you."

"I wouldn't have fallen in love with you without it. And no matter what you do in the future, I will never stop loving you."

He fingered her gold necklace. "I had forgotten about this. Is it the one he gave you?"

"Yes. I hope it doesn't upset you."

Alexander twirled the gold between his fingers. "No, it's good that you wear it. It keeps him with you."

"Then I shall wear it, always." She reached for him, hungry to inhale the sweetness of his skin.

He wrapped her in his warm embrace. "We never did get to share that bath all that time ago in India."

He was again her Alexander—the kind, gentle man she'd fallen in love with. She sighed, happy for his return.

"I seem to recall I was pregnant then as well."

"You make me happy, Roxana. Happy like I used to be before ..." He left the name unspoken.

"Shh." She put her arms around him, not wanting the pain of the past to intrude on their moment. "We're going on, Alexander. Just like he would have wanted."

Chapter Thirty-Six

On her balcony, Roxana admired the curtain of dusk descending from the sky as crowds bearing torches gathered along the shore of the Tigris River. Hephaestion's funeral pyre, built to resemble an Egyptian step pyramid, was ready to send to the gods.

Alexander had sent specific instructions for its design with tiers depicting hunting scenes, battle scenes, and even scenes from Hephaestion's childhood.

"In all my days, I've never seen such a thing." Morella stood next to her, surveying the crowds.

Roxana's gaze rose to the top tier where Hephaestion's body lay decorated with gold. "I don't think anyone will see anything like this ever again."

The blare of trumpets and call of elephants carried from the shore, drawing Roxana's attention.

A single figure stepped forward from the crowd. In the white chiton, purple cloak, and bronze cuirass, Alexander looked decidedly Macedonian.

She couldn't see his face, but she could imagine the heaviness pressing on his chest because she felt it in her own. Before tonight, Hephaestion had been with both of them in some small way as his body waited for the burning. When Alexander set his torch to the bottom tier stacked with kindling, a single teardrop snuck down her cheek. It meant her friend was truly dead.

It didn't take long for the flames to climb up to the top until the fire seemed to embrace Hephaestion with red and orange arms. The tremendous heat forced back many of the well-wishers gathered at the base.

Alexander had a seat on the beach. He appeared entranced by the blazing pyramid, lost in the embers rising into the sky.

She stayed on her balcony through the night, keeping watch over her husband, until almost the entire structure had crumbled into red embers. She wished she could go to him, give him words of encouragement, but he needed to be alone.

Just as the first glimpse of sunlight crept over the horizon, he left the remains of the pyre behind and walked back to the palace.

Roxana noted her husband's determined stride and knew in her heart that Alexander had finally said goodbye.

A stiff wind came off the river as Roxana stood on the sprawling dock, part of the new harbor construction at Babylon. It had only been a few weeks since the funeral, and already hundreds of men worked to enlarge the waterways and erect bigger docks for the newly constructed fleet.

"The progress is astounding, Alexander. It's bigger than the harbor at Nicaea and Bucephala."

Her husband shaded his eyes from the sun while scouring the frenzy of activity. "It has to be to accommodate the new warships I'm building. We will have to check back in a few days to see how it's coming."

We. He'd used the term more and more—*we* need to do this, and *we* need to check on that. It had started after the funeral when he'd come to her at the end of his day and informed her of what happened in his meetings. His insistence on walking tours of the city and palace grounds was new as well. He'd wanted to show her his building plans for the harbor and temples. Her expanding girth made keeping up with her husband a challenge, but she vowed to do whatever necessary to share the time with him.

"How are the plans for your invasion of Arabia coming?"

He took her hand, encouraging her along the dock. "We've been fortifying our troops with newly trained Persian soldiers and more arms for the men. I've been assigning them to mixed officer corps with both Persian and Macedonian soldiers. I'm hoping to fuse the two together without much difficulty before we set out for Arabia."

They walked among his men, holding hands. There were no hostile looks or whispers. For Roxana, it was a measure of acceptance. They were like any other couple in the king's camp.

"Your plan will succeed. All your plans succeed." Roxana inspected the blue water. "It seems like quite an undertaking, this harbor."

"Yes, I'm trying to inspire the men. I've even made competitions to keep the men motivated and prepare them for Arabia. 'Wherever there is competition there is victory,' Aristotle used to say. It's working, too. They're training harder than ever."

She noticed how quickly he got out of breath.

"How hard are you working yourself, Alexander?"

"As hard as I work my men." He peered out over the harbor. "It's what's expected of me."

"But your men aren't planning invasions by day, meeting dignitaries in the afternoon, or hosting political suppers, dramatic readings, plays, and games at night. You're wearing me out with all the activities you have going on around here, and I'm not even one of your generals."

He gave her a tolerant grin. "Well, you should be one of my generals."

She didn't like the rosy color on his cheeks.

She touched his brow. "You're warm, Alexander."

He removed her hand and kissed it. "Nonsense. It's only the sun."

Dead birds filled the streets of Babylon, fires would not stay lit in the temples, and strange lights hung in the western sky over the next few days. The number of dire predictions floating around the palace troubled Roxana.

"Something unfortunate happened today during work on the harbor," Morella related during Roxana's lunch. "The king's sun hat with the royal headband on it blew off and landed on some reeds next to one of the tombs of the Assyrian kings. A workman jumped into the water to fetch it, then placed the hat on his head before he swam back to the king. The priests are very upset. They say it's a bad omen."

Roxana pushed her plate away. "These bad omens are everywhere. People haven't stopped talking about them."

Morella collected her plate. "Then there's a story about the man who walked into the throne room and sat on the king's empty throne while he was out."

She stood, too nervous to stay seated. "When did this happen?"

"Yesterday. The king refused to have the stranger beheaded for his crime."

Roxana went to her windows. "He never mentioned any of this to me."

"You're with child, my lady. The king doesn't want to upset you."

She viewed the charred spot where the pyre had burned, fingering her gold necklace. She searched her memories of Hephaestion for advice, some comment on how to help Alexander through this crisis, but there was nothing. Hephaestion had known the king during a time when his luck never seemed to wane, but Roxana sensed it already had. And that, more than the frightening omens, terrified her. A king without luck, would not remain a king for long.

She faced her maid overcome with a sudden urgency to see her husband. "Morella, ask the guard outside if he knows where to find the king. I need to speak to him."

"He's in the palace library. Meeting with that admiral. His cook told me she was sending up their lunch to the library as per his request."

At a brisk walk—anything else was uncomfortable—she made her way through the maze of corridors to the library. She had traveled the same path numerous times before in search of new reading material.

Done in sheets of tigers-eye, the doors touted carved depictions of war elephants locking tusks. Sunlight streaming in through four large windows on either side of the corridor landed on the king's guard outside the doors. She relaxed a little, knowing he was safe inside the library.

Once the guards opened the massive doors, a musty aroma tickled her nose.

With beamed ceilings and dozens of windows, the library contained stone shelves which housed thousands of books and scrolls.

At the end of the rectangular room, at a table scattered with maps, Alexander glanced up at her. Beside him was the noble admiral from Crete with the brilliant blue eyes, Nearchus.

Alexander's boyish smile lit up his face. He strutted down the long aisle to join her.

"What are you doing here?"

She became concerned when she saw his flushed face. "I wanted to see you. Is that all right?"

"I always want you with me." He took her hand. "I was just going over my invasion plans with Nearchus. Did you know Arabia has fertile lands filled with myrrh, frankincense, and cinnamon?"

He escorted her down the aisle, praising the information his naval expedition had gathered on Arabia. She kept wanting to butt in, to ask him about the omens, but as they got closer to the table and the admiral, she hesitated.

Nearchus dipped his head. "I hope you are well, my lady."

Her hand instinctually went to her belly, and then her embarrassment warmed her cheeks. She was still in her long robe and nightgown.

"You're very kind, General Nearchus, but I had a question for the king that could not wait. I hope you will forgive the intrusion."

"We don't mind, do we, old friend? We can talk some more at the banquet tonight." Alexander turned back to his wife. "I'm having a feast to honor our admiral before our Arabia campaign. The celebrations are the only thing I could think of to appease all the damned soothsayers who keep speaking of evil omens."

"Ah, yes." She jumped on the opportunity. "I've heard about these omens. It's the reason I came. They frighten me."

Alexander rested his hip against the table, cocking his head as he studied her. "Frighten you? I thought you didn't believe in such things."

She warily eyed Nearchus. "I don't, but your men do. There has been talk of—"

"I've told you before never to believe idle gossip." Alexander's irritation crept into his voice. "I've made numerous sacrifices to the gods and employed several soothsayers to lift this bad shadow from me."

"It's true, my lady." Nearchus stepped away from the table. "The king has been working tirelessly with the priests in the city. Hopefully, we've pleased the gods so we may be victorious in Arabia."

The king's ruddy complexion deepened her concern. "I know whatever the king does always pleases the gods, General."

Alexander came alongside her. "There. See? Nothing to worry about." He extended his arm. "I'll see you back to your rooms, my wife."

But Roxana's growing sense of dread would not be appeased. "Maybe I should see you to yours. You need to be in bed. You have a fever, don't you?"

Alexander hooked her hand on his arm. "I'm fine. I have too much to do to stay in bed."

They strolled the great corridor that ran the length of the palace. Murals of a woman in white robes, Spenta Armaiti—the goddess of devotion to family and truth—looked on as they passed.

"While I'm away in Arabia, I want you to take care." He patted her bump. "And our son."

She rested her head against his shoulder. "How long will you be gone this time?"

"As long as it takes."

She stopped walking and faced him, her stomach a conflagration of knots. "I'm afraid, Alexander. These omens are all over the city. What if they mean something may happen to you in Arabia?"

He wrinkled his brow, darkening the piercing quality of his eyes. "Where is this coming from? I've had bad omens haunt me before, and I'm still here."

Her hands on his chest, she struggled for the right words. "It's never been like this. Everyone in the palace senses the poison in the air. I'm begging you to postpone Arabia, at least until the omens change."

He held her hands against him. "Postpone? I can't do that. I've told you a thousand times, I must lead by example. If I become afraid of bad omens, what will my men think?"

"The same as I—that you heed the warnings of the gods."

He stepped toward the window. The sunlight coming through it caught his hair, creating a golden halo.

Roxana paused, taking in the sign from the gods.

"I love you, Roxana, I always have, and I would do anything for you, but don't ask me to change my destiny. I'm a warrior, and I can only be happy when there are worlds to conquer. Take that away from me, and I will be lost. Perhaps when I'm too old to lift my sword, then I can remain in a palace." He raised his head and inspected the ceiling. "Maybe this one. And we can spend our old age together, enjoying our grandchildren. But until then, I must plan, I must fight, and I must go. I would rather live a short life, filled with greatness, than a long and mediocre one."

Then the shadow of a cloud drifting across the sky blotted out the sunlight and a dark shade enveloped her husband's head. She froze, terrified by the omen.

Alexander eased closer. "But I will return to you, little star. I always do."

Not wanting to show him any fear, she gave him a dazzling smile.

"Oh, that smile! It will be the death of me."

She cupped his cheek, the warmth of his skin still vexed her. "No wine tonight at your dinner. Promise me? It will make this fever worse."

He gave her hand a loving squeeze. "If it will make you stop worrying, then I will drink only water. But there is no fever, just the flush of too much activity."

They strolled the rest of the way to the women's quarters, holding each other. When they reached the confines of her reception rooms, Roxana gave Alexander a long, tender kiss.

"I want you to be careful in Arabia. And always remember how much I love you."

"I will come to see you before I go. Until then I will have generals to meet and plans to see to, and—"

"I understand," she interrupted. "You will be busy."

He went to her chamber doors, and right before he opened them, Alexander turned back to her. "I used to wonder if I did the right thing by marrying you. Now I know I did. Of all the treasures Persia has given me, you are the only one I cherish."

He walked out, and Roxana stood in the middle of her elegant room smothering the impulse to go after him.

No matter what she said or did, he would march out to meet his fate. Letting him go would be the hardest thing she'd ever done, but he was Alexander, and his destiny had already been set by the gods long before the stars had blanketed the night's sky.

CHAPTER THIRTY-SEVEN

Roxana spent a quiet afternoon on her balcony with a book, soaking in the cool river breezes. The burden of her pregnancy kept her indoors most days, seeking relief from the summer heat.

There was another reason she'd not ventured out—news of ill omens. She'd even banned Morella from informing her of the gossip from the kitchens. But she could not shut the world out forever.

"Roxana, I must speak with you."

General Perdiccas appeared at the doorway to her private balcony. His rumpled white tunic, untrimmed beard, and disheveled hair perplexed her.

"What is it, Perdiccas? You look a fright."

He helped her from her chair. "The king is ill with fever. He's been taken across the Tiber River to the garden island of the kings. He refuses a doctor and says he will only have you."

She didn't question him, but went inside and grabbed a shawl to cover her head, ignoring a wide-eyed Morella.

"My lady, what is it?"

She didn't stop to explain but hurried through her doors with Perdiccas. Her two bodyguards quickly followed.

They reached the dock leading to the Great King's garden island where a flatboat waited for them. Perdiccas helped Roxana into the boat. Once she had taken a seat on the bench, she turned to the hard-nosed general.

"When did this happen?"

Perdiccas had a seat next to her while the two soldiers assigned to protect her climbed on board. "Last night he complained of fever when he met with us to discuss Arabia. This morning he could not get out of bed. He ordered his men to take him to the island because it was cooler." Perdiccas shook his head. "You know how he is. He will have nothing to do with doctors. Ptolemy suggested you tend to him and he agreed."

She cast her gaze to the approaching island. "I should have been told earlier about this."

"He didn't want us to bother you. Especially with a child on the way."

The boat jerked to a stop at a short dock. Perdiccas stepped onto the pier and lifted Roxana out of the boat.

After progressing through a palm-covered walkway with pools of water on either side, Roxana climbed several steps to the first terrace of the gardens. She passed beneath a mud-bricked doorway and emerged in a blue-tiled hall that ran the length of the first floor. Perdiccas motioned for her to follow. He turned down one of the corridors and entered a white marble room.

Inside generals gathered around a simple cot. Propped on pillows and barking orders in a hoarse voice was her Alexander.

Her trepidation escalated at the sight of his pale skin and labored breathing. She prayed not to fall apart. She needed to be strong for her husband and the baby in her womb.

"Make sure the Companion Cavalry is drilled with their maneuvers for this campaign. Our early expeditions report these nomads are fearless horsemen." His voice barely carried beyond the room. He grinned as Roxana came up to his cot. "My physician has arrived."

She knelt and felt his brow. "Alexander, you're burning up." She raised her head to Bagoas, who stood to the side of the cot.

"I'll need cool water and wine to wipe him down … and some linens to make compresses."

After Bagoas left the room, she faced the generals.

"No more. He must rest."

Alexander waved to his generals. "You heard her. Be back in the morning to go over more details for Arabia."

The men ambled from the room, talking amongst themselves. When the last one had left, she pulled the damp sheets off him.

He held her hand. "I told them not to say anything to you."

"Oh, I could kick you, you arrogant, spoiled, selfish ass."

Alexander laughed, and as he did, he held his side. Then an attack of coughing came over him. It took a few moments before he could catch his breath again.

She eased him back against his pillows. "I told you to rest, that you were doing too much. Why didn't you listen?"

"I thought it was nothing. Just a chill." He closed his eyes. "I've seen worse."

Roxana flashed back to the last time she'd seen Hephaestion alive. He had uttered almost the same words.

She covered her mouth, the lump in her throat getting bigger as she took in the pallor of his skin, and the perspiration on his brow. She swallowed hard and sniffled, keeping her tears at bay.

"Rest, my love." She ran her fingers across his red cheeks. "I will be right here. I'm not going anywhere."

She remained by his side, wiping him down with wine mixed with water to cool his fever. He slept fitfully that night. He talked to someone in his dreams. Roxana listened attentively, hoping to detect a name, but she could guess who it was. Hephaestion was never far from his thoughts.

In the morning, he seemed better and insisted he must see to his religious duties at the temple on the other side of the island. Despite her objections, he went, carried on a litter, and when he returned, his generals were waiting.

"Looks like his old self," Ptolemy said, sounding upbeat.

Roxana wasn't convinced. His fever had gone down but had not gone away.

By evening, after barely sleeping for more than a day, her exhaustion thwarted her ability to care for her husband. At Alexander's insistence, she napped on an uncomfortable cot in a room next to his, and when she awoke, she caught Alexander, sitting up in his cot and playing dice with some of his generals. She could tell by his pale coloring and his labored breath the activity wore him out.

"Ah, there's my beautiful wife."

His voice sounded weaker.

"I told Bagoas to let you sleep. After all, you are sleeping for two, and you must protect the health of our son."

She snatched the dice from his hand. "I must also protect the health of his father. You should be sleeping, not playing games."

He frowned, his gray eyes smoldering with frustration. "I didn't feel like sleeping. And we had a good game on. I'm winning."

The childlike exuberance in his raspy voice didn't match the dullness in his eyes. He wasn't getting better, she could tell, but what kind of fever grabs hold like this?

"I want to consult with your doctors about this fever."

He glowered at her. "No doctors. Is that clear?"

She gave in, knowing anger would only make him sicker, but her inability to help him overwhelmed her.

Determined to get a handle on his care, she turned to his generals crowding the bed. "You should go."

The tightlipped men averted her insistent glare as they left the room. They reminded her more of precocious boys in need of a firm hand rather than fierce warriors. Or perhaps she was the one who had changed.

"You've become my mother." Alexander chuckled behind her, and then a fit of coughing overtook him.

When he settled down, Roxana noticed how quickly the brief episode had tired him, draining the color from his face. He reclined on his pillows and closed his eyes while she kept a wary eye on his breathing.

For the first time since his soldiers had climbed the great rock and taken her family, she was terrified of a future without Alexander.

CHAPTER THIRTY-EIGHT

A warm morning breeze meandered through the room, sweeping across Alexander's bare chest, eliciting a shiver. Roxana sat quietly by his side, her fingertips on the thready pulse in his wrist.

"How did this happen?" Perdiccas came alongside her, taking in the scene.

He helped Roxana from her chair and led her to an empty corner of the room. "He's not improving, is he?"

"The coughing attacks are getting worse every day. I'm afraid he's collecting fluid in his lungs."

The unflappable general's jaw dropped. "Are you saying Alexander is dying?"

Roxana turned away, unable to take his expression. "At night, the king sleeps erratically. The fever has caused bouts of delirium. I've tried to calm him and relieve his fever with cool compresses to the chest, but it's not helping."

Bagoas came in with a pitcher of fresh water. The king tossed on his cot, mumbling incoherently. The attendant's astonishment was the same as the general's standing next to her.

Roxana never wanted anyone to get wind of her husband's weakness. He could never appear less than a king to his subjects. She had to limit those who came in contact with him, to protect him for as long as she could.

"Why don't you get some rest, Bagoas. I will tend to the king."

He nodded and set the pitcher on a table.

Perdiccas waited until the eunuch had left the room before he spoke. "You should rest, too."

"I can't leave my husband. He needs me."

"Think of your child."

Her lower lip quivered. "I've thought of little else for days. Without my husband, what will become of our child?"

"If he's a son, he will be our next king." Perdiccas put a comforting hand on her shoulder. "Another Alexander to lead his men. That must bring you some comfort?"

Roxana refrained from telling him the future he proposed scared her to death. Without his father to defend him, her son would have an uphill battle to be accepted as a Greek king.

The general gave Alexander a worried glance before he left the room.

At her husband's bedside, Roxana rested her head on Alexander's chest and listened to his racing heart. His breath rattled as he struggled to get in enough air. He was beyond her healing knowledge, and even the doctors she'd secretly consulted were at a loss for his treatment.

Her heart ached every moment of the day and night. She couldn't lose him now. She wanted nothing more than for Alexander to hold their child in his arms and share a few moments of happiness.

Tendrils of early morning light stretched across Alexander's ashen face, sunken eyes, and gaunt cheeks.

Roxana dabbed a wet cloth across his dusky, cracked lips.

He stirred, his head listing toward her.

"Roxana …" he rasped.

"Shh. Save your strength." She caressed the reddish stubble on his jaw. "The men need their king. And I need my husband."

Someone cleared their throat behind her.

Ptolemy and Seleucus, the infantry's general, waited at the doorway. He, as well as the other commanders, had been coming in and out the past few days, updating their king on preparations for the Arabian campaign.

Seleucus crossed the room and arched over Roxana's shoulder so he could speak directly to Alexander. "The soldiers have heard of your illness. Many are demanding to see you. They're crying, wandering about the streets of Babylon calling for you. What do we tell them?"

Roxana scowled, biting back her protest. How dare he upset her husband?

Devotion to his army sparked in Alexander's eyes.

All the times she had seen him interact with his men came back to her. They were his strength, and perhaps his salvation. If he could rally for anyone, it would be for them.

"Call all the company commanders and battalion leaders," Alexander got out in a wheezy voice. He strained to raise his head. "Have them wait outside the palace."

Ptolemy eased closer. "Alexander, you can barely move. You must not—"

Alexander's flinty gaze silenced his general.

Ptolemy bowed and stepped back from the bed. "I'll inform the other generals."

With Seleucus at his side, Ptolemy plodded to the doorway, bereft of his usual energy.

Roxana fussed with Alexander's bedsheet. "The men can wait until you're well. You'll wear yourself out if they visit you."

Alexander's shaky fingers touched the top of her hand. "No. My men must see you and the baby you carry next to me. Do you understand, little star?"

The request confounded her. "But your men can see me—"

"They must see you with me when they come, and know the child ..." His voice disappeared, and a bout of coughing overpowered him.

Roxana wiped the perspiration from his brow, terrified. "You must not tire yourself so."

He settled back against his cot and caught his breath. "I want you to promise me ... you will fight for our son. Show the men ... what I've always seen in you ... your strength."

The color drained from his cheeks, and her heart sank. She kissed his lips, anxious to do anything to appease him.

"I will do whatever you ask. Rest now, Alexander, please."

While she dabbed his damp face, her gold necklace brushed his arm.

He weakly smiled as it glistened in the faint morning light.

"Hephaestion," barely escaped his lips in a soft sigh.

He drifted into a fitful sleep. She tucked her head next to him, listening to his every ragged breath. She feared he would soon join his dear Hephaestion. How could she go on without him? And how would she be able to fight for their child in a world without her king?

Feet shuffled along the stone walkway as Alexander's generals carried his stretcher to a small dock. Roxana held his hand while they boarded a flatboat that would take them across the river to the palace of Nebuchadnezzar. No longer able to speak, the king signaled with his eyes what he needed or wanted.

The wind stung Roxana's face as the rhythmic dirge of oars sliced through the water. She rested her husband's hand in her lap, her thumb mindlessly grazing his palm.

The boat slowed as they neared the docks to the palace.

Perdiccas came out from a patch of date trees. He waited until the other generals carried the stretcher onto the shore.

"Alexander, the army has gathered—there are hundreds of men."

Roxana searched Alexander's eyes. "What do you want to do?"

He glanced at the palace walls.

She squeezed his hand, letting him know she understood. "Have the men come into the palace. They can file through his chambers once we get him into his bed."

Alexander sighed, sounding relieved, and rested his head on the rough linen covering his stretcher.

Roxana directed the men carrying the king forward. She was about to follow them when Perdiccas placed his hand on her arm.

"Do you know what this will do to him?" he whispered.

"I'm well aware of his condition, but I will not deny him the company of his men. Could you?"

Perdiccas marched into the palace.

The hot sun beat on her back as a procession of priests and servants escorted the king through the courtyard filled with trees and reflecting ponds. They entered the palace gate and made their way through the tiled halls filled with paintings of Persian gods.

The curtains in the king's rooms had been drawn, leaving nothing but shards of afternoon light slicing through the somber darkness. The generals shuffled toward the enormous bed and settled Alexander amid a plethora of soft pillows.

Roxana waited until the men backed away before shooing the servants from the bedside.

Alone with her husband, she positioned pillows under Alexander to help him breathe. Her shaking hands hungered for something to do, but when he gripped her fingers and raised them to his lips, her trembling eased. She'd done all she could.

Bagoas entered the chamber, followed by Alexander's other generals, their stony faces adding to the heaviness in her heart.

She let go of his hand. "I will stay close by so they can see me. I promise."

The men gathered in the room swarmed the bed and forced her to the side. She ended up a few feet away, stuck in the corner. Roxana wanted to protest, tell them of Alexander's intentions, but a flicker of movement drew her attention to the open chamber doors leading to the outer corridor. There, a long line of Greek men, some officers, some commanders, many army regulars, and others without rank or status, stood with forlorn faces, bent on seeing their king. The sight of them reminded her of Alexander's love for his men and their disdain for his Persian bride. Perhaps his army needed to see their king more than his pregnant wife. In time, when he was better, she could win their support. Right now, she needed their collective prayers to beseech the gods to save the man she loved.

The air became stifling as the afternoon wore on. One by one, men filed past their king, many with tears in their eyes. Some men were so overwhelmed that they could not walk without assistance. Alexander greeted each one as if he knew them personally, with a smile, a look, or a gesture.

Roxana's linen dress was soaked through with sweat after hours of standing. Her feet and back ached.

She waited until the last of the men had visited their king before she made her way back to the bedside.

The pink had left Alexander's cheeks, leaving him deathly white. He lay with his eyes closed and his breath, no longer labored, hardly registered as she anxiously checked the rise and fall of his chest.

That his men had taken the last precious dregs of his strength infuriated her. "They've tired you too much."

Perdiccas came up to the bed, not a hint of emotion on his face. "You should rest, Roxana. This isn't good for you or the baby."

She selected a few shreds of linen from the pile left by the servants at a bedside table. "I'm fine."

"No, you're not. You're exhausted. You need to start thinking of your child."

She angrily dipped the linen in a bowl of water and wrung it out. "Do you or any of the other generals think of my child, Perdiccas? What will happen to my baby without the king?"

Their eyes clashed, but Perdiccas turned away.

"That's what I thought." She returned her attention to her husband. "Let me worry about my baby. You and the other generals have more pressing concerns to occupy your minds."

Roxana stayed at her husband's side with his generals as the pleasant evening air chased away the overbearing heat of the day. She remained by his bed throughout the night, continually wiping Alexander down and humming to him.

By sunrise, it was apparent to all, including Alexander, the inevitable had come.

Roxana trembled when Perdiccas came up to the bed and inspected Alexander's face.

He leaned into the king and asked, "To whom do you leave your empire?"

She looked on in hopeless despair as her husband's lips parted, becoming blue.

"To the best," he breathed with all the strength he had left.

A glimmer of his tenacious determination flashed and then faded from his features.

Perdiccas hesitated, then he reached for the king's right hand and slipped the gold seal ring from his finger. He lowered his head and backed away.

She took Alexander's hand, squeezing it as a tear ran down her cheek.

"I can't lose you."

Every memory of their time together flew across her mind. There were so many things she wished to say, so many regrets she wanted to share.

Roxana kissed his forehead, wishing for her last words to give him peace. "I will never stop loving you, and I promise I will never stop fighting for our child."

Relief softened the lines carved into his brow, and his shoulders relaxed, sinking into the pillows.

She gazed once more into his magnificent gray eyes and remembered how they had mystified her from the moment they had met. She smiled—her warmest and best smile—so he could take it with him on his journey.

She held his hand as his breathing slowed. A stunned stillness settled over her heart.

This can't be happening!

The king gave one last long, raspy sigh and was gone.

Roxana rested her head against her husband's lifeless chest and, giving in to her grief, wept inconsolably for her Alexander.

CHAPTER THIRTY-NINE

"T he empire must have a king!"

The shout of a man woke Roxana from her stupor. It came from the reception area outside of Alexander's bedroom.

Numb, she wiped her eyes and listened to the muffled voices of men. She turned to her husband in the big bed.

How peaceful he appeared in death. She'd never seen him so at ease.

She touched a curl of his hair. "I pray Hephaestion is taking care of you."

"Dammit, Ptolemy!"

It sounded like Perdiccas, but she could never imagine the unflappable man raising his voice. Drawn to the heated arguing, she rose from Alexander's bed. Suddenly, her concern for what was happening on the other side of the bedroom door became more important than staying with her husband.

Before she pushed the door open, she glimpsed her wrinkled and dirty black peplos. She'd been wearing the same clothes for the past six days. The hollow ache in her chest intensified. She turned back to her Alexander, anxious to be with him once again.

"We have to wait for the child!"

Ptolemy's gruff voice stopped her.

She placed her hand on her swollen belly. The child. Alexander had wanted her to fight for their baby. And she had promised she would.

With a deep breath, she turned toward the door.

The glare from the oil lamps lit in the room momentarily blinded her as she stepped from Alexander's darkened chamber. She raised her hand, blocking out the light and slinked into the room.

"Are you sure he said the best? Maybe he meant to say Craterus," Ptolemy suggested as he sat with others at Alexander's silver dining table.

She recognized the generals who had known Alexander best in life—along with his stocky secretary, Eumenes.

"It sounded like *kratisto*, or the best, to me." Perdiccas's cheeks reddened. "Or are you just hot to get Craterus back? Can't stand the idea that Alexander left me in charge," Perdiccas added, raising his voice. "I'm his second-in-command."

Ptolemy glared at him. "You've never let any of us forget that."

"Please, gentleman, please." Eumenes rapped his knuckle on the table. "The man has not even turned cold, and you two are already shouting at each other. We have to make arrangements for the succession."

"Perdiccas," a man with one eye called. "Alexander trusted Craterus. He sent him home to be regent of Macedon. Are you sure he didn't mean for Craterus to take over?"

"Antigonus is right." Nearchus arched forward in his chair, his blue eyes blazing. "Perdiccas, are you positive?"

"Enough!" Perdiccas sliced his hand through the air. "We have things to work out. Problems are going to come up. They have to be thought out now. That's what Alexander would have done."

"He was only thirty-two." Ptolemy rubbed his face, his voice teeming with bitterness. "I'm eleven years older than him, and now he's dead." He slammed his fist into the table, startling everyone. "Damn all the gods!"

Roxana rushed forward, stunned. "Gentleman, please stop your shouting. Do you have no respect for your king? Can he not have peace even in death?"

Ptolemy went to Roxana's side and took her elbow. "We have matters to discuss with you that cannot wait." He ushered her to the table and placed her in the chair next to his.

Roxana eased her weary body into her seat. "I understand. We have funeral plans to make. I feel that—"

"That's not what's important right now, Roxana." Perdiccas came around to her chair. "There's an empire that needs attention, and quickly, before things get out of hand."

She gaped around the table at the men's stern faces. She could see it in their eyes—they feared Alexander's empire falling apart.

"What do we do?"

Ptolemy took his seat next to her. "This is what we have been discussing. The Persian factions in this country will demand a Persian heir to the throne, and the Macedonians will want a Macedonian heir. We have to come up with a solution to keep both sides from turning on each other."

His disclosure rekindled her fear for the baby in her womb. "What about my child? He or she is half Macedonian, half Persian."

"And two more months away from being born, and we don't know if it will be male. We need a leader now." Perdiccas stood back from the table, his eyes squinting together. "There are others who can cause problems for us. Alexander considered Stateira his queen; marriage to her could give someone a claim to the throne. Even someone marrying Parysatis as the daughter of Artaxerxes could give any man of noble Persian blood a reason to start one hell of a war or claim succession to Alexander's realm."

A tall man with a rugged face spoke up. "But we have a son of Alexander. Barsine's boy living in Pergamum, Heracles. We could make him king."

"Lysimachus has a point. The king has a son, even if he's a bastard," Nearchus said with a grimace. "And then we can't forget about Arrhidaeus."

Ptolemy groaned. "That dimwitted fool."

"Who?" Roxana asked, overwhelmed by the list of names proposed in opposition to her child.

"Arrhidaeus is Alexander's half-brother," Ptolemy explained. "He's soft in the head and a few years older than Alexander is … was." Ptolemy briefly paused and dropped his head. "He's the only other surviving son of Philip's. Olympias took care of all the rest of Philip's boys by his other wives. She wanted to make sure her son became king."

Alexander had told her of his friends, enemies, and family, but he'd never mentioned a brother. This was far more than she'd expected. Conspirators were everywhere.

"Alexander never said anything about a half-brother. Why was I not told—?"

"I'd forgotten about him. He's been in the city for some time." The surly General Seleucus cut her off, ignoring her. "Alexander kept him close during the campaigns, not wanting to leave him alone back in Macedonia. He had to make sure no one could use him to overthrow him as King of Macedon."

"What about you, Perdiccas?" Roxana turned to the man next to her. "Alexander appointed you his successor. He gave you his ring."

Perdiccas folded his hands, displaying a patient smile beneath his beard. "My lady, in Greek *kratisto*, or best, and Craterus, could sound the same coming from a dying man with no breath. We can't be positive Alexander meant for me to be in charge."

Roxana could not believe it. Her husband's last words had been clear. "But I heard Alexander. He meant—"

"There's only one way to decide this." Eumenes rose to his feet. "The Macedonian way. We put it to the army."

Ptolemy rubbed his chin, lost in thought "That could be dangerous. There are many among the officers who can stir the men and make problems for the succession."

Perdiccas nodded. "We'll have to risk it. Whatever we decide, the army will have to go along with us."

The army. Why had everything in her life come back to the army?

But it all made sense. Their marriage, how his men treated him, the banquet of acceptance, the mutinies in India and Opis—Alexander had never been a king, but a leader. A true king would never have catered to his men. How could the fate of an empire lie in the hands of rabble?

"What of Arabia?" Nearchus tossed up his hands. "Do we go on?"

"Without Alexander, I don't know if the men would be willing to go on to

Arabia," Perdiccas pointed out. "Perhaps we should hold off on expanding an empire we have yet to take control of."

Seleucus inhaled a shaky breath through his broken, yellow teeth. "What do you think Greece will do when news reaches them of the king's death?"

"Revolt, what else?" Ptolemy shrugged in a matter-of-fact fashion. "Craterus and Antipater will have to sort out that problem. In the meantime, we have our own nest of scorpions to deal with."

Lysimachus pushed away from the table. "Then we'd better hurry and put the decision to the men before word gets around the camps about the king. We'll have a riot on our hands if we don't move soon."

Perdiccas stepped behind her chair. "I will call a general assembly of the men in the throne room. It should be big enough to handle everyone."

The rest of the generals made their way toward the doors to the king's chambers.

Roxana, however, didn't get up from her chair. She banged her fist on the table, furious at the disregard the men showed her husband.

"When do we take care of the king?"

Ptolemy stopped at the doors, appearing more perturbed by her statement than remorseful.

"In good time, my lady. We have first to find our new king before we can lay our old one to rest."

Roxana's heart broke all over again. She thought these men, above all others, had loved him, but it would seem like most things associated with Alexander, she was wrong. His death didn't incite sorrow in any of them. They only saw opportunity.

The names, plots of intrigue, challengers to the throne, spun around in her head as if caught in a giant cyclone. Why had Alexander kept this from her?

"It feels as if everything is falling apart."

"Yes, it does." Perdiccas came out from behind her chair. "Alexander is dead, and the world will never be the same. Now we must deal with the aftermath. 'Achilles absent is Achilles still.'"

"From life to legend. How pleased Alexander would be to know he'd achieved everlasting fame."

Perdiccas pulled out the chair next to her.

"We need to discuss something, Roxana."

She turned to face his cold brown eyes, the twisting in her gut becoming more insistent.

"There's another problem." Perdiccas took his seat. "I dispatched a letter to Alexander's other wives two days ago, informing them of his illness. They will arrive in Babylon very soon. A decision must be made about their future."

Roxana sank deeper into her chair, her fatigue quickly overpowering her. "What decision?"

"If these two women were to die suddenly, you would be Alexander's queen. If you bear a son, then the army would not question your son's succession to the throne."

Murder? In all her contemplations about a future without Alexander, she'd never foreseen this. Her first reaction was to shout her vehement rejection, but before she could open her mouth, the child moved. She had to entertain every option to help her hoped-for son—Alexander's son.

"I must be either exhausted, Perdiccas, or overwhelmed by grief even to be having this conversation."

Roxana wondered what Alexander would have made of his faithful generals. Or had he suspected all along that they would be like this?

Resigning herself to her fate, she asked, "Why are you telling me this?"

"Because you need to know what's going to happen. People will die, disputes over territory will break out, and the ugliness of maintaining an empire will shadow your doorstep. Alexander protected you from all this, but you can't remain oblivious any longer. You have to fight for your child and yourself." Perdiccas paused and wiped his fingers across the table's surface. "From now on, be very careful. Watch what you say to everyone, including your maid. Trust no one. You're just as much of a threat to Stateira, Parysatis, and all who would take Alexander's throne, because you carry his only legitimate heir. That makes you very precious to us who wish to honor his memory. So keep the guards with you and have all your food and drink tasted." He stood. "I'm sorry, but the days and months ahead will not be easy for you. I wonder if Alexander truly knew what he did to you the moment he took you for his wife."

He marched to the doors and disappeared into the corridor.

The silence in her husband's reception room seeped into her skin like the worst of the cold in the Hindu Kush. She shivered, overwhelmed with all she'd learned, and all she had to face.

What have you done to me, Alexander?

A few more tears raced down her cheeks as she remembered the man she loved, and her shaking eased. Their short four years together she would not trade for anything. Her hand went to her round bump as she tried to fathom the future, but fear more than happiness crowded her images.

Wiping her nose on her sleeve, she mumbled, "What is to become of us?"

Aching inside and out, Roxana rose from her chair. She made her way to the doors of Alexander's bedroom. Then the wailing of the women from the harem apartments drifted along the corridor to the king's rooms. Beyond that, the shouting from the streets of, "The king is dead!" rose like the din of far-off thunder.

The games have begun.

She walked into his bedroom and went to the windows to open the curtains, allowing in the light.

But instead of the sun, dark, ominous clouds had gathered in the skies—a fitting start to the long days ahead.

The gods have surely abandoned us now.

Alone in the bedroom, Roxana collected fresh water from the running gold taps in the king's bath area and soft white linens from shelves in the rear of his rooms. The weeping and wailing coming from outside the windows, she ignored. The grief of the palace was not hers. They didn't know the man, only the king.

Roxana prepared to bathe her husband and rinse away the sweat and stains of his illness. She worked methodically, without being hindered by her emotions, as she removed his soaked loincloth and stretched his arms out to the side. The contentment of her labors surprised her. There was no sorrow, no grief. It eased her burdens to take care of him and not leave it for a servant or embalmer. This was her duty as his wife.

First, she wiped down his chest, arms, and legs, taking care to dry him with fresh towels. She touched every scar, memorizing the feel. Roxana rubbed oil over his cold skin, wanting to remember the pale color, and note the few freckles on his arms and chest. He no longer smelled like her Alexander. She missed that; it had lulled her to sleep so many times. How would she live without his sweet perfume?

His hands she lingered over, remembering their tender touch as she gently cleaned his knuckles and around his dusky nails. She rubbed oil into the calluses in his palms, wanting to hold on to them for as long as she could.

She delicately dabbed his face with damp linen, anxious to preserve every curve, every wrinkle. A light coating of oil in her hands, she traced his brow, the line of his nose, and ran her fingers along the curve of his jaw, the stubble of his whiskers scraping against her skin.

His hair she rinsed and then opened a window to allow the warm afternoon breeze to dry it. She ached to see his unruly waves one more time.

The last thing she did was change his bed linens, positioned him to lie in state, then sat in a chair next to him, keeping watch.

How long would it be before his men came to see him? And when would the embalmers arrive to preserve him?

The heat of the afternoon gave way to evening and no one came.

Only Morella ducked her head in the bedroom doors.

"You must eat, my lady."

She didn't get up. "Go away."

Roxana wished she could put a sign across his doors with those words to keep the world at bay.

At peace, she hugged her belly, and spoke to her husband, not ready to give him up.

"Do you remember when I first danced for you?" She smiled at the memory. "I was terrified I would do something stupid in front of the king. But the moment I saw your eyes, I knew you were different, special."

She went on recounting their lives together—the good and bad.

The light from the windows faded and night descended, but she never rose from her chair. She stayed with her king as was the duty of his queen.

The thunder of marching feet roused Roxana.

She wiped her face and sat up, the room around her dark, with only a few beams of moonlight streaming in through the open windows.

Pain ran along her back and arms when she moved. Stiff, she stood, and her added weight labored her efforts. The events of the last day siphoned into her head, and she caught sight of the bed where Alexander lay.

"Why has no one come for you?"

Anger surged from her gut as she remembered the generals and their disregard for her husband. She went to the chamber doors, and halted, afraid to leave him.

What if he wasn't there when she got back?

She rested her head against the doors. He wasn't there. Her husband was gone. The stirrings of hunger helped to sweep the cobwebs away. Then her baby kicked, and slowly, she realized she could not stay with him anymore.

The movement of shadows from the reception room sparked her curiosity. Who was out there?

Roxana jerked the heavy doors open.

Four soldiers from the king's guard stood with spears at the ready. When they saw her, they didn't move.

"What is the meaning of this?" she asked, stepping into the light from the adjoining room.

"General Perdiccas sent us to protect the king," a sandy-skinned Persian soldier closest to her said in Greek. "The generals are meeting with the army now, deciding the future of the empire. General Perdiccas felt it best to not leave the king unguarded in case the men got other ideas."

Roxana trembled at the gravity of her situation, and her child's. A sick feeling came over her at the idea of her fate in the hands of an army of men.

"Have any decisions been made?"

"Ah, not exactly, my lady."

CHAPTER FORTY

An anxious Roxana waited in her chambers as the rays of the summer sun carried the torrid heat of the day through her open windows. The fresh linen peplos she'd changed into when returning to her rooms already clung to her skin. Consumed with waiting for word on the army's decision, she had refused all Morella's suggestions to eat or sleep. She was thankful her agitation kept her exhaustion from overwhelming her completely.

While she paced the sun-streaked stone floor of her reception room, Morella sat on a stool, a fretful wrinkle embedded in her brow.

"You must lie down. You haven't slept a full night since the king fell ill. You have to think about your baby."

Roxana glimpsed her maid's dark eyes. "Sleep is the last thing on my mind. There's too much at stake now."

"I know, but—"

A knock at her chamber doors sent Roxana racing ahead of Morella. She yanked open the doors, her stomach a churning mass of doubt.

In the corridor, a rumpled Perdiccas waited. The fatigue etched in the lines on his pale face shook her.

"Roxana, we need to talk."

He came inside, searching the room with his bloodshot eyes. When he caught sight of Morella, he said, "Send her away."

Roxana turned to her, but Morella held up her hand.

"It's all right. I've spent enough time around these Greeks to understand some of what they say." She gave her an encouraging smile. "I'll go to the kitchens and wrestle up a plate of food for you."

After Perdiccas shut the doors, he faced her.

"I think you need to prepare yourself for rough days ahead."

Her legs wobbly, she went to a chair by her refreshment table and sat. She took a breath, then raised her head.

"What is to become of my child and me?"

He curiously tilted his head and ran his hand over his graying beard. "That has yet to be decided."

She rocked back, more unsure than ever of her fate. "Perhaps you should tell me what happened at the meeting."

He walked to the center of the room. "Ptolemy and I met with the members of the army from generals all the way down the chain of command to the rank and file. Alexander's empty throne had his crown, sword, and the shield from Troy set on it for all the men to see. The generals stood by the throne as I announced the king's death to the men. I then told them Alexander gave me his seal ring and left the army to choose the best among us to rule."

She gripped the arms of her chair, hanging on his words. "And then what?"

"All hell broke loose."

Perdiccas wiped a bead of sweat from his forehead and went to her refreshment table. He lifted a jug of wine.

"Have you had this tasted?"

"My maid tested it on a servant from the kitchen. Morella made her drink it twice to make sure."

He selected a goblet and filled it. "You think you know men after fighting alongside them for years, and then during a real crisis, they surprise you."

"What did they say about my child, the king's heir?"

He set down the jug and peered into his drink. "I proposed the assembly back your child, if a male, as king but requested a leader for the army until the child arrives. Then Nearchus, the idiot, shouted for the army to choose Alexander's bastard, Heracles, as the male heir. I told Alexander never to trust him." He sipped his wine. "The men in the room beat their swords against their shields to show their opposition to the idea. Fights broke out, and the men got riled up. Ptolemy stupidly opened up his big mouth and announced to the men a bastard male or the half-breed son of a Persian girl would not rule over them."

Half-breed? Was that how they saw her child? Not even born and already it suffered the stigma of being her child and not the glory of being Alexander's.

"I thought Ptolemy would support me. Before when the generals met, he said he—"

"Ptolemy says a lot of things he doesn't mean. He sensed the men needed assurances. Perhaps they did." Perdiccas swirled his wine. "He was trying to maintain control of the situation. He proposed the army make decisions regarding the empire as we did when Alexander was alive—by a majority vote."

Greek army men deciding the fate of a Persian woman and her half-Persian child brought back the disgruntled voices she'd heard at her wedding feast. The men had hated her then, and nothing had changed, except for their ability to decide if she should live or die.

"And did the men want that?" She swallowed the lump in her throat. "To rule themselves?"

Perdiccas set his goblet on the table. "No. Some men wanted it, some were against it, but most said nothing, meaning they were just as confused about what to do as we were."

She saw a speck of hope in his answer. "So nothing has been decided?"

"Not quite. When one of the men in the room, an officer of low rank, suggested we stick with Alexander's last wishes and keep me in charge, most clapped and cheered. Even when I put Alexander's gold seal ring on my right index finger, the men applauded. But then a high-ranking officer, named Meleager—an impudent troublemaker—spoke out against me. He proposed Arrhidaeus, brother of the king, be the sole heir to the throne. He incited the men, claiming only a pure-blooded son of Philip could be king. Then the throne room became a sea of shouting, brawling, and mayhem."

"Do the men know Arrhidaeus is simple? He can't rule as a king."

Perdiccas sat on the edge of her table. "But he can *be* ruled because he is simple. That's what Meleager and others like him want—a puppet king. If they support Arrhidaeus and the others in the army back him, we will have to do something to shut it down."

She suddenly felt weak. Maybe it was a lack of food or lack of sleep making her lightheaded, or perhaps it was knowing her life could come to an end in the blink of an eye.

"I don't understand any of this." She held her belly, terror-stricken for her child. "What does this mean for us?"

Perdiccas came up to her, a softness lifting his features. "Some dissent was expected after Alexander's passing. This gives us an opportunity to weed out those who will oppose your baby. I've already sent Ptolemy and his division to stop Meleager and his men from getting out of Babylon and stirring the Persian nobility to rebel." He knelt down to face her. "We will deal with this, and then the army will choose me to make decisions until your baby comes."

She wished she could believe him, but Ptolemy's betrayal still hurt. "If my child were pure Macedonian, there would be no question of its succession, but because I'm the mother, there will always be dissent among the men."

Perdiccas stood, his voice taking on a hard edge. "I will not lie to you, many of us begged him to marry and father a child before setting out for Persia. But he didn't and here we are. If I've learned one thing as a soldier, you can never second guess fate."

She clenched her fists, holding in her frustration. "Thank you, General. For supporting my child and me."

"What I do, I do for Alexander. He was a good friend. I want to see his wife and child safe. If you have a boy, and the army sees any of Alexander in him, we will win their support. Then we can get back to the business of putting the empire in order before he comes of age."

"And what happens if it's a girl?"

He wiped his hands together, not a hint of disquiet on his face. "Then she'll be married off to help continue Alexander's line."

"But will a half-Persian boy or girl be accepted in Macedon or Greece? Athens thought Alexander a barbarian; what will they think of my half-Persian child with him?"

He raised his brows. "Who told you that?"

"Hephaestion." She caressed her gold necklace, thinking of all the things he'd taught her. "We often spoke about the world Alexander came from."

"How I wish for both our sakes he was still here." He briskly walked to her doors.

Before reaching for the handle, he stopped. "Stateira and Parysatis have arrived and been placed in the royal harems. Stay in your rooms for the next few days. Do not venture out."

She slumped forward, catching herself on the table. "Why? Am I a prisoner?"

"It's for your safety and your reputation." He pulled one of the doors open. "I don't want suspicion to fall on you when the two women are found poisoned."

The casual manner in which he spoke of killing appalled her. "Is that necessary? They're innocent."

"It doesn't matter what they are. We can't have excess baggage from Alexander's life posing a threat to our affairs."

A strange sense of inevitability washed over her. To survive, she would have to play the game. She would have to please the generals and win them over to assure her child's position. No matter what they asked of her, she had to comply. Even when it came to murder. What had her world come to?

"What happens now, Perdiccas? How do we proceed?"

"We prepare, my lady." Perdiccas stepped outside her doors. "The fighting is about to begin."

Roxana spent her days on her balcony, lounging on a couch stuffed with pillows and avoiding the baking summer heat of her rooms. She longed to stroll the shores of the river and catch any of the cool breezes, but Perdiccas's instructions had been clear, and the safety of her child remained paramount.

Her baby thrived, growing more active with every passing day. Alexander's unborn heir was the only solace from her constant heartache. She missed her husband, and even though they had spent months apart at a time, knowing he would no longer return added to her despair.

Her only lifeline to the outside world was Morella. Her talent for collecting whispers along palace corridors sustained Roxana.

"I have news," Morella announced as she scurried onto Roxana's balcony. "That halfwit, Arrhidaeus, has been appointed king by the soldiers. Calls himself Philip Arrhidaeus, of all things." She rolled her eyes.

The news agitated Roxana's frazzled nerves. *This can't be good.*

"What do the generals say about all this?"

"Not much from what I hear. I guess they had no choice. They even let the simpleton dress in Alexander's armor and crown to receive ambassadors in the throne room. Can you imagine that? A fool dressed as the king."

Roxana struggled to get up from her couch. "I should talk to General Perdiccas."

Morella helped her up. "Oh, I would stay away from him. Rumors are flying around the kitchens about the general."

Roxana stopped inside her balcony doorway. "What rumors?"

Her maid shooed her inside her bedroom. "Some soldiers tried to arrest him for treason the other night."

"Treason? Perdiccas? That's insane." Roxana walked to her makeup table, shaking her head.

"Well, the other members of the army must have agreed with you because he was never arrested, and it created a lot of ill will with the men. Something is brewing. No one knows what, but the city has been cut off from wheat and grain supplies. Farmers from the fields are seeking safety inside the walls because they're afraid of civil war."

Civil war? Roxana went to a bust of Alexander on a pedestal draped in a sheer black cloth. She fingered the soft fabric, questioning what to do. She wanted nothing more than to be alone and mourn her husband, but the restless baby inside her kept reminding her of her duty. If everything fell apart, she and Alexander's child would not survive. Did she defy Perdiccas's orders and leave her rooms to see him or stay and go crazy with worry for her fate?

"Morella, fetch my shawl."

"Why? Where are you going?"

She smoothed her hair back, debating if she could comb it. "To the general's rooms. I have to find out what's going on."

"But it's too dangerous!"

Roxana clasped her shoulders. "Alexander would want me to fight to stay alive. This is the only way I can."

"You're not going without me." Morella put her hands on her hips, staring her down. "After hearing about those two Persian princesses poisoned in their rooms, I'm not letting you out of my sight."

Her guilt over the women's demise hounded her. She had done nothing to save them.

"I'm not going to be poisoned walking to the general's quarters and back. Stop worrying."

Morella lifted one side of her mouth in a cocky smirk. "You aren't walking out of this room unless I go with you."

With Morella close on her heels, and her guards behind her, Roxana walked as fast as she could to the chiliarch's quarters. When she passed the closed gilded doors to her husband's rooms, she expected to see some activity—embalmers carts parked outside, professional mourners, and priests offering prayers on plates laden in myrrh, but there was no one.

Infuriated her husband still lay unattended, she quickened her pace.

They ran into several soldiers patrolling the halls, something Roxana had never seen in a palace before. Men at her door or her husband's she expected, but randomly marching everywhere? This was new.

"I don't like this," Morella whispered as they turned a corner.

Roxana took her hand and pulled her along the corridor to the four guards at attention outside a pair of solid black doors.

"What will you do if they don't let you in?" Morella asked.

"Scream, if I have to."

The sentries blocked the doors with their spears as soon as she got close.

"I'm here to see General Perdiccas."

Awkward glances volleyed between her guards and the ones stationed to protect the general.

"And who are you?" the soldier closest to her demanded.

Not being recognized was a bit of a blow. Since she'd arrived in the camps, the Greeks had known her. In every palace, they'd acknowledged her. Even here in Babylon, she'd been with the king for his last days. How could this be?

Morella stood in front of her, poking out her chest like an angry bullfrog. "This is the lady Roxana, wife to Alexander."

Pensive gazes went back and forth between the four men holding spears at the ready.

"Get the general," the young man in front of her barked.

A soldier ducked inside the thick doors.

Roxana wiped the sweat from her brow, suddenly uncomfortable with her surroundings. It was as if she didn't belong anymore. Alexander had made her one of them, but without him, she was an outsider.

Perdiccas flung the heavy doors open, his mouth a single line of pure rage.

"What in the name of the gods are you doing here?"

His raised voice swept past her like an offensive desert breeze, but she didn't flinch.

"I came to speak with you. I want to know what—"

He raised his finger, stopping her. "Not out here. Come inside."

The guards backed away.

She turned to Morella. "Stay here."

In the sleek reception area of rose-colored Padauk wood, the walls had carvings of archers, chariot teams pulled by horses crowned with feathers, and foot soldiers carrying spears. They engaged in a ferocious battle with men in loincloths and wielding curved swords.

"It's meant to represent the Persian invasion of Greece." Perdiccas came up behind her. "And now a Greek resides here."

He sighed, sounding defeated.

"Why are you here, Roxana? I told you to stay in your rooms."

She turned to him. "Are we on the verge of a civil war?"

Perdiccas inspected her black tunic and matching black cloak. "Everywhere I go lately I see black." He clasped his hands behind his back. "Have you heard Alexander's witless brother has been proclaimed king by that agitator Meleager and his band of thugs? King Philip—I hate calling the wretch that."

She lowered the sheer black shawl from around her head. "I heard you were almost arrested for treason. If they can arrest you, they can certainly do much worse to me."

"I wasn't arrested, and you won't be harmed. And there will be no civil war. The generals and I agreed on what needs to happen. Once these men using King Philip to grab power are out of the way, we will divide the empire to govern. Philip and your unborn child will be under my protection. If you have a boy, he and the halfwit will rule jointly until the time your son can take over his father's throne."

"What happens to Philip then?"

He went to a desk with scrolls neatly arranged in piles and wax tablets stacked to the side. "He will stay alive to keep the army appeased until the time comes when we don't need him anymore."

The statement sickened her, compounding her guilt. "Will you kill him just as you killed the Persian princesses?"

Perdiccas grinned and selected a wax tablet. "If Philip had decided to marry one of Alexander's wives, it could have made things more difficult with the army and the Persians. With their bodies on the way back to Susa, along with Alexander's Persian boy, a multitude of problems have been averted."

The disclosure blindsided her. "Bagoas is gone?"

"Yes, back to the harems where he belongs. Another bit of Alexander's baggage I didn't want hanging around." He lifted a stylus and wrote something on the tablet she could not make out across the room.

His words provoked her concern. Was she another piece of Alexander's baggage Perdiccas did not care for?

The organized desk reflected the personality of the man who used it. She remembered Alexander's small desk cluttered with scrolls and tablets. How different the two men were, but how similar in other ways. Did she trust him? What choice did she have?

"What will you do to these thugs manipulating Philip? Alexander dealt with his enemies swiftly."

The look in his eyes as he slammed the tablet closed sent a chill through her. She caught a glimpse of the ruthless man under the sphinxlike exterior.

"Tomorrow the army will have a purification ceremony. Ptolemy will suggest it to cleanse the army and men of all the discord that's happened since Alexander's death. Meleager and his cronies will be told he is to become one of us, a general, but ..." He walked back to her, holding the tablet.

She saw it in his eyes. "You will kill him."

"We will set an example for the other men in the ranks considering insurrection." He held the tablet against his chest. "There won't be any trouble after that. My troops, as well as Ptolemy's, surround the city as we speak. Order will be restored."

She wanted to leave, wishing she'd never heard of the general's plans, but there was another matter needing attention.

"What about Alexander? I passed his rooms on the way here. No one has bothered with his body since his death."

"When this is over, and we've firmly established control, we will see to him. We will prepare him for his journey home."

"Home?" A surge of nausea overtook her. "I don't understand."

"Every Macedonian king has to be buried by his successor before the next king can take over his office. If you have a son, you, the child, and Philip Arrhidaeus will have to accompany Alexander's body back to our old capital in Aegae for his funeral rights."

All the stories Alexander had told her of his homeland came rushing back. Her nausea intensified as she pictured his palace, his subjects, and his infamous mother.

"I never imagined that I would be going to Macedonia without Alexander."

"If your child is to be king, you will have to. It's a Macedonian tradition." He took her arm. "Stay in your rooms until Meleager is dead. I will send word when it's safe to move about the palace again." He escorted her across the room.

Perdiccas opened his doors and handed the wax tablet to the first soldier he saw. "Take this to the officer of the watch. Tell him I'm assigning two more men to the Lady Roxana's rooms."

In all the time she'd spent with Alexander, on the road and in different palaces, she'd never been afraid. Now she had a sneaking suspicion she was getting a glimpse into her perilous future.

"The extra guards are for your protection." Perdiccas guided her into the hallway. "From now on, all your visitors will be approved by me. We must both be cautious." He bowed to her. "My lady."

When the chamber doors slammed, she shuddered at the sound.

Morella came alongside her. "Are you all right?"

She took her hand, wanting to feel something warm after all the cold talk of death.

"We must return to my rooms," she said, turning to the corridor. "And wait out the gathering storm."

Chapter Forty-One

From her balcony, Roxana admired the morning sun shining down on the orange trees in the palace gardens. She waited for what she wasn't sure—word on the plight of the men who had rebelled against Perdiccas, soldiers running into her rooms set to kill her, or the screaming of women in the harems as news of the bloodshed tumbled through the palace.

Then, in a field adjacent to the palace, she spotted movement. The din of men, whinnying of horses, and cry of elephants carried to her balcony, igniting her curiosity. She climbed from her couch as soldiers, hundreds of them, bearing shields, long spears, swords, and axes lined up on one side of the field. A contingent of cavalry and elephant corps occupied the opposite side.

"What's going on?" Morella asked, coming out on the balcony.

"I'm not sure."

Priests, dressed all in white and leading a white dog, joined the men. Plates of incense hung from chains, wafting plumes of white smoke around the men and animals.

Roxana could guess what was going on. The purification ceremony Perdiccas spoke of was about to take place. But why here, in front of the palace? Whatever statement the general planned to make, she had a feeling it would be momentous.

Morella crept toward the edge of the balcony. "Is it some strange Macedonian ritual?"

Roxana gripped the delicately carved wooden railing. "Not a ritual; a way of life."

The pure white hound bitch was taken to the center of the field and held by the priests. A ceremonial knife cut the animal's throat, and the dog squealed. The priests worked quickly, throwing the entrails between the forces of infantry and cavalry. The men in white raised their hands to the heavens and offered prayers. In a cloud of white smoke, they left the field.

Then, the cavalry horses circled the few hundred infantrymen and phalanx divisions. The elephant corps stayed on the sidelines as horses closed in, nervously pawing the ground, snorting, and tossing their heads.

A sense of doom latched on to Roxana and never let go.

Shouts from the field rose to her balcony as men caught in the middle of the circle of horses, demanded answers for the strange formation. A few tried to run between the horses, but the animals closed in even tighter.

"My lady, what is happening?"

The tension in her maid's voice brought on a rush of guilt.

"Morella, go inside. You don't want to see this."

Her attendant lowered her head and dashed into the bedroom. Roxana went to her balcony doors and with her hands shaking, slammed them closed.

Back at the railing, she watched as the circle closed in on the men. Shouts of anger turned to cries as the foot soldiers realized their fate. Calls for mercy and on occasion, Alexander's name carried in the air. But Alexander had nothing to do with this. Despite his ferocity on the battlefield, he was not a butcher, but apparently, his generals were.

In the center of the circle was the red-plumed helmet of the infantry leader. He pushed through the men as if trying to organize a last stand. But it was too late.

The cavalry opened their ranks to let in a contingent of the elephant corp. The massive beasts raised their trunks and let out battle cries as they went after the trapped soldiers. The first loud shriek came from a man who was lifted into the air by an elephant's trunk and thrown against the palace wall. The *smack* of his body hitting a few feet away repulsed her, but she never withdrew.

The high-pitched shrieks of men, their bones and skulls crushed under the massive feet of the elephants, surrounded her. The green field turned a bright crimson as the elephants went after their prey, their large pads dripping with blood.

She remained on her balcony, forcing herself to watch the heinous killings. Roxana would never have stomached such atrocities in the past. When had she changed? Somewhere along the way, she'd become like the men to which she'd resigned her fate.

The screams stopped, and the thunderous pounding of elephants on the field faded away. Instead of surveying the carnage, she went inside, drained of strength.

Morella came up to her. "It's for the best. You and your child will be safe now."

A numbing indifference squeezed her heart. "My child will never be safe. These men know nothing but killing."

"Forgive me, my lady, but these men would never have conquered the world if they didn't live for the kill. Alexander would never have become Great King unless he loved killing as much as his men. You're in a different world now. You must find a way to live among these people and stay alive."

She closed her eyes while Morella's worlds settled over her. She lived in a den of vipers. How could she ever hope to avoid their bite?

Her mettle waning, Roxana went to her bed, longing for sleep.

She reached underneath her assortment of pillows where she kept her most treasured memento—the silver coin her husband had minted commemorating his battle at Hydaspes. She studied Alexander's profile, desiring to fill her mind with images of him and not the butchery she had witnessed.

Morella came up to the bed. "You look at that coin a lot."

"Alexander gave it to me." She touched the gold chain on her neck. "It was on a night when Hephaestion was with us. It was a happy time."

"Give it to me." Morella gestured for the coin. "And the necklace, too."

Roxana hesitated. "Why?"

"Because they should be together. The king's gift and the kind general's together so you can keep both men close." She winked at Roxana. "I know a jeweler in the palace who can do it for you."

Touched by her thoughtfulness, Roxana handed the mementos to her maid.

"What would I do without you, Morella?"

Her maid clasped the pieces in her hand. "You'll never be without me, my lady. Where you go, I go. Even to the backwaters of Macedonia."

CHAPTER FORTY-TWO

A nervous Roxana joined the council of generals on a hot afternoon in the onyx-lined reception area next to Alexander's bedroom. She took in the battle-hardened faces of twelve men she barely knew as they gathered around a table. Spread out in the center was a map of the empire Alexander had built.

She had no idea what to expect, only that Perdiccas requested her presence since her child might one day lead them. Thank the gods for the two glasses of wine in her system; otherwise, she might never have walked into the room.

The closed doors to Alexander's bedroom, where his body remained unattended, garnered many fleeting glances from the generals. What she read in each man's eyes varied: sadness, anger, indifference, and affection.

"Let's get this over with, Perdiccas." Ptolemy fidgeted.

Perdiccas placed his hands over several scrolls in front of him. "Chaldean and Egyptian embalmers are with the king, preparing him for the long ride home. One of my lieutenants is to oversee the construction of a funeral coach. When the funeral carriage is ready, he will escort the king to Aegae for burial."

The men tapped the table with their knuckles, nodding in approval.

She scanned their faces, mindful of the oppressive atmosphere. One pair of eyes stared back—Cassander. She remembered his violent encounter with the king and questioned his influence with the generals. Of all the men in the room, he was the one who made her most uncomfortable.

"Down to business." Perdiccas lifted each scroll and rolled it across the table to a specific general. "Philip and an unborn infant can't administrate this vast territory, so I propose each of us to take up a portion of the empire and govern it until such a time that either Roxana's hoped-for male heir or Philip can rule alone. Your assigned posts are written on the scrolls I just gave you, but I say we wait for the birth of the child before any of you depart. In case changes need to be made if the child is a female or does not survive."

The generals around the table mumbled their approval.

"Fine, we're agreed." Ptolemy's loud voice resonated as he retrieved the scroll. "This better say Egypt, Perdiccas, or I'll have your hide."

"There's a surprise." General Seleucus laughed. "You always had a soft spot for those Egyptians, Ptolemy."

"Yes, Ptolemy, you have Egypt." Perdiccas rapped on the table, directing the generals' attention back to him. "The rest of you read your scrolls, and we can talk in private if there are any problems."

Cassander didn't pick up his scroll but rhythmically tapped it. "What about my father? Does he get to stay in Macedonia?"

Roxana wrung her hands under the table as tensions climbed.

Perdiccas showed a grimace to Ptolemy before he spoke.

"With the loyalty of the Greek city-states still in question, Antipater and Craterus will have to join forces to retain control over the lands around the Kingdom of Macedon."

Cassander pounded the table with his fist. Roxana flinched.

"Craterus will challenge my father's regency and send us headlong into another war."

"Don't go making wars where none exist, boy." Ptolemy's icy tone reeked of his contempt for Cassander. "Do as you're told and be happy you're being included."

"You'll eat those words one day," Cassander grumbled.

"None of that." Perdiccas raised his voice, gaining control of the meeting.

A nerve-racking silence lingered in the air.

"How will I deal with the problems in Cappadocia?" Eumenes asked, holding up his scroll. "The king there still refuses to align with Macedon."

"Nobody said it would be easy." Ptolemy sneered. "Not bad to go from being a secretary under Philip and Alexander to being a governor, is it, Eumenes?"

Eumenes stuck out his broad chest. "Shove it up your ass, Ptolemy."

Perdiccas slammed his fist on the table. "Ptolemy, enough!"

Aggression ran through the room like a firestorm. Roxana began to wonder if Alexander had picked the right man to lead them.

She'd been in the company of Alexander's generals before, but never felt so ill at ease. How Alexander had kept this hungry pack of wolves in check for ten years amazed her. After spending ten minutes together, she sensed they were ready to rip each other apart.

"The kings of India will remain as appointed by Alexander." Perdiccas indicated a place on the large map. "Oxyartes will retain governorship of the Caucasus region Alexander gave him after his marriage to Roxana. I'm sending his son, Histanes, along with a division of Persian troops, to help align the rest of the territories. The Companion Cavalry goes to Seleucus to use as a back up to the armies of each territory if needed for future battles." He placed his hand on his chest. "I will take over the royal troops assigned to our two kings and head to Macedonia to help oversee the regency." He looked around the table. "All right, that's it. I assume we have—"

A man in a loincloth burst through the doors from Alexander's rooms, screaming. He ran over to the table, wildly waving his hands.

"What in the hell is wrong with him?" Ptolemy asked.

"The embalmers are afraid to touch him," Roxana told the table. "He says the breath of life is still on Alexander's face and he cannot be prepared."

Ptolemy was the first out of his chair, quickly followed by the rest of the men and a waddling Roxana.

She hurried past Perdiccas and into the king's rooms, where Alexander's body had waited six long days for preparation.

Roxana was the first to approach the corpse. She expected some odor of decay, but she detected nothing. There was no wasting about his face or bloat filling the body. He was as he had lived—vital, alive, and even with the faintest ruddiness coloring his cheek.

"What could this mean?" Perdiccas demanded.

The rest of the generals stood behind him, dumbfounded.

Two servants entered the room from the hall, huffing and puffing. They carried the sarcophagus for the king with the story of Alexander's conquests and his greatest battles beaten into the gold. They set the large coffin on the floor and gaped at the small crowd.

"Tell them to get to work," Ptolemy snapped. "Enough of this Oriental superstition."

Roxana's skin crawled. Had she done enough to win the generals over? Perhaps she should have done more.

"Get back to work," Perdiccas ordered in Persian. "The king is dead."

Eumenes motioned to Roxana. "By the gods, Perdiccas, do you have to be so cold?"

The generals departed, leaving the embalmers to their work.

Cassander came up to Roxana. He offered her his arm. "You should not be here, my lady."

Roxana could not tear her gaze from Alexander. "I feel the best part of me has died with him. From now on, I will only be a shadow, existing in this world, waiting for my end so I can return to his side."

"You should not talk of such things, Roxana. You're going to be a mother; mother to a king, hopefully."

Reassured by his kindness, she took his arm. "A king? We shall see."

CHAPTER FORTY-THREE

In the middle of a moonless night during the height of the summer heat, Roxana awoke with a sharp twinge in her back. She almost called out for Morella, who had been sleeping at the foot of her bed, but decided to wait.

She rubbed her belly and winced every time a spasm hit, and when not in pain, she prayed. Roxana asked the gods to protect her baby, to let it be a boy. More than anything, she wanted to hold a piece of Alexander in her arms. To know something of him went on.

By dawn, her discomfort became too intense to ignore. When she tossed back her sheet and stood, her water broke.

"Morella, it's time!"

While Morella shouted for her guards to summon the midwife, doctors, and priests, Roxana sat in a chair by her bed, a strange sense of calm settling over her.

She'd spent half the night worrying about her baby, but as sunlight stretched into her bedroom, she knew everything would be all right. The contentment helped, getting her through each hard contraction.

The midwife strutted in, brandishing a wide grin. She was a heavyset woman with a lazy eye and streaks of gray hair poking out beneath her shawl.

"I am Atasia, my lady. Let's see how you're coming along."

The intrusion of Atasia's long fingers during her examination added to Roxana's misery, but somehow knowing what to expect made it easier for her to concentrate on her child instead of those around her.

The midwife spoke gently, asking her to stand, to walk, and even to squat during her debilitating pains. Roxana felt comfortable with the woman, encouraged by her easygoing manner.

Sweat covered her, her muscles quivered, and at times Roxana's confidence faltered.

"I can't do this!" she cried out after a horrible round of contractions.

Atasia took her face in her hands. "My lady, you will do this. Your baby and your husband need you to be strong."

Remembering Alexander gave her the courage to go on. She battled through each eruption of fire in her belly. She did all the midwife asked without question. When the pressure building in her groin convinced her the baby would soon arrive, the midwife confirmed her suspicions.

"My lady, we must get you to the birthing room."

The serenity she'd held on to during each debilitating spasm suddenly cracked.

"No!" Roxana gripped the arms of her chair, ready to kill anyone who refused her. "I'm not going to sit in another oven-baked room on one of those uncomfortable damn stone tables and have a goat-faced physician staring at me!"

Morella frowned. "But it's tradition. It's what all mothers of kings must do."

A twisting slice went right through her belly. "I said no!"

She sat back in her chair and panted, sorry she'd raised her voice.

"For weeks, I've had generals telling me what to do, where I will live, how I will travel, even who can come into my rooms." She let out a long breath as her cramps eased. "But I will have this baby my way. No doctors, no birthing chairs, no fires, and no priests. Just you and this midwife, here in my room, in my bed."

Atasia took her arm, helping her out of the chair. "Then the child will come where the mother demands."

Morella guided her to the bed. "Even if I've got to beat off a few toady-looking priests with my fists, then so be it."

Their support brought tears to her eyes. "Thank you."

Another big pain came over her, and she moaned as it seemed to go on and on. She swore her body would split in two.

"I can see the head," Atasia said. "Deep breath and push, my lady. It's time to meet your child."

She screamed as a ferocious fire ripped through the lower part of her body, blinding her to everything and everyone around her. The excruciating agony went on and on. Convinced something was wrong, Roxana called for Morella.

A hand held hers. "I'm here, Roxana. Keep pushing."

She gripped Morella's hand as she bore down, forcing the fire out of her body.

Then, as if being swept up by a wave, a rush of relief came over her. The intense pain ended.

Thankful for the reprieve, tears streamed down her face, and then she heard the faintest cry.

Roxana struggled to her elbows, checking between her legs.

The cries grew stronger, and her heart lifted.

Atasia held up a wiggling dark red baby still covered with slimy white paste and attached to the birth cord.

"You have a son, my lady. Alexander has a son."

All the suffering she'd endured melted away as she put her arms around her child. Roxana could hardly see his face through her tears. She wept for the joy of having a son, for the blessing of his being alive and well, but mostly, she cried because his father would not share in the news of his birth.

"He will know you," she whispered. "I promise, Alexander, not one day will pass without your son hearing about your life, your deeds, and our love."

Exhausted but happy, Roxana stood over the ebony crib given to her by the palace staff. She caressed the bridge of her son's nose, smiling as he squirmed. His ruddy hair, heavy forehead and gray-blue eyes, so tiny, yet so like Alexander's. Thank the gods he was blessed with his father's looks. He had a better chance of succeeding to the throne if he resembled the warrior the army adored. But other concerns plagued her—the life he would lead, the battles, the trials, the misery. All the things she'd seen Alexander endure, she wanted to spare her son. But how? Roxana had longed for her baby, but now that he was with her, she lamented over the responsibility he had inherited.

"He's a good baby, my lady," Arnia, her wet nurse, said. "And a healthy eater. Latches on to my teat like he's done it a thousand times before."

Roxana liked the energetic woman with the oval face and deep-set brown eyes. She was stocky, muscular, and attuned to her baby's needs.

"I wish I could have nursed him for longer than a few days."

"Can't ruin your figure with breastfeeding," Arnia folded a towel and placed it next to the crib. "You will need it for your next husband."

Roxana clasped Alexander's silver coin hanging around her neck, remembering his voice, and his enthusiasm. What man could come close to him?

"I will not marry again."

"How can you say such a thing, my lady?"

Arnia's surly tone was unexpected.

"You've only seen twenty summers. You have your beauty and an important son. Of course, you will have other husbands."

Roxana knew better. Her life was no longer hers.

"My duties from this point forward will be to protect and raise Alexander's son as a true Macedonian, in Macedonia. I have no other usefulness to these men."

"But you will need a husband, a protector in the Greek lands." Morella wrinkled her pug nose as she came up to the crib. "I hear it's very primitive there. The women in the palace say the people sleep with their sheep. Do you think that's true?"

Roxana chuckled. "We will be living in a palace. I don't think they will have sheep there."

Morella stroked the infant's cheek. "Any idea what you will call him? He's over a month old now. He needs a name."

Roxana's heart ached as she recalled a night long ago with the king. "His name will be Alexander. That's what his father wanted."

A loud knock on the outer chamber doors made all three women turn away from the crib.

Perdiccas and Ptolemy entered unannounced with a servant scurrying behind them.

Arnia gasped at the intrusion, but Roxana took it in stride. Since Alexander's death, she'd gotten used to the familiarity of the generals and didn't want to discourage them. She needed to do anything she could to keep them close to her son.

"We came to see the new king," Perdiccas said while waiting with Ptolemy at the entrance to her chambers.

She stepped through the open bedroom doors and went to greet the generals. They wore simple white tunics without any armor or swords at their sides. She hoped it meant their call was a social one, and not intended to convey more news of plots or intrigues.

"Fortunately for both of you, the new king just woke up from his nap."

She caught the glint of gold in the hands of the servant behind Perdiccas.

"A gift for the baby. I took it before they packed away the last of Alexander's things." Perdiccas snapped his fingers at the servant and pointed to a table close to Roxana. "It's something his father would have wanted him to have."

The chest was made of gold with silver handles and hinges, and small enough to sit on a desk. She drew closer and a jolt of recognition seared through her. She'd seen it in Alexander's rooms.

She tenderly fingered the impressions of men and horses depicted on the box, aching for the man who had once possessed it. She had thought it a hunting scene, but Alexander had told her it was a depiction of the war at Troy.

"This is very kind of you, Perdiccas."

Gently, she lifted the lid, eager to see if the contents Alexander had once revealed to her were still inside. Then she saw it—Alexander's copy of *The Iliad*.

Roxana touched the smooth calfskin cover, transported back in time. "It was his favorite book."

Ptolemy came forward. "And now it can be your son's."

The baby gurgled from the bedroom, reminding her of her duty. She shut the lid of the chest, promising to come back to the book when she was alone.

Arnia and Morella retreated to a corner of the bedroom while Roxana escorted the generals to the large crib decorated with carvings of griffins.

Perdiccas tickled the child's chin. "He's Alexander's son, alright."

"Thank the gods." Ptolemy's face fell as he realized his blunder. "I mean, thank the gods for the men, Roxana. It's better if he reminds the men of who he comes from."

She placed a reassuring hand on Ptolemy's thick forearm. "It's all right,

General. I understand. I'm also glad he takes after his father. Very glad."

Ptolemy gave the child one last look and then squared his shoulders. "I'll be setting off at first light for Egypt. I just wanted to say goodbye to you and little Alexander."

"Little Alexander?" She furrowed her brow. "I haven't even named him yet."

"Alexander Aegus." Perdiccas rocked his hands behind his back in a dictatorial manner. "The council of generals has decided his name."

Roxana predicted it was the first of many decisions related to her child she would have no part of.

"I'm sure Alexander would approve."

Perdiccas observed the infant with only a slight interest. "Now that your boy is here, the generals will be heading out to their governorships within the next few days. We need to consolidate this empire."

Roxana's hands twitched. The generals would set out for their territories, and without Alexander to keep them anchored, she feared they might never come together again.

"Take care of our little king, Roxana." Ptolemy bowed graciously to her.

"May your gods go with you, Ptolemy. I feel it shall be a very long time before we see each other again."

He gave her a curt nod, and with his purple cape flapping behind him, Ptolemy headed into the corridor.

Why did she suddenly feel abandoned?

"Get your staff in order and give me a list of supplies," Perdiccas intruded on her thoughts. "We will be leaving Babylon in a few weeks."

"I'm going to Macedonia, so soon?" she asked surprised. "Shouldn't we stay here until my child is older?"

"I can't leave you and the young king without an army to protect you. And we won't be heading back to Pella right away. The revolt we anticipated in Athens has begun. Until that war is settled, you're better off with me. We will go to Cappadocia on our way to the Hellespont. While there, I plan to help Eumenes bring a rebellious king to heel. Once we get word it's safe, we will cross the sea to Macedonia."

What he said made sense. Alexander had always insisted on troops traveling with the baggage train, mindful of those who would want to ransom his wife like they had his horse.

"And Alexander, my husband. When will he return to his homeland?"

"That may not be for some time yet." Perdiccas stepped away from the crib. "There's much work to be done on the funeral carriage. Alexander will have to remain in Babylon until it's completed. I'm told they're building quite a monument. It will be covered in gold and decorative reliefs describing the feats of Alexander and pulled by sixty-four mules, each with a gold bell so all will be able to hear the procession coming. A shame we can't see it, but we must push on."

Roxana sensed there was more. He seemed unusually stiff. "Is there something wrong?"

He smiled, trying to reassure her. "It's an old general's worry about his men and coming battle. Our forces are spread pretty thin. I hope nothing else goes wrong." The infant stirred in his crib. "Not to worry. We will take care of Alexander's empire."

CHAPTER FORTY-FOUR

Roxana stood outside the open flap of her large tent, petting Hera's neck as evening faded and pinpoints of light popped up above the inhospitable terrain of Cappadocia. She'd tethered her horse to one of the odd rock formations—a thin pyramid-like shape protruding from the semi-arid basin surrounding the camp. She no longer trusted the grooms to tend to her horse. Her confidence in those around her was not the same as when the king was alive. She put her faith in very few people these days.

Inside her tent, Arnia sat on a bench by a blazing brazier keeping her son warm on her lap.

Roxana went to little Alexander and checked his blanket. He still amazed her, and just looking at him brought her so much joy. He had helped her sorrow during their year on the road. And even though Alexander's memory had never left her, she had a part of her husband to hold on to. At least for a few years.

"Can I visit my nephew?"

The short man stumbling into her tent, with his red hair, deep green eyes, and sharp features was said to be the image of his father, the late King Philip, but she saw nothing of her husband in him. Philip Arrhidaeus had none of the style or grace of his half-brother, nor any of his intelligence. He did, however, always appear incredibly rumpled, with a wrinkled tunic and disheveled hair reminding her of Alexander.

"Of course, Philip." She ushered him to a stool next to Arnia's bench. "Come and sit by the fire."

Philip flopped down, his perpetual grin in place. "Can I hold him?"

At first apprehensive, she relented. He'd always been so good with little Alexander.

"Remember, he's not a doll."

"I know." He bobbed his head. "I'll be careful."

She nodded for Arnia to pass him the child.

Arnia's frown accentuated the alarm in her voice. "Are you sure, my lady?"

Roxana took her son and carried him to Philip.

"Hold him like I showed you."

She waited until he gripped little Alexander firmly and then set the child in his lap.

Philip's eyes lit up. "Hello, nephew."

The boy grabbed his uncle's beard in his small hands. Philip howled with delight.

Roxana noticed things more than people interested Philip, except where her son was concerned. He'd been fascinated since the first day they had met in the baggage train leaving Babylon. It had taken him a while to open up, but soon he'd become her only link to what was happening within the camp and around the empire.

"Have you spoken to Perdiccas?"

"He asked about the little king." He bounced the child on his knee. "I'm good with babies, even though my mother never let me around them. I spent a lot of time with my nurse. My half-sister, Cynane, says Olympias poisoned me when I was born. That's why I understand babies so well. They're like me."

Roxana got nervous for her son. "Cynane shouldn't have said such a thing to you. I'm sure Alexander's mother did not harm you."

"Oh, Olympias had everybody killed." He tickled a laughing Alexander. "Some even say she killed my father. At least, that's what Cynane believes. She doesn't like Olympias, and neither do I. Cynane is Illyrian and very fierce. They let women lead armies in battle in Illyria. Can you imagine?"

She rubbed her forehead, attempting to think of a way to get him back on track. "Did Perdiccas say anything else?"

He reached for a straw-stuffed elephant on her bench—a gift to little Alexander from Perdiccas. "My half-sister, Cleopatra, is going to marry General of Leonnatus of Phrygia. It's at the most western tip of the old Persian empire right before your reach the Hellespont. Did you know that?"

A chill ran through Roxana. "Are you sure about this marriage?"

He dangled the elephant in front of her son. "I even heard Perdiccas talking about it while he was planning the battle with his generals. He was angry. Said he had to find himself another general to run Phrygia because he was going to kill this one." Philip puckered his lips together in a childish pout. "Roxana, why doesn't Perdiccas let me join him in planning battles? I'm the king, right?"

She fought to process everything he'd told her. The players in the game of empire were changing quickly.

"Perdiccas is protecting you. He doesn't want to risk losing you in battle, Philip."

Her mind filled with plots and deceptions happening at the court in Pella. Any Macedonian marrying into Alexander's family, especially a powerful general, could claim Alexander's throne and leave her son without a kingdom. Or worse—dead.

"Did Perdiccas say anything else about this marriage? Like when it will take place?"

"After the Athenians are beaten. He says everyone is fighting them now."

Little Alexander let out a happy giggle.

Philip dropped the toy elephant to the ground. "I went to Athens once with Alexander. When we were little, Alexander would come to my rooms to visit. He always talked to me." Philip sat quietly for a moment, staring blankly at the ceiling. "Perdiccas told me after we finish with King Ariarathes, we're going to move to the cities of Isauria and Larandia because Perdiccas says they're not paying proper tribute to us kings."

She feared for her son and wanted him out of a wagon and in the palace at Pella, but even then, she wasn't sure what awaited them.

"Then do we go on to Macedonia?" Roxana asked.

"I hope so. I would like to be able to sit on a real throne, like the one in Pella. Oh, you will love Pella. My grandfather and father built the palace there. Right above the city, on a high hill. All the people in the land say it is the prettiest palace in Greece."

Philip squealed when he discovered the stuffed elephant at his feet. All talk of his homeland, kings, and battles was forgotten.

She took her son from him, amazed at how quickly his mind went from one topic to another. For Roxana, Philip was like having another child, except this child would never grow up. Oblivious to his predicament, Philip giggled as he smashed Alexander's toy.

Roxana envied his ability to forget about the struggles of the world outside her tent. To have a few moments of peace until the distant blast of the army trumpets rang out, letting them know another battle was underway.

CHAPTER FORTY-FIVE

To Roxana's relief, Perdiccas oversaw a successful campaign in Cappadocia. News swirled around the camps of the brief battle and how the traitorous King Ariarathes ended up crucified and his family slaughtered. No messengers came from Perdiccas, but she assumed with the rule of Cappadocia safely in the hands of Eumenes, the baggage train and army would soon travel farther west across the arid plains of Anatolia.

Ordered onward, Roxana packed her wagon with Arnia, her son, and Morella, but they traveled less than a few weeks before arriving in a barren, cold region home to the disloyal cities of Isauria and Larandia. Occasional patches of pastureland crammed full with wild asses and lots of sheep—more sheep than she had ever seen in her life—entertained Roxana and her growing son, but the rocky terrain and high salt content in the ground created a camping nightmare. Pikes rusted through, and the constant winds brought off the plains kept her tent billowing through the night, making sleep impossible.

Gossip kept Roxana going during the long days, and it was also her only means of staying abreast of the army's activities. Stories floated around the tents of how thousands of families were burned alive inside the city of Isauria, how the entire town of Larandia became enslaved. The army veterans, it was said, were displeased and complained about how Alexander would not have been as harsh with his captives.

She had to agree with them. The atrocities reported made her long for Alexander's way of handling his enemies. He won the respect of those he conquered—her father being one of them. At night, in her tent, her son sleeping next to her, she would think of him, and his impression of the state of affairs. There was so much she didn't know and wished he would have taught her. How could she keep her and her son alive amid the constant backstabbing and war of his generals?

By winter, Perdiccas's army, along with the king's baggage train, was on the road again heading to Sardis—a city very close to the Aegean Sea. She hoped this was the last leg of her journey and Macedonia their final destination, but Perdiccas never sent her messengers or said much to Philip about what lay ahead.

It had been over two years since Alexander's death, and Roxana feared things were not better with his empire but growing steadily worse.

With his army settled outside the city of Sardis, and the baggage train camped close by, Perdiccas made his way to Alexander's old tent with the gold pike on top. He rushed past his sentries, anxious to get to his letters from Antipater.

A sweet perfume filled his reception area. The *clink* of a metal tray compelled him to turn.

She stood in the corner, holding a silver goblet and staring at him with her deep green eyes.

"I thought I would come and wait for you here, instead of in the city."

Her musical voice matched her petite, slender figure and seductively long legs. Her hair reminded him of fall leaves with its deep auburn color. He remembered running his hands through it all those years ago before he left for Persia. He had kissed her short nose, and the few freckles dotting her cheeks and promised to return, but it was her loving smile he'd taken with him to war. Now, she was back in his life.

He drank in the cut of her yellow peplos over her small breasts. "Well, I for one am glad you came, Cleopatra."

She gracefully glided across the floor, bringing him the goblet. "Mother sends her regards. She hopes you are well."

He took the silver cup from her, letting his fingers caress hers. "Did Olympias send you?"

"You know how Mother feels about Antipater. When she found out that the old coot had offered you his daughter in marriage, she had to counter the offer with a promise of marriage to someone more prominent." She winked at him. "Like me."

Perdiccas sipped from his drink, weighing the advantages of having Alexander's sister as his wife.

It will drive Ptolemy mad. Reason enough to do it.

Taking the goblet, he moved toward a couch, trying to stay one step ahead of her and her conniving mother. "Don't you think it's a bit soon to marry, considering the recent death of your intended, Leonnatus? After he ignored my orders to go to Phrygia, I heard he served nobly with Antipater in the war in Greece."

"Well, one does what is necessary to please Mother. She thinks the marriage will be advantageous for both of us."

"What does your cousin think? The current King of Epirus. Does he want this alliance?"

She waved a delicate hand in the air, reminding him of Olympias. "Aeacides is an idiot. He will do as he is told."

He had a seat on the gold couch, wanting to let her down easy without alienating her affection. "Your offer is intriguing, but I won't do Olympias's bidding. I have to marry Nicaea. She's already in Sardis. Antipater sent her over two weeks ago." He sighed and sat back, wishing he hadn't given his word to the old man. "No matter how tempting the idea of marriage to you is, my dear, I have to fulfill my obligation to Antipater. He would be a far more formidable enemy than your mother."

She never showed a hint of disappointment as she sauntered toward his couch. He chalked up her savvy skills to her mother. Olympias had taught both of her children how to be astute politicians.

"You do know that old one-eyed monster, Antigonus, is in Macedonia. He has joined forces with Antipater and Craterus."

Perdiccas cradled his goblet, hiding his irritation. "I know. He went to them after I tried to oust him from his governorship. I should have known he would go right to Antipater for help."

She leaned over to him, a wicked gleam in her eye. "Old One Eye will poison their minds against you. Probably already knows I'm here in Sardis. He has spies traveling with your camp."

Perdiccas chuckled. "And I have spies in his, as well as in the palace at Pella. How else am I to stay informed?"

"He will convince Antipater and Craterus that you want the throne for yourself. You know what an agitator he is."

"And Antipater will eventually turn Ptolemy against me. Which won't be too hard to do considering our feelings for each other. I believe he means to split the generals into factions and weaken my power."

Cleopatra furrowed her brow. "Didn't Ptolemy already do that? When he enlarged his domain by capturing Cyrene, some of the other generals agreed with him, others were angry. Seems to me, Alexander's men have been splitting apart since the moment my brother died."

He set his wine on a table next to his couch, pursed his lips and debated how much to tell her. Her mind was a great deal like her brother's, but she lacked his diplomatic skills and his thirst for conquest.

"To get to me, Antipater and Antigonus will have to make Ptolemy an ally. If they choose sides with him, I will have to—"

"Go to war." She had a seat on the couch next to his. "How many of the generals do you think will support you against Ptolemy?"

He rested his elbows on his knees and clasped his hands, stumped. "I don't know. But as long as I have the kings under my guardianship, then perhaps I can convince the others to join me."

She played with the fabric of her dress, twirling it in her fingers. "You think the men will back a half-breed infant and a simpleton? The other generals will try their best to stay out of a dispute between you, Craterus, Ptolemy, and Antipater. Even with Eumenes's wealth in your purse, men will not want to take part in a civil war."

Perdiccas ran a thumb across the rough calluses on his hand. Wielding a sword was all he'd ever done. A peaceful world was as foreign to him as the Orientals. War was all he knew.

"Then perhaps they will do it for the boy. He's the last tie any of us have to Alexander." He stood from his couch. "I might have to use him to rouse the others to join me in war when the time comes. Macedonians may not want to fight other Macedonians, but they will if they think it's for a wonderful cause. Especially the cause of seeing Alexander's true son on the throne."

"The men might think that cause tainted after your harsh treatment of the people of Isauria and Larandia." Her tsk-tsk floated around the tent. "Was all that killing necessary?"

How dare she presume to question me?

"The Isaurians chose to set themselves, their wives, and their children on fire. The city was burned alive, not at my hands, but at the hands of its people. My men could do nothing but watch as all were lost. As for the people of Larandia, they got what they deserved." He lowered his head, the screams still ringing in his ears. "I'm a general, and at times I have to see and do things that are not well liked but are necessary."

"Alexander would not have approved of your impaling the entire royal family of Cappadocia."

He brought his hands forward, showing her his clenched fists. "Alexander is dead. If we are to stay alive in this free-for-all of an empire, then someone is going to have to take charge, kill a few innocents, and slaughter thousands of not so innocents." He caught himself and took a moment to bring his temper under control. "Forgive me. I didn't mean to vent my frustrations on you. It's just the past several months have been difficult for me."

Cleopatra put on a cheerful smile. "Let's not talk any more of such unpleasant things. Tell me about Roxana. Do you think you can rely on the mother of this child to stand by you?"

"Roxana will do what's best for her son." He eased closer until he stood before her couch. "She's very bright and knows what she has to do to stay alive."

"Like getting rid of Alexander's other wives before he was even cold?" She ran her finger along the front of his bronze cuirass, eyeing him like a hungry lioness. "I know you well enough to sense you had a hand in that nasty affair. Everyone blames the girl for the deaths of Parysatis and Stateira. No one else suspects."

"It was necessary," he whispered.

She scooted over, making room for him on her couch. "Shame you didn't get rid of Barsine and her bastard boy while you were at it. I guess we can deal with those two complications later. For now, we have enough to keep us busy."

Perdiccas settled next to her. "You must go and meet the girl and your nephew." He caressed her right thigh. "You will find her intriguing."

Cleopatra placed her hand over his. "I'm curious to see why my brother found her so alluring. The gods know Alexander was not one to be seduced by a pretty face." She urged his hand up her thigh. "I shall go and meet her tomorrow."

"That gives you tonight to spend with me. Perhaps we can pick up where we left off so long ago."

She pressed his hand into the valley between her legs. "My dear Perdiccas, you must have read my mind."

A trickle of disappointment sailed through Roxana when the former Queen of Epirus, daughter of Philip, and sister of Alexander regally entered her tent. There was little of her brother in her. Draped in gold necklaces and wearing a royal blue ensemble, she appeared refined, graceful, and elegant, but Cleopatra lacked Alexander's magnetism.

"Oh, I'm so glad we finally get to meet. Alexander wrote to me about you all the time." Cleopatra sat in a chair across from Roxana in her reception area. "He said you were quite beautiful. I'm glad to see my brother didn't exaggerate."

Roxana glanced down at little Alexander playing on the reed mats with his toys, overwhelmed with her love for him.

"Alexander spoke of you as well, my lady. He wanted us to meet one day."

"He was the best big brother a girl could ask for." Cleopatra beamed. "He taught me how to hunt snakes, ride, throw a spear, handle a sword—all the things Father didn't want me to learn, Alexander would teach me."

Cleopatra laughed, and Roxana almost melted at its similarity to Alexander's. Her heart heaved, wishing she could hear his light-hearted chuckle one more time.

"Usually it was him, me, and Hephaestion getting into trouble. The gods always favored him."

"I didn't realize you and Hephaestion were so close."

Her sister-in-law rolled her pretty eyes. "I was mad about Hephaestion. All the girls in the palace had a crush on him. I sometimes suspected Alexander was a bit jealous of him, but then Hephaestion worshipped Alexander. They were inseparable."

Little Alexander let out a loud yawn. The women look down, checking on him. Seeing his mother's face, he smiled.

The sight of him reassured her. It was as if Alexander had joined them, listening to their conversation, and sharing the family moment.

"He has your smile." Cleopatra nodded at the boy. "But he has Alexander's eyes."

Roxana admired her son, pleased the best of them had come together in the child. "Alexander would like that."

"My brother and I used to talk about children." Cleopatra caressed little Alexander's cheek. "I asked him about what kind of child he wanted, boy or girl. Of course, he wanted sons to inherit his empire, but he wanted a daughter, too. To teach her to ride and hunt and do all the things boys do so she would be strong-willed and never afraid. He found those things in you. It's why he married you."

Roxana flashed back to a night with Alexander. What his sister said rang true. "Many believed the king married me for lust."

"Lust?" Cleopatra's tight-lipped expression showed her disapproval. "Anyone who knew him was well aware my brother never gave into such things. Alexander grew up watching the tirades of my mother, the sexual and alcoholic escapades of my father, and it affected him. To lose control was to become like my parents." She ran her hand along the smooth fabric of her frock and smiled. "Probably why he was always so serious, like Mother. Whereas, I am like my father. I take nothing seriously and have the hide of an elephant … or so Mother always tells me."

Roxana sensed an opportunity. She needed to find out the intentions of those vowing to support her son's claim to the throne, as well as his family's regard for Alexander's half-Persian child.

"Yes, Alexander was very serious about some things, especially where matters of state were concerned. He always tried to stay ahead of his enemies and the plotting of his generals."

Cleopatra regarded Roxana as if sizing up her intentions. "What do you mean?"

"Forgive me, but there's a rumor about the camp that you're here to marry Perdiccas, even though he plans a wedding to Nicaea, the daughter of Antipater. You must know what would happen if you jeopardize the alliance with Antipater? Not to mention, my son's claim to his father's empire could be challenged if you and the general had a son, a pure Macedonian son."

The slow smile winding its way across her face was just like her famous brother's—mischievous and alluring. It let Roxana know she had guessed correctly—others plotted for the throne and her son needed supporters to further his cause.

"Perdiccas said you had a brain." Cleopatra adjusted one of the gold bracelets on her wrist, hiding her eyes. "I've received numerous proposals from Alexander's other generals, but it's for the future of my brother's empire that marriage to Perdiccas may be required. By allying myself with the guardian of my nephew's throne, I'm weakening the position of others also vying for control over Alexander's realm. Our marriage will help lessen tensions between the generals and keep Antipater from retaining power over Philip and your child."

The political infighting saddened her. "I don't understand. These men were loyal to Alexander. Since his death, it's like they hate each other."

Cleopatra heaved a fake-sounding sigh. It raised an inkling of concern in Roxana. Could she trust this woman?

"These are the war games men play when power is up for grabs. Without Alexander to hold them together, yesterday's friends have become tomorrow's enemies."

"What will you do if Perdiccas marries Nicaea?" Roxana asked. "Will you return to Epirus?"

"I'll stay in Sardis for a while and see what happens." She noticed the child on the floor. "It will give me a chance to get to know you and my nephew."

Roxana longed for her son to have a family. He needed to know his father and something about the lands he would, hopefully, one day rule.

"Yes, I want you to teach him all you can about his father and his family. I have a promise to keep."

CHAPTER FORTY-SIX

In Sardis, Roxana received a suite of rooms in the older, Greek stylized palace. The lack of Persian artwork or breathtaking gardens gave her a hint of what lay ahead as she traveled closer to her new home. She admired murals adorning the walls of the heroes and the gods from Homeric legend, and the clean lines of the architecture which was a far cry from the heavy swirls and dark colors found in many Persian residences. She enjoyed the play of light from the windows set in many of the corridors.

Her spacious three rooms and private garden pleased her.

She waited by a window as the palace servants piled the trunks from her wagon along the bedroom wall.

Little Alexander took in the bustling activity while gripping the skirt of her dress, his elephant tucked under his arm. She admired how he remained composed and refrained from running wild like he was prone to do some days. Stocky, with muscles forming on his small frame, she wondered where her infant son had gone? Just yesterday he was a newborn baby in her arms.

"That snooty Queen of Epirus got the best rooms," Morella whispered next to her.

Roxana picked up little Alexander. "Well, she is royalty."

"And you're the wife of Alexander, mother to the King of Greece and Persia." Morella went to one of the trunks and angrily shoved it open. "Sometimes, ma'am, I swear you're treated as a commoner's wife. No one comes to pay their respects, and no generals keep you informed of their intentions."

"Those days are over." Roxana carried the boy to her maid. "Don't unpack everything. I'm sure we will be moving on to Macedonia soon."

"I like your rooms better than mine." Cleopatra stood in the open doors, staring at her tiled ceiling, which was decorated to resemble a giant dolphin. "I have flowers all over my ceiling."

Morella took the child from her. "I'll give him to his nurse." She scurried to the outer chamber.

Roxana greeted her sister-in-law with a smile. "I hear your rooms are quite lovely."

Cleopatra came up to her, her purple linen ensemble flowing in the afternoon breeze let in by the open window. "Don't believe everything you hear. This is a different part of the world than you're used to, and gossip is sometimes spread to hurt and deceive."

"I'll remember that."

Something nagged at Roxana not to trust her sister-in-law, but also not to discount her friendship. Without Alexander to protect her and her son, she might one day need to ask the former Queen of Epirus for her help.

Cleopatra went to Alexander's gold chest beside Roxana's bed. She traced the raised images of horses and men on the lid.

"I came to tell you there will be another family member joining us for the wedding of Perdiccas and the daughter of Antipater. She arrived in Sardis a few days ago."

Roxana approached the woman, intrigued. "Who is it?"

"My half-sister, Cynane. She's brought her daughter, Eurydice as well. She's loud, demanding, and dangerous. Stay away from her."

The warning fed her curiosity about Alexander's family. "Why should I stay away?"

Cleopatra walked toward Roxana, a wrinkle carved into her creamy brow.

"Cynane coming here, especially after she had to fight her way out of Macedonia against Antipater's orders, means she's up to something. My guess is a marriage for her daughter to gain political clout. You must admit, any member of Alexander's family, no matter how remote, seems appealing to anyone wanting to grab his empire."

"But his empire belongs to his son," Roxana angrily countered. "My son. Anyone else would not be a true heir."

She stopped in front of Roxana and dropped her voice. "Your son has a long way to go until he reaches the age of fourteen and can rule. Until then, the pretenders will do all they can to take away his birthright. You need to stay smart, Roxana. Regard everyone as an enemy and no one as your friend."

Doubt nibbled at her. "Including you?"

Her grin was slight, but it took away the darkness from her eyes. "I'll admit I was not pleased when my brother wrote to me and told me he had married a Persian girl, but having met you, and my nephew … I'm not your enemy. But I'm afraid if things get very messy in this rat's nest of an empire Alexander left us, I will not be able to help you. Find someone who can."

"Roxana?"

Perdiccas bounded into her rooms, brandishing a crumpled scroll.

He stopped in her bedroom doorway. "Ptolemy has gone too far this time."

"Why?" Cleopatra got out before Roxana could. "What is wrong, Perdiccas?"

"He has stolen Alexander's body and taken it to Egypt."

Roxana's knees buckled. "But how? I thought Alexander's sarcophagus would not be ready for another few months."

Perdiccas swiped the scroll across his leg. "I ordered his procession on the road weeks ago. I wanted him out of Babylon before this constant bickering between the generals gets any worse. Ptolemy must have had spies in my camp because he caught my men by surprise in Syria. From there, he took the body back to Egypt." Perdiccas held up the scroll. "Ptolemy told the general leading the funeral procession that Alexander expressed a wish to be buried in Egypt. What utter nonsense!"

"How can your man just hand over the body to Ptolemy?" Roxana's temper rose at the atrocity. "What about the other generals? He has to answer to them."

He sighed, losing some of his bravado. "There weren't enough men to fight off Ptolemy's soldiers. The army is spread pretty thin and protecting the remains of the king has not been a priority. As for the others, I believe Ptolemy is in league with Antipater and Craterus."

Roxana gasped. How could this be happening?

Cleopatra tilted her head exactly like her famous brother. "How do you know?"

"Eumenes warned me of their treachery." Perdiccas rolled the scroll in his hands. "Antigonus and Ptolemy were close. After that one-eyed idiot failed to help us in Cappadocia and fled to Antipater in Macedonia, I suspected Ptolemy of encouraging him. It would be just like that loud-mouthed fool to want to see me fail or get killed in battle."

"I thought we would have more time to stop Antipater, but it seems not." Cleopatra fixed her attention on the starfish mosaic on the floor. "What are you going to do about this? Alexander must go back to Aegae and be buried. You know the tradition."

Roxana's mouth went dry. "What tradition?"

Cleopatra twirled one of her gold necklaces around her finger. "A dead king must be buried by the succeeding king to be legitimate. Superstition states that if a king of Macedon fails to be buried in Aegae, the kingdom will die."

"Ptolemy knows this." Perdiccas casually stepped into her bedroom, twisting his lips into a wry smirk. "It's the one bit of propaganda he could use to help strengthen his power and turn the other generals against me."

Dread burned the back of Roxana's throat. "If Alexander is buried in Egypt—"

"Ptolemy makes a statement about Alexander's heirs," Cleopatra cut in. "Namely, that he's the rightful heir to the empire and your son and Philip are pretenders."

An icy chill swept through her. Roxana went to a nearby table to steady herself.

She'd questioned Ptolemy's allegiance in the past, but this act made his true intentions known. He'd found a way to take away her son's chance to be king and had opened the door for war between Alexander's generals.

"He won't get away with this." Perdiccas walked up to her, radiating his usual cool confidence. "I've called an assembly of the army. I will let them decide where we go first. Either to Egypt to fight Ptolemy, or to join Eumenes and face Antipater and Craterus."

Cleopatra raised her eyebrows. "Which will you talk them into choosing?"

Perdiccas glowered at her cavalier expression. "Egypt of course. I want this situation settled."

"And then what? Another battle?" Roxana tightened her grip on the table, sick at the prospect of her son growing up in a wagon, dragged from one end of the empire to another. "Do you Macedonians ever tire of war? How long can you keep combing this giant empire you created and fighting everyone?"

"Your husband founded this giant empire, my lady, and he knew the only way to hold on to it was through war." Perdiccas lifted her chin. "Your son better get used to living a life on the road and never tiring of battle if he wants to emulate his father. Alexander proved himself to win his men; his son must do the same."

"What about Eumenes?" Cleopatra went around to Perdiccas. "He's on our side and has the funds to help with the war."

"I've already sent him word." Perdiccas gestured to Roxana's trunks. "Don't unpack. You and the kings will come with me." He faced Cleopatra. "I want you to stay in Sardis and await our return from battle. Send word if you or Olympias hear of anything else brewing in Pella. I don't want to have to deal with any more surprises." He spun away and hurried out of Roxana's chambers.

"I must get this news to Mother." Cleopatra glided toward the doors. "The sooner we get control over the Kingdom of Macedon the better."

Roxana stood in her bedroom. The disturbing sound of marching soldiers resonated throughout the palace halls.

Her heart heavy and her limbs lacking strength, she pictured Alexander's beautiful sarcophagus of gold buried in a dark Egyptian temple, lost to her and his son.

"What was that about, my lady?"

Morella stepped into the room, followed by Arnia, carrying little Alexander.

She scoured the trunks and furniture left behind by the servants. "Get everything back on the wagon."

"What in the blazes has happened now?" Morella asked in a disgruntled tone.

"We aren't going to Macedonia." Roxana closed her eyes, holding back tears. "We're heading to Egypt to get Alexander back."

In the hall outside of Roxana's quarters, Perdiccas marched with his guards, impatient to return to his rooms and prepare for the coming campaign against his old adversary.

That son of a bitch!

His dislike for Ptolemy ran deep, but even he hadn't predicted he would betray Alexander in such a way.

Cleopatra caught up to him.

"We have to talk," she said, slightly out of breath.

He stopped, wishing to avoid being seen together. "Can it wait? There is much to do."

"No, it can't wait." She ushered the general to the side and stood in the shadow of a large statue of Diana. "We have another problem. I think Cynane plans to marry that daughter of hers off to one of the generals. To weaken your position."

"By Zeus!" Perdiccas punched the wall. "Damn woman, I knew her being here was bad news."

Cleopatra placed a comforting hand on his arm. "There are options."

Perdiccas liked the way her green eyes sparkled in the faint light. "Go on."

"Make Cynane stay behind with me in Sardis. The daughter is a lot less trouble than the mother. I can take care of her myself when you and your men have pulled out."

"All right. When we're ready to leave, I'll give the order to make sure the silly woman doesn't follow us." He paused, weighing her fortitude. "Are you sure you are up to this?"

"I am the daughter of Olympias, my dear general. I was taught well."

"Yes. I know." Perdiccas kissed her lips. "Keep my place in bed warm for me. I might be a while."

Cleopatra held his chin while running her thumb over his beard. "What about your wedding to Antipater's daughter? You can't go through with it now."

He tossed his arms around him. "Of course not. When I've finished destroying Ptolemy for provoking this war, we shall celebrate our victory by getting married."

She eased against him, her breasts pressing into his chest. "And then you will be the general with the greatest claim to the throne."

He liked her ambition—it matched his own. "And what will we do with Philip and the boy?"

She curled her lips into an alluring smile. "Idiots don't live long as kings, and the boy has years before he can rule. Time for you to insert yourself as his indispensable regent and run the empire in his name."

He wasn't surprised by her ruthlessness, Alexander had possessed the same vindictive streak, even if he'd hated to show it.

"And when he grows up?"

"Do you believe Macedonians will want a half-Persian son of a governor's daughter ruling them?" She traced the outline of his ear with her fingernail. "Once we're married and the other traitorous generals have been weeded out, we can decide what to do with the boy and his mother."

Perdiccas pulled away, a troublesome iciness enveloped him at the idea of executing Roxana and the boy. He had killed to protect the empire, but could he destroy the last reminders of his good friend?

"We shall see, my dear queen. We shall see."

CHAPTER FORTY-SEVEN

The glittering sandstone city of Sardis got steadily smaller in her wagon window. The baggage train, following the army led by Perdiccas, headed away from the western edge of the empire to follow the route along the Great Sea to the dusty shores of the Nile. Distraught over her husband's remains and convinced she would never find a place to settle with her son, Roxana dreaded another long journey through the cold winter months and another precarious battle for her son's realm.

Her faith in Perdiccas and all the generals had waned, taking with it her optimism. How could this band of men hold together her son's empire without killing each other in the process? But even though her hopes floundered on their journey, her son thrived.

He got excited with every stop the long caravan made. He played in the ocean, thrilled at exploring new cities and towns, but most of all, he seemed captivated by the soldiers, and they with him.

The men who approached her as she walked through the camps with the boy amazed her. When alone, they never acknowledged her, but with her son, they were different. Every soldier, from crusty veteran to recruit, wanted to meet the heir of the mighty Alexander.

"He's his father's son," one infantryman with a limp told her when she passed the supply wagon.

"Oh, he will be another Alexander," a pock-faced cavalryman said as he tended to his horse.

Some tousled his hair and others gave him small tokens, carved toys of animals and weapons of war.

Their interest and genuine affection for her son roused her spirits, but it also reminded her of the joy his father would never share. The pride he would never have, the walks he would never take with him among his troops.

There wasn't a day that she didn't think of Alexander. Alone in the little cot in her travel tent was the worst. So many memories came back to her at night, and her ache for him drove her to tears. Between the festering knot of worry in her stomach and her grief, sleep became a wish instead of a reality.

There was another benefit of taking her son with her for walks; the soldiers were a wealth of knowledge about the latest drama in the camp—the fate of Philip's half-sister Cynane.

"I saw her dragged off her horse, kicking and screaming, while her daughter tried to fight the troops sent to arrest her," an officer in the infantry recounted when they stopped in Phrygia. "Many men witnessed it and are afraid of what Perdiccas may do to her. Alexander would never have tolerated such a thing happening to a woman."

The news shocked her. The old veteran was right—Alexander would never have allowed such treatment of his family, but the soldiers' reaction was more worrisome. Perdiccas needed the army to continue her son's regency. Without them, she and her boy were vulnerable.

Back in her tent, she reported the news to Morella.

"I should speak to Perdiccas about this." Roxana kissed her son while he sat on Arnia's lap. "Maybe it's time I got more involved in the affairs of my son's regent."

"Careful, my lady," Morella warned, fixing a hole in one of little Alexander's tunics. "General Perdiccas is a hard man; some say he's even worse now that the other generals have turned on him. Desperate, even."

Roxana warmed her hands in front of her brazier, struggling to remember the things Alexander had told her about his generals, searching for an angle to use on Perdiccas.

"Desperate or not, I have to try. I can't afford for the army to rebel against Perdiccas like they did with Alexander. There's too much at stake."

The next morning, ready to corner Perdiccas, Roxana set out across the men's camp, with her two bodyguards in tow, her sights set on the gold pike of her husband's former tent.

But as she trekked along the well-worn dirt paths, she noticed something. There were no calls from men, no laughter, no murmur of conversation. It remained eerily quiet.

Where were the men? Where had they all gone?

There were no sentries on duty at the entrance to his tent. No officers milling about. The only man there was Perdiccas's old, wiry attendant.

"Where's the general?" She lowered her shawl from around her head.

"He's with the assembly, ma'am. The men have ..." The old man's voice faltered. "The men have rebelled because of the death of Cynane, and they—"

"She's dead?" Disgust raged through her.

"Last night. Her throat was cut. The men were not happy to see old Philip's daughter killed in such a manner. They came to my master's tent and told him they would march no further until he allowed the marriage of King Philip and Cynane's daughter. It was said the woman pleaded with the men before she was killed to let her daughter marry the king. Now the men insist on the marriage to honor her death."

A marriage to Philip—so that is why Cynane had traveled to Sardis and joined the kings. By marrying Philip to her daughter, any issue would not only be royal but pure Macedonian. It could eliminate her son from the royal succession.

Roxana desperately needed to stop the marriage, and her only hope was to convince Perdiccas as regent not to allow it.

"Is Perdiccas still talking to the army?"

The old man's gaze fell to the ground. "Perdiccas is standing by with the assembly witnessing the marriage of King Philip to the poor woman's daughter, Eurydice."

Roxana reached for the servant's hand, overwhelmed.

"Do you need a doctor, my lady?"

She let him go and took a deep breath, terrified of what this meant for her son. "No. Just tell the general I need to speak—"

Perdiccas strutted into his tent, still wearing his ceremonial cuirass.

"Roxana?" He snapped his fingers, dismissing his attendant.

While the old man hobbled out, Perdiccas proceeded to a table where jugs of wine and water sat next to a few silver goblets. After his attendant closed the tent flap, she challenged the general.

"What have you done?" She kept her voice low so none outside could hear. "By allowing those two to marry, you have cut my son off completely from his birthright."

"I had no choice." He lifted a jug of wine and sniffed the contents. "The men were about to mutiny. I can't have things falling apart within the ranks when we're about to go to war with Ptolemy, Craterus, and Antipater."

"What do you mean, Craterus and Antipater? I thought we were going to Egypt to fight Ptolemy."

"Craterus has crossed the Hellespont against Eumenes. Antigonus is with him." He set the jug aside. "They mean to unseat Eumenes from his post and probably give it to Antigonus. It's all being done to hurt me."

"And to hurt my son!" Roxana shouted. "This has escalated from a dispute among generals into a civil war. The army will want little Alexander's head before too long!"

He held up his hands, urging calm. "No, Roxana, no one wishes to harm the son of Alexander. This war is about who will control your son and Philip, not rule in their place."

His certainty after all the betrayal they had encountered amazed her. "And what happens if this girl gets pregnant? What happens if she takes control of Philip and he cuts out my son?"

"Eurydice will have no hold over Philip, trust me." He moved away from the table, grinning. "The man can barely manage feed himself. I seriously doubt he will know what to do with a sixteen-year-old girl." He went to a bench in the corner of his tent. "I may not have been able to stop the wedding, but I can stop the marriage from being consummated. Philip and Eurydice will spend all of their time apart until I finish with this damn war. She's being set up in the women's camp as we speak. I'm sure you will run into her. After I deal with Ptolemy, I'll figure out what to do with the two of them."

Roxana sighed, her strength siphoning out of her. How much more of this could she take? The travel, the feuds between generals, Alexander's family, the fate of her son? Every day, her uncertainty weighed her down and left her spirit depleted. She had lost interest in food, sleep, and longed to run away, but she couldn't. She had a duty to her son and her dead husband. Alexander had told her once to fight if anything should ever happen to him, so she would go on fighting until she had no more blood left.

"When does the war begin?"

He loosened the straps on his cuirass. "We will be within the borders of Egypt in another few weeks. I will meet Ptolemy and his forces sometime after that, I expect."

Her bitterness snuck into her voice. "And what if you lose? What will happen to all of us?"

"Do not doubt me, Roxana. I will not fail. I will bring Alexander home to Macedonia and install your son as king. We will be victorious, but you must trust me."

Trust? The word left a bad taste in her mouth. Her father, Alexander, Hephaestion, now this general charged with her son's regency asked for her trust, and she had none to give.

"If you will forgive me, General, I've given up on trusting. But I will pray to the gods for you and your army. I will pray for peace and an end to all this war."

He loosened the breastplate on his armor, displaying a slight grimace. "I hate to disappoint you, but the war will never end. Ptolemy has set in motion a chain of events that will go on for many years to come. If you're going to pray, pray for victory." The stoic countenance she'd always associated with the man returned. "Peace only comes when we're dead."

Roxana, accompanied by her guards, maneuvered the trails crowded with soldiers through the camp. She arrived back at her tent, slapped the flap aside, and came to a sudden halt. A stranger waited in the middle of her reception area.

She was thin, but muscular, and wore the thick linen cuirass and short sleeveless chiton of a soldier. With lovely pale skin, high cheekbones, and light blonde hair, she was a beauty. Her pursed red lips lifted into a smile.

"Philip says you're very kind."

Her soft voice contradicted her masculine attire. A sneaking suspicion rose in Roxana's gut.

"Eurydice?"

The young woman nodded. "I thought I would be spending my wedding night with my husband, the king, instead, Perdiccas had his men bring me to your tent."

Roxana spotted the trunk and a bedroll at her feet. She ran her hand over her brow, suppressing her scream. Could this get any worse?

"He said the wives of kings should reside together in the camp," Eurydice added, her blue eyes brimming with apprehension. "I told him I didn't want to bother the mighty Roxana."

"The mighty Roxana?"

"I've heard stories about you from others in the camp. How you cured the children of fever, saved the king from his arrow wound, ride, hunt, and have stood up to the generals." Eurydice twisted her hands together. "My mother also taught me to fight and hunt. Perhaps we can hunt together one day."

Morella entered her tent, carrying blankets and a pillow. She stopped in front of Roxana. "It's all over the camp," she said in Persian. "She's become your charge."

Morella handed the girl the blanket and pillow, then winked at Roxana on the way out of the tent. "Our wagon is going to get crowded."

Roxana was unsure of what to say. First Philip, and now his wife would be under her thumb.

"Perdiccas didn't tell me you would be joining my party. I would have made provisions and gotten the supply master to issue you a tent."

"I don't need a tent. I can sleep outside with your guards. I like the fresh air."

"But you are the wife of a king." Roxana tempered her impatience. "You shouldn't be sleeping in the rain like a common soldier."

Eurydice snickered, and the cold, guttural sound traveled around Roxana's tent. "My mother pounded my duty into my head for years. I was to elevate our family and marry above my station. That's why she dragged me to Sardis and insisted I marry Philip. She even got herself killed to ensure I would marry the king. I like Philip, but a husband …?" Her eyes glistened with tears. "I never wanted to marry. I wanted to be free to ride my horses, hunt, and choose my life, but others have chosen for me. I'm helpless to stop it."

Her brittle voice awakened memories of Roxana's life before Alexander. She saw her younger self in the girl. The anger at her predicament petered out. How could she be cross with another victim of Alexander's demise?

She took Eurydice's hands, vowing to give her a chance. "We have a long journey ahead of us to Egypt. It will give us time to get to know each other. And you can ride my horse along the way. Hera could do with the exercise."

Eurydice sniffled and then wiped her nose on her tunic sleeve.

Roxana smiled. Perhaps they had more in common than she'd first surmised.

The cool breezes from the Great Sea helped cut the early spring heat in Roxana's wagon. The baggage train had entered the green lands of northern Syria. She gazed outside the window at the shoreline, noting how their path since leaving Sardis kept them close to the water. She put the book she'd been reading in her lap and turned to her sleeping son. Here she was with Alexander's son, taking almost the same route as his father when he'd conquered his empire.

Roxana ran her fingers over his wavy reddish-brown hair, in awe of the how much her little boy resembled his mighty father. Already two and a half, he had Alexander's boundless energy and his curious nature. He asked questions about every new animal, building, and city they passed through. But he had his father's temper and impatience as well. She could see it when he didn't get his way. His thick brow would crease, and he would raise his voice, insisting on being heard. She wished he had a father to teach him restraint, but the only male influences in his life were the soldiers protecting her and the army men in the camp. Perdiccas would stop by to see the boy, but he was too busy to stay for long.

Growing up in the back of a wagon with nothing but women and soldiers around him wasn't the life she wanted for her son. He would need an education and a place to call home, but all of that would have to wait.

"Roxana?" a voice called through their window.

She pulled back the curtain. Eurydice trotted Hera alongside the wagon.

"Cleitus from the supply wagon wanted me to pass on that one of his twin girls has a cough. He asked if you could check on her."

"When we stop for the night, I will go to her."

Her reputation for tending to the sick had grown since leaving Babylon. Many in the camp sought out her advice for different afflictions, and she was happy to help. Anything to relieve the tedium of the endless days of bumpy dirt roads, and a long line of forgettable cities and towns.

Eurydice held up two dead rabbits. "I caught us something special for dinner."

The idea of fresh game thrilled Roxana. The rations from the wagon had given her little appetite, preferring the wine stores to food.

"You're a better hunter than me."

She secured the wild hares to the blanket across Hera's back.

"It gives me something to do." Eurydice slapped the side of her wagon. "I'd go mad hidden in one of those big monstrosities all day."

She rode off.

Roxana stuck her head out the window to see where she headed.

"She's going to the front of the train," Morella told her, looking up from sewing a new tunic for little Alexander. "She rides with the cavalry officers at the front as we travel."

Roxana came back in the window. "How do you know that?"

"You said to keep an eye on her so …?" Morella shrugged. "I get reports. Many in the camp say she thinks herself a soldier."

Roxana adjusted the pillow behind her back. "As long as she stays away from Philip, I don't care what she does."

"She's trouble, that one. Imagine what she will do when she eventually gets her hooks in that simple man."

"That's why we should be grateful General Perdiccas has kept Philip away from the women's camp."

Morella cut at a piece of thread with her teeth. "Word is he's training with the army, preparing for the battle in Egypt."

Roxana reached for her book. "That's Perdiccas's way of keeping him occupied. You know he can't stay focused on one thing for too long."

Morella held up the tunic, inspecting her work. "And what of the general? What will he find to occupy himself once he's finished in Egypt? Another battle? Another fellow general to overcome?"

Roxana dreaded what Perdiccas had in store after they left the shores of the Nile. "Let's just get through the battle in Egypt. We'll worry about his next move once Ptolemy is subdued."

"I hope the general knows what he's doing. I've got a bad feeling about this war."

Roxana pretended to read her book, not wanting to share that she had the same bad feeling.

Chapter Forty-Eight

B y late spring, the baggage train and army pushed through to the outskirts of
Egypt where a violent sandstorm introduced Roxana to the abysmal landscape
and extreme living conditions. She had to sleep above the ground in a chair to evade
the constant influx of snakes and scorpions into her tent at night. By day, she stayed
inside her wagon to avoid the blistering sun.

One morning, their caravan arrived at a freshwater oasis not far from the city
of Pelusium. Perdiccas ordered the baggage train to remain while he and Philip,
along with the army, horses, and elephants marched to face Ptolemy. The women
rejoiced as they rode away, but Roxana didn't share their enthusiasm.

"Philip has no business going into battle," she said to Morella while changing
for an evening ride on Hera. "I feel responsible for him since he has no family to
look after him."

"The general will make sure no harm comes to him." Morella helped her secure
her trousers around her waist.

"I can't believe Perdiccas rode off with the army leaving us here unprotected.
What if we need him? We have no idea where he plans to surprise Ptolemy's forces,
or how to get word to him." Roxana stepped into her leather shoes, the pressure in
her chest building. "What do we do if he loses this battle? Where do I take my son?
How do——?"

Morella held her hands. "My lady, you've been fretting since the king died
almost three years ago. You can't keep this up. You must take care of yourself." She
let her go. "If something were to happen to you, your boy could end up in the hands
of that simpleton's wife." Morella scowled. "Then I would have no choice but to
kidnap the little king and take him back to Persia to make sure the she-devil never
touches him."

Roxana's shoulders sagged under the weight of her never-ending worry, but she
knew Morella was right.

"Please don't call Eurydice names. She's exuberant. I was the same way at her age."

Morella's surly expression never changed. "You were her age when you married
the king. I don't remember you riding around with the men, eating with them, or
sitting with them by the fires. You should say something to her. The women in the
camp are whispering about her shameful behavior. She's making a lot of enemies."

"I'm thankful she has taken the attention away from me for a change." She
secured a belt with a knife around her waist, preferring to keep one close by since
arriving in Egypt. "Perdiccas gave me the task of making sure she stays away from
Philip, which I've done. Now with Philip off with the army, the girl can do as she

likes. I'm not her nursemaid."

"If you ask me, she could use one. She needs to get off her high horse and start acting like the wife of a king and not like she *is* king. She'll cause problems with the men, mark my word."

Little Alexander came running into her tent with Arnia right behind him. Roxana hugged her son, amazed at how much he had grown.

"Mama, I want to go riding with you," he said with his usual insistence.

She swept a lock of reddish-brown hair from his eyes. "Tomorrow, I will let you ride with me on Hera, but this evening I want to check the lands around our camp for herbs. When you're bigger, you will be able to ride with me on a horse of your own."

Arnia took the boy's hand. "Which will be before this war ends at the rate he's going through clothes."

Roxana gave her a weak smile, the precariousness of their situation returning to the forefront of her thoughts.

"I'll be back." She rushed out of the tent before anyone could see her tears.

Every day, Roxana waited for news from the army. She occupied her time playing with her son, reading her books when she could concentrate, or sewing with Morella. But at night, alone in her tent, she paced and drank the local wine to keep her anxiety at bay.

She wasn't the only one who was apprehensive. Wives and mistresses of the men roamed the camp in the hopes of gleaning any news, but there was none. Roxana empathized with their distress. She worried about Philip, and if Ptolemy had captured him. Would his men descend on the camp wanting to take or kill her son? The waiting was agony.

On the fifth night without any word from Perdiccas, a restless Roxana left her tent intending to walk the camp, but instead, lost herself in the stars. Admiring the night sky kept her from reliving the almost three years of uncertainty she'd endured since Alexander's death. Her thumb rubbed back and forth over the silver coin around her neck as a full summer moon shone down, lighting the familiar world of tents and wagons she'd come to regard as home. This was the legacy Alexander had left her—a life of perpetual travel and endless war.

"I wonder if you know what you've done," she whispered to the coin in her hand. "The cost we're paying for your everlasting fame is incredibly high. Do you regret your choices or have you forgotten about us?"

"My lady?"

With thick shoulders, a deep voice, and a boyish grin, the soldier in front of her tent was one she recognized from her dealings with Perdiccas. He was an officer in his army, but his uniform was crisp, his face clean-shaven, and he didn't have the ragged look of the men she'd seen leaving with the general to fight Ptolemy.

"My name is Peithon. I've been sent by General Ptolemy to—"

"Perdiccas is dead, isn't he?" Roxana interrupted in a matter of fact tone.

He gave a curt nod.

A fleeting pang of sorrow passed through her. The tough, disciplined general had been fair with her, but the years spent following him through the vast territories of the empire had brought her to this.

Roxana suddenly realized her two sentries from the king's guard had disappeared. She felt for the knife secured to a belt under her cloak. Did she need it? The man before her didn't seem like a killer of women and children.

Peithon cleared his throat, a speck of unease glistened in his eyes. "The war is over, my lady. And General Ptolemy has been very gracious with the soldiers. He wanted me to send you his regards and that he will make sure you are well protected." He motioned to a pair of ragged foot soldiers, holding shields and swords, behind him. "No harm will come to you or your son. He gives you his word."

"And Philip?" She feared Ptolemy may not have been as kind to the man he'd denounced more than once in her presence.

"He's back in his tent here in the camp. Rejoined with his bride."

Shocked, she took a step backward, almost running into her tent. "Perdiccas wanted to keep them apart. General Ptolemy has no idea what he has done. If they're together, she will influence him and perhaps even—"

"General Ptolemy didn't put them together. I did." Peithon's friendly smile vanished. "As Perdiccas's second-in-command, the assembly of Macedonian soldiers voted for me to take over the regency of the kings."

"You? Why didn't the assembly ask Ptolemy to take over the regency?"

"They did, but he refused."

Roxana closed her eyes. Of course. He had no interest in seeing Alexander's son on the throne. He didn't care about the empire, only in keeping his piece of it.

"What about Perdiccas? Did he die bravely in battle?"

"No, he did not." Peithon's voice grew colder. "When he tried to cross the Nile to the battle site, not far from here, two thousand soldiers and countless animals were lost, drowned in the river. Perdiccas showed no remorse for his actions. The cavalry officers went to his tent after the men started to mutiny, and they stabbed him to death."

Roxana turned to her tent doorway, overcome by the brutal act. "He was decent to me. I cannot speak ill of him." She rested her hand on her knife, debating her next move. "What happens now? Do we go head to Macedonia or is there another battle to win?"

Peithon came up to her. "We wait here until Antipater sends word."

This surprised her more than hearing about Ptolemy refusing the regency. "Antipater? Is coming here?"

"To take over the regency of the kings. He left Cappadocia after Craterus died in battle against Eumenes. I'm not sure if he's coming to us, or we are going to him."

Roxana recalled the kind general who had walked with her in India and told her stories of Alexander. "Craterus was a good man."

"That he was." Peithon pushed aside the flap of her tent.

The loss of so many good men would have angered Alexander. But if he had lived, there would have been no need for war.

Peithon cleared his throat. Roxana became aware of the other women around her listening in on their conversation.

She stepped into her tent.

Peithon followed her inside and secured the flap.

She stopped in her reception area, frantic for word on Alexander.

"Where is my husband, General? Is he still in Egypt?"

"He's in Memphis. Ptolemy plans on building him a final resting place in Alexandria, close to the bay, where the world may come to know of his accomplishments."

She clenched her fists. How dare Ptolemy keep her husband. He belonged to her, not his general. "But he must return to his homeland. The succeeding king must bury the former one; otherwise, the reign of the new king will be deemed invalid."

"I know of no such custom, my lady, only that the king loved Egypt, and General Ptolemy wishes for him to stay in the land he conquered and be worshiped as a god."

That made her even angrier. "I would like to discuss this with General Ptolemy. I want to see Alexander."

Peithon's loud sigh hung in the air. "The general has returned to Alexandria. I'm sorry, but he wants no further contact with you or the kings."

It was like a slap across the face. She'd hoped he would at least speak with her, but the dismissal told Roxana what Ptolemy thought of her and her son. He had no intention of honoring Alexander's legacy. He was more interested in making his own.

"If you will excuse me." Peithon dipped his head to her. "I must see to the men returning to the camp."

Without another word, he stepped outside and left her alone to absorb the news.

Roxana went to her refreshment table and poured a goblet of wine. She steadily sipped, wanting to take away the sting of the encounter and remember the dead men and how things used to be. The good times, when enemies were friends, and Alexander ruled the world.

CHAPTER FORTY-NINE

Roxana sat on a bench in her stifling tent, melting in the Egyptian heat. Why had she ever dreamed of coming to this ghastly country? All it had given her was sorrow, snakes, bugs, and endless nights without a wink of sleep.

The heat wasn't completely to blame for her nervousness. Since learning of Antipater's arrival, she'd struggled to think of anything else.

She stared into her wine goblet, remembering everything Alexander had told her of his regent, which wasn't much. This new taskmaster of her fate was one she'd never met, unlike Alexander's generals. Not knowing how he felt about Persians, her son, or Alexander's marriage to her added to her increasing unease.

"That general is here, my lady." Morella stepped into her tent. "He wants to speak with you. Or at least, I hope that's what he said. He speaks so fast it's hard to tell."

Roxana arched an eyebrow. "Your Greek is getting better. Before you had no idea what any of them were saying."

Morella took her goblet away, then fussed over her wrinkled clothes. "I can get by with these army types. They don't say much."

Morella went back to the tent flap and held it open for Peithon before darting outside.

"Lady Roxana." He bowed. "I've come to let you know that we will be pulling out at first light tomorrow. Please prepare your belongings."

She got up from her bench, alarmed. "Pulling out? To where?"

"My instructions are to get you and the kings on the road to a settlement in Syria. Antipater is to meet us there and take over the regency." He wiped his brow and slouched his shoulders. "The sooner we get on our way, the better."

Something bothered the man, and she needed to pry it out of him. Any information these days was valuable.

"Are you all right, General?"

He stood at attention. "Just the usual complaints of the camp. I never realized there were so many. General Perdiccas handled a great many things I never knew about."

"Anything I can help you with? I've spent many years in the camps and I'm very familiar with the running of them."

"Yes, I'm sure you are." He paused, searching the ceiling of her tent. "Your sister-in-law, Princess Eurydice, has been making a lot of unusual requests."

She concealed her satisfaction behind an indifferent stare. Eurydice had been a threat ever since she'd moved into Philip's tent. Roxana needed to shut the young woman down before she became pregnant with a new problem.

"What sort of requests does she have?" Roxana coyly asked, making sure to give the general a pleasing smile. "Food? Supplies? Perhaps a horse from the stables since she no longer rides my Hera?"

"No. It's rather awkward." He fidgeted with his hands. "I've been instructed by Eurydice that all correspondence meant for the King Philip is to be given to her."

Roxana put her hands on her hips, ready to tear Eurydice apart.

That she-devil!

"When did she make this request?"

"After she joined her husband in his tent." He wiped his brow again. "Then a few days ago, she told me she plans to train with the men. She wants to get them in shape. I haven't said anything to the division leaders yet. I'm not sure what to say."

It seemed all of Morella's misgivings about the girl had been accurate. She'd turned into a troublemaker.

"What did you tell Eurydice about training with the men?"

"What do I tell her? She's married to the king, and I can't ask King Philip his opinion on this since … Well, his wife's opinion is his, isn't it?"

For the first time in years, Roxana felt like she had the upper hand in a situation. Not since her influence with Alexander had anyone in charge asked her opinion.

How could she undermine the girl's position in the camp? The women already hated her, and if the men felt the same way, it would shut down any chance she had of influencing Antipater or the other generals.

"What harm could it do?" Roxana added a sweetness to her tone, driving her point home. "She's a spirited girl, bored with the camps. I say after a few days of training with the men, she will soon grow bored and return to her wifely pursuits."

Peithon let out a long breath. "Thank you, my lady. I will take your advice. As you say, what harm can she do?" He gave her another quick bow. "If you will excuse me."

The moment he left the tent, Morella came inside, carrying her goblet of wine.

"It seems you're finally getting the hang of this."

Roxana took the drink. "You were listening at the door?"

"That's what you pay me for."

"We need to pack up the wagon." She swirled her wine in her goblet. "Keep tabs on Eurydice as we travel. From now on we have to make sure we know every thought going on in that vixen's brain."

Morella grinned. "Now you're talking, my lady."

The sands of Egypt gave way to majestic palms and fertile fields as the army and baggage train crawled into Syria. Roxana relished the cooler climate and colorful landscape, eager to put the dismal sand dunes behind her. She counted the days until the army arrived at the settlement where the kings would come under Antipater's regency. But instead of dreading the meeting, she now embraced it.

After weeks of debate, she'd decided Antipater had to be a formidable man and a reasonable one. He had put up with Alexander's mother for years but remained loyal to her husband—that said something about the character of the man. He'd served Alexander and his father—a testament to his devotion. The only question still unanswered was his regard for Persians, particularly a half-Persian son of Alexander's.

Once the luster of the green pastures and farms had worn thin, Roxana turned her attention to her little boy. He sat by her feet on the floor of the wagon, under Arnia's watchful eye as he crashed toy carts into each other and squealed with delight.

"We'll have to get him his own wagon and tutor soon, my lady," Arnia asserted. "That is if you are educating him as a Persian. Our boys leave their mother's side at five, but I read in Greece the boys are not taken from their mothers until seven."

She caressed her son's pink cheek. "He will be educated as his father—in the Greek tradition."

Arnia frowned. "Excuse me, ma'am, but he's both Persian and Greek. Shouldn't he know both worlds? To rule this empire, he must be immersed in each side of his blood."

The question had never occurred to Roxana. She'd assumed he would be raised Greek, but Arnia made an excellent point. How could he rule over Persians without knowing much about the culture?

"Then he will have Greek tutors, but his Persian mother will teach him what he needs to know. I may not be educated, but I can remind him of where he comes from."

Morella turned up her pug nose. "Seems to me you two are putting the cart before the horse. Before he can be educated as a Greek, he needs to get to Greece. And to do that, we have to see what happens in Syria."

Morella was right. Since hearing of Antipater's regency over the kings, Roxana had hoped it meant the end of their travels. Three years on the road was enough. Her son needed a home, an education, and she desperately wanted a respite from her ceaseless anxiety over their plight. Would Antipater offer them peace or more war?

Outside her wagon window, Roxana heard shouting.

"What's going on?"

Between her wagon and the one traveling next to hers, a woman sat on a black horse, barking orders at one of Roxana's sentries.

"You should be walking not riding, Soldier. How else do you plan to get in shape for battle?"

The long blonde braid coming out the back of the abrasive woman's helmet immediately revealed her identity.

Eurydice. Why am I not surprised?

"What is it, my lady?" Morella came up to the window and peeked out. "Oh, it's her. She's like a field commander, that one is. Heard she even sleeps out with the men in their tents and won't stay with King Philip anymore."

Eurydice rode on ahead, leaving Roxana's guard to harass another.

"Let her keep digging a hole for herself." Roxana shut the curtain. "She can prance around on horseback all she wants, but unless she gives birth to an heir, the men will grow tired of her. If there's one thing I know, it's the Macedonian army and their fickle allegiances."

Arnia lifted little Alexander to her lap and frowned at his dirty hands. "I don't know how she'll ever get a child off of that silly excuse for a man. He has no more sense than this boy, and Alexander will at least grow out of it."

Morella went back to her bench. "Do you think the general will do anything about her?"

"No, he's afraid of her." Roxana sat back, nursing a smug grin. Her plans for the arrogant girl were unfolding nicely. "My guess is he will leave her for Antipater. I would. If anyone can keep the girl in check, it's him. He's handled Alexander's formidable mother for years; a tiresome girl like Eurydice will be nothing more than a buzzing gnat needing to be squashed."

"I've heard Antipater is called the 'old bear' by many of the men." Morella picked up her sewing. "They say he puts up with no nonsense and hates women."

Roxana's excitement about the coming meeting tickled her belly. "Then the next few days should prove to be quite entertaining. When the old bear and the young lioness square off for control, it might weaken the position of Philip with the men."

Morella gave a short belly laugh. "And make Alexander seem the better choice for king."

Roxana tousled her son's hair. "Yes, I was thinking the exact same thing."

CHAPTER FIFTY

"Ordered?" Morella balked, pinning Roxana's sedate Greek dress into place. "Who orders you around?"

Roxana stood before the copper mirror in her small tent on the outskirts of the settlement of Sun City—or Heliopolis, as the Greeks called it. The chilly night air snuck under the edges of her tent, and she shivered. Was it the cold or nerves making her tremble?

She smoothed the linen of her blue frock. She hoped to impress Antipater by appearing as a proper Greek wife.

"Antipater orders everyone around." She adjusted the blue shawl around her head, making sure to cover her hair like an unassuming matron. "Since we've arrived, the army has been hopping mad about Antipater's demand for discipline. Something our dear Peithon has been unable to maintain."

Morella tucked in a few stray strands of Roxana's hair beneath the shawl. "Between Antipater and the she-devil snapping orders at them, the men don't know who to follow. I'd say we're ripe for another rebellion."

Roxana smiled, delighted at the dire news. "Which is why I was ordered along with my son, Eurydice, and Philip to attend the assembly meeting. Antipater is about to wield that power he has fought so hard to acquire and shut Eurydice down."

Morella lowered her voice. "I head the little nymph is wearing gold armor and bringing a sword to the gathering. Her maid told me she wants to present herself to Antipater as a warrior queen."

Roxana eyed her reflection. "Which do you think the established Greek general will admire? The young female warrior, or the wife of Alexander demurely dressed as a Greek woman holding the hand of her famous husband's son?" She wiped what she thought was a speck of dirt from the corner of her eye, only to discover it was a wrinkle. "The last time I was ordered to do anything was by Alexander. Seems like a lifetime ago."

"I'm glad you've woken up, my lady."

"Woken up?"

Morella fussed with the belt of her dress. "Since the king's death, you've been preoccupied. But since Perdiccas died, you've gotten back in the game, so to speak. You're thinking again, and not following. It's good to see."

Roxana tossed her head to the side, pleased with Morella's observation. Perdiccas's death had opened her eyes. She'd come to realize she needed to take control of her situation and stop depending on the generals.

"From everything I've heard about Antipater, I need to remain sharp."

"You just be careful with this one, ma'am. We go through generals pretty fast these days."

"Yes, Morella, we do. However, this general is known for his staying power. After all, he served Philip and Alexander, and now—"

"An idiot and a toddler." Morella snickered. "I would say that's a bit of a letdown."

Arnia appeared at her tent door, holding Alexander's hand. Pleased the nurse had followed her instructions, she inspected her son's short white tunic, and his little purple and white diadem.

A perfect Greek king.

"Where are we going, Mommy?"

She took his hand. "We are to meet a man who was very important to your father. And who will be very important to you."

The cool evening air evaporated when she entered the massive gathering tent, and hundreds of men turned her way. Heat pressed against Roxana's skin as she followed Philip and Eurydice down the long aisle toward the raised platform. Two thrones, gilded with gold, waited for the kings. A tingle rose up her spine as she glanced around the tent and discovered the object of every man's fascination wasn't her—it was little Alexander.

"He looks just like him," one soldier whispered as she moved past.

"It's Alexander come back to us," another called in an excited voice.

She held her head high, knowing her gamble had paid off. The men saw her son and not Philip. They would rally around their little king, and hopefully soon forget the other and his meddling wife.

Eurydice gave her a scathing glare as they climbed the short steps to the platform. Her gold cuirass and ill-fitting white chiton was almost comical on the slight girl. The sword at her side, made for a man, hung to her knees, adding to her awkward appearance.

Another man quickly joined them on the platform—the oldest man she'd ever seen.

His white hair and beard added a translucent quality to his deep blue eyes. With a long, thin face lined with numerous wrinkles, he seemed better suited for teaching Greek philosophy than running an empire. His white tunic reached to his bony ankles, and his leather sandals were plain and worn. The only hint as to his importance was the gold seal of the Macedonian regency hanging from a gold chain around his neck.

"That's old Antipater," Philip whispered as Roxana took her position next to her son's throne. "He's been regent since back in my father's day. He's a bit rough at first, but once you get to know him, he's not such a bad sort. Antipater taught me how to use a sword."

Antipater tapped Philip's shoulder. "Stop fidgeting."

She flinched at his gravelly, booming voice. She hadn't expected such a sound from an old man.

Philip immediately went as still as a statue.

Roxana bit her lower lip, unsure of what to make of the individual standing next to his throne.

"You're Roxana." Antipater came around Philip's throne to her side.

His invasive stare stirred her butterflies. "Yes, General Antipater."

"Alexander wrote to me frequently about you. I'm glad you and the boy are here." He watched the child playing with the ribbons on his diadem. "He's just like his father."

"The boy is the spitting image of Alexander, Antipater," a general in front of the assembly called out.

"I was not talking to you, Ameliyas," Antipater shouted, but kept his intimidating eyes on Roxana.

She wasn't sure if it was fatigue getting the better of her, but to finally stand in the presence of the man respected by her husband and his generals, filled her with a reassuring calm.

Clasping the seal of regency in his wrinkled hand, Antipater faced the assembly. "It has come to my attention that certain parties here have been denouncing me and my discipline of the army. She has been training with the men, rallying them against me, and performing duties with the army unbecoming of her station. Such actions could be quite catastrophic for the realm. Any, and I repeat, *any* matters of state will be discussed with me and approved by me, as is my right as guardian of the kings and regent to Macedon." He glared at Eurydice. "And if certain people are not happy with the way I run things, they can leave the empire and live in the wilds of Italy."

Eurydice rolled her eyes contemptuously. "Antipater, you're being paranoid again."

He turned to her, his harsh gaze bearing down on the Argead star decorating the breastplate of her cuirass. "After years of living in the palace at Pella with you and your mother, dear girl, how could I be anything else?"

A faint chuckle came from the men.

"I know how you think, Eurydice." He went up to her, towering over her slight figure. "And I will not have you undermine my authority. I have guardianship of the kings. From this moment forward, you will respect the decision of this assembly and all the men in it." Antipater paused and scanned the crowd. "You will have to find someone else to blame for your choice of husband."

The men laughed louder than before. Even Philip got caught up in the merriment. He clapped his hands and giggled with childish delight.

Roxana covered her mouth, hiding her snicker. *This is better than I'd expected.*

Eurydice charged the old man. "How dare you attack my marriage to the king. I am queen."

Antipater silenced her with a raised eyebrow. "Until I say you are what you are, you will do as I say, and when I say it. Is that understood?"

Her teeth clenched in anger, Eurydice became as rigid as a stretched rope, but she nodded in resignation.

"This is all rather exciting, isn't it?" Philip leaned over to her, still grinning. "It's like how it used to be when my brother was alive."

"Philip, mind yourself." Antipater tapped his shoulder, his tone much gentler than the one he had used on the king's wife. "Eurydice, your actions could be misconstrued by the unenlightened to mean you're attempting to take over the throne for yourself. That is treason and punishable by death."

"That's not what I intended." Eurydice hung her head. "I just wanted to …" Her voice drifted away.

Antipater surveyed the mass of faces before the platform. "Philip, take your bride to your tent. And may I suggest, my king, from now on you put your woman on her back and do with her what all men do with their wives, instead of allowing her to play war games."

A loud wave of cheering came from the assembly.

The young woman's reprimand gave Roxana some satisfaction, but it also burned in her gut. Just when she'd thought she was making inroads in her quest to be heard, a reminder of her sex, and the powerlessness that came with it, was tossed in her face.

Eurydice did something Roxana had never seen her do—she blushed. Then Philip took her hand and led her from the platform, still grinning like a little boy.

While they were hurrying down the aisle, Antipater's strong voice washed over the assembly.

"This has been a most unfortunate time for all of us. Many fine Macedonian men have been lost. We must remember our dead and move on. I will make new appointments to replace those brave men who were lost in Egypt. I will meet with the generals individually to go over their new governorships. We will make a treaty to prevent such battles from ever happening again." Antipater waved his hand over the assembly. "If there are any more reports of insubordination or disturbances, men will be prosecuted to the full extent of Macedonian law. Are there any other issues?"

Not a hand went up. The entire assembly was utterly still.

The regard of the men reminded Roxana of her husband. Alexander had the same mesmerizing effect.

"Most of you will remain here and be placed under the command of Antigonus to help fight against the disloyal Eumenes. The rest, prepare to leave with your commanders by dawn. The kings will depart for Pella. You can go back to your posts."

Roxana wanted to cry. Finally, she and her son would see Alexander's homeland. They would have a place to live in peace where her son could receive an education, get to know his lineage, and hopefully, win over his famous grandmother.

Antipater turned his back on the men. Quickly and quietly, the soldiers left the assembly. Assuming she was to leave with the men, Roxana took little Alexander's hand to help him from his throne.

"Why don't you stay?" Antipater held her shoulder. "It will be much easier to talk when there is no audience."

He waited until the last of the men had moved away from the front of the platform before he faced her, leaning on the throne previously occupied by Philip.

"I'm sorry you had to be privy to that, but I needed to clear the air and get the men back in order."

She held on to Alexander's hand, nervous about what the man wanted with her. "Things have been difficult in the camp since the death of Perdiccas. I'm sure the men and Eurydice will fall in line."

"I want to assure you that I have the best intentions for you and your son." He searched her face as if trying to figure her out. "Have you heard from Olympias yet? As grandmother of the king, I would have thought she would be corresponding with you."

The question shocked her. "No. I've never heard from her."

"Consider yourself most fortunate in that respect, my dear. Olympias has been a thorn in the side to many, many people." He spied her gold rope necklace. He lifted the coin hanging from it and admired the detail. "Roxana, of all the players in this funny game of ours, you have been the most silent. I ask you now, where does your allegiance lie?"

"My allegiance?" Roxana held up her son's hand in hers, mystified by the question. "My allegiance lies with Alexander and his son. I have no interest in political games or contests for power if that's what you fear. I wish only to see my son inherit the throne his father left him."

"I wish for that as well." He let go of the coin. "We will be heading for Pella in the morning. We will talk again once you're settled in the palace." Antipater patted the boy's head. "We will have to discuss the future of your son and his throne."

Roxana took her son and walked away from the platform.

"Where are we going now, Mommy?"

She squeezed his hand, hopeful for the first time in years. "We're going home, my love. To our new home, and the place where your daddy grew up. Macedonia."

"How long will we stay there?"

The question pulled at her heart.

"Home is where we will stay. No more traveling, no more tents. You will have your own room in the palace with teachers, and books, and servants to care for you."

His intense gray eyes flashed with excitement. "Can I have a pony when we get there?"

They broached the brisk night air, and her heart lifted with happiness as she hugged her son to her side.

"You can have anything you want, my little Alexander, because in this new home, you will finally be a king."

CHAPTER FIFTY-ONE

Rays of glimmering sunlight hit the water, sending flurries of sparkles into Roxana's eyes as she scrutinized the Macedonian shore. The white sandy beaches backed into rocky ledges of brown and white that staggered upward to jagged cliffs. The sharp slap of the brutally cold winter wind brought tears to her eyes and warmth to her heart.

She'd made it. She'd reached Alexander's homeland. Three years of grief, endless travels, countless battles, and weeks at sea sharing cramped quarters with her son, his nurse, and her maid, had made it possible for her to touch the Macedonian soil. The burden of her long journey lifted from her shoulders, but one thought persisted—he wasn't with her. When Alexander had been alive, she'd often imagined making this trip with him. Now, she made it with his son. The myriad of emotions settling over her tasted bittersweet, and mixed in with her feelings, a twinge of foreboding for what lay ahead.

When the wood plank from the deck of her ship came to rest on the dock, a bevy of servants and carts congregated around it.

The ships carrying Antipater's army also moored next to her vessel, and the small harbor quickly became a mass of confusion with donkeys, oxen, men, women, and children, anxious to reunite with family members.

Amid the endless uproar, Roxana negotiated the crowds while keeping a firm hold of her son's hand. Was this her introduction to this strange country? To be tossed into the mix of people? Unsure of where to go, she stopped in the middle of the pier. Arnia and Morella joined.

"Is this how they do things here?" Arnia asked. "It's chaos."

Roxana felt naked without her guards.

What do I do?

Then, a path cleared, and a small group of men appeared, bowing before Roxana and her son.

"My lady, we are to take your things to the palace," a gray-haired man said in front of the group. "There's a wagon waiting just ahead for you and your party." He pointed to a covered wagon not far from the end of the dock.

Relieved, she turned to Arnia and Morella. "We're to proceed to the palace with the aid of these men," she said in Persian.

"Is this the reception given to the king and his mother?" Morella grumbled in Persian. "Four men and an ox."

Roxana spotted Philip and Eurydice, also caught up in the turmoil. "Philip and Eurydice didn't receive a reception, either. It's a different country. Perhaps they have different customs."

Morella sniffed with displeasure as the servants carried Roxana's things from the ship. "I don't trust these people."

Amused, Roxana smirked at her attendant. "I'm sure they're thinking the same thing about us, Morella. Let's not start another war, shall we?"

She followed the line of servants to the wagon, and her hopes for a warmer welcome to her husband's homeland quickly dwindled.

Smaller than the one she'd known in Persia, it was stuffed with too many pillows and had several holes in the thin canvas, letting in the cold. It barely had enough room for all of them.

Their luggage, along with a few women from their baggage train, followed behind as they maneuvered up the cliffs along the shore. Then they arrived at the edge of a city. The women said little to each other as they got their first glimpse of Pella.

Shimmering white marble temples built in the Greek style stood out against the surrounding wooden huts. Statues of Greek gods crowded street corners and graffiti with advertisements for local businesses and offensive messages covered most of the buildings. The noise of conversation, the screech of birds, the call of animals, the rolling of carts, the pounding of footsteps on cobblestoned streets surrounded their wagon. Roxanne lifted her son to her lap so he could peek out at the activity.

Merchants in open stalls sold an array of items as they passed the city center. Olive growers had huge jugs of olive oil. Farmers had tables of fresh vegetables and pens housing livestock. Bakers displayed tall piles of bread. Tailors touted colorful tunics and fancy woven cloaks. Artists hawked brightly painted statues of the gods. There were spices from India, caged birds for sacrifices; one stall even auctioned slaves from all over the empire.

Soon, the clamor of the city died out, and the wagons started up a narrow, winding road. The landscape changed and the stark and rocky terrain of Macedonia replaced the colorful city structures.

On every crag and cliff, sheep and goats grazed and frolicked—the rough and isolated landscape appeared littered with them. She'd heard her father once say Macedon had started as a kingdom of goat herders, and from what she could see, they still were.

After their wagon made a turn around a huge bluff, the scintillating white palace came into view. Though it was smaller than the ones she'd previously occupied, it was no less opulent. It had a covering of marble with brightly painted frescos around the outer wall. Fruit trees shaded the grounds, and numerous ponds lay in the middle of lush greenery. The architecture was Greek with its high Doric columns, square gardens, and wide porticos.

"Better than I expected." Morella peered through the wagon curtains. "I wonder where they keep the sheep."

Roxana's royal rooms, set in the women's section, had scenes of deer, foxes, and rabbits on the walls. The furniture, made for necessity and not overly decorative, consisted of a few plain chairs, a stool, and a low table in the Greek style of dining finished the room. Tucked away in opposite corners were two poorly done busts of Alexander.

She would have them removed after she settled in.

The bedroom had more wildlife scenes, and the bed had none of the intricately carved detail she'd grown accustomed to in Persia. It was plain and accommodating, just like her rooms.

Morella grimaced as she set Alexander's gold chest down. "It's rather severe."

A soldier, still dusty from his travels and with his helmet tucked beneath his arm, walked into Roxana's rooms, unannounced.

"Antipater wishes to see you, my lady."

Put off by his snippy tone, Roxana gestured to the trunks scattered around the floor. "I haven't finished unpacking."

"Now, ma'am. In his offices." His insistent voice echoed throughout her rooms.

Instead of reprimanding his rudeness, Roxana crooked her finger at Morella.

"I don't need a translation, my lady." Morella wiped the dirt from Roxana's traveling clothes. "You would think you could at least change."

Roxana patted her maid's trembling hand. "I'll be fine. Finish with the unpacking."

She followed the solider into the corridor, struggling to keep up with his long legs, and was surprised to discover no sentries assigned to her rooms. She couldn't remember the last time she'd walked anywhere without the shadow of men with spears around her.

He led her through smoky, dark marbled halls lit with oil lamps where alcoves held flower-decorated statues. By the time she passed the third statue, Roxana's curiosity had piqued. Why were they all of Alexander?

The corridor opened up into a hypostyle hall with smooth white columns on each side. Between the columns were paintings of her husband, tile-mosaics of his feats, tapestries of his fighting prowess, and a few full body statues. He was on the floors, ceilings, and over a few arched doorways. Some portrayed him as a boy—others as a soldier. A few even had him gazing up to the heavens, his head tilted slightly to the left, looking like a god. But none of the impressions elicited the swell of emotion she'd expected when walking through his home. They were not her Alexander. Not the man she loved. They were lifeless recreations and lacked the fire he'd exuded.

She got so caught up in the plethora of Alexanders she didn't notice when the soldier halted before a pair of silver-inlaid doors. She almost ran into him.

One of the two guards posted outside the room snickered.

Then she caught it—that glint of dislike, the sneer of superiority she'd received from the Greek officers on her wedding day.

He opened the doors. "He's expecting you."

Roxana walked across a tiled floor with a vast scene of lions, bears, and wild boars. In the center was Alexander as a young boy, hunting a lion with another boy whose face Roxana didn't recognize.

"It's a very good likeness of him as a young man."

Antipater's commanding voice rolled through the room.

"Philip had it commissioned for Olympias when he added on to this palace. This is her reception area. I use it as an office." The older man rose from behind the desk and motioned to the mosaic. "I hope it doesn't bother you."

"No. I find his image comforting." Roxana scratched her head, perplexed. "But he does seem to be everywhere."

"His mother went a little mad after he left for Persia, but she was never a stable woman. You will find him around every corner and in every room … except for mine." He settled his hands behind his back. "Unlike Olympias, I prefer to live in the present. Alexander is the past. And your son is our future. He's three now, is he not?"

She tried to gauge his thoughts but couldn't. "Yes."

Antipater smiled. "Still young enough for play and toys."

She nervously folded her hands. "Yes, he and his Uncle Philip play quite a lot together."

"How wonderful for Philip to finally find a playmate of his caliber." Antipater chuckled. "I know Philip can be irksome at times, but he's harmless. His wife is another story." He paused for a moment, watching her. "There's something I would like to show you." Antipater took her elbow. "Come."

He ushered her out of his office, and Roxana's upper lip beaded with sweat.

They walked in silence down the long corridor. He stopped in front of two red painted doors. Tied to the handles was a single black ribbon.

"Alexander's rooms," Antipater told her. "I haven't been in them since before his death. There's something little Alexander should have of his father's." He pushed the doors open, and the black ribbon fell to the floor.

Light filtered in through the windows, catching dust scintillating in the air. The first thing commanding her attention was a great battle scene strewn with violence and mayhem. Men with swords and shields fought on a green field. Blood poured from wounds of fallen men, bodies burned on funeral pyres, and black warhorses pulled at the bit as they raced before a magnificent chariot. Around the horses, men captured in contorted movements of pain and frenzied excitement.

"It's from *The Iliad*." Antipater shut the doors. "Alexander wanted his rooms covered with scenes from the book. Philip found a young man from Thebes who was renowned for his battle paintings."

She moved closer to the wall, admiring the detail. "Yes, it was Alexander's favorite book."

"He loved to read. Never was without his nose in a book when he was little. He wrote me that you read Greek."

She was impressed he would remember such a trivial detail. "Yes. My mother taught me."

He studied her with a critical squint. "Has Olympias reached out to you since you've arrived?"

"Ah, no. We just got here." The question confounded her. "Is there a problem?"

He flourished a hand around the room. "Forgive me, but Olympias's spies are everywhere, and this is the last place in the palace where I can speak without fear of being overheard. If she ever contacts you, I must know. She will try something now that you and the boy are here."

"She's never once reached out to me since Alexander's death. What makes you think she will now?"

"She wants war," he said in a pragmatic tone. "Olympias would control her grandson and the Kingdom of Macedon, but she's the least of my concerns. I have rebellious generals in Persia and the constant threat from Athens to keep an eye on."

Roxana rubbed her head, fed up with the seven years of war she'd endured. "Will it ever end? Since I married Alexander, all I've known is war."

"War is a way of life to the Macedonian. Alexander grew up with it. So will his son."

Her patience snapped. "His son is already well-acquainted with war. He's known little else since he was born. What I want for him is a childhood without it."

Antipater's amiable demeanor never faltered. "You're a mother who has tried to raise her son in spite of war. It was an admirable feat, but you no longer need to concern yourself with your child's upbringing. I will be overseeing his needs from now on."

The fire in her belly ignited into an inferno. "You expect me to do what, stand aside while you take my child away from me? I'm his mother, and I have—"

"You are his Persian mother!" His booming voice rumbled throughout the room. "A Persian mother many in Greece prefer to forget. If we are to raise your son to be a Greek king, he must act Greek, be educated by Greeks, be seen as every inch the son of Alexander with no memory of his mother to create even one iota of apprehension in his subjects. If you do not leave your son in my care, he will die."

Roxana's obstinacy receded—something she'd never experienced before.

"But I want to be a part of his life, teach him things from my country, show him Persian traditions to go along with all the Greek ones you will no doubt pound into his head. How can he rule both lands without knowing about them?"

He went to an old wooden trunk along the wall and flung it open. The hinges creaked loudly with protest.

"Whatever he learns of Persia must be from a Greek perspective, not yours."

She knew the hazards of being Persian in a Greek world—she'd lived the nightmare and wanted none of it for her son. But she'd promised Alexander to fight for their child. How could she stand up for him when the sight of her would only hurt his chances of being accepted as king?

He retrieved a small black object from the depths of the trunk. "I must know you will go along with my plans. I've spent most of my life fighting with Olympias. I will not have those tumultuous times repeated."

She warily appraised his stony features. "And if I refuse?"

Antipater slowly walked up to her. "Then you will be sent back to your homeland and never see your son again."

Her heart crumbled. Of all the torments, that was one she never wished to endure. How could she win? Roxana had no choice but to bide her time and bit her tongue.

The crudely sewn stuffed black horse in his hands caught her interest. It had two wooden eyes, and even though the paint had faded, she could still see the red color. There were black ribbons for the mane and tail and little wooden hooves.

"Alexander was about your son's age when he first got this." Antipater handed her the toy. "His nurse, Lanice, made it for him. When he was going off to school with Leonidas, his first tutor, he placed it carefully in this trunk." He tapped the doll in her hand with his forefinger. "If anyone asks why we were here, tell them I wanted your son to have something of his father's."

"And who will ask?"

Antipater wiped the dust from his hands. "Those who have no interest in keeping your son on the throne."

She held the small horse close to her heart, wishing her husband were here with her, fighting for her and her son. She was so tired of going at it alone.

"I've heard enough about Alexander's mother to assure you I will not be like her. I want my son to be a great Greek king, and whatever you advise, I will do."

"Then the purpose of our meeting has been attained. I needed to hear your assurances before you settled in. I wish I could say this would be easy, but it won't. Alexander left behind not just your son, but a group of ambitious generals who want to see their fates as great as their king's. They will carve their empires out of your son's future if we don't stand together."

She questioned if she could trust the man. Her instincts, once sharp, had been dulled by years of disappointment and betrayal.

"Are you like those ambitious generals, Antipater? Are you eager to make a name for yourself?"

"I only wish to hold together your son's empire for as long as the gods allow." He eyed the streaks of afternoon sunlight stretching across the floor. "It's getting late. I'm sure you have much unpacking to do."

"Thank you for your honesty and this." She held up the toy horse.

Antipater's smile briefly lifted his face, making him appear years younger. "I will send for you again when it's time to plan your little boy's future. We have much to discuss if we are to raise another Alexander."

CHAPTER FIFTY-TWO

Weeks trudged by, and spring snuck up on the palace, blanketing the craggy lands surrounding it with colorful wildflowers. Roxana enjoyed the change of seasons, glad to be rid of the damp cold. She'd adjusted to her new life in Pella, but the occasional stares from servants and staff still bothered her.

"The Persian wife," they would whisper as she went by.

Some things never changed.

Rumors from the few Persian staff in the palace reported Antipater was busy, mending broken fences with Alexander's generals, and making plans for new wars, but there was little else she could learn. Antipater frowned on gossip, and many feared his wrath. Isolated, she existed on the snippets Morella could dig up.

"Doubt I'll get much, my lady," her maid said one morning when she asked about the news from Persia. "Their lips are about as tight as a poor man's purse."

A powerless fixture subject to Antipater's whims, she'd decided to concentrate her energies on the one thing she still had control over—her son.

Little Alexander grew stronger and taller with every passing month. His laugh was the most beautiful thing she'd ever heard, and his determined face, the most handsome she'd ever seen. He thrived in the palace. Giving him a room of his own and something of a family had offset the years of fear and frustration their travels had created.

Roxana often brought Little Alexander to the stables when she went to exercise Hera. She let him sit alone atop the gentle mare's back as she walked the horse around the enclosed paddock surrounded by walls of stone. Soon, he was trotting Hera about and then running her in the open fields. It was as if he'd been born on a horse, just like his father.

"Mommy, can I have a great black horse like Bucephalus?" Alexander asked her one late autumn day as they headed back to the palace from the stables.

She brushed his wavy hair from his eyes, marveling at the color. "How did you know about that? I never told you about your father's horse."

"The servants talk about him. They say my father tamed him when he was little like me and rode him into battle. Is that true, Mommy?"

"Yes." Roxana stooped and pulled the chain with the coin out from under her tunic top. "Here's his picture with your father on his back after they won a great battle in India."

He cocked his head as if deep in thought, just like his father. "And who was Hephaestion?"

She fingered the gold chain. "Where did you hear about him?"

"Some workmen in the palace told me. They said he and my father were very close."

His serious face troubled her. He seemed to be always thinking for one so young. Was this a result of too much war or his young life on the road? Her guilt kept her up at night.

She caressed his cheek, wishing to see his bright smile. "He was your father's general, second-in-command, and best friend. Hephaestion was Patroclus, and your father was Achilles, and they—"

"Who was Achilles?"

"Achilles was a great hero from a very famous book called *The Iliad*." She stood and took his hand. "Let's go back and have something to eat, and I'll read some of this book to you. It was your father's favorite."

"I would like to hear more about this Achilles and Pat ... ro ...."

"Patroclus, my son." Roxana beamed, proud of his interest. "It's time I taught you about your father. I think you're ready to learn about his amazing life."

When the rains of summer arrived, Alexander terrorized many in the palace by releasing his boundless energy by running up and down the corridors. Often the guards joined him, their shouts echoing throughout the royal residence.

He made friends in the Macedonian court, inviting them to play games in his rooms under the supervision of his nurse.

One day, Roxana walked into the nursery to find her son on the floor, concentrating intently on a game of dice, with none other than Antipater's son, Cassander.

"Ha!" Cassander counted the dice on the floor. "I win again."

"You don't play right. Antonius showed me the dice game and—" Alexander stopped when he saw his mother. "Mommy!" He ran to greet her.

Roxana wrapped her son in her arms and held him close, her soul rejuvenated by his warmth. She wished it could last forever.

Alexander pulled away. "Uncle Cassander was showing me the way he plays dice, but I think he cheats."

"I do not!" Cassander got up, wiping his short tunic.

Roxana waited for Alexander to run back to his dice before she spoke to Cassander. His appearance in her son's rooms concerned her.

"I didn't know you came to visit Alexander."

He gave her an indulgent smile, the kind she remembered her husband giving her frequently.

"Antipater told me it was time I got to know my king. He brought me by some time ago, and we've become fast friends."

"Uncle Cassander plays better games than Uncle Philip," Alexander said from the floor. "Uncle Philip only wants to play baby games."

Roxana frowned at her son. "Alexander, but you can't hurt Uncle Philip's feelings. You're his friend, too."

"Yes, Philip needs his friends." Cassander turned to the boy. "We must all look after him." Cassander came closer, lowering his voice. "He's very bright. Just like Alexander. It's all right, isn't it? My playing with him?"

Roxana hid her suspicions behind her brilliant smile.

"Of course. Alexander doesn't have any boys his age to play with. I'm sure he would love to get to know his Uncle Cassander better."

"Yes, well, Father and I were talking about that." Cassander casually took Roxana by the arm and eased her away from her son. "Father and I think it's time to recruit the king's Companions. The men he will use as council, train as generals, and depend on when he's king. Father and I have gone over a list of suitable candidates from the privileged families in the kingdom. We thought we would bring them to Pella in the fall, after the boy's fourth birthday."

She maintained her friendly smile, but on the inside, she seethed. "If that's what Antipater thinks is best, who am I to argue?"

"It's what we both feel is best for the king," Cassander corrected.

Alexander rolled the dice across the floor. "Uncle Cassander was telling me about the time when he and Father went hunting lions in the forest."

Cassander turned back to the boy. "Yes, I was. Your father and I caught this huge lion, the biggest lion anybody had ever seen. Alexander said it was a sign from the gods."

The boy's gray eyes shifted to her. "Did Father tell you about the lion, Mommy?"

Roxana's heart twisted with regret. There were so many things Alexander had never told her, so many stories she'd missed.

"Yes," she lied. "Your father told me all about the great lion. He said it was as big as an elephant."

"Oh, much bigger," Cassander claimed, rolling his eyes for emphasis. "Then there was the time your father took me to see the great city of Athens. He was very excited by Athens."

"Mother, were you in Athens, too?"

"No, Alexander. I met your father long after Athens."

Cassander clapped his hands, drawing the child's attention back to him. "There was the time in Egypt when Alexander came across this great lion statue with a man's head in the sands by the pyramids. We went to—"

A knock at the nursery door interrupted him.

Arnia opened the doors.

To Roxana's astonishment, Antipater entered the room, carrying a wooden horse on wheels.

"Ah, there he is." Antipater made a surprised face for the boy. "I brought it. The Trojan horse I promised you."

Alexander took the toy from Antipater. He was about to turn around and run back to his spot on the floor when he abruptly halted. "Thank you, sir," he said and bowed his head gracefully.

Roxana's seething turned into rage. Months without a word from the regent, but he'd spent time with the boy without her knowledge or consent. Little Alexander may have been their king, but he was still her son.

Antipater crooked his finger at her and slipped into the corridor.

Roxana checked on Alexander, who rolled the toy around in front of him as Cassander neighed like a horse.

"It's not a real horse, Uncle Cassander," Alexander asserted. "Men are supposed to hide inside of it. They jump out and take Troy."

Roxana summoned her calm, ready to confront Antipater.

He gave her a welcoming smile as she joined him next to a bust of her husband.

"The boy is of an age where he needs to develop relationships with others, his elders. He has been on his own for far too long."

She clenched her fists. "He's had his nurse and me."

"He needs men to teach him about being a soldier, going to war, and ruling as a king. Cassander and I have been talking about his future."

"Yes, he told me." She didn't disguise the aggravation in her voice. "You want to select his Companions."

"I've decided to do much more than that." Antipater hesitated as he appraised her stiff posture. "I've assigned him a riding instructor, a sword master, and a tutor to teach him history and Greek. From now on, his mornings will be spent riding and sword fighting, his afternoons devoted to his lessons, and at night, I will have dinner with the boy to teach him the finer points of diplomacy. You can spend breakfast and lunch with him."

Roxana bit back her fury. "I thought we were going to discuss this."

He tossed up an uncaring hand. "There's nothing to discuss. I have to see he grows up to be like his father."

The constant comparisons to his famous father haunted her day and night. "What if he's not like Alexander? What then?"

The condescending gleam in his eye irked her even more.

"I'm sure he will be a strong king who will rule his country and lead his people with compassion."

She glimpsed the nursery doors. "Do I get no say in his life? Are you going to dress him, plan his meals, hold him when he falls down, soothe his nightmares, listen to his stories?"

"The things you advocate will make him weak. He needs strength to rule. A tough heart and a sound mind. I can give him that. Your job is done."

The words hit her heart like a hammer. "My job will never be done!"

The hard line across Antipater's lips lifted, and he sighed. "I may not have agreed with Olympias about many things, but at least she knew when to let Alexander go and encouraged him to be capable without smothering him. You must learn to do the same. We have to make sure … no, *I* have to make sure … I've done everything in my power to see he sits on his father's throne."

The change in him, the speck of doubt in his eyes, turned her anger to unease. "Is there something you're not telling me?"

His smile was slight but did not appease her. "I'm simply an old man dealing with far too many power struggles. Not to worry. It will all work out in the end."

Would it? She wasn't so sure. She had enough experience with Alexander's generals to be concerned about their plans. Perhaps she'd been in the background for far too long at Pella, but she sensed the tides of power shifting once again. Roxana needed to get reacquainted with all the players vying for the realm, so if the time ever came, she'd be ready to fight for her son's interests.

CHAPTER FIFTY-THREE

The warmth from blazing fire pits set throughout the palace accompanied a nervous Roxana one chilly evening as she walked down a long corridor toward Antipater's chambers. In a fitted green peplos, highlighting the color of her eyes, she hoped the outfit appropriate for a proper Greek dinner.

The invitation from the old man had been unexpected, and as she passed underneath an arch decorated with a mosaic tile portrait of her husband, she questioned why she'd received it in the first place.

She arrived at Antipater's olive wood doors, and an officer talking to one of the sentries caught her eye.

His muscular, tanned arms appealed to her, as did his broad shoulders, clean-shaven jaw, and gray-streaked brown hair. He turned, inspecting her with a pair of vivid light blue eyes. When a somewhat sarcastic smile brightened his striking face, an odd tingle awakened in her belly.

Where did that come from?

She was the mother of the king, wife of Alexander, and had no business having any interest in a man.

The officer dipped his head to her. "Lady Roxana."

His smooth voice reminded her of Persian wine—deep, dark, and delightful.

"I am General Polyperchon."

She flashed her best smile. "General, it's a pleasure."

He drank in every curve of her face; her cheeks flushed, and a funny fluttering engulfed her heart.

"We finally meet. I felt I've known you for some time."

The knotted doors to Antipater's rooms opened, and a befuddled secretary, weighted down with scrolls and wax tablets, bolted from the chambers.

The secretary stopped in front of Polyperchon. "You can go in now, sir. He's waiting for you."

Polyperchon waved Roxana inside. "Shall we?"

She walked into a lavishly furnished apartment with light, elegant wooden Greek couches sitting next to intricately carved Persian chairs adorned with gold. The black painted ceiling had dozens of copper oil lamps hanging from chains. Magnificent tile mosaics of hunting scenes and wild game covered the walls and floors, and nowhere was there a single bust of Alexander.

Antipater rose from an ornate gold-leaf desk in the corner. "You've both arrived on time ... perfect. I hope you didn't have to wait long."

"No, sir." Polyperchon stopped and stood at attention. "Roxana and I were just becoming acquainted when your secretary came out."

Antipater's keen eyes traveled from the commander to Roxana. "How delightful you look this evening, my lady."

"Thank you." She examined the walls. "These mosaics are stunning."

He came out from behind the desk. "These were once Philip's rooms. I prefer to keep them because they're far removed from the noise of the palace." Antipater slowly walked to a dining table made in the Persian fashion. "How have you been these past few months, Roxana?"

She followed the regent to the table. "I'm well, thank you. I've tried to keep busy. Not as busy as my son, of course, but I make do."

Polyperchon came alongside her. "You're very Greek tonight. I thought perhaps you would dress more in the Persian style."

She found the intensity of his gaze disconcerting. "Like my husband, I'm comfortable in both the Greek and Persian attire."

Antipater took his chair at the head of the table. "Roxana is quite versatile, Polyperchon. She's at home on both sides of the Hellespont."

"This is quite a treat for me." Polyperchon pulled out a chair to the right of the regent. "I haven't seen Roxana since I left with Craterus."

Roxana took her chair to the left of Antipater, struggling to remember the officer. "You served with my husband?"

"I was at your wedding, my lady." He settled into his chair. "I even remember the outfit of gold you wore the night you first danced for Alexander."

The funny tingle returned in her belly.

"Polyperchon came from Persia as a second to Craterus," Antipater explained.

The regent suffered a bout of coughing and then cleared his throat.

Polyperchon patted the old man's back. "You must slow down, Antipater. You're not well."

Roxana looked from Antipater to the officer beside him. Did he know something she didn't?

"I'm fine." Antipater stretched across the table for his wine. He took a sip, and his eyes lingered on Roxana. "I'm sure you're wondering why I invited you to dinner tonight."

Roxana folded her hands, avoiding her wine, preferring to stay sharp. "It had crossed my mind."

Antipater set his drink down. "I want to talk to you about the succession and what will happen after I'm gone. Polyperchon will take over the regency of the kings and the army when I'm dead. He's a good man. He knows my way of doing things, and he can run the army with a firm hand. They respect him, and to rule Macedon—"

"You must rule the army," Roxana edged in.

Antipater appeared amused by her statement. "I didn't realize you were so well versed in our ways."

"I spent seven years traveling with your army, so I understand your reasons for Polyperchon as your heir. But what about your son?"

Antipater frowned, fingering the stem of his goblet. "He's not competent enough to run the empire and its army. The men need one of their own in charge. That's why Polyperchon will be my heir. Cassander will be chiliarch under Polyperchon."

Polyperchon rested his folded hands on the table, drawing her attention.

"Antipater feels Cassander will not be reliable when it comes to protecting the interests of your son and Philip."

Roxana flashed back to the brutality she'd witnessed during the turmoil after Alexander's death. She did not wish to see another horrific grab for power after Antipater's demise.

"And Cassander? Does he know of your plans?"

Antipater's frown deepened. "He will in time. I wished you and the general to meet first. I want to assure you Polyperchon will take care of you and your son."

The attractive general leaned into the table, his striking eyes focused on her. "I have nothing but the best intentions to keep Antipater's policies and organizational institutions in place. I would like us to be friends, Roxana. To work together for the future of your son."

His leering grin made her snap up her goblet, hoping to hide her burning cheeks.

"You will have my support." She lifted her goblet to the old man. "But I'm sure such a day will not come for a very long time."

"Yes, a very long time indeed," Polyperchon agreed, toasting the regent.

Antipater smiled, appearing pleased. "Thank you, but whenever my time comes, I'm at peace knowing the future of the kings is in good hands."

Roxana drank from her cup, staring over the brim at the captivating general. Not only was her son's future in capable hands, but hers could be as well.

Polyperchon stood by the entrance as a guard escorted the intoxicating Roxana down the corridor to her rooms. The scent of jasmine lingered in the air, the musical essence of her voice hummed in his ear, and the sway of her hips, the silky way she moved fascinated him.

He wiped his brow, ashamed of the way he could not keep his eyes off her at dinner, but also praying he'd made his intentions known. He walked back to

Antipater's table, gathering his thoughts and putting her image out of his head.

The servants cleared the dishes as he collected his goblet, anxious for the wine to cut the ache she'd left in him.

"She's a beautiful woman," Polyperchon said as the servants closed the chamber doors.

Antipater bobbed his head, smiling. "I saw you noticing. I don't blame you."

Polyperchon refilled his goblet. "Now will you tell me the real reason why you set up this dinner?"

"You needed to meet her. To get to know her, and by the way you were looking at her, I'd say you will know her well soon enough. The man who controls Roxana controls the kings, both of them. Philip listens to her and the boy … well, a boy always listens to his mother."

He lifted his goblet to his lips, the suggestion not lost on him. "Like Alexander listened to Olympias?"

"Make sure she doesn't turn into another meddling menace like Olympias. From now on, keep her close to you, very close, so you can control her."

Polyperchon didn't care for the general's intimation. He didn't need to sleep with a woman to control her but having Roxana in his bed would be a perk.

He leaned forward and appraised Antipater's cold gaze. "I'll think about it."

Antipater struggled to his feet. "Don't take too long. Cassander may have the same ideas about her. I wouldn't want to see that young woman and her son come under his control when I'm gone. I love my son, but he's the most ruthless son of a bitch I've ever known."

Polyperchon peered into his wine, concerned about the increasing frailty he saw in the regent. "Coming from you, that's saying something."

Antipater grinned. "Yes, it is."

CHAPTER FIFTY-FOUR

Her heart pounding, Roxana ran, her slippers skidding on the smooth marble floors. The icy wind from the open windows tore through her thin linen robe, but she paid no mind to the cold—she had to find out the truth. She rushed beneath the arched entrance to the royal quarters and hurried to the regent's rooms.

A soldier stationed outside the knotted doors held up his hand, asking her to stop.

"Is he here?" she asked, between mouthfuls of air. "I have to see him."

"My lady, you can't go in—"

Polyperchon opened the doors. "Roxana?"

She turned to him, dreading what she might hear. "Is it true? Is Antipater dead?"

His grim, downturned mouth and bloodshot eyes told her it was true. She stood back, gutted. With Antipater, she'd been able to put her worries behind her. Now they were back.

The general eased closer to her. "How did you know?"

His voice was no longer smooth and seductive. He was a soldier—all business.

"My maid." She wiped beads of sweat from her forehead. "The kitchen staff knows, and several servants in the palace are spreading the news."

He took her elbow. "Get in here."

He pulled her into the darkened rooms. The curtains drawn, the lamps remained unlit, and the odor of sour wine hung in the air.

Polyperchon guided her to the desk once used by Antipater.

Sealed scrolls lay strewn across the surface; one was sitting open, apart from the rest. She squinted to make out the contents, but he pushed her into a chair before she could.

"He was found dead this morning by his secretary." He turned to the darkened bedroom off to the side of the desk. "I haven't moved him yet. I was waiting for Cassander to come. I thought you were him."

She could just make out the blanket-covered figure on the bed.

"I heard the news, and I had to make sure it wasn't a rumor. With Antipater gone, my son's life will change."

He knelt before her, holding her hands. "Nothing will change. I will continue running the empire as he would have."

The zing traveling up her arm astounded her. How could she be attracted to the man at such a time? Then she spotted the regent's seal hanging from his neck.

She withdrew her hand and sat back, putting some distance between them.

"I've witnessed enough power struggles to know this transition will not be an easy one. These generals see death as an opportunity, and with Antipater out of the way, and you as regent, they will vie for who gets control of the kings."

He stood, his face like one of the statues cluttering the corridors. "I have control of the kings. Antipater left it to me and any—"

The chamber doors flew open.

Roxana jumped to her feet, surprised by the intrusion.

Cassander appeared in the doorway. His face red, he held up a scroll in his clenched fist.

"What is this insanity?" He threw the scroll across the room. "Why did he leave you in charge?"

Roxana sensed she should leave before the discussion got ugly. "I'll go back to my rooms."

Polyperchon angrily pointed at the floor. "No! You're staying here."

She held her breath as he went across the room, his feet pounding on the marble.

He pulled Cassander inside and shut the doors with a loud *bang*.

Polyperchon motioned to the darkened bedchamber where Antipater lay. "Your father had his reasons for picking me. He did what he thought was best for the empire. You're to be my second-in-command. Why can't you be happy with that?"

Cassander got right in his face. "I am his son. I have a right to—"

"You have the right to nothing," Polyperchon shouted. "You know damn well why you're not regent. Don't make me embarrass you in front of Roxana with a litany of your screw-ups. Your father has had to do a lot of scrambling to cover for you with the king over the years."

Cassander staggered backward. "You conniving bastard."

Polyperchon grabbed the top of his tunic. "You've alienated the generals. Your father knew none of them would back you as regent. He was trying to avoid more war by appointing me. You know that!" He shoved him back.

Cassander leveled his murderous gaze on her.

"For the sake of your son, you'd better think long and hard about which side you take in this affair."

The hate festering in his black eyes sent a chill through her soul. It was as if someone had walked on her grave. She couldn't afford to make enemies but feared Cassander would see her as one from that moment on.

"I'm sorry, but I'm not choosing a side. I'm simply doing what I have to for my son."

Cassander cackled, sounding like something that had climbed from the pits of

Hades.

"I should have expected nothing less from the wife of Alexander." He shook his finger at Polyperchon. "You've not heard the last from me on this matter."

The commander opened the doors and snapped his fingers to the guards. "Get him out of here."

The sentries seized Cassander. He did not resist. He allowed the men to escort him from the room.

"He will cause trouble for you," she said after the doors closed. "He will try to win over the generals and turn them against you."

"I can handle Cassander." Polyperchon turned to her. "The generals know why Antipater chose me. He wrote to all of them before he died informing them of his decision. Cassander will have a hard time convincing them otherwise."

She was about to ask what he planned to do if the generals backed Cassander when the doors opened.

Roxana's hand went to her throat, not sure what to expect.

Two women entered, all in black, carrying large bowls of water and jars of oil, their heads bowed.

They ignored the general and her, slipping into the darkened bedroom to clean and anoint the dead regent.

The women lit the oil lamps to prepare for their task. A memory of cleaning and anointing Alexander's body sent a pain across her chest, and then it was gone.

"Come with me." A hand tugged her out of the room.

When she came to a standstill in the corridor, he was in front of her. She itched to get away from him and retreat to her rooms.

"There will be much to do, but in the coming weeks, when things settle down, perhaps we could dine together and talk about your son's future."

Talk? Roxana's heart was in her throat. Could she entertain the interests of another man? Was she still Alexander's or was there room for another? There was only one way to find out.

"I would be very pleased to dine with you, General."

She dashed away and left him in the corridor before she changed her mind.

Roxana walked along a pillared corridor to the palace's dining hall, butterflies in her belly. She patted her hair, twisted above her head in the Greek fashion, and then ran her hands over the front of her long, light blue peplos and blue Persian coat.

"You look like you can't make up your mind if you are Greek or Persian, my lady," Morella had said before she had left her rooms.

But to Roxana, the blend of styles reflected what she felt—out of place.

Here she was about to have dinner with a man who controlled her son's future, and she had no idea what to say or how to handle him. In the past, she'd learned what she could about Alexander's generals to win them over, but this man was a mystery. In the weeks since Antipater's death, she'd discovered little more than he was a widower, ambitious, and had been spending a great deal of time with Philip.

She passed beneath the arched marble entrance to the dining hall and came to a halt. Ahead, a central fire pit was stacked with logs and surrounded by low tables with cushions around them. But there were no large groups of palace officials and high-ranking officers dining, as per the Macedonian custom. The only other guest was Polyperchon.

"I ordered the cooks to close the hall tonight, so we could have some peace. I've grown tired of rowdy drinking feasts."

In a short tunic and without the regent's gold seal around his neck, he appeared as any other palace official. The only sign of his importance to the realm were the two members of the king's guard stationed inside the doorway.

"Why not order the dinner in your private rooms instead of denying the hungry their dining hall?"

"Dinners can be held just as comfortably in dining halls. However, when one is trying to make a point ..." He waved to the empty room.

The heady blend of olive oil and wine teased her nose. "What point are you trying to make?"

His smile eroded her confidence in keeping him at a distance.

"We're both in a precarious position. People will talk about tonight and what was said. I want to ensure your virtue, and my integrity, remain intact by staging our dinner in a very public setting."

"You're my son's regent and protector. Why should people be concerned if we dine together in private or like this?" She eased around the table and took her place next to him.

"Because you're a beautiful widow and I'm an older widower. If we are alone together, I'm afraid it would be dangerous ... for both of us."

A barefoot servant girl brought a platter of roasted goat to the table.

Roxana waited until she'd gone before she spoke again.

"I thought Macedonian men thrived on danger."

"The perils of battle are nothing compared to the forbidden arms of a beautiful woman."

Roxana's insides quivered. Why did he have this control over her and how could she fight it? "Perhaps, General, with so many ears listening to our conversation, we should change the subject."

Polyperchon's warm musical laugh spurred her growing attraction. He took a hefty portion of goat from the platter. "As you wish." He dropped the meat on her plate. "Have you heard from Cassander?"

The mention of Cassander dulled her appetite. She pushed her plate to the side. "No. The palace gossips say he left for Athens after his father's death."

"He has friends there, and he will try to ally himself with Antigonus and Ptolemy." He reached for more goat. "He wants to use their power against me to take over the guardianship of the kings."

Roxana gripped the edge of the table, terrified. "Antipater appointed you his successor. Surely, that will keep the generals loyal to you."

"Possibly, but I have also written to Queen Olympias and Eumenes, asking them to join our cause."

She recoiled at the mention of the ambitious secretary. "Eumenes? He didn't help Perdiccas; how will he help you?"

Polyperchon picked at the meat on his plate. "He has all of Alexander's treasure from conquering Persia. He can fund armies and ships for me, securing my stronghold over Greece and shutting Cassander down. In exchange, I've had Philip pen a letter pledging the royal army and his power as king to Eumenes. Ptolemy and Antigonus may not be too pleased about that, but ..." He popped the meat into his mouth.

A stab of revulsion cut through her like a well-aimed sword. "You've been using Philip to pit the generals against each other. No wonder you've been spending so much time with him. You're planning to go to war."

"This confrontation will force a conclusion to the squabbling between all the generals since Antipater died." Polyperchon clasped the jug of wine on the table. "It will also secure my position as regent."

She watched him fill her goblet horrified by what he proposed. "What if you lose?"

"I have no choice." He set the jug aside. "Cassander is rallying troops and generals in Greece. The Greek cities will choose sides. I must show them I'm the true regent, not Cassander."

Teeming with disgust, Roxana rose from her pillows. "If you will excuse me, I have no more stomach for war."

"Roxana, please." He got up in one swift motion. "I told you these things not to upset you, but to inform you of what will be. I want you to know I intend to do everything I can for your son."

"The methods you've chosen to secure his throne are ..." She shut her mouth, afraid to speak her mind.

She could not afford to alienate the only person she had left to fight for her son. Perhaps it was best to walk away instead of risking saying too much.

She turned to go when he grabbed her wrist.

"I will escort you back to your rooms."

Roxana had the urge to shake off his hand, but there was something about the steely glint in his eyes warning her not to.

"It will give us a chance to talk more," he added, hooking her hand over his arm.

He accompanied her across the dining hall, his footfalls like claps of thunder shooting through her. The touch of his hand, his musky scent, the heat of his skin, tortured and tantalized.

"What's bothering you?" he asked when they reached the pillared corridor. "I can't imagine the talk of another war would frighten the wife of Alexander."

She yanked her hand away, fed up with men and their propensity for death. "How many more wars? How many more have to die? And what about my son? Will he be left as king when you generals have finished slicing up his empire for yourselves?"

His calm composure never wavered. "You son is also the son of Alexander. No general ever loyal to your husband would ever harm the child. As for men dying, that's what happens in war. You've seen enough of it. I know, I was there that day when you came to the king's tent after the Mallians attacked him. You're not afraid of anything. What has changed?"

Shivering, she backed into a pillar behind her. Without thinking, she felt for the coin and chain hidden beneath her tunic.

"I don't want to lose any more people I love. And you're wrong about me. I've lived in fear since the day Alexander's troops arrived at the great rock in my homeland. Since then, all I've known is war. Where does all this fighting get you?"

Polyperchon sighed. "That's what the gods want for us—glory and a life filled with exemplary deeds."

"But would starting another war please the gods?"

"War is inevitable." He took her elbow, encouraging her onward. "We can't stop it."

A dark shadow crossed her heart as if foreshadowing their future.

"We won't win."

The lines around his eyes bunched together. "What makes you say that? Alexander faced worse opposition than we and still, he rallied his men, believed victory was his. And in the end, he was unconquerable."

Like raindrops from the sky, a thousand images of Alexander cascaded through her mind, but only one vision lingered—the last moment she'd seen him alive. Soaked in sweat, pale, and at the doors of death, she'd given him one last smile.

"He wasn't unconquerable. He had to bend to the will of the gods. I fear if you go ahead with this war, you will incur their wrath." She read the incredulity in his blue eyes and dipped her head. "I'm sorry. I've angered you. I shouldn't have said that. I will go."

A group of soldiers rounded a corner. On seeing Polyperchon they halted, saluted, and then quickly moved on.

Polyperchon waited until the soldiers walked past, and then he eased closer to her.

"This is not how I envisioned our evening ending. I don't want you walking away thinking I'm angry. Far from it. Since the day I first saw you dance for Alexander, I've never been able to stop thinking about you. I used to watch you with him at banquets and about the camps. I always wondered what it would be like to talk to you, to get to know you … and now the gods have answered my prayers."

She didn't know what to say. Her sorrow was still so fresh, and yet, something stirred inside of her.

"You flatter me, General." She lowered her head, butterflies tumbling about in her stomach.

"That was not my intention." He placed his hand beneath her chin and lifted her head. "I was offering you an invitation. An alliance, if you will, for the two of us to join forces." His lips came so close to hers that his breath caressed her cheek. "Tell me to go away, Roxana, and I will. But tell me to stay, and I will devote every fiber of my being to you and your son."

Roxana opened her mouth to tell him to forget about her, but the words never came.

He retreated from her side. "Let's leave the subject open for further discussion, eh?" He gestured to the corridor, imploring her to move on. "For a time when we are both ready to decide an answer."

CHAPTER FIFTY-FIVE

From her bedroom window, Roxana admired the change in the sky from black to red as the sun climbed into the east. Streaks of light stretched across the fields around the palace, bringing to life beasts and men. And as the magical orb trekked upward, changing from red to yellow, the sound of clashing swords and shields rose to her open window.

Soldiers, hordes of them, gathered on the palace grounds, readying themselves for their journey to battle. Guilt-ridden, she considered their fate on a muddy, blood-soaked battlefield, fighting for her son and Polyperchon.

But the general's proposition was the real reason for her inability to sleep. She'd kept to women's quarters in the palace, vacillating on what to do.

"There are so many of them," Morella brought her a steaming ceramic cup.

She inspected the contents. "Polyperchon must be preparing to go soon." Roxana sniffed the drink.

"He likes you, mistress. One can see it when he looks at you."

"He's an ass." She held up the cup. "What's this?"

"Mountain tea. Cook swears by it for calming nerves." She tilted her head and smirked. "By the way you've been acting, I figured you could use it."

"I have no idea what you're talking about." She sipped the tea, desperate to avoid any mention of the confounding man.

"It's all right to like a man who's not the king." Morella patted her arm. "It doesn't mean you love him any less."

A commotion outside her doors made her set the cup aside.

Polyperchon threw her doors wide open with his strong arms, startling her and sending Morella to her knees. In his bronze cuirass decorated with a lion's head, he was an imposing figure.

When her eyes connected with his, she tugged her robe closer over her nightgown, covering herself as best she could.

"You've been ignoring me for weeks, so I thought I should come to you." He snapped his fingers at Morella. "Leave. I need to speak to your mistress alone."

Morella grinned, but Roxana encouraged her to go with a curt nod.

She waited until her maid pulled the chamber doors closed before she found the courage to face him.

He stood with his hands behind his back and a crease across his brow.

She knew that look. It usually went along with bad news.

"I've just received word." He lowered his voice. "Cassander has an army in

Greece. Antigonus has sent him men and ships to fight against us."

She sighed, knowing what it meant—war had found them once again. "When do you leave?"

"Day after tomorrow." The crease in his forehead deepened. "Eurydice has asked to return to her estates. I believe she wants to get away from Philip."

Roxana didn't like the idea. "Do you trust her not to start trouble while you're away?"

"No, but I would feel better with her out of my hair." The lines on his face softened. "You and the kings, on the other hand, will come with me."

"Where are we heading?"

"I'm setting up camp in Phocis—a central location in Greece. It will be easier to send troops to rebellious cities from there." He went to her window and surveyed his men. "I've also invited your mother-in-law to join us, but she's refused to set foot in Macedonia to help us."

That didn't surprise her. "I'm beginning to wonder if she has any regard for her grandson."

"Oh, she's very concerned about her grandson and anxious to meet him, but she chooses to remain in Epirus with her army. Which is good because knowing her, as I do, the first thing she would advise is for you not to trust me." He came up to her and rested his hands on her shoulders. "But I need you to trust me."

His proximity, the scent of sweat and oil on his skin, and her lack of dress made her uncomfortable.

"Every single general who asked me to trust them is dead. You hold my son's throne—his very life—in your hands, and you ask me to trust you?" She let a long breath, finding her answer. "I don't have a choice."

His nostrils flared. "You have a choice; you either trust Cassander or me. I promise you my terms of surrender will be a lot more pleasurable than his."

Angry and frustrated with her attraction to the man, she lashed out.

"Do you think you can bully me into bed with you? Justify sleeping with you out of some duty to save my son?"

"Do me a favor, Roxana. Don't pretend you don't want me." He cupped her right cheek. "I don't have the patience to wait for you to come to me. I'm not proposing marriage or even love. This is desire."

Roxana jerked her head away. "I don't want you!"

"Ah, there's that fight of yours." Polyperchon grinned. "I first saw it when you punched that doctor of Alexander's in the nose. You've been hiding it away since your arrival in Pella, but I need you to wake up and fight again."

The challenge in his voice roused her fury. "Did you ever consider perhaps

I'm tired of fighting?"

"Fighting is something we do the moment we leave the womb and continue until we breathe our last. Life is a fight, my lady. Get used to it."

Roxana was about to retreat when he grabbed her wrist. He pulled her close and wrapped his arms around her.

"What are you so afraid of?"

Roxana struggled to get away from him. "I'm not afraid of you."

He held her tight. "I never said you were afraid of me, but of this ..." Then he kissed her.

The strangeness of a man's lips on hers after so long was not what she expected. There was no all-consuming rush of heat and no sweeping passion. He was rough, almost clumsy. Alexander's kisses had been skillful, exuding a confidence the general lacked.

When he backed away, she was more bewildered than ever. Why had his kiss left her so empty?

"I'm sorry, but I've wanted to do that for a very long time." He bowed to her. "I hope my intentions for you are now perfectly clear."

He strutted from her rooms, his purple cloak flapping behind him. Suddenly, she realized he was right. She'd been asleep since arriving in Pella, afraid to rock the boat and change her settled existence.

She went to the window, breathing in the morning air and sweeping aside the uncertainty his kiss had created.

She stomped her foot. "Now what do I do about him?"

Morella appeared, carrying a tray stacked with wine jugs. She eyed the empty room.

"You didn't throw him out the window, did you?"

Roxana moved toward her maid, the old fire of determination stoking in her gut. "No, but I wish I had."

Morella set the tray on a table. "Seems to me you already know what to do, my lady. You have a chance at happiness again. You should take it. It's been five years. You've grieved your husband long enough."

"Is there a time limit on grief?" Roxana inspected the tray. "I think not. It doesn't matter how many years have passed, I will still miss him."

"Then miss him but start a new life with another."

Roxana's fingertips grazed the rough surface of the clay wine jug. "It's not so easy for me, but thank you for your concern. Through the years, and all our travels, yours has been the only voice of reason for me. You've been the one constant in my life, Morella."

"As you have been in mine, my lady." She poured wine into a goblet. "Did the general give you any news about the coming conflict?"

Roxana mulled over everything Polyperchon had told her. "We'll be leaving with the army for Phocis in two days."

"Phocis?" Morella crinkled her pug nose while handing Roxana the goblet. "Where in the blazes is that?"

CHAPTER FIFTY-SIX

R oxana took in the muddy fields, broken roads, and rocky shores of Greece from her wagon window. The smoke from meat cooking, the hum of conversations, the trill of a flute, and the occasional call of an elephant, carried into her tent. It was all so familiar.

She never ventured out among the men and kept to her quarters in the men's section of the camp with only Morella and her son for company. The cities, the skirmishes with locals, even the muddy fields all looked the same after a while. But she pushed on with the army, chasing Cassander across Greece.

With the camp settled outside another massive walled city threatening to support Cassander, Roxana warmed her hands on a brazier as she waited for Morella to bring her supper from the supply wagon.

"What's this word?" Alexander asked as he sat on a stool across from her, struggling with poems from Pindar.

He appeared so grown up in his chiton and the purple cloak Morella had made to duplicate the ones worn by his father and his Companions. Where had the baby gone she'd carried across Persia?

"Blessed." She read above his finger. "'And blessed are their days.'"

He sighed, sounding bored. "Why can't I go to the stables? I want to see how the new horse Polyperchon gave me is doing."

"Alexander, you've already been to the stables three times this morning." She fixed his crooked tunic hem.

"Alexander Aegus," her son insisted in his high voice. "You promised to call me that from now on."

"I'm sorry. I forgot."

He smiled at her, and she saw her husband when he was happy. He resembled his father more with each passing day, and though she thanked the gods every time she held him, Roxana still mourned the man who had given him to her.

Keen to get his mind back on his studies, she tapped the open page in his book. "After your finish two more poems, you can go to the stables."

The groan he gave her elicited a slight chuckle.

Just like his father.

Morella stepped into the tent. Her eyes darted from mother to son, and her hands twisted together.

Roxana went to her. "What is it?"

Morella nodded for her to follow her outside.

Roxana checked on her son, then slipped from the tent.

The dreary skies above threatened rain, and a brisk wind blew in from the nearby Chief Sea surrounding the mainland of Greece. Around her, men packed up horses, cleaned and sharpened weapons, and doused their campfires.

"Are we moving on?"

"The siege the general had planned here failed." Morella kept her voice right above a whisper. "Word about the camps is that more Greeks across the mainland have gone over to Cassander. They say he's winning many supporters because of his honorable and just leadership. We're heading back to Macedonia tonight."

Roxana searched the frenzied activity in the camp. "I have to speak to Polyperchon."

Through thick trails of mud and manure, she pushed through men and animals, keeping her sights on the gold pike high above the city of tents. A sprinkling of rain touched her cheeks, and she pulled her shawl over her head.

Outside of Polyperchon's tent, Roxana glowered impatiently at the soldiers stationed there, waiting for them to announce her to the general. When Polyperchon finally appeared, he took her hand and tugged her inside.

"What is it, Roxana?" He went back to a work table in the corner. He picked up a scroll and sat down. "I'm extremely busy at the moment."

She unwrapped the heavy woolen fabric from her head, annoyed with his brusque manner. "The Greeks have gone over to Cassander?"

"So, you've heard." He popped the seal on the scroll. "Cassander has taken a little jaunt into Macedonia. The reason why the men are packing up. We're going after him."

Astounded things had fallen apart so quickly, she wanted to blame Polyperchon for the blunder but refrained.

"When did this happen?"

"Since I've been preoccupied here in Megalopolis." He picked up an open scroll and held it out to her. "He and Eurydice have made an arrangement. She claims she and Philip support Cassander as guardian to the kings."

Her stomach dropped to her knees. "How can Philip support her when he's still with us?"

"Cassander doesn't care about that. Eurydice has been buying support for Cassander from the wealthy families allied to the Kingdom of Macedon. Turning them against me."

She went to his desk, the familiar churn of panic sweeping through her. "What do we do?"

He stood, cocking an eyebrow at her. "We? Now it's we. I thought you didn't trust me."

Her fingers and toes tingled as they usually did whenever he was near. "I'm here with you, aren't I?" She directed her attention to the papers on his desk. "What do you have planned?"

He retrieved a scroll and held it out to her.

"It's from Olympias. She's agreed to take over the regency. She and her nephew, Aeacides, King of Epirus, will meet our army at the border between Macedonia and Epirus. Then we will march into Macedonia to the lands of Euia to confront Eurydice and her armies."

Hope sprang to life in her heart. Her son could still have his throne. "What do we tell Philip? You know how much he dislikes Olympias."

"He will have to go with his wife."

No! She could not live with that. "You can't! He's a simple man. We can't leave him to—"

"It's what Olympias wants." He put down the scroll and rubbed his hand across his darkly shadowed jaw. "Philip must go with Eurydice. We need him out of the way so your son can rule alone. By allying herself with Cassander, Eurydice has signed her death warrant and Philip's."

"Where's Philip?" Roxana demanded, terrified for her brother-in-law. "Does he know you're sending him to die?"

"He's already gone. He left this morning. I told him he was joining his wife." His sad smile mirrored the pain in her chest. "He seemed happy to go. He said he missed her."

Roxana went to a stool in front of his desk and sat, drained. "How can you be so calm about sending an innocent man to his death?"

He came up to her. "Because I was never in this for Philip. You and Alexander Aegus are all that matter to me."

She hunted for a hint of reassurance in his gaze. "When Cassander meets us in Euia, will it finally be over?"

"He won't be there. He's busy securing the alliances of the Greek cities who betrayed me. Athens and the rest have gone to him. And it seems so has my navy." He picked up an open scroll from his desk. "I got word that one-eyed jackal, Antigonus, defeated my ships, taking away my control of the sea around Macedonia." The message tumbled from his hand. "Cassander knows we have no choice but to head to Epirus, but he's sending us Eurydice as a peace offering. He's hoping we eliminate her, so one less king is standing between him and the throne."

She almost toppled from her stool. "Is that what my son is to him? The next king standing in the way of the throne?"

Polyperchon didn't answer. He went to a serving table and poured a goblet of wine.

When he brought the wine to Roxana, her mouth went dry.

"Do I need this?"

He nudged it closer. "You look like you do."

She clasped her shaking hands together, refusing the wine. "How long have you known about Cassander? That he means to kill my son and not set him on the throne."

"Antipater feared he would. One of the many reasons he chose me to be regent." Polyperchon knelt in front of her. "He knew I had no desire for fame, for the empire, or to conquer the world." He set the goblet aside. "He knew I would only desire you."

That primal urge to get lost in the arms of a man jarred her, but something held her back.

He gripped her hands. "We're two lonely people who have lost our loves, but we're still alive. We can share so much. Share yourself with me, Roxana."

She leaned forward, wanting to kiss him, mesmerized by his eyes. Then the gold chain around her neck slid out from beneath the folds of her clothes.

Polyperchon lifted the silver coin on the end of the chain. Turning it over, he smiled.

"Even now, he's still with you. Isn't he?"

And then she knew. The doubt holding her back wasn't fear, it was love. Polyperchon was right; Alexander was still with her. Deep within the reaches of her soul, he lived on, and her duty to please him, to honor what they had shared still burned. No man would ever be him, and no matter how much she wanted one night of pleasure in the arms of the general, it would taint her memories of her king.

She pushed his hands away, no longer confused. "I will always belong to Alexander. My life began with him, and in many ways, it ended that summer's day in Babylon. I have no room in my heart for another. I'm sorry."

"Permission to enter, sir," the sentry outside called into his tent.

He climbed to his feet. "Just a moment."

The spell broken, Roxana arranged her shawl over her head.

"You'd better go." He clamped his hands behind him as if fighting to keep from touching her. "I have plans to see to before we make for Epirus, and I can't think when you're close to me."

Back in her tent, she went straight to her sleeping area, avoiding talking with her son or Morella.

She sat on her bed. A single teardrop rolled down her cheek and landed on the silver coin around her neck.

Roxana threw herself onto the bed and held up the coin, taking in every facet of Alexander's image.

I'm such a fool.

CHAPTER FIFTY-SEVEN

After a long day's march in the rain, Roxana gratefully settled into her small tent, exhausted. She'd sent Morella in search of something to eat when an envoy appeared. Wearing the thick linen breastplate decorated with the colors of Polyperchon's division, the young man kept his head lowered as he addressed her.

"You're to come to the general's tent immediately. The queen has ordered it."

Roxana patted the dust from her long coat, not sure if she had heard him correctly. "The queen?"

The soldier's gaze never rose higher than her leather shoes. "Queen Olympias, ma'am. She wants you to come right away to the general's tent."

Olympias is here?

Something Craterus once said came back to her. *May the gods help us if the day ever comes when we must bow to Olympias.*

It seemed the dreaded day had finally arrived.

She collected her shawl and faced the young man. "Take me to the queen."

Roxana followed the soldier around campfires and past groups of men complaining about the hurried pace of their march. When she finally spotted the gold pike of Polyperchon's tent, her resolve disintegrated.

What if she doesn't like my son or me?

Outside the entrance, she was greeted by troops in vibrant red chitons and dashing blue cloaks.

"Epirus royal guards, my lady," the young man said.

Before entering the tent, a litany of advice, descriptors, and warnings about Olympias inundated her. The last time she'd been so nervous about meeting anyone was when she had danced for Alexander. She shoved the cautionary tales from her mind and stepped inside.

The flickering oil lamps sent streams of acrid smoke across the tent. In the center, next to the pole supporting the gold pike, Polyperchon spoke to a woman. Her azure cape trailed the dusty ground. She had her silver hair twisted into a bun atop her head, and a gold diadem graced her brow.

The pair stopped talking when Roxana drew closer.

She stood as tall as Polyperchon, and her deep-set gray eyes sparked a million memories for Roxana. They were Alexander's eyes, filled with all the distrust and shrewdness she had seen in him, but without his warmth. Her face was long, with a proud chin and smooth, creamy skin, but deep lines of worry marred her forehead.

"So, you are Roxana."

Her harsh voice matched her eyes.

"I am Olympias, mother to your husband, the mighty Alexander."

Roxana bowed, wishing she'd taken the time to change. She prepared for an icy reception.

"Alexander wrote to me many times about you. He said you were the most beautiful woman in Persia." A faint smile crossed her thin lips. "I can see he did not exaggerate."

She decided on a diplomatic response. "Thank you, my lady. Alexander often spoke of you as well."

Olympias let out a loud, crone-like cackle that belayed her queenly exterior.

"Oh, I bet he did. I'm sure he complained to everyone about how I drove him crazy with my letters and demands." She shrugged as the laughter left her face. "Well, that is … was my job, to watch out for him. Men will call you a bitch or harpy when you fight to protect your son, but they will never understand your devotion."

She tilted her head slightly to the left, reminding Roxana so much of Alexander.

"It doesn't seem fair. You raise them, give them all the love you possess, and then they leave. They go in search of their glory, their destiny, and all you are left with are memories. Being a mother is a thankless job, you shall see." She motioned to two Greek couches off to the side. "Here, sit. You must be tired after the day's journey."

"Perhaps I should leave you two ladies to get better acquainted." Polyperchon dashed to the doorway.

"We still need to discuss the details of my return to Pella, Polyperchon." Olympias's impressive voice filled the tent. "Bring Alexander Aegus to us while you're out. I want to meet my grandson."

Polyperchon gave Roxana one last apologetic smile before he scurried out of the tent.

She could kill him for leaving her alone with the woman.

"I wanted to meet you before your son. I thought it best if we were not strangers when he first sees me." She moved closer to Roxana. "He is well, Alexander Aegus?"

The woman's concern for little Alexander disturbed her. *Why now?* "Yes, he's very well, ma'am. He's obsessed with horses, his sword lessons, and likes hanging out with men from the army."

"Ah, just like his father." She took a seat on one of the couches. "Alexander relished anything having to do with war."

Roxana settled on the opposite couch, mindful of everything she said. "He's very much like Alexander, in temperament as well as looks."

"Alexander was always a very fussy child. I had to change nurses four times before he settled down. You have a good nurse?"

"Yes, my lady, she's Persian. She came from Babylon—"

"Oh, that won't do." Olympias waved off Roxana's praise. "We will have to get him a proper Macedonian nurse."

Roxana cringed. After so many years of such comments, she should have been used to it, but coming from Alexander's mother had been unexpected.

"Arnia has been with him since he was an infant. He loves her so."

With a flick of her wrist, Olympias dismissed her comment. "Your nurse will be sent back to Persia and well paid for her trouble. You are in Macedonia, Roxana. You need to assume the role of a Macedonian matron if you're to raise a true Macedonian king."

She seethed at the suggestion. "He's a half-Persian king, my lady. Alexander wanted his son to be raised knowing both cultures."

"He said you had fire but I thought he exaggerated like most men in lust do." Olympias wrinkled her brow, making her appear older. "This boy is Alexander's heir and will be raised as his father was raised, as a Macedonian. There can be no other alternative. A king of Greece must be Greek and not some half-breed."

The term made her blood boil, and her restraint evaporated. "Are you to take over my son's life? First, it was Perdiccas, then Antipater, then Polyperchon, and now you? Am I only to be the decorative barbarian mother, or will you eventually send me back to Persia, too?"

Olympias grinned. "Very good, Roxana. You speak your mind. I admire spirit just as my son did." She reclined on her couch. "I would not dream of sending you back to Persia. To what? Be used by some backwater governor as a way to the throne? No, my child, you will stay with your son. And you will have a say in the way he's raised but do us both a favor—leave the details of his education, his tutoring, and his training to me. I raised one Alexander, and I can raise another. Is that understood?"

Roxana suddenly grasped the overbearing side Alexander had alluded to when he'd spoken about his mother.

"I trust your knowledge, my queen, but my son doesn't have the advantages Alexander had. He doesn't have a father. Your son had Philip."

"A half drunken, oversexed, incompetent mule could be a better father than Philip."

She cackled again and the sound grated against Roxana's nerves.

"The only thing my husband did for Alexander was give him an army. Alexander did the rest. Don't worry. We will do better without another Philip around to muck up the situation."

Roxana was about to respond when the tent flap flew open.

Polyperchon walked in, his arm around Alexander Aegus's shoulders.

In his wrinkled short tunic, his reddish-brown hair about his shoulders, he was the spitting image of his father.

Alexander Aegus peered up at his grandmother.

"Hello, Mother," he said in Persian to Roxana without taking his gaze from Olympias.

The older woman rose slowly from her couch, affection warming her features.

Roxana could only imagine what she must have been thinking—her beloved son had come back to her. She empathized with Olympias's joy and heartache because Roxana felt the same way every time she looked at her child.

Olympias stepped closer to the boy. "Hello, Alexander."

"Alexander Aegus," he corrected in Greek.

"You have your father's determination; that's good. Never let people call you by a name that doesn't suit you." She knelt and held out her hand. "I am your grandmother, Alexander Aegus. Olympias of Epirus."

Roxana rose from her couch and went to his side. "Your grandmother has come to see you." Roxana softened her voice, wanting to alleviate the apprehension she noticed in his round face.

Alexander Aegus turned to the older woman, stood on his toes and kissed her cheek.

"Greetings, Grandmother," Alexander Aegus pronounced carefully in Greek.

Olympias rose to her feet, beaming at her grandson. "You will be as great as your father. You will carry on his work and run his vast empire when you come of age, my grandson. We must set out to find you a suitable girl to marry right away. He must be trained in all the things his father learned. We will get him the best teachers. He must occupy his father's old rooms at Pella. I know the perfect place—"

"Alexander Aegus," Polyperchon interrupted the queen. "Why don't you take your grandmother to the stables and show her your new horse?"

"You have a new horse?" Olympias's harsh voice was gone. A loving, grandmotherly tone had replaced it.

"Polyperchon gave him to me." The little boy held out his hand to her. "Would you like to see him, Grandmother? I named him Patroclus. He's black like my father's horse, Bucephalus."

Alexander Aegus took his grandmother's hand and led her out of the tent.

Polyperchon lowered the tent flap. "She was getting a little carried away there, but the stables should keep them both occupied for a while."

"You could have warned me." Roxana wiped her damp brow.

"I didn't know she was coming to meet us ahead of her army and King Aeacides. She just showed up." He hesitated, grimacing. "And she wants to dine with us tonight. I have to arrange quarters for her and her men. The old woman brought half her belongings by the looks of the wagons. And bring the king tonight. She wants to see how well he's progressed in his studies."

Roxana remained overwhelmed by the encounter. "My poor son. He finally gets to meet his famous grandmother, and she will quiz him like a schoolmaster."

"No, she will quiz him to find out what Antipater and I have filled his head with. You saw her with the boy; she thinks she can recreate her son in this child." Polyperchon rubbed his chin as he drank in her figure beneath her rumpled clothes. "I need to go before you tempt me further." He winked and pushed the tent flap aside, barking orders at his guards.

Roxana plopped onto her couch. "It's going to be a very long night."

CHAPTER FIFTY-EIGHT

In the bedroom of her great tent, Roxana waited while Morella set the gold pins on her long, pleated tunic. White, trimmed with gold thread, and belted snuggly around her tiny waist, it complemented her figure.

"I like your hair up in the Greek way, my lady. Makes you look very queen-like," Morella praised.

"Ah, you are ready?"

Olympias stood at the curtain to her bedroom. Her bright blue peplos, made from fabric so light it seemed to float, matched the cloak over her right shoulder. A stunning gold pin of two lions preparing to do battle secured the cloth to her dress.

Morella gasped and sank to the floor, adding to Roxana's humiliation.

Olympias gestured to the servant. "Oh, do tell the child that we don't do that in the Macedonian court. A simple bow will do."

Morella stood up. "Thank you, my lady."

Olympias raised her dark eyebrows. "You speak Greek?"

"Yes, my lady. I picked it up through the years."

"Good. It will make you useful." Olympias fingered the gold cloak Morella had laid out on her bed. "I had hoped to see you attired in the Persian fashion this evening."

"I thought you wanted me to be more Greek."

"What is that?" Olympias pointed to the silver coin hanging around her neck. "Why do you wear him like a keepsake?"

She touched the coin. "It was a gift from your son. I treasure it."

Olympias took in her bedroom. "You have no statues of my son. There should be something more than a coin."

Roxana folded her hands, squeezing tight as she remembered the endless corridors filled with images of Alexander at Pella. "I have a few statues of him, but they're packed away."

"And what of the gods? Where are they?" Olympias feigned an indulgent smile. "Where do you sacrifice to them?"

Roxana snapped up the cloak from the bed. "I do not say prayers."

"What about little Alexander?"

The shock in her voice agitated Roxana. "With the life we've lived on the road, I have not had—"

Olympias dramatically threw a hand into the air. "His father was devoted since childhood. My grandson must be the same way!"

Roxana fumbled while wrapping the cumbersome cloth around her chest and shoulders. "And what good did Alexander's devotion do for him? During his last days, when he had no voice, no energy to move, he was carried to his temple so he could make his sacrifices. But his gods did not save him."

The queen's scowl accentuated the deep lines on her forehead. "Alexander knew what he owed the gods. Imagine if Alexander had been like you, then he would never have conquered the world."

Fed up, Roxana yanked off her cloak and threw it on the bed.

"I did everything I could, but I couldn't save him in the end, and your gods did nothing to help me." Her voice broke as she fought to hold in her emotions. "My world was ripped apart, and since he died, I've been surrounded by ambitious generals, greed, and war. Do you believe I should thank the gods for all of that? I owe the gods nothing, and they will receive nothing from me!"

The mother of Alexander pressed her hand against her chest. "How dare you? He was my son. I loved him more than my own life. When he died I was destroyed, but—"

"Then where were you? When Alexander died, and I had a son, there was no word from you. No letter, no interest. I traveled with Perdiccas for three years wondering when I would go to Pella. Then Antipater took us there. And since his death, I've been with Polyperchon and still no word from you until now. Why?"

The queen stood before her, her eyes no longer gray, but black like the deepest ocean.

"Because I hated you," she said without the slightest hint of remorse.

Her admission added to the dull ache creeping through Roxana's bones. She sat on the bed, numb.

"I always wrote you off as a passing fancy of Alexander's. A pampered Persian plaything he married to anger me. He knew how much I disliked your people." Olympias flicked her hand, the golden bracelets on her wrist tinkled. "But you were nothing of the kind. I could tell by the way he wrote about how much he loved you. I didn't want to believe it. Accepting a son's love for another woman is hard. It makes you feel discarded in a way."

All the times she'd feared for her life and the life of her son, and the one person who could have reached out to help them hadn't because she was jealous.

"And what has changed, my lady? I'm still Persian. Still the woman your son loved." She dropped her hand to the bed, robbed of strength. "Why did you finally come for us?"

She sat next to her on the bed. "Because someone asked me to. Before now, I've been at the mercy of my son's generals just as much as you. You may have thought I didn't care about you or your son, but I made inquiries, which was all I could do at the time. I may be a queen, and the mother of a mighty warrior king, but my opinion is discounted because I'm a woman."

She'd always assumed her circumstances were different from her mother-in-law's, but they were the same. They both had been shouting at the top of their lungs in a room full of men all of their lives.

"It seems we've both been at the mercy of others for a very long time."

"And always will be." Olympias patted her thigh. "The only way to avoid being cast aside is to make yourself indispensable to those who wield power. I've learned over the years how to read my enemies and my friends, and I advise you to do the same. You should be considering what use you can be to the likes of Cassander or Polyperchon or even me." She stood. "Finish getting ready. I will see you at dinner. Perhaps next time we can talk about my son without the shouting."

Olympias sauntered from the tent, leaving Roxana more confused than ever about her intentions and her sanity.

She closed her eyes, dreading the evening ahead. "You should have warned me, Alexander. You should have warned me about the whole bloody lot of them."

In her wagon, Roxana and the rest of the army slowly navigated the harsh hill country along the border of Macedonia. Relentless winds created treacherous conditions during the day, and at night, toppled tents and smothered fires.

The size of the army swelled as the forces of King Aeacides of Epirus joined Polyperchon's camp. The cramped quarters with boisterous men, calls of animals, and tents crammed together made her long for an escape.

She often retreated to the stables to ride Hera and think. The mounting concerns about her son, her mother-in-law, and the continued threat of Cassander preoccupied her.

One afternoon while putting Hera through her paces, she got so caught up in her worry for her son's future she didn't notice someone approaching from the camp.

"Roxana? Why are you out here?"

With his feet covered in mud and his cloak over his head, Polyperchon stood at the edge of a grassy knoll.

She pulled her horse alongside him. "You're all wet."

"It's raining."

She raised her face, reveling in the raindrops tickling her skin. "Glorious, isn't it? I used to love to ride in the rain as a child."

"We have to get out of this mess."

She held out her hand. "Climb on. It will be faster if we both ride her in."

He hesitated at first. Then he gripped her hand. She waited as he easily swung onto Hera's back, positioning himself right behind her.

Once beneath the shelter of the open tent used for the stables, Polyperchon helped Roxana from her horse.

He handed the reins off to a groom. "You should leave your horse for others to exercise. A lady of your station doesn't ride in the rain."

The suggestion irked her. "Alexander gave me my horse because he wanted me to ride—rain or shine. Oh, I do all the other things required of my station—I read, I sew, and I get glimpses of my son whenever he's not in the middle of some required lessons for reading, horsemanship, battle, etiquette, or whatever else his grandmother thinks he needs."

He wiped his face. "What did you expect? You know how difficult she is."

"Difficult?" Her raised voice spooked a few of the horses. "I barely recognize my son anymore. He's moody, snaps at the servants, and barely speaks to me. And when he does say anything, his every word is about his grandmother. How she will hire the best tutors in Greece for him. Move him into his father's rooms, have armor made for him, portraits done of him. Did you know she introduced him to a possible future wife? Alexander was terrified he might have to actually marry the girl. Then she tells my son to have me educate him on how babies are made!"

He chuckled, a glimmer of cheerfulness in his sober face. "Yes, I heard." The light left his eyes. "In spite of her methods, Olympias means well."

"She means to keep me out of his life!" Disgusted, she ran her hands through her wet hair. "To her, I'm not royal enough to have an opinion on his upbringing, but not lowly enough to ship back to Persia along with his nurse. But I'm still his mother."

He clasped her arms, forcing her to look at him. "Listen to me; we need to keep her happy. Without her troops, we can't beat Eurydice's forces. We both must appease Olympias, no matter how much she annoys us."

"Is that why you're here? Because you're afraid I'll say something to her?"

"No, of course not." He let her go and searched the stables. "I've come to warn you. Olympias has taken control of more than your son's future. She's inserted herself in the planning for the battle. She's brought her generals to the table and is even ordering my men around." The circles rimming his eyes stood out. "With Cassander forming alliances with all the Greek cities against me, I can't afford to stop her, but I'm afraid she will require a great deal more from us before this is over. She won't rest until she's ruling the empire through your son."

"All this time I thought it was only men who craved power." She rubbed her hands along her arms. "How long before we reach the plains of Euia?"

"Two days. When we arrive, the battle must be planned, and there will be much to do, but I will send you word when I can on our progress. Please refrain from listening to the camp gossip."

She snickered at the notion. "After years of living on little else, it's a hard habit to give up."

The slight grin on his face lifted her foul mood. There were moments when her attraction for him got the better of her.

He moved closer, the heat coming off him chased away the chill around her.

"Roxana, do you think one day, there will ever be a chance for us? I'm willing to live in Alexander's shadow if you'll have me."

She rested her hand on his chest, moved by his declaration, and not wanting to send a man into battle without hope. "Someday, when there's no more war and my son is secured on his throne, then there can be time for us."

He held her hand against his wet tunic. "I will protect you and honor you always. Everything I do is to help you and your son, remember that. No matter what happens, I am with you."

A small contingent of the royal guards from Epirus steadily approached the stable, their colorful attire standing out against the dreary sky.

Polyperchon stepped away. "It seems the queen wants me, yet again. I fear this is becoming a battle not between two factions, but between two determined women." He dipped his head to her. "My lady."

When he walked out in the rain and ran to meet the soldiers, an overwhelming sense of sorrow overtook her. It was as if their days of desperation careened to a fateful climax. How would it end? Only the gods knew for sure.

CHAPTER FIFTY-NINE

In the green rolling hills of Euia, beneath a glorious blue sky, the queen's forces met those of Eurydice. Roxana paced the confines of her tent as the trumpets of war rang out from the field of battle. She debated her son's future, both at the hands of his grandmother and Cassander.

Gossip about the confrontation flew through the camp, and she instructed Morella to ignore it as per Polyperchon's instructions. But day rolled into evening, and the stars rose with still no word from the general. Succumbing to her desperation, she sent Morella in search of news.

"There was no battle," Morella told her when she returned. "Olympias marched out at first light and while beating a drum, showed herself to the opposing forces. When the men found out that the mother of Alexander was leading the opposing army, soldiers laid down their weapons and walked across the field to Polyperchon's side. Almost the entire army of Macedonians under Eurydice's command has gone over to Olympias."

Roxana clasped her hands and raised them above her head. "Thank the gods. Alexander Aegus and his future are safe."

Polyperchon bounded into her tent. She wanted to run to him, relieved he'd come back but stopped short when she caught lines of distress cutting into his features.

Morella left her alone with the general.

"Where have you been?"

"The queen kept me detained." He went to the tent entrance and closed the flap. "But I left to come to you. Olympias is about to send for you, but there are things you need to know before you see her."

"Something's wrong. I can see it in your eyes."

He walked up and placed his lips close to her ear. "Olympias has gone mad with power. She had Philip stabbed by her royal guards. Eurydice was forced to commit suicide by hanging herself."

She put her hand to her mouth, forcing back the bile rising in her throat. Philip's kind face flashed across her mind. He'd been the stepbrother of Alexander. His callous assassination meant any one of his relatives could be just as easily slaughtered, including her son.

Polyperchon put his arm around her waist and helped her to a bench. "There's more."

A single tear rolled down her cheek. "What else?"

He set her gently on the seat. "Olympias ordered the death of Cassander's family. She dispatched her Thracian death guard to kill him a few days ago. I just got word his brother is dead."

Roxana's grief gave way to confusion. "Why? What has his family got to do with any of this?"

"She thinks they were part of a plot to poison Alexander."

She shook her head, stymied. "Alexander wasn't poisoned. How could Olympias believe such a silly conspiracy against her son?"

"She doesn't, but she's using the story as an excuse to eliminate all of Cassander's family and supporters. He's Antipater's son, and this is revenge for all the years of fights and standoffs she had with the old man. The stupid woman thought by killing innocent people, she'd win support, but she hasn't. She's alienated the men and many of the Macedonian people. Cassander will have little resistance when he sets foot in Macedonia."

The strength left her limbs, and she almost tipped forward to the floor. "If he returns, he will eliminate my son. You said so yourself."

He gripped her shoulders, holding her up. "He has to win first, and I will not let that happen. Once he's handed a few defeats in battle, Cassander can be reasoned with."

"Men are never reasonable when there's an empire at stake. I was there when Alexander died. I saw how all his loyal and loving generals tore each other apart trying to take control. Cassander is no different."

He sighed, sounding dejected. "You should prepare to leave."

His defeatist attitude astonished her. "And go where? Back to Bactria?"

"Olympias will take you somewhere safe. Since she's regent, you will have to go with her—you and Alexander Aegus. I wish there were some way I could keep you with me, but she won't allow it."

"What about you?" The walls of her tent closed in and panic quickened her heart. "You have sided with Olympias. Cassander will be just as interested in you as in my son and me. Where will you go?"

"I will go where I belong, with the army. I'm to head out to Perrhaebia tonight. There, I can recruit more men for our cause." He gazed longingly into her eyes. "No matter what Olympias says and does, keep your options open. In the end, her fate must not be yours. Wherever you go, I will find you. I promise I'll never stop fighting for you and your son."

A shadow darkened her doorway. A soldier entered her tent, unannounced. He wore the bright uniform of a royal guard of Epirus.

"I came to collect you, Lady Roxana. The queen bids you to come to her tent."

Roxana turned to Polyperchon. She didn't want to go. After hearing the atrocities her mother-in-law had committed, she couldn't face her.

He gave her an encouraging nod. "Go on. It will be all right."

Before she ducked out of the tent, she halted. A sickening feeling gripped her—they would never see each other again.

She gave him one last smile and said, "Thank you, Polyperchon, for everything."

Roxana trekked through the sloppy narrow paths, regretting her fidelity to her husband. Perhaps if she had given into the general's desires, he would refuse to send her off with Olympias. It seemed her love for her king still decided her fate. Six years after his death, and she was not free of him, and in her heart, she knew she never would be.

On top of a knoll, Roxana arrived at a red tent made of a tightly woven material, aglow with lamplight. It stood out from the rest of the dingy, goat-hair tents in the camp, representing the tastes of the eccentric queen who occupied it.

Once shown inside, she waited by the entrance. The guard who escorted her went to the queen and whispered in her ear. Seated around a meeting table in their battle armor, her Macedonian generals pored over several maps.

Roxana perused the spacious tent and recognized a familiar face.

Alexander filled every nook and cranny. Busts sat on pedestals, tapestries with the king's likeness hung from the walls, and ornaments with his image dangled from the ceiling.

Olympias sat back in her chair and addressed her generals. "Leave me with my daughter-in-law. We can resume discussion of the battle plans in the morning."

The officers rose, and each bowed respectfully to Roxana as they left. After the last of the men had gone, the guard posted outside closed the flap.

Wary about what would happen next, Roxana drew closer to the table. She peeked at the maps, trying to make sense of terrain painted on the animal skins.

"Cassander is on his way to Macedonia to confront us," Olympias announced with all the emotion of a seasoned general. "To guarantee your safety and the safety of my grandson, we will be leaving in a few days with my troops for Pydna."

"Where is that?"

Olympias touched a point on the map next to the blue sea. "It has a big fortress backing against the sea. My generals feel we will be safe there."

"For how long?"

"Do not fret, my dear." Olympias kept her cunning eyes on Roxana as if waiting for her to crack. "For now, Cassander is a pest, just as Antigonus The One-Eyed in Persia has been to Eumenes. These generals hold no power against the royal family."

Roxana sized up the queen's integrity, debating how far she should push the unstable woman.

"Even the smallest wasp, my lady, can have a very sharp sting. Cassander is a wasp you have made angry by killing his kinsman. He will seek revenge. Like your son, he's not a man to forget a slight."

Olympias grinned. "Despite what Polyperchon told you in your tent a little while ago, the murders of Cassander's kinsmen and supporters were necessary to protect the throne for my grandson."

So her royal guards were also spies—she should have known. Roxana felt like a fly caught in a spider's web.

"And what about Philip? He was an innocent man. He did not deserve to die."

"Philip was a puppet Cassander was going to use to take away the throne from my grandson." Olympias drummed her tapered fingers on a map. "He took my son from me. I will not lose my grandson, too."

"Cassander had nothing to do with Alexander's death. There was no conspiracy to—"

"I will not hear any more!" She thumped the table with her fist, rocking the goblets left there by the generals. "All those who slighted my son, who mocked him, who wished him harm, will pay."

"By avenging your son, you endanger mine!" Roxana sent the maps flying from the table. "Then all of this will mean nothing. Is that what you want?"

The mother of Alexander pulled her mouth taut in a grimace, the blue veins in her slender neck popped out against pale skin.

"He was my son!"

She calmly regarded the icon she'd once feared. "Your son is dead. No amount of revenge is going to bring him back. Unless you have the ear of those gods you so ardently worship, you have sealed our fates. You have killed us all."

She turned from the table, shutting her ears to any more ravings from the queen.

Fate would determine what happened next. Her life and the life of her son were now in the hands of a madwoman.

CHAPTER SIXTY

Sea air mixed with the pungent odor of livestock wafted past as Roxana's wagon halted at the steps to the palace at Pydna. Her hopes for the type of accommodations she'd enjoyed at Pella sank when she spotted a massive reinforced tower. The high, impregnable walls resembled a fort, not a palace. There were no gardens, or fountains, or even a place to stretch her legs. The oppressive structure offered no views of the surrounding hillsides—just the sea, the adjoining town, and endless blue skies.

"Now this is Greek," Morella joked when she entered Roxana's quarters.

With simple sea scenes of fish and birds painted on the walls, Roxana found the small sitting room confining. Her only solace—a single window in her cramped bedroom overlooking the town.

Morella set Alexander's small gold chest on the table next to a plain cedar bed. "This reminds me of Susa."

Roxana tested the mattress. "But I don't have to compete with other wives here."

"No, just other in-laws." Morella wiped her fingerprints off the gold chest. "Did you see them coming out of the wagons? I wonder how many more people from the court at Pella the crazy woman will invite to join us."

Roxana eyed the chest, thinking of Alexander and all the things he'd kept from her about his mother, his family, and his generals.

"I can't imagine any of them are from Alexander's family. Other than his mother and his sister, Cleopatra, who is left?"

"There's only one—a half-sister." Morella told her while opening a trunk. "I saw her on the way in, settling in rooms next to yours. A servant with the queen told me her name is Thessalonice. She was the last child born to your husband's father, King Philip. They say her mother and Olympias were friends, and the queen has overseen her upbringing."

Roxana moved toward her small window and glimpsed the town below.

The inhabitants of the quaint hamlet walked the narrow streets on their way to shops, the central marketplace, or to their stone and wood houses. She envied their ignorance. If only she could forget about why they had traveled to the remote destination and the man who wanted her son's crown.

"This ghastly place makes me long for Pella."

The *thunk* of a sword on armor echoed from the hallway outside. Her chamber doors flew open, and Olympias strutted into her rooms, appearing fresh despite the days of arduous travel.

"All settled in?"

Morella's hand flew to her chest, and she backed away from the bed to a corner.

Roxana rested against the window sill, not bothering to bow—she didn't respect her mother-in-law enough for that.

"How long will we be here?"

Olympias wiped her hands, taking in the paltry rooms. "That depends on Cassander. He plans to lay siege to our little fort, but we will prevail." She walked toward the window. "My nephew and his forces from Epirus are on the way to assist us. I've sent one of my generals on to the fort at Amphipolis to engage some more men for us there. Then we have Eumenes and his armies to help us. We will be fine." She noticed the gold chest next to Roxana's bed.

"Are the forces here prepared for a long siege? When my family encamped on the Sogdiana Rock to wait out Alexander, my father had us prepare enough food and water for a year. Do we have that here?"

"I have some men seeing to it." Olympias caressed the impressions of men and horses depicted on the chest. "This was Alexander's, wasn't it?"

Roxana ignored the question. She was more concerned about their precarious circumstances. "Shouldn't you be overseeing the preparations, or at least have someone you trust making sure we have—"

"I gave him this chest when he was a little boy." She lovingly admired the gold box. "I told him to keep his treasures in it."

The dreamy look in her eyes compounded the sinking feeling in Roxana's stomach.

"Do we have enough food to feed the troops here? How deep is the well? Are there any tunnels below the fort for escape, or any holes in the walls surrounding the town?" Roxana moved toward the bed, fear pressing down on her. "My lady, we need to see to these things immediately."

Olympias raised her head as if coming out of a trance. "We have food, water, and enough supplies to outlast Cassander, I assure you. The local guards and all the army elephants and horses we brought with us will make it rather cramped and smelly for a while, but that is all. You shouldn't worry your pretty little head about such things, my dear. It's most unbecoming." She turned from the bed. "I'll leave you to your unpacking."

Like a graceful muse, the queen glided out of the room, giving a dismissive flick of her hand to the guard at the doors.

Morella emerged from a shadow in the corner of the room. "She's a rather cool customer."

"Yes, too cool." Roxana rubbed her arms, trying to chase away the cold enveloping her. "I don't believe she has any idea what's about to happen."

Gentle autumn winds transformed into blistering mountain gusts, and Roxana's hopes for a quick resolution to Cassander's siege drowned beneath the biting sting of her fear. Smoke from his army campfires billowed over the city walls, filling her rooms. The ever-present reminder of the conflict added to her escalating sense of doom.

She sought relief from the confines of the palace by taking short walks around the grounds. But the constant noise of the troops and stink of urine and feces from the animals housed inside the fortress wore on her nerves.

Her only solace was the gossip Morella collected.

"Some of the men in the palace have deserted to Cassander," her maid reported one frigid afternoon.

Roxana turned from her window, the walls of the room once again closing in. If the army men were bailing, things had to be getting worse.

"When did you hear this?"

"Today, in the kitchens." She went to Roxana's side. "Cassander is offering them food and warm lodgings."

The mention of food roused her curiosity. "Do the men have enough to eat?"

"Their rations have been cut, my lady."

The news sucked the air from her lungs. The palace food stores had to be getting low to cut the men's rations. How much longer could they hold out?

"Let's not tell Alexander Aegus any of this. I don't want him to worry."

Morella rested against the sill. "I won't say a word. The king's been upset enough lately. First losing Philip, then Arnia, and finally Polyperchon. The boy looked up to the general a great deal. He's been a little lost since we came to this place."

Roxana raised her head, the sting in her heart watering her eyes. "I've been a little lost, too." She patted Morella's hand. "Thank the gods, I have you."

Morella smiled, wrinkling her pug nose. "You'll always have me, my lady. Not to worry. I'm not going anywhere."

With every passing day, Roxana became more concerned about their state of affairs. Both sides remained steadfast, lessening any chance for a peaceful resolution to the siege. She spent her time pacing in her rooms and worrying about the future.

Then, one wintry evening, when Morella arrived with her dinner tray, Roxana's worst fears came to fruition.

She sized up the skimpy portion of dried fish and bread on her supper plate. "Are we now on diminished rations like the troops?"

Morella nodded. "Cook says the queen ordered her to cut the royal family's portions."

It was only a question of time before starvation forced their surrender.

Morella wrung her hands, adding to the gloomy atmosphere haunting her rooms.

"I also have news on the war, my lady. Polyperchon and his army tried to break through forces outside the city walls but failed. Most of his men have gone over to Cassander."

She could not move, could not think. Her only thoughts were of her son and the fate of the man with the beautiful blue eyes.

"And Polyperchon? Where is he?"

Morella dropped her head. "He's alive, but he's been humiliated. They say he's boarded a ship for Persia."

He's left us! The words repeated over and over in her head. Heartsick, she went to the bed and sat down before her legs gave out.

He'd been her last hope. Her protector, the one man she'd believed in, and now he had run away, leaving her and her son at the mercy of a mad old woman, and a cold-blooded commander with a thirst for kingship.

Roxana covered her face with her hands. For the first time since arriving at the desolate locale, she wept.

Morella put a consoling arm around her shoulders. "Please, my lady. Don't give up. You're the wife of Alexander. That still means something to these people."

Had it ever meant anything to anyone? She doubted it. In all her dealings with the Greeks, from Alexander's mother to his generals, she'd been an outsider, an Oriental, not worthy of their respect. With things at their worst, she would be expendable. But what about her son?

Roxana wiped her eyes. "The other forces the queen summoned, where are they?"

Morella frowned. "They're not coming. Polyperchon and his troops were our only hope. The Queen's nephew is fighting a civil war in Epirus, and her other generals have gone over to Cassander. Cook says we're on our own."

Helpless and trapped, she didn't know where to turn, or how to help her boy. A rush of fire flowed through her at the thought of anyone hurting her child. She still had a knife and would kill anyone who came near him.

"I must protect my son."

"He has a guard at his door. No one will touch the king." Morella held her hand. "Cassander wants to be regent over the boy, not to hurt him. It's the crazy old lady he wants to kill."

"Do you believe that?" she asked, on the verge of hysterics.

Morella offered a sunny smile. "Yes, I do. He's Alexander's son, and they would never want to anger the gods by hurting one of their own."

Her maid's reassurances calmed her. Here she was at the end of her rope, and the only person by her side was her devoted Morella.

"You have always been so good to me."

"And you have been very good to me. Like a friend, my lady."

"You are my friend, Morella." She squeezed her hand. "And from now on, you must call me Roxana. No more my lady."

"Then may I suggest you eat your meal before it gets cold, Roxana." Morella encouraged her to the table.

Once seated, Roxana inspected her meager plate.

How much worse will it get?

CHAPTER SIXTY-ONE

Roxana braved the cold of her open window to distract herself with the everyday lives of the people of Pydna. Their routines kept her grounded, but as the dismal days of winter and the siege wore on, the activity of the town's residents changed. They became listless, roaming the streets and cowering in doorways as the food and livestock stalls in the market dried up. Merchants closed shops, and the horses, goats, and herds of sheep once seen cluttering the stone streets vanished.

The crying of babies carried up to her window day and night, and then the noises stopped. The happy laughter of children disappeared completely. Like rats, the people skulked about, snatching up whatever food they could find.

The first bodies surfaced a short time later, wrapped in sacks. Family members wept as they laid them in the abandoned marketplace away from the houses. After days in the sun, the stench of rotting flesh and decomposition made it to her room. She shut her window, but her macabre fascination with the devastation drew her back.

Soon, the bodies were no longer wrapped in sacks, but tossed, half-clothed or naked, on the piles of dead. She expected to see the rats and dogs hovering around the carcasses, but any animal that ventured near ended up clubbed by the starving inhabitants and dragged away for food.

A horse bolted through the city streets one rainy afternoon as several emaciated children chased it down and stabbed it to death with knives and swords. The creature's abominable screams sent her to her knees, crying at its suffering.

By the time warmer weather arrived, the townsfolk had resorted to rummaging through the dead, ripping off limbs and eating the raw flesh of their neighbors. The corpses outnumbered the living to a point where the once happy town of men, women, and children resembled a massive graveyard.

Unable to take the gruesome scenes any longer, she left her window to walk the palace grounds, but when she reached the bottom of the stairs leading to the outer courtyard, the appalling smell brought her to a grinding halt.

Persian soldiers and Greeks stood over starved corpses of elephants, hacking away at limbs and skinning the dead creatures. Others sat around large fires with the hocks of horses, their hooves still attached, roasting over the flames. And bones, mounds of them, lined the walls inside the courtyard. Remains of elephants, horses, goats, and sheep sat as grotesque memorials to their plight.

She turned back to the stairs, eager to run to her rooms. On her way, she passed a group of Persian soldiers hunkering under an arch out of the bright sunlight and whispering amongst themselves in her native language. She attempted to eavesdrop, and when she was just about to climb the steps, something on their small fire caught her eye. She squinted to make it out, and then covered her mouth, aghast. It was a human leg.

Terrified, she bounded up the steps two at a time to the inner palace gates. Once inside, she ran along the empty corridors to her rooms. She was almost to her doors when one of the sentries posted outside stopped her.

"What's the matter, my lady?"

She peered down the long hall, the atrocities she'd seen awakening another fear.

"Go to the stables and see to my horse ... and my son's horse, too. See if ..." She couldn't bring herself to say the words.

The soldier bowed. "Yes, my lady."

Morella came out into the corridor, putting her arm around Roxana's waist. "What is it? You're trembling."

Roxana turned to her, a lump in her throat.

"Get my son. Bring him to my rooms." She pushed away from Morella once inside her doors. "And tell him to bring his sword with him, and any other weapons he has."

Morella clasped her arm. "You're white. What has happened?"

She wasn't ready to relay the abysmal sights she'd witnessed. "Please go. Get my son. I want him with me from now on."

Morella left, pulling the doors closed.

While she waited, Roxana clutched her stomach, sick at the realization she couldn't rely on her guards to keep her son safe anymore. When men succumbed to eating human flesh, they were beyond reason.

Soon the army, town, and palace would be Cassander's. There was nothing she could do to. No more generals to appeal to, no armies to summon, no one to help her. They had reached the end.

The only question left was what would Cassander do to them?

A knock made her jump. She cracked the thick wooden doors and the soldier she'd sent to the stables reappeared, his lean face grim.

"I'm sorry, my lady. A groom in the palace told me all the horses are dead. Your mare and your son's horse, both died of starvation several days ago. The queen ordered all the dead animals distributed as food for the army."

She wretched, disgusted by the idea of her beloved horse ending up in a soldier's belly.

"Not my Hera." Roxana whimpered as tears blinded her. "She was a gift from Alexander. He gave her to me. She was all I had left."

Appearing uncomfortable with her emotional display, the guard shut the doors.

Roxana crumpled to the floor.

All the sorrow she'd experienced—the loss of her first son, Hephaestion, Alexander, the slaughter of innocents at Babylon, Perdiccas, Antipater, Philip, Polyperchon—came rushing back and she relived each heartbreak in that instant. The pain eviscerated her will to live.

"Roxana?" Morella appeared at her side, touching her shoulder. "The guard told me what happened."

She wiped her eyes, her protective instincts sweeping aside all other concerns. "Where's my son?"

Morella sat on the floor with her. "A servant is packing up his things. They will be here soon."

She hugged her maid, crying into her shoulder. "It's all so horrible. What are we going to do? How are we going to survive this?"

Morella patted her back. "There, there. We'll figure out something. We'll find a way to get all of us out of here."

Morella balanced the four goblets of wine on her silver tray as she hurried down the dark corridor to the queen's rooms. She tugged at her loose-fitting brown Greek tunic.

I can't believe I have to wear this thing.

She stopped outside the doors and glared up at the sentries, their spears crossed before her, barring entry.

"Well, open the door for me," she insisted in Greek. "The queen wants her wine."

"Where's the usual girl who serves the queen?" the shorter soldier asked. "We've never seen you before."

She frowned. "The usual girl is probably sick like all the others. They've got no one left in the kitchens, so I'm helping out."

The soldier glared at her, sneering. "And who are you?"

Morella hiked her eyebrows at his intimidating voice. "I work for Lady Roxana. Right down the hall." She rolled her eyes when he didn't budge. "Either go ask her yourself or open the door. This tray ain't getting any lighter."

The other soldier, who had not said a word, pulled back his spear and turned the handle on the door.

"She's the Persian woman's maid, all right. I've seen her before."

She bristled at the *Persian woman* comment and headed inside.

"My lady, it's been over two months since we've heard any word from your generals outside of the city," a towering man said as he stood over a table set up in the middle of a sitting room.

Morella snuck toward the table, creeped out by all the images of the dead king.

"I've had no reports that my generals have handed Pella or Amphipolis over to Cassander," Olympias said. "Polyperchon writes he's still gathering troops for our cause. He's not as easily swayed by hardship as you, Pausinas."

A short, muscular, and hairy man stood and struck the table. "Are you and the ladies of the court not aware of what's going on?"

She glowered at his fist. "I don't need your theatrics to remind me, Demetrius. I know what the army men have been doing with the flesh of the dead."

Morella tried to remain invisible as she set a goblet in front of the queen.

General Demetrius met Olympias's cold stare. "You cannot expect the men to be loyal when their stomachs are empty. Cassander is willing to take in all deserters. He's offered to feed them and send them off to fight for him. The men want to go, and I can't blame them."

"We have all suffered!" She snapped up her wine. "That's no excuse for leaving your post."

Morella set the goblets in front of the generals. She clasped the tray to her chest and crept to a dark corner, anxious to hear more.

Demetrius went to the queen's side. He knelt next to her and lowered his head.

"I'm begging you, mistress, let my men go. Allow them to take their families from the city so they can feed them and bury their dead. We are at our end. We will all go mad; at least this way, those who are left behind might stand a better chance."

Moved by his speech, Morella waited to see what the queen would say.

Olympias set her drink aside and gracefully rose from her chair. "I understand, Demetrius. Your men are free to leave the city, but I will have their names written down. I will know who they are and I will not be so lenient in the future. Make sure they are aware of that."

A weary Demetrius gripped the table to get to his feet. "You can add my name to that list, my queen. I will be joining those men going over to Cassander. I have no more stomach for such misery." He bowed and slowly walked out the chamber door.

"What a sorry excuse for a man." Olympias shifted her focus to her other military leaders. "Are you two going to leave me, too?"

A man with a black and gray beard lifted his goblet to the queen. "No, ma'am. Pausinas and I have sworn to protect you until death, but there are others to consider. Your grandson has suffered, as well as your daughter-in-law. Your whole court is starving. Your family has grown very thin. Perhaps it's time to end this."

She sat and carefully studied the general for a moment.

"What did you have in mind, Tacitus?"

The man named Pausinas slid her goblet toward her. "You must leave Pydna. You could escape to Persia or join your daughter in Sardis."

She refused her drink. "I have stood by as friends and family have been coerced by Cassander, bribed by Cassander, and even killed by him. I cannot, and will not, give in to that man." She pushed her chair back. "But you're right, Pausinas. It's time to make my way to Persia where I can continue my fight." She eyed her commanders. "You have served me well. Prepare a ship for my family and me. We will leave as soon as the tide allows." Olympias glided out of the room.

Morella debated leaving, her job done, the wine served, but her nose told her to stick around. There might be more she could learn.

Tacitus threw his head back and laughed. "She's mad!"

Can't argue with him there.

Pausinas went to the doors and shut them. "She's a cornered rat on a sinking ship, my friend."

Tacitus let a long, slow hiss escape from his lips. "Can't the silly old woman see all hope is lost?" He cast a wary eye to the other general. "Are you going to make a ship ready for her?"

"Already done." Pausinas plucked his goblet from the table. "There's a quinquereme waiting at the harbor with enough room for her and some of her family. But she will never make it out to the open sea."

Morella perked up. *Oh no?*

Pausinas rested his hip on the table. "I'm going to tell Cassander of her plans when I leave and go over to his men."

"She won't like that, my friend. But then again, Cassander will like it, very much. He might even be so grateful as to give you a rank in his army."

"Now you're starting to think like a Macedonian general." Pausinas gulped more of his wine. "What else do you think we could do to please Cassander?"

Tacitus picked up his drink. "I'll get word to the other generals that the queen has surrendered and to give up control of Pella and Amphipolis. Do you think that will get me a commission in Cassander's cavalry?"

"It just might be enough to save our hides." Pausinas held out his empty cup to Morella. "Girl, get us more wine."

CHAPTER SIXTY-TWO

Cassander ignored the noisy billowing of his tent as a steady, brisk breeze battered against it. Perched on his stool in the middle of his reception area, he focused on the messenger in front of him. The short, bearded man was gaunt, and his deep brown eyes were sunken and empty. Cassander gave him a thorough examination while keeping himself from showing his emotions, just as his father had taught him to do.

He'd won. He'd beaten the old bitch. It was all his, but there was business to take care of first. When he was back in Pella, the army with him and his enemies dead, he could celebrate.

"When was the last time you had a good meal, Hector?"

The messenger cracked a half-smile. "It's been a very long time, sir."

How could she have let this go on for so long?

"Arrange for some food to be brought for this man," he called to a guard in his doorway.

He turned back to the queen's envoy. "Eat first, then go back to Olympias and tell her this. I ask that she put all of her interests into my hands. No exceptions. I must take over the guardianship of the king."

Hector bowed his head. "I will tell her, sir."

Cassander stood, keeping up his calm demeanor. No point in terrifying them all just yet.

"I would like you to bring this message to the Lady Roxana. Let her know I mean her and her son no harm. She has nothing to fear from me. Take her and the boy some food when you return to Pydna. Now go."

Hector was shown outside by one of Cassander's soldiers.

"Do you think the old cow will give in to your demands?"

Cassander scowled at General Molyccus, a thick tree of a man with scars on his cheeks.

"Does it matter?" Cassander waved off the general's concern. "She can come to me now or later. It makes little difference to me." He went to a table filled with scrolls and tablets.

Molyccus cleared his throat. "When will you tell her Antigonus has killed Eumenes?"

Cassander never looked up. "When it is to my advantage to do so."

He pulled out a letter and read it, mindful to keep up his guarded expression.

"What do we do with the royal family?" his general asked.

Cassander mulled over the bounty he'd captured with Olympias's family. "The girl, Thessalonice, intrigues me. A daughter of Philip, step-sister of Alexander—marriage to her could solidify any man's claim to the throne." He gleaned more of his scroll and turned to his general. "I want the boy and Roxana brought to me as soon as the old witch has agreed to my terms."

"Yes, Cassander."

"Make sure the boy and his mother are well treated." Cassander grinned. "I must repay the kindness the wife of Alexander once showed me."

Roxana waited in her sitting room, pacing and wringing her hands as she went over what Cassander's capture of the palace meant for her and her son. She ran through scenarios to keep them alive, ways to please the general, she even considered giving herself to the man if he would spare her child. She didn't care. Alexander Aegus was all that mattered. She was beyond humiliation.

She remained in her sitting area, retracing her steps, not wanting to upset her boy. The lack of food and the death of his horse had devastated him, taking the light from his eyes. She would do anything, even die, to bring her happy, carefree son back to life.

"My lady?"

Morella came up to her, a stocky, bearded man in a dirty white tunic at her side, carrying a sackcloth.

When had he come into her rooms?

"Who is this?"

He bowed. "Hector, my lady. I'm a messenger for the queen." He held up the sackcloth. "Cassander gave me food when I went to see him. He wanted you and the boy to have something to eat."

He handed the sackcloth to Roxana as Morella kept a watchful eye.

Her hunger pains told her to eat, to accept the food and feed her son, but Roxana didn't trust the messenger. Cassander could have sent her and her son poison. If he wanted to take over the throne, it would be the easiest way.

"Thank you." She refused the food. "The general has made it quite clear what he means to do—"

Morella snatched the sackcloth and opened it. "I'll taste it and make sure it isn't poisoned. Your son needs to eat."

Roxana's mouth watered while her maid took bites of the lumps of bread, cheese, and meat. She ached to grab and eat it all for herself.

Morella glanced from Roxana to Hector. "No pains. No nausea. No poison, my lady."

Overcome, she wilted with relief. "Wake Alexander Aegus and make sure he eats."

Morella went to her bed in the adjoining room. When her groggy child saw the food, he snatched up the cheese and bread like a common street urchin.

The sight of her starving child brought tears to her eyes. She should have done more to keep him safe.

"Cassander wants the best for you and your son, my lady."

She faced the messenger, not trusting a word. "Cassander's intentions for my son have been known to me for quite some time."

Hector took a step closer. "He sends you word—he means no harm to either you or your boy. You have nothing to fear. I think it sat better with him that you didn't attempt to leave with the queen."

"I heard she tried to escape in one of her ships and was caught outside the harbor. That she didn't want to take her grandson with her—" Roxana's hands shook as she pictured the old woman leaving her and Alexander Aegus behind.

Hector dipped his head, offering a sad smile. "She left the boy because she knew he would come to harm in Persia. Despite how it may appear, the queen wants nothing but the best for her grandson."

The best? How many times had she heard that before? She didn't believe any Macedonian alive had her son's best interests at heart. He'd been a part of the game to all of them. Something to use so they could gain power.

She put her hand to her brow, wishing away her pounding headache. "What of Olympias? I can guess what Cassander plans to do with her."

"He never said. We're all at his mercy now."

Hector bowed and slipped out her doors.

The idea of being at Cassander's mercy sent a shiver through her. It was not a question of if they would die, but when.

Am I so afraid of death anymore?

She'd been running from it for so long, she questioned if giving in and joining her husband would be better. But then Morella's soft voice drifted through the sitting room doors, and she pictured her son. She'd sworn to protect him, promised his father. Roxana could never leave him, no matter how tempting an existence without pain or heartache seemed.

She resolved to go on and walked into her bedroom anxious to check on her beloved boy.

Alexander Aegus sat up on the edge of the bed, eating his cheese. His face had grown quite thin, and his once muscular and agile body appeared spindly and fragile.

"Come and eat some cheese with me." He held out the chunk of white goat's cheese.

In spite of her lightheadedness, and the poke of her bones through her clothes, watching her son eat was better than any meal.

"No, Alexander Aegus. You eat it."

"Where did he get the food, Mother?"

She sat on the edge of the bed. "Your Uncle Cassander sent it. He and your grandmother have made arrangements for a great peace."

Morella's dark eyes rounded. Roxana detected her maid's fear.

"Will I see Uncle Cassander soon?" His gaunt face came alive.

"Yes, I'm sure you will." Roxana held him to her, comforting him in a loving voice. "I'm sure we both will."

Cassander sat at his small wooden desk in his dull white palace rooms as sounds from the town filtered through his window. The rumble of carts filled with food, the clip-clop of horses arriving to replace the ones lost, the laughter of children and happy voices of those who had survived the siege circled him.

Fools.

He stood from his chair, and with a perturbed scowl, shut the window.

Back at his desk, he sorted through the pile of scrolls from governors and city leaders across Greece. He'd watched his father manage the Kingdom of Macedon for years, and now it was his.

A soft knock on his door interrupted his reading.

"Come."

Cassander sighed as Molyccus strolled up to his desk. It was either bad news or good—with the man he could never tell.

Molyccus stopped, flipped his purple cloak behind his back, and held up a scroll.

"The assembly has voted. They've condemned the queen to death as per your wishes."

"Good." Cassander took the scroll and tossed it to pile. "Stupid woman didn't believe the men would condemn her."

"Should I send the guard to kill her? There should be nothing stopping you."

Cassander folded his hands, weighing all his options. He liked the crusty general, but the man's inability to see the big picture when it came to power struggles baffled him. Probably what made him better in battle than at negotiations.

"Many things are stopping me. I can't just send a unit to her quarters and have her killed. That would make me rash." He was determined to get rid of the insufferable woman but remembered his father's frequent calls for patience when dealing with enemies. "I have to make it appear as if I tried to help the mother of Alexander, tried to save her from her eventual fate. Soldiers prefer their leaders to be compassionate."

Molyccus grinned, looking more malevolent than kind. "You've thought of something. I can tell."

Cassander stroked his grizzled beard, joyful over the old woman's impending demise.

"You know me well, old friend. I will give the queen a way out. I will offer her exile—Athens, let's say. Unfortunately, she will never make it there, having been killed in a terrible accident aboard ship. Then my problems will be over."

Molyccus cocked an eyebrow. "What about the little king and his mother? Will we deal with them in the same way?"

"Let's take care of Olympias first, then I'll worry about the son of Alexander and his widow." Cassander softened his hard scowl, hoping to appear genuinely concerned. "I want no harm to come to either Roxana or the boy. I need them."

"What about Polyperchon? He vows to keep fighting for the young king. He still has some troops at his disposal. Do you want him killed as well?"

Cassander debated the fate of the man who had taken away his legacy. The funny thing was, now that he had everything he desired, he no longer cared about the general.

"Leave Polyperchon to his fate. He can gather all the troops he wants. He will never be a threat to me. I hold the king and I will make damn sure he never gets the boy back." He picked up another letter. "Send Roxana to me. It's time we had a little chat."

He waited by the window, peering at the cliffs and admiring the pristine blue sky. Cassander was anxious to see Roxana, to see the fear in her eyes, to have her in the palms of his hands. But he didn't want to intimidate her—not at first anyway. He needed her help and using Roxana would add to the sweetness of his revenge.

Who is the king now, Alexander?

The door to his rooms opened and he turned, greeting her with a well-rehearsed smile.

"Roxana." The hint of dread in her gorgeous green eyes delighted him. "I'm so glad we could speak privately." He noted her hollow cheek and the way her long blue tunic hung on her figure. "You're too thin. You must eat more. Perhaps I should send my cooks to your quarters to make—"

"I'm fine, Cassander, thank you." She rubbed her hands together. "You've been more than generous with my son and me. We have more than enough to eat and are recovering from the ordeal."

"Yes, it was an ordeal, wasn't it?" He escorted her to a couch set up by his desk, making sure to keep his voice cheery. "It wasn't my choosing. Olympias is the one who insisted on holding out here. She didn't think to supply herself for such a siege, but what would the woman know of such things. She's not a general." He stopped at the couch. "Please sit. There's something I need your help with."

He marveled at the way she moved. He could see why Alexander had married her. She was a charming creature. It was a pity he couldn't claim her for a wife.

"Olympias has been condemned to death by the Macedonian assembly." He took a breath and waited for her reaction.

She kept her eyes on him, not showing a smidgen of regret or sorrow. "I expected it. Isn't that what Macedonians do to traitors?"

Brains and beauty. Alexander was a lucky man.

"But I do not wish to kill the mother of Alexander. I want her to live. However, she will not be able to live in Macedonia now that the assembly has passed judgment. But she could live in exile in … Athens, let's say."

A crack appeared in her outer shell. A little light entered her sunken eyes. She would do as he wanted.

"Could you do that?" she asked.

Cassander took a seat next to her, enjoying the role of benevolent general. "I've arranged for a ship to take Olympias to Athens. There she could live out the rest of her life, but she has refused my offer of exile." He threw up his hands, adding to his pretense. "I've tried to have others talk to her, but she won't listen. I was wondering, perhaps, if you could speak to her. Tell her to take the ship, to leave Macedonia, and live a quiet life away from here."

He could almost see her weighing his sincerity. She didn't trust him, he picked that up instantly, but she wavered on if she should.

"I will do what I can."

The thrill of triumph coursed through him. His deception had worked.

"That's all I ask."

Roxana stood, but he hadn't finished with her.

"Do tell Alexander Aegus I will come and see him soon. I want to find out if he's gotten any better at dice."

"I will."

Roxana smiled, but it wasn't heartfelt. He'd practiced the same smile on so many through the years, he quickly recognized it on someone else.

She hesitated. He sensed she had another question. He knew what it was, by the way her knuckles shone white on her folded hands.

"What do you plan to do with my son and me?"

Cassander's smile grew, hiding his smugness. He stood next to her and placed his hand on her arm, offering his sincerest reassurance.

"Have no fear, Roxana. I am your friend."

CHAPTER SIXTY-THREE

Roxana left Cassander's rooms with his guards shadowing her every move. They escorted her through the bustling palace while around her, servants cleaned floors and rooms that lay abandoned for weeks during the siege. But when they turned a corner to a musty corridor, the servants disappeared.

Her visit with Cassander didn't sit well with her. She didn't trust him and figured this attempt to reason with Olympias hid another motive. Unfortunately, she wasn't in a position to refuse him.

At the door to the queen's new apartment, an armed sentry barred her way. A bulky man with two swords on his person, he gave her a thorough inspection with his impertinent brown eyes.

"Do you have any swords or poisons on your person, my lady?"

Flabbergasted, Roxana stared, openmouthed, at the man. "No. Why do you ask me such a thing?"

"So the queen does not have means to kill herself."

Roxana had no fears of the queen harming herself. Olympias was too proud to take her own life and would go out fighting, just like her famous son.

Once ushered inside, Roxana tensed. Her formal tent was bigger than the lodgings allocated to the queen. The walls, a pale shade of yellow, had no decoration, and the furniture consisted of a simple wooden bed and a single chair. All that remained of her collections of mementos of Alexander was one portrait bust, proudly displayed on a corner pedestal.

Roxana ached for her. What greater hell could she face than being removed from all her cherished reminders of her famous son?

"He has sent you?" Olympias's harsh voice resonated in the confined space. "I would have thought Cassander would have given up by now."

She emerged from a darkened corner next to the window looking out on a masonry wall.

"Cassander offers you a way out." Roxana kept to her spot by the door, undone by the awkward encounter. "You should take it."

Olympias made her way into the light. Her clothes hung from her bony frame. Her creamy skin had turned sallow and stretched taut over her protruding cheekbones. Her silver hair was dull, her eyes listless. Even her slender, long neck had withered away to no more than a spindly twig of bone and sinew. A shell of the woman she used to be, the regal, elegant woman had disappeared.

"I want no deals with Cassander." She trudged toward her chair. "I will not give the hairy toad the satisfaction."

"What about Alexander Aegus?" Roxana pleaded. "You could go to Athens for him."

She flicked her hand, dismissing the suggestion in her cavalier way, and sat. "I can't help you or the boy now. I wish I could, but I'm done."

Roxana balled up her hands. She'd endured months of wretchedness because of this woman, and when given a way out of her impossible situation, the crazy old bat refused it.

"So that's it? You're just going to let them kill you?"

Olympias smiled, placing her hands on her lap. "They can't kill me. I'm the mother of a god." She shrugged. "At least he's a god in Egypt."

The thunder of many footsteps in the hall sent her heart into a tailspin.

"Olympias, please!" Roxana rushed to her chair. "You must not let all you have done come to this."

"We are the life we lived, not the ending—that's what I taught my son."

The door to the chamber flew open, banging against the stone wall, startling Roxana. Dozens of soldiers with their swords drawn stood at the entrance. They looked as though they were going into battle.

Time stood still. She registered every breath, every beat of her heart, but as the moment went on, the numb shock morphed into the icy stranglehold of fear.

A single man stepped out from the others. Scarred, stocky he walked with a limp and brandished a sword with a silver handle.

"By order of the people, you're hereby convicted of the unlawful murders of King Philip and Queen Eurydice of Macedon, as well as those of the friends and family of the regent Cassander. We're here to carry out your sentence of death."

"No!" Roxana stood before the queen desperate to save her.

The escorts who had brought her to the room restrained her. She struggled as they carried her to the door.

"Stop!" Olympias stood, her eyes burning with the same intensity as her son's. "Don't you dare touch the wife of Alexander in such a manner!"

The guards instantly let her go as if realizing their mistake.

Her hands shaking, and her legs about to give out, Roxana scrambled to get back Olympias. She gripped the back of her chair, holding herself up as she faced the soldiers. Staring down their craggy, empty faces had been the most terrifying thing Roxana had ever done.

"I have my orders, my queen," the soldier standing before her said.

Olympias held her head high. "I understand your orders, but my daughter-in-law is not to be harmed."

The leader angrily gestured for the men at the door to join him.

The men tentatively approached the legendary Olympias, their swords flagging, their steps faltering. Their attention darted from the intended victim to their leader.

Their uncertainty was palpable, and in it, Roxana felt a smidgen of hope. She'd lived in the company of army men long enough to know they had to be inspired to kill, not ordered. Her heartbeat exploded in her ears as she held her breath, waiting for their next move.

A young boy among the soldiers stopped. His freckled face scrunched in disgust, he threw his sword to the floor.

The *clank* made the other men halt.

"I will not kill the mother of Alexander," he shouted.

Another man next to him sheathed his sword. "I'm a soldier, not a murderer."

A lanky man grabbed the sword arm of their leader. "This isn't right. I will not kill in cold blood."

The others mumbled their assent. Roxana's tight grip on the chair eased, and then one by one, the men sheathed their blades, their grim faces focused not on the mother of Alexander, but on the man who still pointed his sword at the queen.

Without asking permission, the men turned their backs on their leader and filed out of the room.

Roxana wanted to give in to the weakness in her legs and sink to the floor, but the old man, his sword still drawn, remained.

Instead of charging forward, the last man in the room dropped his head. Finally, he lowered his weapon and bowed to Olympias.

"I served with your son, my lady. I vow the army of Alexander will not touch Queen Olympias. Cassander can find someone else to do his dirty work."

He slinked from the room, quietly shutting the door and leaving the two women in peace.

Roxana wiped the sweat from her brow and sucked in a few deep breaths. "I can't believe it."

She flinched when Olympias's loud cackle sliced through the air.

"Believe it, girl! I live today." The brief moment of light in her eyes faded. "Tomorrow will be another story."

Her behavior baffled Roxana. "How can you be so brave?"

"When one has accepted death, one lets go of fear. My son taught me that." She sighed and sat in her chair. "We may not have not seen eye-to-eye, but I want you to know, I'm glad Alexander married you."

Touched by her regard, she kissed Olympias tenderly on the cheek. "Thank you."

"You take care of yourself, Roxana. Give Alexander Aegus my love."

A single tear crept down her cheek as she took one last look at her mother-in-law, knowing she would never see her again.

The old woman smiled and wiped her tear away. "None of that. I'm going to be with my son, and nothing could make me happier. Now go." She motioned to the door.

With no more words left to say, Roxana bowed one last time to Olympias, Queen of Macedon, and then walked out of the dingy little room, closing the door on the bravest woman she'd ever known.

With the lively voices from the thriving town coming through her bedroom window, Roxana stood over her son's chair as he read aloud from his book on Greek heroes. With uncertainty clouding her head like smoke from a thousand campfires, she listened with only a passing interest to his lessons.

Throughout the morning, she'd felt ill at ease. The torment over what lay ahead kept her from sitting still. Endless worry consumed her, eroding her strength. The only thing keeping her going was the hope that Cassander meant to return her and her son to Pella.

But the eerie lack of servants, even the disappearance of her dear Morella, added to her mounting uncertainty. She prayed no harm had come to her kind maid. When she questioned the sentries outside her door about their servants, they encouraged her to go back inside and not come out again.

Why were they confined to their rooms?

Her eyes kept darting to the sword resting against a chair in the corner of her bedroom.

"Mother, I'm hungry." Alexander Aegus looked up from his book. "Why has no one brought us any food or wine this morning?"

The distress in his voice sent her to the bed. She ruffled his head of thick hair, fighting to appear at ease despite the battle raging inside her.

"I don't know, but I'm sure there's an explanation."

Her chamber doors opened without a knock or warning.

Roxana tossed her arms around her son, expecting to see a line of men marching into her sitting room with their swords drawn. She buried the boy's head in her chest, ready to beg for her son's life.

Cassander stood in her doorway, smiling.

"May I come to call?"

She stumbled backward, letting go of her boy, too stunned to speak.

Alexander Aegus perked up, and a happy grin lifted his features. The change in him astounded her. It had been ages since she'd seen his smile.

"Uncle Cassander!" He ran to greet him.

Cassander eagerly hugged the boy, then held him back. "How big you've gotten. How old are you now?"

Alexander Aegus raised his chin. "Seven this summer."

The warm reunion didn't seem real. The constant highs and lows of her emotions, the fear of death and the normalcy of life, eroded at her soul, leaving a hollow pit behind. How much more could she take?

Cassander stepped inside. "Seven? Where does the time go?" He waved to a muscular man waiting in the hall. "Why don't you go and see my friend, Glaucias, while I speak to your mother? He has some interesting stories about your father."

Her throat constricted. She summoned the courage to ask what was about to happen to them.

"It's fine, Roxana," Cassander whispered as if reading her thoughts. "I only wish to speak to you alone. Glaucias will not harm him."

Roxana nodded for her son to join the intimidating man.

Alexander Aegus walked into the hall. Her heart rose in her throat when Glaucias put his arm around her beloved child.

"He's just like Alexander." Cassander closed the doors and shifted his attention to her, his amiable smile collapsing. He walked toward her with a purposeful stride. "I'm afraid Olympias is dead. The families of those she had murdered through the years have done the deed. They stoned her to death on the palace grounds. I was told she met her end nobly, as the mother of Alexander should."

The way he spoke, the ease in which he relayed the news, sickened her. Alexander would never have let a woman die in such a manner.

"I wonder how the army will feel knowing the mother of Alexander met such an end."

"Does that matter?" His shrug revealed his indifference for the men whose future he now controlled. "She was sentenced to death by the assembly for her crimes. How she died will make little difference to them."

Roxana plodded back to her son's chair and sat down. "You're right. It makes little difference now."

"I'm glad we have the bad news out of the way." His loud clap rolled around her rooms. "I will need you and the king to pack."

"Of course. I'm sure it's time we all returned to Pella." Roxana pushed herself up from her chair, grateful he meant to bring them back to her husband's home. "When I find my servant, Morella, I will be happy to oblige."

"She's gone, Roxana. I shipped her to Pella this morning. Her command of Greek and Persian will make her useful to me."

"Morella? But why?" Dismay tensed her limbs. "Why send her ahead of us?"

He fingered the regent's gold seal hanging from a chain around his neck, his face a mask of stone. "You're not returning to Pella. You and Alexander Aegus will be given a new place to live in Amphipolis." He eased closer, a cool disregard in his black eyes. "Pack lightly. You will not need much. You will live simply among the people of the citadel there. You will no longer have royal treatment and will be considered a person of a private station."

She held her stomach as the knives of anxiety twisted deeper. "I thought you were our friend. Why are you doing this?"

"I'm helping you, Roxana. I'm protecting you and the boy from people who would wish to use him as a way to gain power over the Kingdom of Macedon. Look at it as being in confinement, until it is safe to return to Pella."

She didn't believe him, but the carrot dangled in front of her helped to keep her terror in check.

"How long will this confinement last? How long before I can expect the guard to come and kill my son and me?"

His sinister laughter echoed throughout her rooms, shredding to pieces any faith she had in the man's integrity.

"I'm not going to kill you or Alexander Aegus. I'm just going to get you out of the way for a while."

CHAPTER SIXTY-FOUR

In a rickety cart pulled by a pony, Roxana and her son approached a desolate citadel nestled next to a steep rockface and away from the walled city of Amphipolis. Ahead of them in another cart was Glaucias, the royal guard sent to protect them and the officer in charge of their care.

"Why are we going to this place, Mother?" Alexander Aegus peered up at a pair of high, depressing towers.

She put her arm around her shivering son, aching to give him comfort. She kept up a rosy attitude, hoping it would ease his fright.

"Uncle Cassander says we will be safe here. You'll see. It will be fine."

After climbing a winding stairwell into one of the towers, they arrived at three connected rooms within the citadel. With stone walls and hardwood floors, the rustic two-bedroom apartment shared a sitting area. It reminded Roxana more of a soldiers' barracks than a place for a woman and child.

A musty odor hung in the air, and while she clung to her son, browsing the thick wood beams above, she recalled all the wonderful palaces where she'd resided. The world she'd traveled, the adventures she'd known, the dangers, the intrigues, and the battles. How had any of those things brought her to this remote stronghold in a forgotten region of her husband's kingdom?

Did you ever foresee this for us, Alexander?

A bulky guard walked past her and set their trunks on the floor, along with the silver and gold chest with which she'd refused to part.

"That's too nice a piece to leave alone around here, my lady." The guard sized up the chest with his greedy eyes.

Roxana's defiance flared. "It belonged to Alexander. It was given to me by General Perdiccas for his son. Would you dare anger my husband's spirit and take it away?"

At the mention of Alexander's name, the guard bowed. "Forgive me. I served with Alexander in Persia. There's never been another like him."

Glaucias came in behind the guard and smacked the back of his head. "If I catch you eyeing her things again, I'll rip your throat out."

The guard backed out of the room.

Glaucias stuck out his chest, his thick body bulging beneath his tunic. "None of the men will touch your possessions. You have my word, my lady. You will come to no harm under my protection."

Roxana tried her best to smile, but she was beyond trusting anyone's word anymore. She still kept expecting an army of soldiers to barge into the rooms to kill them. She doubted such a fear would ever leave her in the dank and dismal place.

"Breakfast is served at sun up." Glaucias's deep voice filled the sitting room. "Dinner is at sundown. The men are usually on their own for lunch in the town, but I will have the cook make you and the boy something every day. Laundry is done by the staff once a week so you may want to save your fancy clothes for another time. The women here would not know what to do with such things. Women wear plain wool work tunics here without any jewelry or pins. You and the king are expected to do the same." He shifted his attention to the Alexander Aegus. "You're confined to the area inside the citadel at night. During the day, you can go about the grounds, but not without a guard—for your protection."

"I understand." Roxana dragged her toe along a deep gouge in the battered wooden floors.

"If you have needs, complaints, or any other service, you ask the guard to fetch me and discuss them only with me. I will check in with you once a week." Glaucias pointed at the heavy wooden door at the entrance to their rooms. "The door will be bolted every night after supper ... for your protection."

He gave her a last nod and left.

The *wham* of the door shutting sent a shudder through her. She turned to the one window in the sitting room. She touched the rusty iron bars over it and examined the cliffs below.

Glaucias had not used the word prison, but it felt like one to her.

"Mother, how long do we have to stay here?" Alexander Aegus gripped her hand.

She had to make this work for her son. She had come from a humble family and would make the best of their circumstances. What choice did she have?

"I don't know, Alexander Aegus, but I've stayed in worse places when I traveled with your father." She squeezed his hand and smiled. "We will make this our adventure, and one day, we will look back on our time here and remember it fondly."

Chapter Sixty-Five

Seven years later.

Roxana raised her head to the brilliant blue sky and walked across the small clearing. The last traces of winter sill hung in the air, but new shoots of spring had arrived, and she looked forward to more time outside and away from her rooms in the citadel.

A stiff breeze batted at her long woolen tunic. Her hair brushed against her face, and then she noticed the streaks of gray. She couldn't remember the last time she checked her reflection in a copper mirror. Perhaps it was a good thing. She didn't want to see her wrinkles and preferred to remember how she had been—the young woman Alexander had loved.

The afternoon sun touched the chain around her neck, sending a glimmer of gold along the citadel wall. Instinctively, she held the coin in her hand, comforted by her memories.

She came to the edge of the wall where the clearing opened up, offering a breathtaking view of the mountains. The *clink* of swords clashing erupted around her. Roxana walked to where two boys sparred.

"Alexander Aegus!"

He ignored her as he lunged at the boy from the village. She admired how he had grown so much over the last few years. His hair still like the disheveled mane of his father, he had Alexander's eyes and prominent brow, but his lips were small like hers. Slender, muscular, and graceful—he was Alexander all over again, even down to his determination in battle.

"No, hold the sword up higher, boy." Glaucias walked up to her son and lifted his arm, tightening his grip on the sword. "Like this. It gives you more thrust with your lunge."

"I got it." Alexander Aegus squared off against his partner.

Her son's changing voice had deepened quickly over the past few months. Her heart grieved, knowing his boyhood was at an end.

She went and stood next to Glaucias while he supervised the sword fight.

"Who's winning?"

His hearty, deep chuckle shook his broad shoulders. "Your boy has got a real eye for the sword. He's grown so in the past year. Now he's better able to handle weapons."

"He'll be fourteen in a few months. Hard to believe he's almost a man."

"At fourteen, Macedonian boys are expected to go to war and become men."

Glaucias arched a black eyebrow at her. "Perhaps it's time to teach him how to use the Macedonian spear."

While she watched her beloved boy, Roxana's pride surged. In spite of everything, the years living in tents, at Pella, and here in the citadel, he'd thrived. She still worried about his future, where he would go, what was in store for him, but she believed he had a firm foundation to be anything he wanted, even a king.

"You've been kind to encourage him these past few years," she said to Glaucias. "It's hard on a young boy with nothing to do around here."

He stroked his gray beard, never taking his eyes off the boys. "It's been a real pleasure for me."

She tugged at her woolen shawl. "Well, it's time for his lunch, so if the Olympic events have come to an end …" She turned to her son and raised her voice. "I've made lunch, Alexander Aegus."

"Just another few minutes, Mother. Please?" he begged, his voice cracking.

She edged closer to Glaucias. "When the conqueror of the world is finished, send him to me before his soup gets cold."

"I will, Roxana." He checked on her son's progress and then shouted, "Up, Alexander Aegus, keep your sword up."

Dust billowed in the distance as she made her way back to the citadel. A rider headed through the gates.

The man dismounted, removed a pouch from his horse's back, and proceeded inside the citadel.

Roxana set out across the clearing toward the entrance to her rooms. Over the years, numerous riders had come and gone; none of them had ever carried anything for her or her son.

The green grass tickled her toes through her simple leather sandals as she gazed up at the walled tower. Her predicament had been hard initially, with her constant fear for her son's life. But as time progressed, she'd gotten to know the guards and her apprehension for Alexander Aegus had diminished. The isolated locale had become more of a home than prison after her years there. Short of her childhood in Bactria, the citadel had been her residence longer than any other place she'd known. The longed-for roots she'd hoped for weren't what she expected, but her life had not gone according to plan, either. She had loved, traveled, and experienced far more than her simple aspirations. Maybe the gods had blessed her after all.

In his tent, seated at his desk, Polyperchon read the scroll in his hand as the din of soldiers, horses, servants, and rolling wagons swelled around him. He pulled the oil lamp on his desk closer, trying to make out the words.

"Damn my old eyes."

"Sir!" A soldier marched up to his desk. "We have more information coming in from the scouts."

Polyperchon dropped the scroll. The impressive young man sparked his sense of pride. "You don't have to call me *sir* when we're alone, Alexander. Father is fine."

His son's clenched jaw relaxed. "Cassander's forces are heading our way. A day, maybe two from here."

Polyperchon pulled the cloak around his shoulders closer, feeling a chill. "Good. I want to annihilate him this time and march on to Amphipolis to rescue Roxana and the king."

Alexander relaxed. "Do you think she's still alive after all these years?"

He picked up the scroll. "My informant in Pella tells me she and the boy are both alive. Imprisoned in the citadel, but very much alive."

"You never told me you had an informant in Pella. How did you pull that one off?"

"I know someone very close to Cassander. She also wants the king and his mother rescued and has been very helpful with gathering information."

Alexander raised his brows. "She?"

Polyperchon gave him a cagey smile. "Go and tell the other generals Cassander is on his way."

"Are you doing this for the boy or for her, Father? I don't mind everyone calling you the mighty defender of the son of Alexander, but when this is all over, will you pursue her again?"

Polyperchon stood, his knees creaking, and rested his hand on his son's shoulder.

"I fight for the rightful heir to the throne, and for Roxana. I promised her I would keep fighting for her and her son, and that's one promise I intend to keep."

"Are you sure?"

Glaucias didn't know how to take the message from the courier standing before his desk.

The news wasn't unexpected, but he'd thought Cassander would at least wait until after the boy's birthday.

The lean man nodded. "That was all he said. It is time."

Glaucias turned to his office window, debating how to carry out his orders with the least amount of fuss.

"Where is he?"

"Somewhere along the border of the kingdom, facing the armies of Polyperchon."

Glaucias chuckled. "Polyperchon always was a fool. I wonder if he realizes what he's done by attacking Cassander."

"They say he has raised a mighty army. It seems many men still want Alexander Aegus to be king." The messenger cleared his throat. "Do you have a reply for me to take back to Pella?"

Glaucias had no reply. What was there to say? He'd agreed to his task when Cassander had given him the duty of watching over Roxana and the boy.

"See my man outside. He will set you up with some food. Prepare to ride with my message after your meal."

The man hurried from the cramped office.

Glaucias rose from his chair, reaching for the sword he kept to the side of his desk. He shut off his thoughts and concentrated on his duty.

"Marcus," he barked at the door.

A tall guard in a dirty chiton came inside.

"Yes, sir."

Glaucias tested the edge of the sword on his thumb, checking the sharpness of the blade. "Get your men. There's something we must do."

Glaucias stuck out his chest, following his guard down the narrow corridor to the tower. He was ready to put an end to his years at the fort. He'd done enough babysitting for one lifetime. It was time to get back to war.

Outside a heavy wooden door, he waited for his men to gather. He sized up each one of them, hoping they had the stomachs to do what was necessary. He would have preferred seasoned veterans for such a task, but the young recruits would get their first taste of blood whether they were ready or not.

"Be quick and clean." Glaucias kept his voice low. "Cassander doesn't want them to suffer."

Roxana ruffled her son's hair as he read from his father's copy of *The Iliad*. She sat next to him on the floor, checking over his shoulder to make sure he pronounced everything correctly. He was such a wonderful boy. He had become her greatest treasure,

The door to their sitting room flew open. Glaucias and two guards stood in the threshold, cold determination etched on their faces.

A shiver ran through her. "What are you doing here?"

The glint of the afternoon sun streaming through her window bounced off their drawn swords.

Terror ran through her like a lightning bolt. She jumped up and took a protective stance in front of her son.

"You can't do this. He's your king!"

"Mother, what's happening?"

"Run, Alexander. Run!" She pushed him away, desperately hoping he would find a way out of the small room.

Footfalls on the battered wooden floor surrounded them.

"You will not harm us." Alexander Aegus's voice deepened with anger as he stood to defend his mother.

She threw her arms around her boy. "Whatever happens, know that I love you more than anything."

Alexander Aegus fought her, attempting to climb to his feet. He was strong—she could barely hold him—and when he broke free of her grip, she shouted after him.

"Alexander, no!"

"I'm sorry, Roxana." With a swift stroke of his blade, Glaucias sliced across the base of her son's neck.

Gasping for breath, he fell to the floor, helpless, one hand trying to stem the crimson seeping through his fingers while the other reached for her.

Please, not like this! Not like this!

She raced to her son and pressed her hand to his throat, pushing the blood back, willing him to live.

"No! Not my baby! Not Alexander's son!"

Enraged, she let out a guttural cry and charged Glaucias, the bloodied knuckles of her fists white.

With a quick thrust, Glaucias plunged his knife into her belly. He twisted the hilt before pulling the blade from her.

The white-hot searing pain overpowered her. The ichor of life spurted from her. She covered the burning wound with her hands, fighting to stay alive.

No!

Her legs wobbled as she clutched her abdomen. She dropped to her knees and then to the floor, her head listing to one side.

Roxana struggled to reach her son, her blood mingling with his on the battered floor.

Tears fell, and black spots swarmed her eyes. She ached to caress her son's beautiful face.

So like his father.

His eyes faded and dimmed until their light disappeared.

Feet covered in grimy, torn, leather sandals, stepped in front of her. Glaucias knelt down and gently turned her head to him.

She tried to fight him, but he stilled her by taking hold of her hand.

"Forgive me, my lady. I did what had to be done."

He shouted for his men to clear the room. After giving her one final look, Glaucias turned and walked away.

With the last dregs of life seeping from her limbs, Roxana crawled toward the lifeless body of her son, desperate to touch him one last time. She endeavored to raise her hand to his jaw, but it fell to the floor.

"Forgive me, Alexander," she whispered with her final breath. "I wasn't strong enough to protect him."

She trembled as darkness closed in around her. Her head sank into a pool of blood. The cold retreated, and an incredible warmth blanketed her, taking away all her sadness and pain.

Happy to be leaving a world where she'd existed for so long as a shadow, Roxana waited for her end, rejuvenated by the hope of finally joining her Alexander in those golden Elysian Fields.

EPILOGUE

Cassander sat at his wooden desk in his study, a fresh batch of scrolls from his army before him. He scratched his fat belly as he read the one in his hand about Polyperchon's movements. He put the dispatch down and stroked his gray beard, considering how to respond.

A loud knock broke his concentration. "Enter."

The door swung open, and Glaucias marched into the study. Mud still clung to his sandals, and dirt streaked his cheeks.

He approached the desk, holding something in his hand.

Cassander went back to reading about Polyperchon's exploits while Glaucias placed a silver coin attached to a gold necklace on his desk.

The sparkle of the metal made him put his letter down.

"When did you arrive?"

"Just now." Glaucias removed his dusty cloak and tossed it to a nearby chair.

Cassander fingered the delicate gold rope chain. "And their bodies?"

"Here. I escorted them personally, as you ordered. They're being prepared for the funeral rites. The royal tombs in Aegae are being opened as we speak."

Cassander picked up a goblet from the corner of his desk. "Good. One less king to get in my way."

"What about Alexander's bastard, Heracles?"

"That arrived from Pergamum this morning." Cassander pointed at a scroll on his desk. "It's from Polyperchon. Barsine and Heracles are dead. At least the gullible general proved useful to me in the end." Cassander looked over his henchman. "You need a drink after your long ride." He turned to a dark corner. "Wine for my friend."

A woman with silvery hair, a pug nose, and wearing the dark brown tunic of a servant, brought a tray with a single goblet.

"How did you convince Polyperchon to kill Heracles?" Glaucias asked, snapping up his drink.

The servant retreated into the shadows.

Cassander rolled his goblet in his hands, grinning. "My spy in his camp told me he'd discovered where I held Roxana and the boy. I couldn't have him stealing them out from under me, so before my troops confronted his, I put him off by sending him a letter promising to place Alexander Aegus on the throne when his half-brother and competitor for the kingdom was removed." Cassander glanced at the necklace, remembering the beautiful woman who had once possessed it. "What he set out to defend, he inevitably helped to destroy. Divine retribution, I would say."

Glaucias wiped his mouth with the back of his hand, removing the stain of wine from his beard. "How did he find out they were at Amphipolis? It wasn't my men."

Cassander guzzled the last of his wine, still stewing about the spy in his midst. "Probably someone in the palace. I'll find them one day and slit their belly."

"There's still Alexander's sister to contend with. Ptolemy means to marry her. What are you going to do about Cleopatra?" Glaucias asked.

Cassander picked up the gold necklace, enthralled by the way it glistened in the lamplight. "Not to worry. My sources have assured me she will never leave Sardis alive."

"Then that's the last of his family. What do you want me to do now?"

Cassander inspected the silver decadrachm commemorating Alexander's victory at the Hydaspes River. He placed the shiny coin in his hand and closed his fist around it.

"Send word to the other generals: Ptolemy, Seleucus, Lysimachus, and Antigonus. Tell them, now we are kings."

Glaucias chuckled and raised his drink. "To the new kings of Alexander's empire."

Cassander went to sip his wine and frowned.

He held up the empty goblet and turned to the servant in the corner.

"Morella, more wine."

Morella stood at the railing of a merchant's vessel that was heading west across the blue Chief Sea. While the salty sea spray lashed her face, she gazed up at a few puffy white clouds, enjoying the taste of freedom. It had been a long time since she'd been on her own. Soon she would be back in her homeland, ready to start anew.

She removed the thin shawl covering her head, letting the brisk wind run through her hair. Over the side of the ship, two dolphins leaped in and out of the water.

Pictures of the dolphins painted on the floors of the palace at Opis came to mind. It seemed like a lifetime ago. The beautiful woman with the breathtaking smile brought a tear to her eye.

Such fire. Such strength. Such a waste.

She reached inside her tunic and pulled out the silver coin hanging from the gold rope chain.

"What you got there?"

A young man with black curly hair poking out from beneath his red cap stood next to her, sizing up the coin.

She quickly tucked the necklace back under her tunic. "It was a gift from my lady. I served her for many years."

"Who was your lady? Some rich Greek?"

Morella chuckled at the irony. "No. She was the wife of the king."

"The king?" The sailor removed his cap and rested his elbow on the railing. "What king?"

Morella gauged the interest in his dark eyes. She didn't feel like hiding who she was or where she'd come from anymore. Cassander could never find her—not where she was going—and it would be days before he discovered Roxana's necklace missing. Besides, she had such an incredible tale to tell.

She held up her head, brimming with pride. "I served the Lady Roxana, wife to King Alexander."

"Alexander?" The sailor gave her a wide-eyed expression. "The Alexander? Alexander the Great?"

"The very same."

The young man scratched his head and put his cap back on. "He had a wife? I've never heard of her."

Morella gripped the railing as the ship gently rocked. "The Lady Roxana lived a life like no other and was deeply loved by the mighty Alexander."

He eased closer, flourishing a boyish grin. "What else can you tell me about the Great King? Did you see any of his famous battles or visit the cities he built?"

The questions didn't surprise her. Alexander's fame would never die, but what about Roxana's? How would the world remember her?

Morella pressed her hand against the coin tucked safely inside her long, drab frock. "You already know his story. I'm going to tell you hers."

ACKNOWLEDGEMENTS

Realm was a labor of love for me, and the team at Vesuvian Books who helped launch it will always have my deepest gratitude.

To Beth Isaacs and Holly Atkinson for your excellent words of advice for getting my baby edited. To Katie Harder-Schauer, my wonder proofer. To Scotty Roberts for your endless patience putting together my map. To Liana Gardner for all your efforts to get this Herculean monster to press. To Michael Canales for my beautiful cover.

To two strong and wonderful women—Mary Ting and Italia Gandolfo. You have both moved mountains for me, believed in me, and your efforts made this book possible. I will be forever grateful for your friendship.

ABOUT THE AUTHOR

 **Alexandrea Weis,** RN-CS, Ph.D., is a multi-award-winning author, advanced practice registered nurse, and historian who was born and raised in the French Quarter of New Orleans. Brought up in the motion picture industry as the daughter of a director, she learned to tell stories from a different perspective and began writing at the age of eight. Infusing the rich tapestry of her hometown into her novels, she believes that creating vivid characters makes a story moving and memorable.

A permitted/certified wildlife rehabber with the Louisiana Wildlife and Fisheries, Weis rescues orphaned and injured animals. She lives with her husband and pets in New Orleans. Weis writes historical, suspense, thrillers, crime fiction, and romance.

www.alexandreaweis.com